Man of Action

BOOK TWO OF THE FAMILY BUSINESS SERIES

ELLE RIVERS

This book is a work of fiction. Any similarities to real individuals are purely coincidental. All events are from the imagination of the author and are not to be taken as realistic.

Cover Design by Allie McGilberry

Edited by Kasey Kubica

Proofread by Amanda Oraha

Contents

A Note from Elle

This work contains themes that some might find disturbing. In this novel, alcoholism and parental emotional abuse are discovered, and there are allusions to marital physical abuse on page. No alcohol abuse occurs on page. There is one support group scene where people who have chosen to quit drinking talk about how it has affected their lives, including divorce and health issues stemming from alcohol abuse. A character is homophobic in one scene but is immediately fired for those comments. Childhood abandonment is discussed, as well. One character is diagnosed as autistic, and another is suspected. I have done my best to represent these issues with care and compassion. These are my experiences with autism and are not representative of all people on the spectrum. If you have questions or suspect you have autism, I encourage you to speak to a professional.

As always, if you feel that there is a warning I missed, please reach out to me at elle@ellerivers.com and I will rectify the situation.

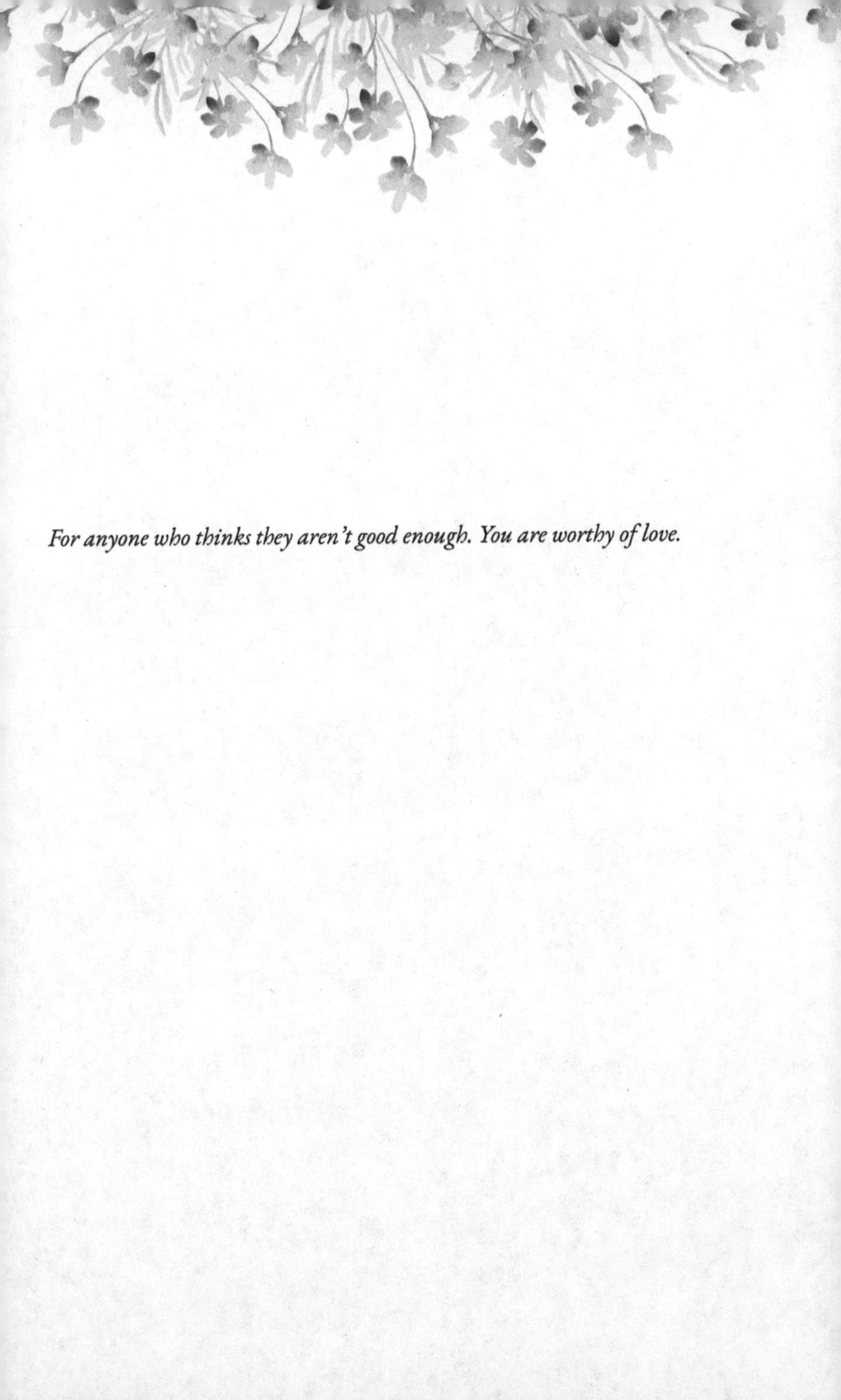

For anyone who thinks they aren't good enough. You are worthy of love.

Prologue

Selena

A soft, dreamy song played in the coffee shop. I could barely hear it over the loud machines and customer conversations, but it was there. It perfectly matched the vibe of the romance novel I'd just finished reading.

I lived my life in books, spending all my time with words rather than with reality. Afterward, I'd draw out all the images in my head on paper to remember them by. I could lose days to my imagination if I let myself.

Usually, I focused on my schoolwork, especially since I'd been accepted into a very expensive college. But I'd been studying a lot, so I had allowed myself to indulge for one day. Then one day turned into three, and I knew I'd have to return to my assignments soon, or else Mom would ask what was going on when I inevitably let it slip again that my grades were dropping. One of these days, I was going to have to figure out how to hide things better to avoid her worried questions. Or worse, her strong opinions on how to fix everything.

I'd already accidentally mentioned how I no longer had straight As. I was firmly in the Bs club my first year in college, and now, in my second, I was no stranger to Cs. I'd covered it up with a quick lie that it was just challenging coursework, not the fact that I couldn't seem to focus in class to save my life.

Mom's attention felt wrong to me. This was the year my younger sister, Luna, was graduating. I didn't want to take away from that with my own problems.

Besides, Luna needed the attention. She was the wilder of the two of us and didn't seem to have a problem being on the receiving end of Mom's ire. I, on the other hand, was usually better at hiding my messes and failures so Mom could devote her energy to Luna.

I was okay with that. I'd known my place since childhood and I could survive without the extra help. Most people would hate to be the background character in anyone's life, let alone their own, but I melted into it like it was meant for me. I took no issue with it and there was no jealousy to be had. I was comfortable exactly where I was.

Even my life goals were those of a background character. All I wanted was to get a business degree and an office job that paid the bills. It was boring but safe.

To do that, however, I needed to focus on my schoolwork, and that just wasn't happening.

Even though I'd long since passed my one day off, I continued drawing the last scene in the book I'd just finished reading. I was working on the main male character, trying to picture his face in my mind.

The bell over the door jingled and I heard the girl at the table next to me whisper to her friend, "It's *him*. Tom Murray is here."

"The guy Rebecca slept with last week?"

"Yes. If only she were here."

I looked up.

Tom Murray was a legend. My roommates, who were far more into partying than I was, talked about how he was at every social event on campus drinking the night away. He was so charismatic that he ended up with a different woman every night. Apparently, this Rebecca had been one of them.

He sounded like my sister's type. She'd had six boyfriends in her senior year alone.

Secretly, I wondered if maybe he was one of those romance heroes who was a playboy simply waiting for his perfect match to break him of his ways.

I'd never seen him in person, but I'd heard stories of his piercing green eyes and dark, wavy hair. Supposedly, when he smiled, he had dimples—a rare sight, unless he was cutting loose at a party. During the day, he was serious, focused, and a dedicated dean's list student, and no smiles could be found on his face.

My type had never been men as popular as he was, but he still made my heart skip a beat when he walked in. He was tall, wearing a perfect button-up shirt and jeans that looked tailored to his body. He took off his sunglasses when he entered the room and I suddenly knew why women whispered about those eyes. They were stunning, like a gemstone aching to be set into a ring.

I tore my own eyes away before they could linger on him any more than they already had. It wouldn't do me any good to try anything with him. He was way out of my league. I could see my best friend, Hadley, or my sister taking charge and being the main character, but I was not like them.

My notepad sat in front of me, the male character's face a blank canvas. Moments ago, I wasn't sure what I wanted to do with it. Now, I knew exactly what to draw.

Just one look at him and my brain wouldn't let him go. It reminded me of when I met Hadley. She had been so stunning that I couldn't help but draw her too.

Maybe I had a knack for finding main characters.

As I sketched him, I lost myself in my work. I didn't notice anything other than what was directly in front of me.

I didn't even notice when someone approached me.

"Is that me?" a deep voice asked.

I froze in my sketching.

No. It couldn't be.

I slowly looked up and saw the same man I'd put on my page. His head was tilted as he looked at my notepad and my hand instinctually came to cover my work.

"Oh, God." The words rushed out of me.

"My name is actually Tom."

"You never saw this."

"The drawing?" he asked. "I definitely did. You did a great job, but you didn't sign it."

"That's for people who want others to see it. This is just a hobby."

"That's a shame, because it would have been nice to know your name."

"You want my name? Why?" Was there someone he could report me to for being weird?

He seemed thrown off by my suspicion. "B-because you're pretty?"

I didn't give an answer. I could only blink at him and he winced as if he regretted his words.

I knew the expression all too well, and seeing someone like *him* feel as awkward as I did gave me the courage to finally speak.

"Sorry, socializing is hard for me sometimes," I explained. "I'll tell you my name. But you have to agree to forget you saw me drawing you. I'd hate for you to have to report me to the board."

"Board of what?"

"Board of...people who police public privacy?"

He smiled. "I don't think that exists."

"Maybe it does. I don't know what laws exist, so I need a promise."

"Those definitely don't hold up in a court of law."

"It'll make me feel better. And you'd get my name."

"Fine. I promise not to hold it against you that you drew me, but I can't promise to forget it. Your art is too good."

Heat rose to my cheeks. *Yeah*, I could see why he was with a different woman each night.

"That works for me," I said, and my voice was a little breathless. "My name is Selena."

"Beautiful name." He smiled, and yep, he definitely had dimples. I should have played the lottery today because I might just be the luckiest woman in the world to get that sight at a coffee shop and not a party.

The one on his right cheek was deeper and I had the urge to add that to my drawing.

But then his smile fell at my silence. "S-sorry, I must be off my game."

"Oh, no. It's not you. It's me. Like I said, socializing is hard and…I also don't get why you're talking to me."

"Because I want to, and you gave me the perfect opportunity to with your beautiful drawing."

"You don't have to flatter me."

"It's not flattery. It's simply the truth."

The room grew stuffier. I was *not* used to this much perfection looking at me. I fanned myself. "Wow, is it hot in here?"

"Maybe it's the sweater," he said. "As cute as it is, it might be making you hot."

No, it was definitely him. I might die if he didn't stop. His looks, plus this adorable, almost nervous personality, were really working on me.

"Can I sit?" he asked.

"Oh, yeah—" I went to gesture for him to take a seat, but my hand brushed against my tea, making the cup wobble and nearly sending it all over the table.

Thankfully, I caught it with only a few drops escaping.

"Are you sure you want to sit next to me?" I asked, laughing awkwardly. "I might wind up dumping my tea on your nice clothes."

"I'll take my chances."

"That shirt looks like it probably costs more than my whole wardrobe. I'm warning you, I can be a danger to everyone around me."

"You say that like it's a bad thing."

My eyes raked over him. "I don't see you as the kind of guy who likes messy things."

"And I don't see you as the kind of girl that I wouldn't like."

I blinked, heart pounding in my ears.

I could see it all. I'd be the one who came into his life like a tornado. We'd be opposites, yet it would somehow work. He'd tone down my chaos and I'd show him that he didn't always have to wear perfectly pressed jeans.

Maybe...this was *different*. Maybe I *could* be the main character.

"Can I have the drawing?" he asked.

"R-really? You want it?"

"It's very good work."

My best friend always said the same thing, but I figured she *had to* since we were friends.

I ripped out the page from my notebook and gave it to him. When my hand brushed his, I was shocked—literally—by the static in the air.

"Ouch," I said, pulling my hand back quickly.

"Your touch is electrifying."

"I think it's the dry air."

"Maybe," he said. I expected him to leave, but instead, he added, "But call me a romantic."

He used the R word. This was it. This was the start of my happy ending.

"So, are you a graphic design major or something?" he asked.

"No," I said. "Business major."

"Do you like business?"

"I don't know. It just seems like a safe choice."

"You probably should have a major that you like."

"What's *your* major?"

"Business," he said, one corner of his mouth turning upward.

"And do you like it?"

"I have to. My parents want me to work for the family business."

"Same here. But my mom is a house cleaner and I'm...allergic to cleaning."

"Deathly?"

"It feels like it sometimes."

"Sometimes, socializing can feel like that for me. When I'm like this, that is." His mouth was a flat line.

"Like this?"

"Sober."

"I like this side of you," I said.

"Are you sure you like me like this? You'd probably like me better about four beers in."

"I'm happy where I'm at. Until you get bored of me, of course."

"I don't think I will."

"Then what do we do? We can't stay in the coffee shop forever. They close in a few, and besides, I've had my fill of the smell of coffee. It's not my favorite."

"We could go back to my place."

My heart skipped a beat.

I hadn't had sex before, but Hadley had. She described it as a sordid affair. Luna did the same.

But if this was the start of my happily ever after, then it wouldn't be like that. And I knew that Tom Murray was very good at pleasing women.

"We could do that now if you'd like," I offered.

"Yeah?"

"Yeah, I think it'd be fun to see where the legendary Tom Murray sleeps."

Tom

I couldn't believe that had gone as well as it had.

Usually, sober me didn't do well with talking to people. I was either too curt or too awkward.

Normally, I wouldn't even attempt to talk to anyone, but when I saw one of the most beautiful women on the planet drawing *me*, of all people, I had to say something.

She'd been sitting there, head hung low. Her tan skin nearly glowed despite the coffee shop's fluorescent lighting, and a sunbeam had shown me the beautiful array of brown in her hair. When she looked up, I'd been floored by a heart-shaped face and round cheeks.

And her smile sealed the deal.

Her impressive drawing of me was tucked in my wallet and I looked forward to studying it later. But for now, she was in front of me and I could tell she was the type of person who could keep anyone's attention.

I opened the door to my dorm for her.

"It's...clean," she said as we walked in. "Well, half of it is, anyway."

"That would be my roommate. Nice guy."

"I'm surprised you can live with it. Most of the tidy people I know can't."

"I'm not really here too much anyway."

"Right," she said. "You have busy nights."

My nights were the only time I could catch a breath. When I was out, I didn't have the weight of being Dad's favorite son hanging over me. I didn't have the responsibility of shielding my siblings from his schemes on me. I was just a college student, having fun.

"You should come to a party sometime."

"Oh no. It's not my scene. I don't dance."

"Would you believe me if I said the same?"

She raised an eyebrow at me. "Not at all."

"I usually need a little liquid courage."

"So it helps you," she said, "in a weird way."

"Yes, it does. I'll be honest, I never do this when sober."

"Do what?"

"Talk to someone like you." I could see a subtle hint of pink on her cheeks. "I could show you the more fun side of me, if you wanted."

Her eyes met mine and she shook her head. "No. I like this side of you."

My heart picked up speed in my chest. I could have thought through every way this would go wrong, but when I looked into the endless depth of her brown eyes, I couldn't seem to.

"So, how do we do this?" she asked.

"Do what?"

"A one-night stand."

"You want that? With me?"

"I thought that's what you meant when you said we could come back to your place. But I could have picked up the wrong signal. I do that a lot."

Her eyes met mine, eyebrow still raised with the question of what we were going to do. I saw myself mirrored in her gaze—a silent fear that she'd gotten something wrong.

"I would be very happy to do what you thought."

I could see her nervousness leave her as she exhaled. "Good. That would have been awkward. Where do we start?"

"Well," I said, her beauty and my nervous energy moving my hand, "first, I usually start with a kiss."

My hand grazed her cheek, and her skin was a kind of softness I was used to. "I'm waiting," she said, her lips curling into a smile.

I wasted no time in leaning down to press my lips to hers. She tasted like mint tea and she smelled like lavender. The hand touching her face moved to cup her cheek and my other found its way to her hip. I brought her to me, already feeling reluctant to let her go.

It was rare for me to lose myself in anything. Even when buzzed, I couldn't let go of things. My life seemed to be a list of things I was doing wrong.

But this kiss consumed my mind. All I could focus on was our lips touching and the feel of her body against mine.

She was a little inexperienced, but not in a bad way. Her lips were slower to react and she seemed to be following my lead. If I pulled her closer to me, then her hands would bunch in my shirt and pull me even tighter to her. If I nipped her lip, then she would bite mine back.

One swipe of my tongue across her bottom lip got her to open up to me, and the kiss turned frenzied. Our tongues clashed as I began to gently walk her to the bed, eager to peel every layer of clothing off of her. She let out a squeak as we fell, as if she didn't know where we were going. The kiss broke only for a second so I could catch myself with my hands before I landed on her.

She gazed up at me, eyes wide. I had her caged in with my arms. For a second, my mind grew loud. What if this wasn't what she wanted? What if I was pushing it too far?

But then her hands reached up for me and pulled me down to her. Her hands tangled through my hair, her electric touch setting every nerve ending in my scalp on fire. I wanted her hands to never leave my head, but I also desperately wanted them on other parts of me.

Instead of my mind thinking of all the things I was doing wrong, it was filled with all the things she was doing right.

It was an addictive sensation.

My cock was already hard and I pressed it against her lower stomach, desperate for any sort of friction. Her gasp of surprise was quickly swallowed by my kiss. But she angled herself away from me and I let her go.

Shit. Did I take it too far?

"N-now is probably a good time to tell you that I'm a virgin."

I blinked down at her. "You are?"

"Yes. Sorry if that's a turnoff, but I want this," she said. "I might just...not know *how*."

I gazed at her. I wanted her, desperately so. I wanted to kiss every inch of her body and feel her tighten around me, but I didn't mess around with virgins because I would always wonder if I was too rough the day after.

But I also wanted this. I wanted *her*. It was the one thing I was sure about—despite my soberness.

There was no other option; I was breaking my own rule for her.

"Okay," I said. "But I need to know you're sure about this."

"Yes," she said. "I am very sure."

"Then we do this my way."

"And what's your way?"

"Slow," I replied. "My goal is making this good for you."

I brought her mouth to mine again, eager to quiet my nervous mind. I was worried I'd hurt her, worried I'd fail her, worried I'd mess up as I did with anything I tried while sober.

But her lips did exactly what I needed. Her soft breathing through her nose brushed against my cheek. Her hips rocked up into my hardness. Her hands were in my hair again. I wanted to lose myself in her, and that was exactly what I planned to do.

I slid a hand under her sweatshirt, feeling the warm skin of her stomach. My mouth moved from hers, kissing the skin of her jawline and neck. She gasped as my hand touched her bra. I glanced up at her, looking for any signs of fear and regret.

"Y-you can take it off," she said.

"Are you—" Before I could finish my sentence, she ripped off her sweatshirt and threw it across the room.

"I'm sure," she replied, her eyes locked on mine. She was only in her bra and I couldn't help but bring my mouth to the tanned skin revealed to me. It was golden, like the sunrise after a calm night. I toyed with her bra for only a moment, giving her a chance to tell me to stop, but then I slowly dragged it off of her, revealing hard nipples and the beautiful swell of her breast. "I hope they're—"

Her words stuttered to a stop as I brought my mouth onto one of the hard peaks, teasing it with my tongue. She gasped again, arching her chest up into the sensation. I kept my mouth there until she whimpered. Then I moved lower.

"You're *really* good with your mouth," she murmured.

"It's even better in other places."

"Are you talking about...you know?"

I looked up at her. "If you mean am I going to put my mouth on your clit and make you come, then yes. Would you like that?"

She blankly stared at me and I wondered if I'd been too bold. Maybe I should take it back. Maybe I should apologize.

"Do you...want to?" she asked.

"I wouldn't ask if I didn't." I gave her three seconds to turn me down. Then I'd move on and remember this as what *not* to do when sober and sleeping with someone. At her momentary hesitation, I was reminded that the drunk version of me never struggled with this.

"Then, yes," she said. "I just don't know what it feels like."

My worries lessened. "Will you let me know if you like it?"

She nodded and I made my way down to her hips, pulling off her leggings. Her center was unshaven and dark curls hid exactly what I wanted my mouth on.

I gave her one exploratory taste and listened for her sharp intake of air. Her legs parted more, giving me better access to her. Her hands roamed my hair as I started off with pressure on her clit.

"Too much," she said, suddenly moving away. "Can you be softer?"

I hummed a yes, grateful for the clear direction. I gave less pressure, moving around her center rather than pressing on it directly.

"Yes," she gasped, rocking her hips into me. Her hands returned to my hair, nails scraping my scalp.

As I moved my tongue, she guided me right where she wanted me, and I graciously gave her the attention she wanted. I kept up my tempo, listening for every soft moan she let out.

Eventually, her movements became more desperate and her hips jerked harder. I provided more pressure, listening as her breaths came out faster and her body seemed to be moving toward exactly what we both wanted.

Selena came with a cry, her body lifting off the bed. I continued to move until she tore herself away, sensitive from her climax.

I straightened my spine. "How was that for your first orgasm?"

"I'm a virgin, not a nun," she said. "I've had orgasms before, just not with anyone else. And maybe not as good as that one."

"I aim to please."

"Now it's your turn. How much is this going to hurt?"

"We're still going slow," I said. "I want this to be just as enjoyable for you as it is for me."

I kissed her neck, tongue darting out to lick the skin there.

"O-okay," she said. "How do we make this enjoyable then? From what I've heard, getting penetrated isn't fun the first time you do it."

I couldn't help but laugh. "That's such a clinical word."

"I'm just saying it's what I've heard. Do you have a better word? Impaled? Shafted?"

I shook my head, bringing my mouth to hers before she could find an even odder word to describe me fucking her. As we kissed, my hand drifted down, first touching her breast, then her hip, and finally, her core.

She let out a sigh when I gently ran my finger up and down her folds, but then I stopped at her pussy, gently pressing in.

God, she was so wet for me already, and I was half tempted to immediately exchange my fingers for my dick.

But then I felt her hands grab my shoulders as she tensed up.

"It's okay," I said into her ear. "I'm not going to hurt you. I'll stop if I do."

"You promise?"

"Yes," I said. "I won't go any further if it hurts you."

"Okay, that helps." She took a few deep breaths. I could feel her body slowly relax under my touch.

I waited until she kissed me back before I pressed my finger inside of her again. I gingerly moved it in and out, feeling her muscles clench around me.

Slowly, I added more in, only doing so when she was ready. Her wetness grew around my fingers.

"Hang on," she said. "Touch me right here." She moved my hand to where I was barely dipping into her. When I did so, her breath hitched.

"Like that?"

"Yes, just like that."

She was gorgeous in this state, writhing and moving against my hand. Her mouth met mine; I could feel her quivering breaths. She bucked against me and I gave her more of what she needed until she shattered for another time.

"Oh, *fuck*."

"I think you're ready," I said.

"I think I agree," she replied. "Are you going to get as naked as me?"

She wasted no time pulling off my shirt and jeans, her eyes hungrily watching me. When my cock sprung free of my boxers, she bit her lip.

"It's going to be fine," I assured her. "I won't hurt you."

"Can I...try something?" she asked, sitting up.

I wasn't sure what she was planning, but then her mouth closed around my dick, enveloping it in warmth.

She struggled with it for only a moment, but she caught on quickly, moving up and down my member with her delicious mouth.

I let her continue for only a few moments before I gently pulled her away.

"If you keep doing that," I said, "then this isn't going to last very long."

"So, it wasn't bad?"

"Nothing about this is bad."

I threw on one of the condoms I kept in my bedside drawer.

She smiled and kissed me again.

I lined myself up at her center, feeling the head of my cock catch on her entrance. I stayed true to my word and went slowly, pressing in inch by inch, pausing whenever her face twisted in discomfort.

When I was finally fully seated in her, my head spun from her tightness. "You ready?"

She nodded, a smile playing on her lips. I moved carefully, fully pulling out and pushing back in. She moved in tandem with me, her hips pushing against each of my thrusts. Her inner muscles clenched around me and her soft moans sent me barreling toward my own release.

"T-Tom, I'm gonna—" Her sentence abruptly stopped as I heard her suck in a sharp breath. Her core tightened around me as she came again.

And I couldn't hold off any longer. I exploded within her, my vision going white as heat licked its way up my spine. I pressed my lips into hers, needing to be closer, and I swallowed her gasps as my movements finally stilled.

"That was..." I trailed off, brain struggling to produce words as I recovered from one of the most intense orgasms of my life.

"It was good," she said, smiling. "Probably the best first time in history."

I hoped she wasn't lying. We separated for a few moments to clean up in my dorm's attached bathroom.

When we were done, I was trying to think of a way to ask her to go back to that coffee shop with me tomorrow and make it a date this time.

She was pulling on her leggings as I still searched for the words.

"Where is my sweatshirt?" she asked, looking around the room.

"No clue," I said. "Want one of mine?"

"That would be nice."

I handed her one from my drawer, still at a loss for something to say. She turned to me, lips pursed as if she was doing the exact same thing as me.

Then her phone buzzed.

"Oh, *shit*," she said. "I have an exam tomorrow and I have to go. Sorry to just run, but...yeah."

I opened my mouth, trying to figure out exactly how to ask her for her number, but she was gone before I could.

Damn it.

Vanderbilt was a huge school and I knew I didn't share any classes or social circles with her.

I'd gotten lucky meeting Selena today, but I wondered if I would be able to make that happen again. I was usually a one-time kind of guy, but I could see myself doing more than that with her. But, as always, my own mind got in the way.

This was why I didn't do these kinds of things sober.

Selena

"So...what do two lines mean?" Hadley held the test that determined my fate in her hands.

"You're joking," I said. She had to be, because if she wasn't, then I was truly *fucked*.

With a wince, she turned the test around. "I'm not."

"No," I muttered as I saw the two lines. "How could I have let this happen?"

I couldn't believe I was pregnant after having sex one fucking time. Luna did it every night. How did I manage to have this happen after only doing it *once*?

Hadley was the only one who knew what had gone down a month ago. Her jaw had fallen to the floor when she found out who it was, but then her first question had been if we used protection. And we had. I remembered Tom grabbing a condom.

And yet, here I was. Pregnant.

This was not how life was supposed to go for me. I never imagined myself even being a mom. At least, not until I was with the person I thought I'd spend forever with.

"Wh-what do I do?"

"First things first: you should drink some water. You haven't all day." Hadley handed me my water bottle, which was still full from when I'd filled it up in the hallway before my business law class.

I took a few grateful sips, heart pounding. "Great. I can't even take care of myself. How am I supposed to take care of a child?"

"You *can* take care of yourself. You've been doing it since you moved into the dorms."

"I know. I just feel like an idiot right now."

"You're not an idiot. You got unlucky."

Unlucky sounded so negative, but there was no other word for it.

"You should probably decide if you're keeping it or not."

It. That felt so impersonal.

I was barely twenty. My biggest problems were my homework and trying to earn scholarships to lessen the astronomical amount of student debt I was going to have. I didn't have a job and couldn't support a child on my own.

Maybe I shouldn't have a baby. Maybe I should give them up for adoption. But as I thought about it, my heart tightened at the idea.

"You want to keep it, don't you?"

"How did you know?"

"I know you. You consume those surprise pregnancy romance novels like they're candy."

I did. I loved the idea of two people finding each other due to the unexpected. I just never thought it would happen to *me*.

But the problem now was that I'd left before getting Tom's number, and though I had dreams of what could have been, a part of me had wondered, even then, if he'd even want to see me again.

Now, he had a reason to. We could raise this baby together.

"You're right. And I need to tell Tom. Maybe I'll get lucky and he's always secretly wanted kids."

"Worst case: he just pays child support. People say his family has money. You should call him up."

"Yeah, but I don't have his number."

"Well, we have his school email address."

"Do we?"

"It's not that hard to figure out. It's his first and last name. Let's email him."

To: Tom Murray

From: Selena Martinez

Subject: About what happened last month...

Hi, Tom. I'm not sure how to say this, so I'll just get to the point. I'm pregnant. You're the dad. I'm sorry to tell you like this. I don't have your phone number. Want to maybe meet up for coffee and talk about what to do?

To: Selena Martinez

From: Tom Murray

Subject: About what happened last month...

How do I know it's mine?

To: Tom Murray

From: Selena Martinez

Subject: About what happened last month...

I haven't been with anyone else. I'm happy to do a DNA test, though. In the interest of honesty, though, if we go that route, I'll want to get a formal child support arrangement set up. It's what my mom is telling me would be best.

"What—are we just supposed to wait forever on this mystery man?" Mom paced her living room. Three weeks had passed with no other answer from Tom. I had dreaded giving her that news. "Whoever this man is, it's obvious he isn't going to step up!"

My eyes were glued to the floor. I'd never made Mom angry like this. Usually, Luna was the one that had her walking in circles. But Mom's tone hadn't affected her in years.

"Things would be easier if you just told Mom who it was," Luna piped in as she sat inspecting her nails.

I was tempted to say, but while waiting for his response, I'd looked up who Tom's family was. All I knew was that they had way more money than we did, and money meant power. His father had been in court cases about unpaid overtime. I didn't understand the technicalities of it, but the article had said that somehow, Todd Murray won those cases, even when it should have been impossible.

And I wondered what he would do to us.

But Mom wouldn't care. She saw someone doing something unfair to one of her kids and wanted justice. Nothing else mattered.

Maybe Tom *would* step up. My brain had been full of images of him coming to the door, telling me he just needed time to process, that he was sorry for leaving me hanging, and that he was ready to be here for this baby, and for me. He'd give me that dimpled grin and we'd start our own happily ever after.

But as time passed, I began to wonder if maybe I'd gotten him wrong. He'd been perfect in his dorm. His attentiveness and soft voice made me wonder if maybe he was the man of my dreams. But then he didn't respond, and the way he insinuated that I could be lying about the legitimacy of his child with just six simple words felt cruel.

Realistically, however, he didn't have to do a damn thing. He didn't have to carry the baby inside of him for nine months, nor did he have to pay the medical bills that would come from it. This was my choice to keep the baby and I had to face the consequences that came with it.

I had no clue if I could finish my degree while juggling a baby and a job, but I would make it work one way or another.

Mom had offered to help after she had gotten over her poorly hidden disappointment in me. After some insisting on her part, I had moved back home and had begun looking for a source of income.

While Mom was still yelling, a knock came from the front door. Luna was too busy picking at her cuticles—and she never answered the door anyway—so I took it upon myself to get up and see who it was.

It could be Tom here to sweep me off my feet.

But it was a stranger instead of the man that had been on my mind for weeks. He asked for my name, and then my ID, before he shoved an envelope into my hands. It was addressed to me, which was strange, considering I never received mail.

I gazed over the handwriting. It had no return address and it wasn't delivered by a postal worker. The person drove away in a truck with Murray and Sons on the back of it. Wait, *Murray?*

My eyes widened. Was this from Tom?

Maybe this was some sort of romantic "I'm sorry for knocking you up and never answering your emails" letter.

It was definitely not that.

To Selena Martinez,

I am aware of your claims of me fathering your child. I have no wish to take this to court for child support like you desire. I need to tend to my future to ensure my own success, not be concerned over a baby that I do not need or want. I've attached a check for you to make this problem of mine go away. Cashing it means you agree to never contact me again or discuss this with anyone else. Your silence is expected. Otherwise, I will ask for you to return my investment.

Sincerely, Tom Murray

Chapter One

TWELVE YEARS LATER

"I know we've seen the Athena statue a hundred times," Max said as we walked out of the Parthenon in Centennial Park, "but I love it every time. Thanks for letting us go. I needed to get out of the house for a bit."

I did too. Life had become a slog of taking on clients and struggling to help Max with his homework. After this summer proved to be the furthest thing from relaxing, I'd hoped our lives would calm down after we got back into our routine.

That had not happened.

"You're welcome," I said. "I needed to too. There's something about looking at Greek architecture that always gets me inspired."

I could classify the cost of admission as a business expense, though drawing cover art didn't seem like much of a business. I was barely making enough to pay our bills, especially since I no longer had any help from my boyfriend who I'd kicked out months ago. I didn't really even have the money for this excursion, but I couldn't find it in me to regret it. I'd seen more smiles today than I had in a while.

"Come on, Mom!" he called, already way ahead of me. "I want to go see where the train used to be."

I broke out into a jog, but quickly realized I was wearing the worst bra for such an activity. Curse my aversion to wired ones.

"Hang on!" I called back, switching to a power walk. I had to pause and catch my breath once I was next to him again. "How do you walk so fast?"

"I have to, in order to make it to class on time."

I couldn't believe he was old enough to be shuffling through different class periods during the day, but apparently they started that in sixth grade now.

He was growing too fast.

"So you've just learned to be a speed demon."

"It's easier for me than it is someone who's...older."

"Excuse me," I huffed. "I'm not old. I'm only thirty-two."

He smiled at me. "Didn't you find a gray hair the other day?"

"Yes, but only because I worry about you so much." I ruffled his hair.

"No," he moaned. "I spent all morning fixing my hair!"

"It's a mess now."

"I've been betrayed." The continued smile on his face told me he felt otherwise.

"Let's get to where the train was." I gestured for him to go ahead.

Even I could admit, the park was peaceful this time of year. There were a few park-goers out with their dogs, but the lingering October heat kept people away. I didn't bother double-checking if anyone was coming when we crossed one of the many pedestrian paths.

"Mom, look out!"

And that was when I collided with a hard chest.

I knew instantly that I was going to hit the ground. Hadley described my falls as watching a slow-motion blooper real. I never managed to catch myself, only making the fall worse.

"Shit," I heard a man say, and I felt arms wrapping around me. Instead of falling flat on my face like I anticipated, I was upright, in a warm, tight embrace.

"Whoa!" Max exclaimed. "Nice catch!"

The first thing I saw was a naked chest. Whoever my savior was, he was shirtless. And he had abs that shimmered with sweat.

I took in a choked breath. He was tanned from the sun and his breathing was fast, though not as fast as mine.

The back part of my brain, the illogical romantic in me—the one that never seemed to learn a lesson—said this was a meet-cute in progress.

The smarter half of my brain stopped the thought before it could get ahead of itself.

Romance novels were only on paper. They didn't happen in real life.

"Sorry," he said in a voice that stopped my heart. "I wasn't watching where I was going."

Icy horror made its way down my spine, but I couldn't look away. In fact, my eyes did the worst thing in the world: they trailed up to meet his.

And they were as green as ever.

Tom Murray had somehow grown. He was tall and well-built. His skin was glistening in the late summer heat. I dimly noted that he was probably out for a run.

I never thought I'd see him again. After his curt email, I did my job and never contacted him.

But I'd always imagined this. I'd played out a reunion with him a million times during my sleepless nights. The most realistic one was that he would run when he saw me. That was what he'd done when he found out about Max.

My favorite dream was that I'd run him over with a monster truck while Max cheered me on.

Neither of those things happened, however. His eyebrows were low on his forehead as he said, "It's you."

"Hi, Tom." I forewent my usual, obligatory "It's good to see you," since it definitely wasn't, in any capacity, good to see him.

"You're...here?"

"Do you know each other?" Max asked. If he were any other kid, he might notice just how similar he looked to this man. But Max didn't think that way. Even with Tom's green eyes and hair type, he wouldn't notice unless someone pointed it out to him.

Tom, however, saw it instantly. He slowly looked over at Max and did a double take, acting like he'd just been smacked in the face. His eyes were wide and his grip on me tightened.

I had forgotten he'd even been touching me. I wrenched myself out of his arms.

"He's a college acquaintance," I said.

Tom's eyes darted between Max and me as if he were watching a tennis match.

That's right, I thought. *Look at the child you abandoned and feel bad about it.*

"Go on ahead to where the train used to be," I said to Max. "I'll meet you there."

"Are you sure?"

"I'm fine," I assured him. "Just give me a minute."

"All right, Mom," he said. "I'll see you in, like, five minutes."

I nodded and watched Max disappear on the trail into the trees.

"How old is he?" Tom asked breathlessly.

"You know good and well how old he is," I hissed, turning to him.

Tom took a step back. "No, I truly don't."

"I'm sure you lost track of time as you *tended to your future.*"

"Is he...is he mine?" His eyes were wide as they bore into mine. Dimly, I noted I should have been sympathetic to this kind of expression. Tom looked like

Luna did when she'd wrecked Mom's car, or when she'd gotten caught drinking underage.

But I refused to let myself feel anything toward him.

"You told me to never talk about him again," I said. "I will hold true to my agreement. Goodbye, Tom."

"Selena, wait."

The use of my name made my fists ball. "What could you possibly say to make up for basically telling me to leave you alone when I said I was pregnant?"

"I...I did what?"

My anger slipped. He didn't remember? How could he not?

But then I shook myself out of it.

"You're not going to get me to feel sorry for you," I snapped. "You told me never to mention it or..."

Or else the money would need to be returned.

I stood straighter, horror dawning on me. I shouldn't have mentioned any of this. Technically, I hadn't contacted him. I had run into him, but I didn't think he would play fair.

"Never mind," I said. "We shouldn't be talking about this at all."

"No, don't—" He reached out and I stumbled over myself to get away from him.

"Don't touch me. Just go back to the life you have. I kept my end of the deal. So stay away from me."

And I turned around and rushed off before he could say anything else. When I caught up with Max, I told him we needed to leave and we hightailed it out of the park.

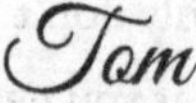

My heart pounded as my sister, Ruth, took in the news. It pounded just like it had when the woman who haunted my dreams ran off with an air of finality after telling me I turned away my son.

It was never my plan to tell anyone about what had transpired. But Ruth had come over, somehow knowing I wasn't in a good place. I had been determined to make her leave, but she simply said no.

And she'd saved me from obliterating my sobriety, so maybe I owed her one.

But now that she knew, I wondered if this would be the thing that made her disown me entirely, much like my younger brother seemed to have done years ago.

"You...have a *child*."

"The math adds up."

"How do you know for sure?"

"He has our green eyes." It was a trait that was strong with Ruth, me, and our dad. One look at us and anyone could tell we were related, just like I could tell with Max.

"That doesn't say for certain that he's—"

"Ruth, it's obvious. I don't need a DNA test to know."

"Did she admit it?"

"She heavily alluded to it."

"Then we don't know for sure. We need to know more. Can't you Facebook-stalk her to find out more about her?"

"I don't even have a Facebook. Do you?"

"No. Only Instagram. Maybe she's on there. What's her name?"

"All I know is that it's Selena."

"No last name?"

"Nope."

"Okay, I'll try it." She opened her phone, but shook her head. "That is definitely not enough information. Did you really not get her last name?"

"When was I supposed to?"

"I don't know, when she told you about the kid? She *did* tell you, right?"

"I don't remember."

"Seriously?"

"Seriously."

"How?" she asked. "Someone saying they're pregnant isn't something you just forget."

"I don't remember most of college."

"Why not?"

"Because I was drunk all the time. If I wasn't drunk, then I was listening to Dad go on and on about what he—" I shook my head. Ruth had already had it worse with our father. It may have been a couple of months since he told her that she'd never amount to anything simply because she was a woman, but that kind of hurt lasted a long time. Besides, I was Dad's favorite; I'd experienced the least of his displeasure. I didn't have a place to complain. "It doesn't matter."

"I think it does," she replied. "What was Dad telling you?"

"He was detailing his plan for Barry and me."

"Why?"

"I asked for bits of the plan every dinner we had. It kept him off you guys."

"Wait, I thought you were holed up with Dad talking shop because you *wanted* to be."

"No. Dad was a jackass, especially to you about things. Distracting him seemed to help."

"You did it even in college?"

"He wanted to tell you to get over your high school rivalry and find someone to marry. I figured it wouldn't have been good to hear at the time. Or ever, for that matter."

"Well, no, but…I had no idea. I thought you liked talking to him and that was part of why you were the favorite."

"It doesn't mean much to be the favorite of the worst person we know." I looked down at my feet. "And besides, it didn't work. He still thought what he did about you, pushed Barry into school, and I drank so much that I can't remember when Selena told me about my child, or if she even did.”

Ruth let out a heavy breath. “Our parents fucking suck. That’s all I can say. But we’re away from them, which means you can change. You can take that energy you were using on Dad to focus on figuring out if this child is yours, and if he is, then doing better.”

“Let’s say that hypothetically, he is. His mother doesn’t want anything to do with me. It’s pointless.”

“Then, *hypothetically*, you need to try. At least find her and meet your son.”

“No, I’m not the kind of person he would want as a father. I need to stay away from him. From them.”

“But—”

“Ruth, *no*. I’m not good with kids. Or adults. Or *people*. The last thing I need is to fuck up my child like Dad did to us.”

She was silent for a long time. “If you are his dad, then how do you know you’re going to mess this up?”

“Because it’s what I always do.”

“So, you’re just going to leave it? You’re going to let a child who could possibly be yours grow up without you?”

The idea sent a knife into my chest, but I shook my head. “Maybe it’s better that he doesn’t know me. There’re a million people who could be better for him.”

“Or you could fucking grow a pair, investigate the claim to find out if it’s true, and if it is, *be* the man he deserves. Did you ever consider that option?”

“I can’t change what’s happened. I can’t change the man I’ve become.”

“Yes you can.”

“How? The damage is done. Once you’ve messed up like I have, there is no coming back from it.”

“You owe him to be better. You can start with one choice. Then another. And then another. Over time, it adds up. You didn’t get here because you had one drink in college. You got here because you started with one and then kept going."

"But—"

"No arguing. You're at a crossroads here, Tom. You can be an asshole and stay away and not *try* to fix it. Or you can do something. Which one is going to help you sleep at night?"

The right answer was in front of me. Ruth, as always, knew how to lead me right to it.

"I don't know how to find her," I said.

"Come on. The family business doesn't have some connection who can hunt someone down?"

I thought about it. "There is one person."

"There you go."

"But I doubt she'll want to do me a favor."

"Come on, Tom. You're the acting CEO of Murray and Sons and almost a billionaire. I think there's something you can fucking do."

Francine Doberman was a legend at Murray and Sons. She was the go-to woman whenever a driver wasn't responding to messages. She could track them down within minutes.

As a no-nonsense woman in her sixties, I knew she had garnered respect in the company. Most people looked up to her. She was cutthroat, yet somehow, caring to those who needed her guidance. She was also the only person I'd ever seen who could roll her eyes at Dad and get away with it.

Why she stayed, no one knew. Maybe it was all the employees she'd taken under her wing throughout her tenure. Maybe she was just trying to make it to retirement.

I had stayed away from her since becoming acting CEO. Ever since Dad was escorted out of the building kicking and screaming, people looked to me to be the enforcer during his absence.

What they didn't know was that I was the one who got him kicked out in the first place. Once I'd focused on sobriety, I saw how he treated the women who worked for him. I found inappropriate emails to two of them, and they agreed to take up a case for workplace harassment. He should have been fired months ago, but he'd been fighting it tooth and nail.

I was sure most people expected me to be on Dad's side. After all, I was the one who was made in his image. But it would look worse if people knew what I'd done. When I'd reported him, my goal hadn't been to become CEO—but they wouldn't see it that way.

Francine definitely wouldn't. I'd heard rumors that she hated Dad, and in turn, me. It was terrifying walking to her office, but Ruth's words were playing over and over in my head. I needed to do something and Francine was the one who could help.

She had her own office in the back of the building. She'd never been assigned it, but when the man that used to occupy the room quit, Francine used the space to yell at a driver and had worked there ever since.

I knocked on her door while she was taking a bite of a breakfast sandwich. Her desk faced away from where I stood, and she chose to look out the window at the Nashville skyline.

"I told you not to bother me unless someone was murdered," she said, turning to glare at whoever dared to interrupt her.

When she saw it was me, she did exactly as I suspected she would. Her mouth thinned and she gently set down her sandwich.

"Mr. Murray," she said, her voice only marginally kinder than it had been before. "What a surprise."

"Hello, Francine. How's work?"

"It's fine. Everything is going smoothly."

I nodded and my mind stumbled over how to ask her for something. I'd done the obligatory small talk, but her hard stare shook me to my core.

"Now, I know you didn't check in for no reason," she added. "What can I do for you?"

I was more than grateful that she'd figured it out.

"I need you to find someone for me."

"I wasn't lying when I said things were going smoothly. Every load we have is on time and accounted for."

I took one breath, and then a second. "This isn't for work. This is a personal request."

Her head jerked back in shock and she could only blink at me for a moment. I wondered if she would find a way to turn me down. I would have, if I were her.

"What kind of personal request?"

"I need you to find someone. It's a woman that I used to know."

She squinted at me. "Why?"

"Because I...I need to talk to her."

"I'm not in the business of giving men random women's contact information."

"I can send a letter, for you to deliver it. I won't know anything. I would pay you for it too."

"So, you want me to be your delivery woman?"

"Just this once."

"I'd get paid per mile?"

"Yes," I said.

"And what about after?"

My chest tightened. "What else do you want?"

"A salary increase when our evaluation comes around in three months. Since things have been...tight these last few years, I've not even gotten a merit raise for my tenure."

"We gave out merit increases, though."

"To *senior* employees. I'm technically entry-level."

That didn't make sense. "Why are you still in an entry-level position?"

"My evaluations from your father cite my attitude. Because of that, I've never been able to be promoted."

"Then why are you still here?"

Francine's mouth pressed into a tight line. "I've been here since before your dad took over. I have a pension plan that I don't want to give up—*unless* I become a glorified delivery woman and don't even get my three percent on top of it. Make it five and I will guarantee that not a soul in this place will ever hear a peep about this."

Five percent. That was pocket change.

"What are you making now?" I asked.

She told me an amount that was under the poverty line in Nashville.

I had to grit my teeth to keep from groaning. I knew Dad was miserly about salaries, but I couldn't believe it was *this* bad.

Francine watched me carefully. "I'm not asking for much. I am even fine staying as a customer service advocate. I just want fair pay."

Son of a bitch. She was stuck in *that* title too?

I needed to do something to change this. *It starts with one choice,* Ruth had said. And I would start here.

"You're no longer a customer service advocate."

"You better not be *firing* me."

"Far from it. From now on you'll be a...logistics coordinator."

She stared blankly at me. "Is that even a real job?"

"It is now. I'll make a stop by HR on my way back to my office. I'm going to make it a mid-level position, and because of your experience and track record around here, I'm tripling your salary."

Her jaw dropped. "Are you being serious?"

"I know what you do for this company, Francine. I'd do more, but I have to cover my tracks considering I'm only acting as the CEO, and I have a distinct feeling this is a decision my father would disagree with. But this is something you should have had a long time ago."

She gulped and her eyes were wide. "That is very...generous of you, sir."

One kind thing down.

"It's what you deserve. And between you and me, my father can't see past it when any woman is smarter than him."

Maybe I shouldn't have said that, but it garnered a smile from her.

"I know the type," she said. "Now, will I lose the pension if I move into this position?"

"Why would you lose that?"

"Todd had a rule about me changing positions and losing it."

"Consider that canceled. I'll send you a written email detailing what this job will entail. If by some miracle my father does return, then you'll have a paper trail."

"Thank you," she said. "Now...tell me who I'm finding."

Chapter Two

Selena

I watched the sunrise from the window of my living room with our cat, Meow-cifer, nestled in my lap.

I'd tried to go to bed at a normal hour, but instead of getting any rest, I had a dream that Tom knocked on my door, apologized for everything, and got down on one knee to propose to make up for it.

And I didn't want to go back to sleep after that ridiculous, illogical manifestation of a future that would never exist.

Instead, I got some work done.

I didn't have a regular job. I tried to, but I was so exhausted after every shift that I was vastly unproductive any time I was home. And since I didn't have a degree, I was paid minimum wage no matter where I worked.

When I still had someone living with me, I could focus solely on designing covers for novels, which brought in a little income. Now that I lived alone again, it didn't feel like enough, but I knew that I couldn't return to a cashier job. I'd lose precious energy that I needed to be using on being the best mom I could be for Max.

The obvious solution was to take on more work. I didn't mind it because I loved what I did. Especially when my clients were romance authors.

Despite my rude awakening twelve years ago when Tom sent that letter, I still loved romance novels. They may have been works of fiction, but I needed that escape from the heaviness of real life. Those novels all had happy endings and that was what kept me reading.

I worked with authors to either design covers or to create art of their characters to use in their marketing. It brought me joy in ways no other career had, even when my own life felt like it was falling apart.

I just hoped I could continue paying my bills with it.

The sound of a Lila Wilde song pulled me out of my work. If music was playing, it meant Max was awake.

"Hey, kiddo," I said as he walked downstairs. "Happy Monday." Meowcifer leaped off my legs and beelined her way over to Max, the only other human she liked.

"Sure," he said, yawning.

"Are you still tired?" I asked. "You went to bed at nine."

"I was woken up in the middle of a dream. I never feel rested when that happens."

"Me too."

"Did you get any more sleep?" he asked.

I blinked. My son had the talent of turning all the concern and love I had for him right back at me. It was like he knew I was always my last priority.

"Not this time. Maybe tonight. I should probably clean."

The house was a mess, as per usual. Most days, I was able to keep it tidy in case Mom made a surprise visit. She associated disorganization with poor mental health and I refused to worry her.

"Mom," he said.

"I'm fine! Totally fine."

"Is this where you say you're fine but you're really not?"

"And how would you know I do that? Is it because you do the same thing?"

He shrugged.

"How is gym class?"

He immediately groaned in response.

My ex-boyfriend, Jax, was the last person I wanted as Max's teacher. Last school year, Jax had proven not to be able to keep his personal and work life separate and would often talk to Max about me during class. I knew it was only going to get worse after I'd broken up with him. At the start of this school year, I tried to have Max removed from Jax's class, but unless I could prove he was being negatively impacted in some way, he would have to stay put.

So far, I had nothing tangible.

"Is this because of Jax or because you're not a fan of gym?"

"Can I say both?"

I narrowed my eyes. "Has he done anything?"

"Um, not really. It's just weird having him be my teacher when he used to live with us. I mean, I've seen his *feet*. How can I go on knowing I've seen something like that?"

"His feet were pretty gross."

"It'll be fine. I'll adjust. You don't have to worry."

He'd been adjusting ever since school started back two months ago. I wondered how long it would take. Max was the kind of kid that was slow to change.

But I didn't get long to mull it over because the doorbell rang.

"Want me to get it?" Max asked.

"No, I've got it. You just get your lunch and backpack."

He nodded and went back upstairs to retrieve his bag from his room. I walked to the door and opened it.

A middle-aged woman stood on the front stoop. On instinct, I checked to be sure this was from a reputable delivery service, but froze when I saw the truck in the driveway.

"You're from Murray and Sons," I breathed, looking at the woman.

"Kind of. This is a personal mission. I just use the truck when I have to go knock the sense into someone."

I gripped the door handle tightly. Did I have anything I could use as a weapon if I needed to? I glanced to my right. How hard could I swing an umbrella?

Or maybe I could use Meowcifer. She could take down anyone with her claws.

"Oh, honey, not *you*," she said. "Trust me, I'm here for your benefit."

"It's a little hard to believe that considering the name on that truck."

"Ah, so you've heard of the Murrays?" she asked. "Can't say I'm surprised."

"What do you want?"

"I have a delivery for you."

My heart sank. This had to be because of our run-in at the park.

"He wants me to pay it back, doesn't he?"

"I have no idea what is in this letter," the woman said. "Sort of. I did put a few things together as I found your address. A son, huh?"

"I'm not supposed to mention it."

"Oh, of course. You can never mention when a Murray screws you over."

I pressed my lips into a thin line to keep myself from either screaming or crying. I didn't know which I wanted to do, but I did know what I *had* to do.

I stuck out my palm. "I'll take the letter."

My mind raced at the thought of the words that could be inside of it. The white envelope was thicker than I thought it would be. "I didn't give him your address, by the way. So, if it's bad news, he doesn't know where you live."

"I'm sure he'd find a way to know."

"You don't have to open it, you know. I doubt he'll do this again. He looked like he was getting teeth pulled when he asked this of me. Then again, that's just how he looks."

Long ago, naive me thought that face was cute.

"Thanks for not giving him my address."

"Us ladies have to stick together. If he *does* ask again, I'll stall him. Or maybe divert him to some other poor schmuck he hates at work." She shrugged. "I have options. You take care, sweetie."

The woman walked away and I waited for her to drive off before I headed back inside. I stared at the letter as if it were a bomb that could go off at any moment.

I needed to rip it open and get the suspense over with, but I didn't get the chance to.

"What's that?" Max asked.

"Oh, nothing. Just an ad." I threw it on the coffee table as if it truly were junk mail I didn't care about.

"Are you sure?"

"Do you have your math homework? We left it on the kitchen table last night after we finished working on it."

"Oh, yeah. I have it."

Sooner than later, my diversion tactics weren't going to work. But I would continue to use them until then.

"Then let's get going."

Max walked out to the car and I followed.

We lived in a small home in south Nashville. It wasn't anything fancy, but it was safe enough to raise a child in. Tom's money had helped me out in ways I didn't like to admit. It was such a large amount that I'd been able to pay off my medical bills from having Max and put a down payment on the very house I lived in now.

Mom lived with us before Jax moved in. I'd always had someone to pay half the bills, but ever since I broke it off with him, I was reluctant to admit to Mom that I needed the help once again.

Besides, she was dealing with Luna dating some older rich man whom she didn't approve of. That alone held all of her attention.

I'd figure something out. I *had* to.

But it was hard. Everything was more expensive, whether it was food, clothes, or gas. I thought not working a full-time job would be the dream, but not having money had turned it into a nightmare.

It didn't help that Max's school was across town and my car ate through gas like no one's business.

Max put on his usual Lila playlist and I tried to get lost in her music the same way he could. But all I could think about was my own lack of money, and that envelope at home.

"Whoa, Mom." Max's urgent voice brought me out of my thoughts. "Watch out for the cursed stop sign!"

I slammed on the brakes, barely coming to a stop in time. I glared over at the worst-placed stop sign in town. It was at the bottom of a massive hill and had a tree branch covering it.

"Sorry," I said. "I'll pay better attention."

Max went back to being quiet and my thoughts quickly returned to the letter. I drove on autopilot.

"Are you okay?" he asked as we pulled into school.

"Never better," I muttered. "I just have to do a few things when I get home."

"Can I help?"

"I'm fine. You just worry about school." Max's shoulders fell. He knew I wasn't fine. "We'll talk when you get home, okay?"

"Is anything bad happening?"

I hated that I didn't know.

"I'll handle it. I promise."

He gave me a hug before he headed inside. I took an unsteady breath before driving home.

My brain continued to conjure up words that the letter could say. I once thought that the original one he sent me was the worst thing I would ever read, but time could make an evil man eviler. I could picture the letter demanding back the money he'd given me, threatening me with court proceedings I couldn't afford to fight if I didn't comply.

I immediately went to the letter the moment I got home. I lifted it with nervous hands and tore into it. I expected this to be a letter sent to intimidate me.

Selena,

I've tried to write this many times, but I simply do not know what to say. I suppose the first thing should be that I'm sorry. I'm sorry I didn't know. I'm sorry for what I must have said to you after. I have no memory of it due to how much I partied in college. If I could go back, I would.

It's still no excuse for what I've done to you. Letting you raise a child by yourself will forever be one of my biggest regrets. I'd understand if you never want him to know me, or the kind of person I am. I deserve that.

But I also can't continue to let you do this by yourself. I am willing to agree to some amount of child support, plus any back payments I have missed over my years of being a failure. I spoke with my lawyer and the only thing they might need would be a DNA test to ensure he is mine. I do not have any doubts, though. My number is at the bottom of this letter if you ever need m e.

I know that route might cause questions from him, however. I've enclosed a credit card for you to use. You can sign my name. If you're not comfortable with that, I will open one in yours.

Sincerely, Tom Murray

I felt the card as I got to the end of the letter, and I dropped it as if it were on fire. A thick, black, plastic rectangle was on the floor, looking up at me as if it weren't from the man I'd despised for twelve years.

Gently kneeling, I picked it up. Was he being serious? Who sends a credit card to a stranger?

Was this some sort of test to see if I would take advantage of him?

I returned to the letter and read it multiple times, thinking maybe there was a code I could decipher.

He had no memory of paying me off? Then why say anything? Why even send a letter at all?

I knew one thing. If this was a test, then I wasn't going to fail. He'd get his stupid little card back today, and I'd continue on with my life as if I never ran into him. The letter was on the Murray and Sons letterhead, and I had no doubt he worked at his family's office. That would be where I would find him.

I hit pay on the stupid website the parking garage made me navigate to for the ridiculous ten-dollar parking fee and squeezed my car into a tiny spot, leaving me even more heated than I already was. I didn't even stop to look at the building. All I knew was the task in front of me.

Find Tom.

He was planning something. I didn't know what it was yet, but I was going to find out. There was no way he could suddenly be so kind after turning us away all those years ago.

My eyes caught glimpses of marble and deep-toned wood as I walked in, and there was a receptionist sitting behind a far-too-opulent desk. But I wasn't there to admire the scenery.

"I need to see Tom Murray," I said to the woman.

She looked at my old leggings and T-shirt with a raised eyebrow. "Do you have an appointment?"

"N-no. But I'm Selena Martinez."

"I don't recognize the name."

"He sent me a letter and gave me something I need to give back. I just need to see him for one second."

"Sorry. Random people don't get to see the acting CEO unless there's an appointment."

Of course. I should have known he was at the top of his family's company. This was like the start of every book I'd ever read. *The CEO and the Wallflower,* starring Tom Murray and Selena Martinez.

Except instead of a happy ending, I was only going to get burned.

I considered throwing the card on the desk and leaving, but then anyone could have it, and I refused to be complacent in his poor card security any more than I had to be.

But I also refused to use the number he gave me. My previous electronic communications with him had left something to be desired.

My mind was slow to come up with a solution to my problem, and the receptionist probably wasn't going to tolerate much more of me hanging around.

"Fine," I said. "Tell him I was here then. Please."

The receptionist smiled. "Sure. I'll do that."

There was a tone in her voice, one that Hadley would call sarcastic. Damn it. I didn't have the energy for this.

The nearby elevator dinged, pulling me out of my thoughts. I let out a long breath and turned, wondering if simply shredding the card should have been my first choice. Rage was an emotion that I struggled with. Usually, it made me make impulsive, stupid decisions.

I was prepared to berate myself for my own stupidity, but then I saw who was walking out of the elevator.

Tom Murray looked just as good with a shirt on as he did without it. He was dressed in a suit and tie, looking like he owned the world. And within these four walls, he did.

When he saw me, he froze, green eyes wide. I gritted my teeth, wondering if he would turn me away just like the receptionist had.

"Oh, sir," the receptionist called. "Welcome back from lunch. You didn't receive any new messages while you were out."

I turned to glare. Seriously?

"Selena?" he asked, his eyes still on me.

I turned back. "Yes. I came here to give you this back." I held up the card. "But I guess I didn't realize I needed an appointment."

"Julia," Tom started, leaning around me to look at the receptionist, "from now on, she is the exception to this rule. She can see me any time she wants."

"What?" Julia asked. "But you've never..."

"She is exceptionally important to me. Do you understand?"

Julia nodded.

My heart pounded in my ears. That was almost...*no*.

This sincerity had to be a trick of some sort. There had to be something I wasn't seeing here, some joke I was blind to.

"Let's go to my office."

I followed him through the sea of employees. People avoided him like he was the plague. Even I could see how they all hunched over their desks, never making eye contact and pretending to be busy.

That was the reminder I needed that he was not a kind man. After that display with Julia, it was getting hard to remember.

We walked into an office with floor-to-ceiling windows looking over the skyline.

"Did you park in the lot?" he asked. "I can validate your—"

"I'm not here to talk about parking," I said. I held up the card again. "What is this?"

"A credit card."

"*Your* credit card."

"Yes, it has my name on it."

"No, what does it *mean*? Is it a test to see if I'm some sort of gold digger? Is it to get me arrested for fraud or something?"

His eyes met mine. "There is no ulterior motive. It's there if you ever need it."

Tom's gaze didn't waver and his voice remained steady. There were none of the signs that I'd taught myself to look for when I needed to know if someone was being dishonest.

I could imagine taking him up on the offer. Maybe I could get Max new shirts, ones that didn't have tags that bothered him all day. Maybe I could afford to treat him to pizza occasionally instead of cooking at home every single night.

Maybe things wouldn't be so tight.

"I can't use this," I said. "I refuse to open myself up to liability by signing your name."

"I'll open one in your name, then, and have all the bills sent to me."

"Why would you do that? I could ruin your finances."

"I somehow doubt you would," he said. "And even if you did, it's a fair price to pay for not being there."

What a line. It was so good it knocked loose my defenses.

I hated that I was in a position to even need this. Whenever I imagined seeing him again, it was when I had my shit together. And sure, it sometimes looked like I did, but I was running on empty, both mentally and financially.

"I will give you whatever you want," he added. "I deeply regret what I did."

I was pretty sure he'd said that exact line in one of my dreams.

"Do you have a time machine?" I asked. "Because it would have been nice to have you there twelve years ago."

Immediately, I could see how the words affected him. He let out a slow sigh and looked at his feet. "I know," he said. "I know I messed up."

"Yeah, you did. And now you're being nice which is so...*weird*. You told me my silence was expected. We're not supposed to even be here talking about this."

"I asked you to stay silent?" He sighed again, rubbing his forehead. "Why would I...unless it was because of my dad."

"You really don't remember?"

"No. But with the things I've done since college, I'd believe it."

Wow. This really felt genuine. But the 'apology' was missing one thing. "And how am I supposed to know you've changed? You haven't even said sorry to my face. You sent me a credit card, but it's not like you're on your *knees* apologizing to me or anything."

His eyes turned to me. "Is that what you want?"

I let out a humorless laugh. "It's a good start, at least."

Tom walked to me, standing only a few inches away. My traitorous heart took in his scent of moss and oak, which was somehow better than I remembered. Despite the alluring smell invading my nose, I kept my eyes on him, ready to hear his apology with my own ears.

What I didn't expect was for him to take my words literally.

Tom sank to his knees, his gaze focused on me the whole time. My eyes grew wide as I saw something impossible play out in front of me.

"Selena, I am so sorry for all that I've done. I'm sorry I didn't accept full responsibility for my actions all those years ago, and I'm sorry that you had to do it alone for so long. It would be the greatest honor to be able to help you in any way."

My heart pounded.

Red alert!, the romantic in me screamed. *This is something out of your favorite novel!*

Tom wasn't supposed to apologize like this. He was supposed to turn me away like he had all those years ago.

While I worked out what I could possibly say, he waited patiently on his knees. He didn't sigh or roll his eyes or rush me. If he was the man I thought he was, that absolutely would have been what he would do.

But this had to be fake. Absolutely *had* to be.

"I-I don't know what to say."

"You don't have to say anything. I don't expect you to forgive me. I just...*want* to be better. The only thing I can do is prove it to you by giving you action. Not empty promises."

It would have been easier to say no if I didn't *need* the help. Accepting his offer might blow up in my face. In fact, I was *sure* it was going to.

But the smallest, dumbest part of me said that maybe this was one step in the right direction of my happy ending.

After all, this was what I'd wanted all along.

"I'll accept *some* help. But I can't use a card in your name."

"Then I'll give you one in yours."

"And I'm only using it for Max," I added. And only what I could pay back if Tom screwed me over.

"I understand. We can work on opening one now...if you're okay with me getting up."

"Y-yeah, I'm okay with that."

He lifted himself to his feet. I knew that the memory of this moment would be burned into my brain forever. I would probably lose sleep over this.

No, I *definitely* was going to lose sleep over this.

"I'm going to the AmEx site. I'll let you add yourself as an authorized user."

I nodded and watched as he did exactly what he said. When the screen prompted for my information, he moved away to let me type in my details.

"Have you given any thought to the other thing? The child support? I know a DNA test might be hard to explain to Max, but—"

"We can do the DNA test. I'll tell him it's about his ancestry."

"Okay, then we can work on child support."

"I don't want child support. I'll do the DNA test so you know I'm not lying, but I don't need to take this to court." I focused on typing in my full name and clicked the next button when I finished. "I'm done with this, by the way."

"But—"

"Tom," I said. "The answer is no. Besides, don't you want to know he's yours?"

"I think I know the answer."

"Well, you'll know for sure in a few days. That's all I'm willing to do right now."

His lips pressed together, but he didn't argue any further. "Fine. Then I'll finish up the credit application. You'll get a card in the mail."

"I'll send you a text with everything I buy. Including the at-home DNA test. And maybe an ancestry one to cover it up."

"You don't have to send me receipts."

"I definitely will. The last thing I need is for you to question something and not want to pay it."

"I won't do that, even if you bought a house with it."

"Is the limit even that high?"

"I could probably authorize it."

I was tempted to take him up on his offer. So tempted, but the last thing I needed was him demanding the money back if he ever came to regret this—just like he'd threatened to if I'd ever discussed Max.

"But I also want you to do whatever makes you comfortable."

I nodded, knowing it was time to leave so I could overthink this in peace. I began to walk for the door.

"Selena?"

"What?"

"Thank you for coming by."

My body still felt warm. I hightailed it out of the office before my mind could remind me that I knew exactly how he felt when he had nothing on.

As I approached my car, I checked my watch. It was still hours before I had to pick up Max from school. What I should have done was get back to work. I had plenty of projects that needed completing.

But I was so frazzled that my hands were shaking too much to do any drawing.

Maybe I needed to talk this out, and there was no one I trusted more than my best friend.

Hadley now lived in a new-built home in an up-and-coming suburb of Nashville. Her husband, Allen, bought it when they found out she was pregnant. It was massive, with vaulted ceilings and white walls that made everything feel bigger. Almost too big. I'd once joked about Allen buying her something so huge, like he was trying to keep her locked away in a castle, but he'd taken offense to that. I had tried to apologize for what I'd said, but the damage was done. It added to the list of reasons why he didn't like me.

When I pulled up to the house, she was pressure washing the driveway. Despite my stress, I couldn't resist smiling at her.

Nesting must have been hitting her hard.

"It's perfectly safe while pregnant!" she called as I pulled to the curb.

"No judgment from me!" I wasn't sure she heard me over the loud machine, but I'd come at just the right time—she was almost done.

"Whew!" she exclaimed. "And don't even say the word *nesting*. It's not nesting if it needs to be done."

"Sure," I said. "Ready to go into your perfectly clean not-nest?"

"Yes. I need a snack." She walked to the door without another word and held it open for me. As usual, Hadley's house was spotless. She'd always been the tidy one in our friendship.

She had her shit together and could read people in ways I would never be able to. She'd met her husband while traveling in Europe and they'd had a perfect fairy-tale romance.

Hadley, much like Luna, was everyone's main character, and I loved her for it. She deserved this beautiful house for her family. And while her husband may not like me all that much, if she was happy, then I was too. She'd gotten her happy ending.

But at the thought of happy endings, my brain reverted to the image of Tom on his knees, and the apology I'd always dreamed of.

"Is everything okay?" she asked as she shoved grapes into her mouth. "You seem a little off."

"Um, yeah. I think everything is fine, for now."

"What happened?"

"I ran into Tom Murray the other day."

Hadley's eyes went wide. "Seriously?"

I told her everything: how Tom said he didn't remember me reaching out about Max and how he'd had a letter he wrote hand delivered to me, which resulted in me going to see him.

She listened with rapt attention, eyes only growing wider as I spoke.

"Okay, first off, if anything this wild happens again, you have to call or text me immediately. I don't care if I'm in labor."

"I think you'll think differently once you're actually *in* labor."

"That's not the point! You can tell me anything at any time. You know I care about you."

"But you've been busy with getting ready for the baby, and when I was pregnant, I didn't want anyone to even *look* at me."

"You had a hard pregnancy with Max. I'm in a different position. As long as I have a steady stream of food, I'm good."

Or not with Allen, I wanted to add. But I held it in. I didn't want to cause any more problems in their relationship than I already had.

"Okay. I'll be sure to let you know if anything like this happens again."

"Good. Now onto the next part. I know you watched that man's body language. Tell me everything he did."

And I did. This was how I figured out people. I told someone who was good at reading people, usually Hadley, and they told me what it might mean.

"Wait," she stopped me. "He apologized on his *knees*?"

"Yes. On his knees. In his office. He made eye contact the whole time."

"Whoa. I didn't think men could even do that. I have a hard time getting Allen to apologize when he leaves the toilet seat up."

"I know! It seemed genuine."

"It *sounds* genuine."

"Could he be?"

"I have no clue. Body language wise, yes. History wise? I don't know. He seems to be able to pivot on a dime."

"Do you think it's the drinking?" I asked.

"It's hard to say. I know you've wanted Max to have a father figure in his life, even if it wasn't his actual dad, so maybe this is a good thing. But I'm also worried he's going to leave again. And this time, it'll hurt Max too."

My eyes fell to my hands. "I want to see what he does with the card. If he pays that off without coming after me for it, then I'll try something more. And then maybe I'll let him meet Max. On a *very* trial basis. Max won't even know who Tom is."

"That might be for the best. It didn't take long for Tom to show his true colors last time."

"It didn't. And I refuse to let anything happen to Max."

"Exactly," she said. "So, what are you going to buy first?"

"Besides a DNA test? I was thinking socks."

"Oh, come on! That's so boring! At least ask for the calculator Max needs too."

"I'll start with the socks. Then maybe the calculator if Tom stays true to his word."

"That's fair. The last thing you need is him sticking you with a bill you can't afford."

"Exactly. I'm prepared for the worst-case scenario."

And I was. Worst case, he would leave again and I'd deal with the disappointment that I'd already felt before. I didn't like the idea, but I at least knew how to handle it now. Max would be none the wiser.

Despite the plan, I couldn't shake the worry that I was somehow making the biggest mistake of my life by letting this man back in. But I also knew I'd be making a worse one if I didn't at least concede to the near-impossible chance that Tom could be a good man.

Tom

I didn't hear from her for a few days, but finally, after the card was delivered, she sent a text.

Unknown: Bought Max socks along with the DNA tests. He needed them. Here is the receipt. I suppose we'll need to meet up at some point so I can give you your swab.

I told her it was fine and that I would pay it off, plus gave her some options on where we could meet. When she didn't respond, I wondered if maybe I'd done something wrong while messaging her. Maybe I should have said something different.

I needed to talk to someone, and the first people that came to mind was my siblings.

But I doubted that they would want to hear from me, not after how many times I'd screwed up. They'd be better off not answering my calls and going on with their lives. Barry was good at that.

Ruth, not so much.

Would she answer if I called? Would she even care to know an update?

She came to check on you, I reminded myself.

She had to care about me in some sort of way. And I wasn't able to deal with this situation alone.

The phone rang four times, and then she answered. "Tom? Is something wrong with the PATH deal again? Who do I need to yell at?"

"This isn't about work," I said, ignoring my racing heart. "Especially not the deal with your company. It's more about life."

"Oh," she said. "Wait, really?"

"Is that okay?"

"Of course it is."

"Okay, then—"

"Hang on. I don't want to catch up over the phone. You free for lunch?"

"I can make it happen. Aren't you at work?"

"PATH values a work-life balance, so I can leave for lunch if I want to. How about we meet up?"

When was the last time I even had a meal with my family that didn't take place in our parents' house?

"Sure. Just let me know where."

She suggested a place that was between her office and mine. As I walked down the hall, I instinctually checked Dad's office to be sure he wasn't somehow lurking in the shadows, ready to tell me to work more.

Thankfully, he wasn't.

When I entered the restaurant, Ruth was already seated at a table by the front door, patiently waiting.

"How did you get here so fast?" I asked.

"I power walked."

I didn't know how she managed it in her heels, but she always seemed to be able to do the impossible. She'd been wearing them since she was in high school, when Barry had grown taller than her.

"Is your day going well?"

"Are you, Tom Murray, trying to make small talk with me?"

"Isn't that what's polite?"

"Yes, but you and Barry are the worst at even *attempting* what's polite."

Shame heated my cheeks. I hated that my reputation proceeded me.

"But you're trying to be better," she added. "Which I appreciate. Good job."

"I...don't know how to take a compliment from you."

"I'm not surprised, considering how our parents were, but usually I smile and say thank you."

"Thank you," I managed, but a smile didn't happen.

"You got halfway there," she said. "Still good."

"So," I began, trying to function after the compliment derailment. "Your day?"

"My day has been great. It's a little odd coming from a place where I had to fight to do everything. Some days, I feel lost when people listen to me."

"Was your last job that bad?"

"It was terrible, but that old CEO got forced to step down once half the staff quit at the same time. I found out the news last week when I hired someone else from there."

"How happy are you?"

"Ecstatic." A radiant smile accompanied the admission. "It's very fulfilling to see a place that screwed you over crash and burn."

"I felt the same way when Dad was escorted out."

"Is anything else fulfilling you? Like maybe a relationship with your *hypothetical* son?"

"It's only been a few days. His mother is...wary, to say the least."

"So you found her."

"I did. Francine Doberman is a miracle worker."

"I think I know that name." She frowned as she thought about it. "Oh! Is she the woman who finds missing trucks?"

"Yes. Did you know Dad had her stuck in a customer service position because of her 'attitude'?"

"You better have fixed that. Otherwise, she'll have a message from PATH tomorrow offering her a job."

"I did. I tripled her salary."

"See? You do have a heart." She smiled and opened her mouth to say something else, but the waitress came over to take our orders. Ruth continued as if we'd never been interrupted. "So, how did contacting Selena go?"

"Okay, I think. I sent her a letter apologizing for how stupid I'd been, and my

AmEx card in case she needs it."

"You *what*?" she asked. "You sent someone you don't know your credit card?"

"I figured she wouldn't want to give me the time of day, but I had to do something."

"That's bold, Tom, but also a *huge* financial risk."

"It didn't do much. She came to the office today to give it back to me."

"She could have spent a lot of money on that thing."

"I'd deserve it," I said. "But she's far nobler than many."

"It seems like it. It almost makes me want to meet her."

"I sincerely doubt she wants anything to do with me. Max, either, for that matter."

"But you're trying. Staying sober and being patient is the way to fix this."

"It's miserable," I said, sighing. "But it's the consequence of my actions, so I need to deal with it. I'm trying not to think about the ways I've messed this up, but it's hard."

"The point is that you're trying. Let's not forget that. Compartmentalize the bad and focus on being better."

"That's a good idea."

"I have those every now again. Now, tell me more about Selena."

"What else is there?"

"How about what she looks like?"

"She's..." I struggled with words. I thought back to her red sweater and leggings, and how she was the only one in the office not dressed up; due to the strict dress code Dad forced on employees, we were all required to come to work in business formal attire. She'd looked angry—rightfully so—but something I'd done had cut through her standoffishness, making her jaw drop. I hoped it meant I was doing something right.

"Tom?" Ruth asked.

"She's...pretty."

I hoped she didn't notice how I stumbled over the words, but Ruth never missed a thing.

"Are you flustered?"

"No."

"I think you are."

"I mean...I remember her. The good parts, that is."

"The good parts? Wait, if this is about the sex, I don't want to know."

"I wasn't just meaning that. I met her when I was sober. It was in the coffee shop at Vanderbilt, before it was converted into a major chain."

"And you stayed sober the whole time?"

"Yes. I was very nervous, but she was, I don't know...calming."

"Calming? Did you have feelings for her?"

"I didn't know her long enough for that. I met her once and that was it. After, I apparently sent her a letter that said I didn't want anything to do with her, or the baby, which was..." I closed my eyes as emotions hit me. "...a huge mistake. I can't even imagine being in the headspace to *do* that."

"Didn't you say you were talking to Dad about business?"

"Yes."

"And Barry was acting out around then."

"I...I think I remember that. Dad was so angry he wasn't even trying in school. He kept saying that he was disappointed that I was the only one of his kids who made something of myself."

"And, of course, I wasn't a part of it." Ruth rolled her eyes. "Whatever. He's a sexist asshole."

"Yeah. I probably panicked and said whatever I could." I sighed, annoyed. "I wish I could remember it all."

Ruth let out a long breath. "I can see why you'd be mad that you don't remember."

"More like I can see why *Selena* would be mad. I'm the dumbass who fucked it all up."

"You were also under a ton of pressure to be the best, just like the rest of us were. You're allowed to be angry about that."

"I am, but when it comes to talking about *him*, my possible son, I can't even think of being angry."

"Why?"

"I don't know. I just don't want anger anywhere near him."

"Do you mean *your* anger?"

"Yes," I replied. "I can't...I won't be how Dad was to me. *If* I ever get to properly meet Max, then I know I can never be cutthroat like Dad was. I can't imagine calling him up at midnight and threatening to send him to jail for underage drinking if he didn't get As on his finals."

"God, *fuck* Dad. Every time I hear anything else about him, I hate him more."

"He's awful," I said. "And he made me awful."

"An awful person wouldn't care about what they've done. I can tell just by the look on your face that you regret what happened. Do you think Dad regrets anything?"

"Absolutely not."

"Then you're already a step ahead of him," she said. "Don't take that for granted."

"Do you think I could even be a decent father?"

She considered it, and my pulse raced as I thought about what she would say to me.

"I think you can do anything if you work for it," she said. "And that includes being a good dad."

I nodded, unsure of what to say in response to her vote of confidence. "Maybe."

"One of these days, you'll learn how to do that whole 'smile-and-say-thank-you' thing when you get a compliment."

"I don't even think I remember how to smile," I said. "Not anymore."

"I'm sure you'll figure it out."

I opened my mouth to answer, but I was interrupted by a text.

Selena: Max also needs a calculator. It's pricey.

Tom: Get it. I'll pay it off.

Selena: Okay. Done.

"Who has your attention like that?" Ruth asked, leaning over to take a peek at my phone.

"Selena," I said. "She asked for something else for Max."

"How does it feel to actually be doing something instead of staying away?"

"Good."

And it did. So much so that the corner of my mouth tilted up infinitesimally, and as always, Ruth caught it.

"See? You can smile after all! Well, sort of. It was a start. Keep at it."

Chapter Three

Selena

"Wait, is this a *new* calculator?" Max asked as I handed him the package.

"Um, yes?"

"But I thought these were like...really expensive. I was going to have Tess ask his older brother for his."

My brain struggled to come up with a better reply than *"Your father feels bad for abandoning you so now I have a credit card I shouldn't have to pay back and you don't have to ask your best friend's brother for one."*

"I got a good deal."

"Are you sure? Shouldn't we have saved this money for food or something?"

"It's okay! You need it. Enjoy it."

He looked down at the package once more. "Okay. Thank you."

A small smile made its way onto his face. It wasn't often that he got to have new things. We were a house of hand-me-downs.

"Maybe this will help you in math."

"Maybe," he said with a sigh. "It would help if Mrs. Mulligan would slow down."

Math had been hard for him ever since he started middle school. They were having students do more and more complex things at younger ages. He'd surpassed my math skills in elementary school, which both amazed me at how well he learned and worried me that I had the knowledge of an elementary student in the art of numbers.

"It's so cool that it doesn't have someone else's stickers on it. I can decorate it myself."

"I'm glad I found that deal, then," I replied. "I also got another thing. Remember how you saw a commercial for an ancestry DNA test?"

"You got one?"

"I did." I held up two swabs. One was for the ancestry kit. The other was for the paternity test; that one came with two swabs for father and child, and it was a reminder that I still needed to buck up and text Tom back about it. "I thought it would be fun."

"Yes!" he exclaimed. "Let's do it right now."

"Don't we need to leave for school?"

"We can be a few minutes late," he said as he sat in front of me.

I did both, thankfully without too many questions, and he excitedly asked when we'd get the results.

It would be a few weeks for the test he knew about, but the paternity would be a matter of days once I had Tom's sample in hand. After we finished swabbing his cheeks and tucked them away, we left for school, Max excitedly telling me about one of his friends who'd done it too, and all about the results they'd gotten from the test.

But then he stopped abruptly. "Is that Jax doing car rider duty?"

"I-I guess so."

Jax had always made a show of getting out of his duty to direct traffic. He thought it was boring and he didn't like being outside for longer than he had to be. Since our breakup, I'd been under the assumption that he would continue that practice.

He walked in front of my car as I cursed how it easily stuck out. I'd gotten a good deal on this thing years ago from one of Mom's clients, but the Subaru Baja was definitely a unique vehicle as it was a mix of a truck and a car.

Smirking, Jax motioned for me to step out. I begrudgingly did.

I'd managed to go through the first two months of school without talking to him. It seemed my fortune was changing.

"What is he doing?" Max asked under his breath.

"I'll handle this," I replied through the open window. "You make a break for it."

"Thanks. Love you!" As soon as his door was open, he was dashing away.

"Hey!" Jax called. "Don't run in front of cars."

Max did not pause, and he hadn't been in any danger. None of the cars were moving, as the only traffic director on duty had walked over to talk to me.

"Did you tell him to do that?" Jax asked.

"He probably just wants to see his friends."

"Come on, Sel. How long are we doing this cold shoulder thing?"

Ugh. There was the nickname I hated.

"Do you need something?"

"I need to talk to you."

"About school?" I pressed. *Please,* I silently begged. *Just leave.*

A car horn honked, adding to my anxiety.

This was a staunch reminder of how our relationship used to be. He would push and I would give in. Once upon a time, I thought it was good for me to let him take over. I'd thought he had our best interests at heart.

Then he hurt Max, and I refused to stay with him.

"Hang on!" Jax called. I winced against the loud noise. He'd always projected his voice when he talked. But his yell truly was earsplitting. "Are you free tonight? We could hang out."

"I'm not free."

"Come on. You don't work. Of course you're free."

"I have Max."

"He loves me."

I knew, for a fact, that he didn't.

But I wasn't good with confrontation and wouldn't say as much, so I just shook my head. "Sorry. I have plans with someone else."

"Who? Hadley?"

"It's none of your business."

Another car horn rang out and Jax glared at them.

"You're busy," I said. "I need to go."

"I'll come by at seven."

"I said I have plans."

"I know you don't."

"How could you know that?"

"Because I know you, and you lie to get out of saying no. But I'm good for you, Sel. You just need to see that."

There was that pushing again. It made my stomach swirl with deeper anxiety. I quickly climbed into my car, locking it to prevent him from getting in. Other people were growing more impatient and I heard Jax snap at them again. I didn't stick around to hear the rest of it. I knew I needed to get home, to get away from him.

The best course of action was to call someone to hang out with me in case Jax did show up. But Allen would be home with Hadley, and he didn't think my neighborhood was safe. He also would object to Max and me coming over.

Mom would love to see us, but Jax knew where she lived, and with his threat of coming to the house, I wondered if he would have the gall to stop by her place to see if I was there.

Luna was with her new boyfriend, and I wasn't sure if I wanted to meet him yet.

Those were all of my options. I had no one else to call.

I drove home white-knuckled. I needed to get some work done, but all I could think about were my made-up dinner plans.

Meowcifer jumped up on my lap, distracting me further.

She purred innocently, green eyes on my hand to signal she wanted more attention.

"I should have trusted you when you wouldn't let Jax anywhere near you," I said. "He's completely ruined my day."

She purred and leaned into my touch.

"Maybe I need a new rule. I only invest romantically into people you like. Which would mean no one."

I could have sworn she nodded.

"I'm losing it," I muttered. "I need to figure out my next move."

My phone buzzed with an alert.

When I'd set up the credit card, I also had balance notifications sent to my phone. It was an easy way to keep tabs on whether or not Tom was paying off my purchases; I wouldn't want to accrue a bill I couldn't afford. As of now, the card balance was zero.

"Hm, looks like Tom's keeping his word. *God*, I really need to meet up with him about the DNA swab. Maybe I can take Max to dinner, just to get out of the house tonight, and I could have Tom meet us at the restaurant."

Meowcifer didn't answer.

"It would seem a little rude not to invite Tom in to share a meal with us, though..." Visions of him on his knees invaded my mind, a sharp blow to my defenses. "Should I just invite him to have dinner with us? Even though that would mean letting him meet Max, and so soon?"

The cat headbutted my hand to demand that I keep petting her. I gave in.

"He's been *so* nice. Maybe he could be nice at dinner too."

This elicited a purr from Meowcifer.

"I'm not ready for Max to know Tom's his father. But we don't *have* to tell him. Tom could just be...a friend."

The purring only grew louder.

Meowcifer must have been softening my hard edges because I was *seriously* considering this.

"Screw it. I'm doing it. I don't know if I don't try."

Selena: We can meet tonight.

Tom answered in minutes.

Tom: When and where?

Selena: Max and I will be getting dinner. I'll let you meet him if you agree not to be introduced as his father. We're just meeting as friends, and beforehand, I'll give you the swab.

Tom: Absolutely.

"Yep," I told the cat. "I've lost it."

After Tom and I agreed on the place, I attempted to work to get my mind off things. I got some of it done, but I was buried under anxiety because of Jax's thinly veiled threat. And because I'd agreed to meet up with Tom.

This was probably going to bite me in the behind, but if I caught Tom in a good mood, maybe he'd still be the man I met in his office.

Tom

I had to focus on the rumble of my truck's engine to keep my mind off of my nervousness about this dinner. It had already manifested one of the strongest desires to drink since running into Selena, and I couldn't afford that tonight.

The noise was barely enough to make the craving pass. I slowly climbed out of the old Chevy I'd had since just after high school, slamming the door as I usually did. A few people turned to look at my antique.

Dad hated that I liked cars, but I'd been living on my own when I bought the truck. A lot of the people Murray and Sons bought out loved talking cars, so I managed to use it in business.

And that was the only thing that kept Dad off my ass about it.

"Is that a C10?" a woman's voice asked.

I turned to face the woman who had addressed me. She had copper hair that glistened in the streetlights. I used to love having a woman come and ask me about my truck. Usually, I'd offer to give her a ride in it and then take her back to my place.

"It is," I replied.

"It's in great shape. Did you do the work yourself?"

"Yes." Short, curt responses were all I could manage.

Damn it. How was I supposed to meet Max when I was like this? If Ruth were here, she'd say I had the personality of wet cardboard.

"I love it," she said, running her hand over the paint. "You know what I'd love more? Getting your number to talk cars."

In my peripheral, I saw Selena in front of the restaurant. Her red sweater was hard to miss. She was watching me, eyes narrowed.

And the moment I saw her, she was all I could notice.

"Sorry," I said. "I'm here for her."

My head gestured in Selena's direction and the woman turned. "Oh, sorry. I didn't realize you were taken."

I should have corrected her, but I wanted this conversation to be over. I nodded and she apologized once more before scurrying off. As soon as I was alone, I made my way over to Selena.

"Found your plans for after this?" she asked.

"No," I replied. "I'm here for you and Max."

Selena's eyes went to the woman. "Why is she giving me a thumbs-up?"

I turned, but the woman's hand shot to her side. She hurried away, and by how quickly she moved, it was obvious she didn't want me to see what she had been doing.

"I think it was because she thinks I'm here *with* you."

"You are here with me."

"With as in...together."

Selena's eyes widened. "Oh. That kind of with me."

"S-sorry. I didn't know what to say."

"*You* didn't know what to say? In college, you could seduce a brick wall."

"That was when I was drunk," I said. "And I am not right now."

"That's right. I think I remember you saying something like that." Her eyes moved up and down me, and I wondered what she was thinking. "Can we keep it that way for this dinner?"

"Of course." There was no other option anymore. "But fair warning, I'll be pretty quiet."

"Max should talk enough to cover you. Oh! Before I forget, here's this." She handed me a swab. "Rub your cheeks, please."

That was the strangest sentence I'd heard today. I was almost tempted to laugh, but her serious expression told me she meant business.

She gave me quick instructions before taking back the swab.

"Is there anything else I should know? About Max, I mean."

"Like what?"

"Like a..." What did Ruth call it when she stood up to Dad? "A boundary."

Selena only stared, and I took in just how deep her brown eyes truly were. *Not now,* I told myself.

"You're asking me about boundaries?"

"I hear they're healthy to have."

"Yes, they are. People usually don't ask."

"I want this to go well. So tell me the boundaries."

She bit her lip as she thought about it. "No talking down about his interests. No getting into his personal space, which means only hug him if *he* asks or offers. And...no drinking around him. Not just tonight. Ever."

"Understood," I said, committing the three items to memory.

"And no saying who you are. At least not yet. The last thing I want is for this to end badly and him get hurt."

I slowly nodded. While I wanted him to know, I couldn't deny that him knowing me as a stranger sounded easier than him knowing me as I truly was. At least for this meeting, he wouldn't hate me.

"I won't tell him until you tell me I can."

"Good. Then let's go in."

My heart raced as she led me to the back of the restaurant where Max was already sitting. I could see our similarities from a mile away, but up close, it made my knees weak.

He had my eyes, that was for sure. They were striking against his tan skin, even in the lower light of the restaurant. He had wavy, dark hair that laid in a mess on his smaller head. He still had baby fat on his face, making his cheeks round. If I pulled out a photo of me at his age, we would be nearly identical.

"Hi," Max said. "You must be Mr. Murray."

Flashes of Dad invaded my mind.

"Oh no," I said, shaking my head. "Just Tom. Please."

"I like to be polite."

"Mr. Murray is my father, and I'm not him."

Selena cleared her throat. I knew I'd stepped on a live wire by mentioning the word "father."

But Max didn't seem bothered. "Okay. What about Mr. Tom? Is that a good compromise?"

"I can work with that." I gave him a nod.

"So," Max said, putting down his menu. "Tell me your life story."

A shocked laugh escaped Selena. "That's an intense first question," she said.

"I want to get to know him. What's better than knowing *everything*?"

"I don't have that much to say," I replied. "My life isn't that interesting."

"Come on, it's got to be better than mine. I'm only eleven, so there isn't much."

"You're almost twelve," Selena said. "That's a little more time."

"Not enough to be interesting." He turned back to me, waiting for an answer.

How did I tell him that I didn't remember most of my life? Or that I'd wasted it away by trying to drink to forget everything?

"Max likes Lila Wilde," Selena interjected. "So, there's that."

"Oh, really?" I asked. I tried to think of anything Ruth had maybe told me about her, since I knew she was a fan, but then I remembered that she and I never really talked about those kinds of things.

"Mom," Max said, cheeks turning red. "I didn't want to start with that."

"Why not?" Selena said, frowning. "Normally, you love talking about her."

"Yeah, but not everyone likes her."

"I don't usually listen to music," I admitted, "but I know of her. What do you like about her?"

"It's really fine, Mr. Tom. I have other interests."

"Ones that you like more than her?"

"Um..." Max paused as he thought about it. "Okay, no. She's my biggest thing."

"Then tell me about her."

Max smiled at me and my heart skipped a beat.

Was I doing something right for once?

He launched into a long-winded explanation about Lila's life, including how she was born in the middle of nowhere in Canada and it didn't take long for her to find fame. Most of her songs were inspired by her long-time boyfriend, who had been credited as her inspiration for nearly everything she wrote. She lived a glamorous life, but could somehow disappear without any paparazzi being able to find her.

I listened to every word, giving him my full attention.

Max only paused when the waitress came to ask for our drink order.

"Shoot," he said after ordering. "I should figure out what I want to eat."

I looked down at my own menu. My stomach was in knots from meeting him, so I didn't know if I would even be able to touch anything.

"They have chicken tenders," Selena said.

"I was thinking about being adventurous," Max said. "They have a bacon mac and cheese, which I like...in theory."

"I'd offer to eat it if you don't like it," Selena said, "but I don't like bacon. It tastes like salty paper to me."

Max gasped dramatically. "How could you say something so bold? You just offended every bacon lover out there."

"Sorry. I speak my truth."

Impossibly, I felt the corner of my mouth lift fully. When was the last time I smiled like this? And how were the two of them making me want to?

Max blew out a breath, eyes focusing back on his menu. "Yeah, I'm probably just going to stick with my usual."

"I'll get it," I offered. "And you can try some."

"Really?" he asked.

"Sure. I like both mac and cheese and bacon."

"Are you sure it doesn't taste like salty paper?"

"I don't think it does."

"You're the best. Thank you, Mr. Tom."

I nodded at him and then risked a glance over at Selena. She was staring at me with her lips pursed. I couldn't tell how she thought I was doing.

Max continued to talk about his favorite pop star, unaware of how Selena was looking at me. I nodded along, trying to focus on his words and not all the ways I felt like I was too stiff for this. My nerves made me want something to drink, and as time went on, it was harder to ignore.

But I refused to let it stop me from knowing Max. I could compartmentalize. I had to—because I wasn't wasting this chance.

He finally stopped once the food was sitting in front of us. "Wow, I really went on about Lila Wilde, huh?"

He glanced at me, his shoulders hunched. As I marveled at his shyness, I wondered how the hell Dad could have ever done what he had.

"It's fine."

"You're not bored?"

"Definitely not."

"Some adults get quiet when they're bored."

Shit. Of course my inability to think of what to say would bite me in the ass. "I'm just a quiet person. It's not you."

"Okay, cool. I can handle quiet."

I offered him my plate. He happily reached over with his fork. He took a bite, considered it, and frowned. "That's a lot of bacon. You try some."

Giving it a taste, I mulled over the flavor. "It's pretty strong on the bacon. It's smoky, and pretty greasy." I couldn't remember the last time I even thought about how what I ate tasted. It was always just fuel to get me through the workday and back to the alcohol waiting for me at home.

"Yeah, it's a little weird. I'd rather taste cheese *and* bacon. But all I get is bacon."

"I think I agree."

"Aw, but you got it because of me."

"We could order something else," Selena offered.

"No, I'll be fine. I can just turn my brain off while I'm eating."

"Really? I wish I could do that." Max looked down at his plate and grabbed a chicken tender. "But here, you should have this just in case you can't."

I took the chicken. This was possibly the kindest thing I'd ever seen a kid do.

And probably the only thing. But still. Were all kids like this? If not, then it had to be from Selena. That kind of kindness didn't run in my family.

I risked another glance at her. She was still staring at me and hadn't even looked at her food. I wasn't sure what I was doing wrong, but I knew it had to be something. It always was.

My body ached for something to drink and I pushed it back once again. A darker part of my mind told me that I would be much friendlier, that this would be easier, if I was halfway drunk.

Nope. Not tonight and not ever.

"Um, Mom?" Max asked. His eyes had followed mine. "Are we out of paint?"

I blinked, trying to understand the odd question.

It must have been something the two of them shared, because she didn't find it odd at all.

"Our paint levels are fine," she said, shaking her head. "Let's just finish our food."

Max nodded and his eyes fell to me. "We haven't talked about you yet."

"We don't need to. I'm really not that interesting."

"I'm sure we can find something." He brought out a notebook.

"When did you bring that in?" Selena asked.

"I had it the whole time. I'm going to start bringing it whenever I meet a new person so I can make small talk."

"Is that what it's for?" she asked.

"Yes. I'm terrible at conversations, so I have this. My friends at school helped me come up with it."

"Maybe I need something like that," I said.

"It's *so* helpful. Okay. Here's one." Max leaned forward. "Would you...cut off your pinky toe for a million dollars?"

"Oh, hm. No, I don't think I would."

"Really? A million dollars is a lot of money."

"I like my toe."

"More than a million dollars?"

"Yeah, maybe."

"What about a billion dollars?"

"The better question might be: what billionaire is willing to give away that much money for a toe?"

"Toe-ny Stark?"

A chuckle escaped me. "Good point."

"So, are you going to give up your pinky toe for a billion dollars from Toe-ny Stark?"

"No. I'll keep my toe. What about you? Are you giving up your pinky toe?"

"For that much money? Yes. Easy decision. Pinky toes are useless. And they always get stuck in the seams of socks."

"I suppose that's true."

"I'd be a billionaire *and* be free of the torture of seams on socks. It's a win-win." Max once again smiled at me and I couldn't help but smile back.

When had I talked to anyone like this? When had I not cared about expectations and simply let myself go with the conversation?

Never. That was the answer.

Selena cleared her throat. "Tom," she said lowly, "can I speak to you for a second?"

Shit. I knew how this would play out. She would tell me to leave and I would have to walk out of Max's life. I should have known more about Lila Wilde. I should have listened better. I should have gotten control of my worry and just acted *normal*.

"What is going on?" she asked. "Are you tricking me or something? Is this a joke?"

"The...the toe thing was a joke, but that's the only one that's been made tonight."

She paced the hallway by the bathrooms. It took me a moment to realize that she wasn't angry—she was confused.

"Selena, I'm only trying to connect with him."

"After not being here for twelve years?"

"If I could change that, I would."

"So, is this some sort of play to get me to let you in his life?"

"No," I said. "This is a one-time thing. I know that. I only want his one memory of me to be a good one."

"Dang it," she muttered. Apparently, that was a bad answer.

"What am I doing wrong? I'll do whatever you need."

"No, *no*. You're not supposed to be *nice*. You're supposed to be a jerk."

"Not with him," I said. "*Never* with him."

"I knew I was going to regret this," she muttered.

"Selena, what did I *do*?"

"Nothing! You've done nothing wrong. You've been *great* throughout this entire dinner."

"Then why did you pull me away?"

"Because you're making me question if this should be a one-time thing!"

I froze. "R-really?"

"Maybe," she said, running her hands through her hair. "How do I know you're not going to hurt us?"

"You don't," I said. "But I will try my best to be the kind of person you two would want to be around. And my best is all I can offer."

Selena sighed and looked at her feet as if in thought. "Is this your best?"

"I...think so. Maybe I could be better."

"Okay, *fine*. You can be in his life," she said slowly. "On a *trial* run. I need to see that you're going to stay before we tell him who you are."

"That's fine. More than fine, actually."

She took in a breath and leaned against the wall.

"Are you okay?"

"It's been a long day," she said. "And this was not how I expected it to end."

"Me neither, but thank you. For giving me a chance."

She nodded. "Let's go back to the table."

Max smiled when we returned, telling me about how good his food was. We finished eating while I listened to him talk about random details of his life.

It was so easy to listen. Why had Dad never done this for us?

"All done?" the waitress asked when we'd finished our food. "Is this one check or separate?"

"One check," I said, just as Selena said, "Separate."

The waitress looked back and forth between us, unsure.

"I'll get it," I said. "My treat."

"That's really nice!" Max replied. "Thank you."

"Yes, thank you," Selena added.

We left the table all at once and I walked them to their car. "Is that a Subaru Baja?"

"Um, yes," Selena said.

"These are unique." I ran my hand over the bed of the vehicle. It was a mix of a car and a truck, something produced for only a short time.

The green paint was peeling in some areas, but it could easily be restored.

"I call it a cruck," Max said.

"Let me guess, a mixture of truck and car?" I asked.

"Yes. Isn't it a good name?"

"It rolls off the tongue," I said. "And it's a perfect descriptor."

"I could be a poet. Especially if I liked writing."

"We need to get back," Selena said. "You have school tomorrow."

"Don't remind me," Max said, and he turned to give me a smile. "It was nice to meet you, Mr. Tom."

"You too."

He climbed into the car and waved. When his door shut, Selena turned to me.

"Please don't let me down this time." She opened her door and immediately started the engine.

"I won't," I said. As she drove away, my future shifted. For so long, it was all about tearing down Dad, and while I still wanted him to get what he deserved, I also wanted to know my child. I wanted to be there for him in every way I could, in every way Dad couldn't.

My heart had grown and split into two over the course of one dinner.

One part remained in my chest, trying to beat out from within my rib cage, and the other part was driving away from me in that car.

Chapter Four

Selena

"Is that the one Max needs?" Hadley asked.

"It's the one the school would give him if they weren't running out of free tablets for low-income students." I bit my lip as I looked at the small device. "Why does it have to be so expensive?"

"Probably because it's name brand," she said.

"But it's what the school uses," I reiterated. "If I get one for him, he doesn't have to deal with the learning curve of a different one."

"What if I—"

"No, you know my rule about expensive gifts between friends. I can't ask you to get this for Max."

"You're not asking, I'm offering. You don't need to put yourself into a financial hole to get it." She paused and then snapped her fingers. "Oh, I know! Ask Tom. Something like this should be no problem for him."

The card was still burning a hole in my pocket. The calculator and the DNA tests had already been a lot. "I...I don't know."

"Okay," Hadley said. "Then I'll get it."

"Hadley, *no*. Allen gets mad whenever you spend money on me."

"But you deserve it."

"Let me at least ask Tom first. I don't want to cause more problems between you and your husband."

I'd been the subject of their fights before and I wasn't eager to be in the center of it again. I pulled out my phone and navigated to the short text chain I had with Tom.

Selena: Max needs a tablet for school.

Tom: Get whichever one he needs.

"He said yes," I said, sighing. "So I'll get it and it'll be fine."

Tom: You've only gotten things for Max so far, which I admire. But if you want something for yourself, I'd be happy to purchase that too.

I stared at the text, jaw on the floor.

"What did he say?" Hadley asked and then read over my shoulder. "He's offering to get you something too? Perfect. I know exactly what it should be."

She ran off before I could stop her. For a pregnant lady, she was *fast*.

After a few moments, Hadley returned with a Kindle.

"I don't need this."

"Yours broke ages ago. And if he doesn't get it, I'm going to. You love reading."

"You're going to get me in trouble."

"He said to get something for yourself."

"Not this expensive."

"He's rich, Selena. This probably isn't even expensive to him."

"We don't know that."

"You're right. Ask him."

I sighed and took a picture of the Kindle. With shaking hands, I sent it to him along with the price.

Tom: Get it.

"Ha!" Hadley exclaimed. "I told you!"

Tom: But if you're reading, I suppose you'll also be needing this.

And then he sent a massive gift card for it.

"Oh my God," I said. "I think I'm gonna pass out."

"Okay, maybe I'm starting to see why you liked him so long ago," Hadley said. "He's certainly doing more than Jax ever did."

It was true. Jax had never once gotten me a gift. If he did have extra money, he used it on things for himself that he would share with me if he was in a good mood.

But I steeled myself. Tom doing these things was simply reparations for him leaving me all those years ago. I didn't need to get lost in the gifts and forget what he'd done.

His kindness to Max played back in my mind, how he had listened to him when he went on and on about Lila Wilde.

It was what he should do, but it was still so sweet.

"Selena?" Hadley asked. "You good? You look like you're at war with yourself."

"Maybe I am," I muttered. "Let's get checked out."

"Want to go get hot chocolate after this?" she asked. "I'm dying for one."

My bank account was down to single digits, so that was not an option.

"I...think I have to skip out."

"Are you sure? I could get you a cup."

I remembered the time Allen not-so-subtly implied that I was a freeloader. It had been when Jax and I first broke up and Hadley had treated Max and me to dinner.

"We can't pay for your friend's dinner if we're starting a family," he'd said.

"Um, no. It's fine. I seriously need to do other things after this."

"Okay," she said, her smile falling. "Let me know if you change your mind."

"I will," I said, even though I knew I wouldn't.

We went separate ways after checking out, but not before she asked me one last time if I wanted to go; I still refused.

When I got to the car, I texted Tom again.

Selena: Thank you.

Tom: You're welcome.

As much as I tried to get my mind away from my confliction over Tom, it circled back the moment I was alone. It didn't help that Max had already asked when we would see him again. He liked him, which made this all the more complicated.

My phone buzzed and I blanched when I saw an overdraft alert from my bank. *Shit.* I thought I'd canceled all of my automatic bills that weren't absolutely necessary.

But then I saw that Netflix had come out of my account, and that my bank was charging a fee on top of it. I couldn't get it reversed because I had also overdrawn last month.

I groaned. I'd told Jax to cancel that when we had broken up. I never really watched TV, but he said he needed it to relax. He was of the opinion that if he was helping me pay half my mortgage, then I should at least cover something that he wanted.

I bet he was still using it.

But a twenty-dollar charge shouldn't make me go into the negative. As much as I was angry with Jax, I knew I was the one who forgot to cancel it in time.

I racked my brain for any other projects that I could take on for extra money. One came to mind, but it wasn't something I was excited about.

Luna was all in on this new man of hers. Mom was not. So, when Luna asked if I could draw a portrait of them, I initially turned her down.

But she'd said she would offer double my normal rate. That, plus knowing I could get it done in about a week, made it a no-brainer.

"Hello?" Luna answered. "Selena?"

"Hey."

"I haven't heard from you in forever."

"I'm sorry. I've been...busy."

"Oh, really? All that drawing keeping you from at least calling?"

I winced. The real reason I hadn't called was because I didn't want to get in the middle of whatever she and Mom were fighting about. But I'd never tell her that.

"Do you still want that portrait?" I asked.

"Seriously? I thought Mom told you not to do it because it would be 'supporting my poor choices.'"

"She did, but—"

"You do everything Mom says. *Everything.*"

"Not this time. I need the money, and I can get it done fast."

"So, you're rebelling in the face of being broke. I can respect that. I definitely still want it done. When he eventually asks me to marry him, I want it to be on our wedding invitations."

"You're talking about marriage?"

"He's not. *Yet.* But I'll wear him down. Come on over. What all do you need to do it?"

"Just a photo of you two that I can use as a reference. I don't even have to come over, you could just send it to me."

"Nonsense," she insisted. "I want someone other than Mom to meet this guy. Come over and take it yourself. I'll give you a deposit if you do."

Apparently, all my loyalty to Mom went out the window when it came to money. "Fine. I can come now."

"We'll be ready. Do you have my address?"

"I still have it from when you moved in and sent us pictures."

She'd bragged about it for days. It was a glitzy new apartment, and even I had to admit it looked nice from the photos.

Never in my wildest dreams did I imagine I would ever be going there, but things never happened how I imagined them.

I knocked on her door and listened as someone shuffled through the apartment.

She answered wearing only a sheet.

"You're here!" she exclaimed.

"Why are you only in a sheet and answering your door?" I pushed her inside and shut the door behind me.

Even in her state of undress, she glimmered in a way I could never. She had bleached her hair blonde a long time ago and had the kind of personality that could draw in anyone. She didn't get tired from talking to strangers like I did, and life had obviously rewarded her for that. She had all the best friends, all the boyfriends—even if Mom didn't like this one.

She, like Hadley, was the main character of her life.

"Because I want this to be *classy*. Nothing says class more than Greek inspiration."

"I could have just drawn that in after."

"Well, I'm not changing now," she said. "Willie! Come on out!"

Please don't be in a sheet. Please no more sheets.

But when he came out of the back room, I didn't even register his clothes. I registered his age. He had to be at least thirty years older than Luna.

Now I saw why Mom was so mad.

"Who's here?" Willie asked. "Your sister?"

"Yes. Willie, this is Selena. Selena, Willie."

I pressed my lips together to keep my thoughts inside. "Nice to meet you."

"You too. You know, without the baggy shirt, you'd look a lot like your sister."

I was tempted to cover myself. "Um, thanks?"

"She's addicted to looking like she's in a potato sack," Luna said. "But her art is beautiful. Wait, aren't you supposed to be dressed like I am?"

I finally saw that he was not in a sheet, but a tank top and old basketball shorts.

"Oh, yeah. You wanted this to be classy, right?" He pulled at his shirt, about to take it off. "Maybe we can just share the—"

"No need!" I called out, laughing awkwardly. "I really can draw togas on you guys. The reference image is mainly so I can get the faces right."

"But—" Luna began, but I cut her off.

"Why don't you guys show me the poses?" I suggested. "We can do five or so and you guys can choose your favorite."

"Fine." Luna stuck out her bottom lip. "But the sheet would have been more fun."

She turned to Willie and directed him to where she wanted him. To his credit, he didn't complain, but I saw his eyes stick to the cleavage showing when her sheet fell a little.

This was my own personal nightmare.

As I snapped the photos, I knew Mom was going to kill me. Even I could admit that this guy seemed to be a loser, but Luna didn't want to see that.

But I also knew that she wouldn't see sense until she was ready to. She always eventually did, but Mom hadn't quite figured that out.

"Okay," I said, putting away my phone. "I have enough. I'll send them to you and you can pick your favorite."

"Great! Willie, why don't you go lie down? I'll be back in a few."

"Be sure to lose the sheet," he said, winking.

I nearly gagged.

"How much do you want for this? Two hundred? Four?"

"For the deposit? How much is he letting you pay?"

"He doesn't know I'm paying, but he gives me an allowance and this is coming from that."

"An allowance?"

Luna gave me a flat stare. "Don't start. I already heard it from Mom. I'm happy, okay? I'm not hurting anyone, so just let me be happy."

This whole situation screamed daddy issues, but mine wasn't any better. I'd dated my fair share of losers, mainly Jax, and he didn't even have the money that this guy did.

I swallowed all of my comments and said, "Okay, you're right. I definitely want you to be happy. And just pay me what you think is fair. I've never really done a large portrait of a couple."

"So, four hundred for the deposit. Got it."

"That's way too much."

"I know you need it," she said. "And besides, I've seen what you can do. Make him look, you know, good, and I'll throw in extra."

"How many wrinkles constitutes as good?"

"We're going for silver fox."

I nodded, though I knew I'd need to look that up when I got home. "Got it."

I wrote down everything she told me before leaving. I put the money in my account on the way home, grateful not to be in the negative.

Tom

It only took a few days for Selena to get the results of the paternity test and forward them to me. As I read over the results, which told me he was my child, I wasn't surprised. The longer I'd looked at him at that dinner, the more I'd just *known*.

The results propelled me to do even more for him now that I knew for sure. And that started with looking into his main interest. I used to like music once upon a time, and knowing that my child did too made me want to give it another try.

When I searched Lila Wilde, I was so overwhelmed that I didn't know where to start. I asked Ruth, but she said she was more of a casual fan and that our brother might know more. And, sure, Barry owned a popular bar in downtown Nashville, but I didn't know if he knew anything more than Ruth did. Neither of us did because he kept to himself. I didn't even know if he had a partner or the names of any of his friends. Did he even have friends?

But he was still the best option since he'd let it slip that he had met Lila last summer. Ruth had been seeing her own famous boyfriend, and Barry had told us only to make her feel better about us knowing about Knox—who had technically been her boss at the time.

All of this led me to texting him randomly—something I hadn't done in years.

Tom: Can you tell me about Lila Wilde?

Barry: Exactly what do you want to know about her?

I sighed when I read his stiff response. I didn't expect him to have anything kind to say to me, but I'd hoped that he could guide me into this conversation, and if I was lucky, tell me more about her. I just needed to know where to start, so maybe I could have something more useful to say when I got to see Max again.

But now I saw that reaching out to Barry was a bad choice. I didn't answer, not wanting to provoke him any further by sending anything else. For years, our relationship had felt like an exposed live wire, ready to electrocute us at any time. Maybe if I'd gotten my head out of my ass sooner, we would have had a chance to repair it.

Thirty minutes later, there was a sharp knock at the door and I straightened at the sound.

Was it Dad? I didn't think he knew where I lived. Even when we were close, I purposely told him the wrong building.

But it wasn't him. It was Barry, wearing a leather jacket and a glare I knew all too well. He was leaning on my doorframe in an attempt to look casual, but I could see the tenseness in his shoulders.

"Why did you ask about Lila Wilde, of all people?" he asked immediately. "What do you know?"

I blinked. "What? I don't know anything except that she was in your bar."

"Then why would you be asking about her? You don't even listen to music."

"I'm getting into it."

"That isn't like you. Why?"

"For reasons."

"Really?" He leaned close, taking a deep breath.

"Are you smelling me?"

"I'm making sure you're not drunk."

"I quit."

"You could have broken, but I forgot how stubborn you and Ruth can be. Just forget I was here." He turned away, but I reached out and grabbed his shoulder.

"Why would you come visit me because I asked about Lila Wilde? Was it just to see if I was drunk?"

He shrugged off my hand and I moved it like it was burnt. "It's nothing," he replied.

"It?" I knew I shouldn't push. It wasn't going to end well.

"Since when is what I do of any interest to you? Aren't you too busy running the family business?"

"It's not that hard to run it."

"Dad made it seem that way."

"I'm not Dad."

"Head of the company? Telling me running it isn't hard? Could have fooled me."

The words hurt. I looked at the ground. It would be *so* easy to snap back and make him regret what he said.

But that wouldn't accomplish a damn thing.

"Fair enough," I said. "You don't have to tell me anything. I'm sorry I bothered you."

He turned. "Really?"

"Yes. I already asked Ruth about her and she told me to come to you, but I should have known you wouldn't want to be bothered. I'm sorry. For both bothering you and for pushing you to talk about your life."

Barry considered me for a long moment. Then he sighed. "No, I'm the one who should be sorry. I came over here in the wrong headspace."

"Because I asked about Lila Wilde?"

"Yes. You asking—you even just texting me—came out of nowhere. I thought that if you were drunk, you might be using the fact that she's been in the bar to get something from me. But that's a Dad move. Not you."

"Why would anyone care if she's been in a bar?"

"A major pop star? In a small bar in Nashville? It's not like her. Her fans would pick it apart and they'd find me. Do you know what would happen if Lila was connected to anyone other than that boyfriend of hers?"

"I don't."

"It would be like what happened with Ruth, but twenty times worse."

"Okay, I can see why that would be a problem. But I'm not going to tell anyone. Your life is your life."

"I agree, but I remember a time when everyone told me what I *should* be. Including you."

He wasn't wrong. When he rebelled, I thought that getting him in line would make things easier on all of us.

It didn't.

"I won't do that again," I said. "I was genuinely curious."

"Why? You're busier than ever now that you run the company."

His question made my chest tighten. "I work all day and come home to a quiet apartment. I just thought...music would fill the void."

"That doesn't sound like you. Are you trying to hide something from me?"

Damn it. Barry was smarter than he'd ever been given credit for.

But I dreaded telling him the truth. I knew Barry would be far less forgiving than Ruth was.

"Someone I care about likes her," I hedged.

"Like a girlfriend? I didn't think you did commitment."

"It's not a girlfriend...It's complicated."

"Does it have anything to do with why Ruth's been acting weird?"

"How do you know Ruth is acting weird?"

He shrugged. "We talk. Sometimes."

"Really?"

"I'm trying, okay? So whatever this is…just tell me. You give a little, I'll give a little. About Lila, I mean."

"I seriously doubt that," I muttered. "In fact, you'll probably find it funny for two seconds and then hate me."

"The only thing I'd find funny is if you were wearing heels to be taller than me."

"I—why would I do that?"

"Ruth does. *Dad* does."

"He what?"

"I snuck into his closet one day and found them. All of his boots have heels so he's as tall as Mom."

"How did I never know this?"

"You and Ruth zoned out when I got yelled at for hinting I knew about them. It was worth it, though."

"Huh. That must be why he never took them off at home."

"We got off topic again." Barry shook his head. "I believe you were about to give me information?"

I knew I couldn't hide it any longer. "I need to know for a…child."

"A child?"

"*My*…child."

For a second, he did not react. Silence stretched out and only my pounding heart echoed in my ears. "You have a kid?"

"Yes."

"How old?"

"Eleven. Almost twelve."

"Fuck," Barry said. "Almost twelve? You managed to keep that a secret for this long?"

"I didn't know about him."

"What do you mean you didn't *know*?" His voice was hard, and I cursed the backslide this conversation had taken.

"I mean, I was told. But I turned her away, I guess."

"There isn't any guessing here, Tom."

"She told me through an email that I don't remember," I explained. "I've tried to, but I don't. I don't remember most of college."

"I wonder why," Barry said, rolling his eyes. "Alcohol is a dangerous thing. A little is fine, but you were getting smashed every night for years. That does lasting damage."

"I know. And I've stopped."

"Yeah. Good for you. Except it's twelve years too late. Knowing about Lila Wilde, even if this kid is her biggest fan, isn't going to fix this, you know."

I was silent for a moment as he said the words I had already been telling myself. He wasn't wrong, and I deserved the harshness—but it still hurt.

The urge to hide from this was so strong that I didn't know if I could fight it. But I had this one chance. And I was going to have to put all the regret in a box and be better.

"I know," I said slowly. "There is no apology, no gift, *nothing*, that can make up for it. All I can hope for is to know him for the time that his mother is tolerating me. I can't make up for what I've done, what I've missed, but I can't sit here knowing about him now and leave him."

"Then how could you have done it all those years ago?"

"I don't know!" I snapped. "I don't *fucking* know. She was...I remember her. I remember the one day we had like it was yesterday but *nothing* else. I wish I had done something different. If I could go back in time and shake some sense into younger me, then I would. But all I know is at that time, Dad was on my ass about being the only Murray he deemed worthy, and I probably hid it so I wouldn't disappoint him, or worse, get smacked around by him. It's not an excuse, but I just want to *try* to be a good person this time. And I don't know if I can."

I expected Barry to snap back like he always did. This fight wouldn't end until we were in each other's faces, especially since Ruth wasn't here to calm us down.

Barry blew out a breath. "That's the most words I've ever heard you say."

"What? Aren't you supposed to yell at me some more?"

"I could, but you seem to know how bad you fucked up." He then looked away. "And that was around the time that I started acting out so...maybe that was why Dad was harder on you. So, I'm sorry for that."

"It's not your fault. It's Dad's, and it's mine. I own up to it."

"You're being more mature than most." He sighed and walked into my apartment, taking off his jacket. "Which is why I'll tell you more about Lila, even the things most people don't know."

"I appreciate it," I said. "But they have to be kid appropriate."

"Duh," he said, rolling his eyes. "I mean the things real fans know."

"How about which album to start with? I'm wanting to listen to her, and to music in general. It's just overwhelming."

"Why?"

"You don't remember when Dad laid into me at dinner when he thought me listening to music caused me to get a B on a final?"

"I dimly remember it. All of Dad's yelling blends together."

"It ruined music for me. And now I don't even know where to start."

"Maybe start with her softer stuff. It's not as popular, but her deep cuts are what are really interesting. She has this way of subtly hinting at something going wrong in life. If you were to like anything, it would be that."

"What songs?"

"I'll make you a list," he said. "I think it's cool that you're trying to get into your kid's interests."

"He's worth it."

"It's weird for me to say 'your kid.'" He shook his head. "That's gonna take some adjusting to. So, a boy then?"

"His name is Max."

"I have a nephew."

"And Ruth is an aunt."

Barry laughed, a welcome sound considering the years of strain we endured.

"She's going to hate that."

Chapter Five

I instantly salivated the moment we entered Mom's townhouse and smelled what she was cooking.

Since focusing solely on work, dinners were low priority. Max and I had been eating a repetitive slew of Crock-Pot meals and I knew he was getting tired of them.

Mom was an amazing cook, and since Luna and I moved out, she always talked about how much she wanted us to come over and eat with her. With how hard I'd been working, I knew I couldn't say no.

"This smells so good, abuela," Max said. "What is it?"

"Enmoladas," she said. "Your favorite."

"Thank you for cooking, Mom," I said, giving her a hug.

"You look like you need it. Have you been sleeping?"

I opened my mouth to lie and say I had, but Max called me out.

"Nope. She's still bad at it."

"Thanks," I said flatly.

"What's going on?" she asked. "Can I help?"

"Just dreams," I said. "Weird ones."

"Dreams about what?"

Tom. Him being around. Him never leaving that first time.

And now, him on his knees.

"Just weird things." I shrugged. "I'm sure it will pass."

Mom frowned, but then the door opened, saving me from further questions.

"Luna!" Mom called. "How are you?"

"Did you really say I couldn't invite my boyfriend?" Luna asked.

"I said *you* were welcome."

"You're lucky he's working," she huffed. "Or else I wouldn't have come at all."

I stepped over to Max, letting Mom and Luna squabble without me being in the middle of it.

"Am I missing something?" Max whispered.

"Luna's dating an old man."

"Oh. Gross."

"Shh," I said. "She's defensive."

Max nodded and I turned my attention back to the table where Luna was still glaring daggers at Mom.

Things had always been this way. Luna had a way of pushing Mom's buttons and I did my best not to add to her plate. Mom had always been stretched so thin being a single parent. It was easier for me to pretend I was fine rather than have her fuss over me when there were bigger problems afoot.

We all sat at the tiny dining table. I always sat on the end farthest from her while Luna sat directly to her right. Max had taken the other side. It was for the best. Mom had the people who needed the most attention closest to her.

"So," Luna said as she dug into the food, "Selena came to the apartment."

"Wait, what?"

"Luna, don't," I tried to cut her off, but she was determined.

"She's doing a portrait of Willie and me."

Mom's jaw fell. "You met him? And you're okay with doing art for them?"

"I mean, I can't tell her *no*."

"Yes, you can! This man is taking advantage of her!"

"He is not," Luna said. "I love him and he loves me."

"Selena, tell your sister she's wrong. I know you agree with me."

I froze. I didn't do well under pressure and I hated it when Mom used me as an example. Luna raised an eyebrow at me, as if daring me to say anything negative toward her.

"Guys, let's all just—"

"Mom, you should support me."

"No! You're making a mistake."

I needed to stop this before it got any worse, but I felt like a kid again, stuck in the middle of their stubbornness.

"Hey, abuela?" Max interjected.

He was possibly the only person who could get her attention when she and Luna were fighting. "Yes, mijo?"

"Did you use a new herb in this? It's *so* good."

"Oh, you're so sweet. I got this new brand from the store."

Max was a genius, an adorable genius. His question gave me a second to collect my thoughts, and by the time Luna opened her mouth to argue again, I changed the subject to ask if she made the mole from scratch or used store-bought. I definitely knew the answer, but it kept the conversation going in a different direction.

Luna rolled her eyes at me, and I knew she was aware of what I was doing, but it had worked. We made it through the dinner without the fight getting worse.

Which felt like a blessing.

My hand cramped from how much I'd been writing, but I ignored it.

I'd been listening to one of Lila's albums for hours, analyzing every lyric. I decided to buy a decent record player to go along with the vinyl, allowing me to hear every detail of the music; plus, the larger surface of the cover allowed me to place sticky notes of my annotated thoughts.

It hadn't disappointed. It was two in the morning, and while I was tired, I didn't want to drink. I kept finding new details in the songs, more layers to listen to, which curbed any of my nighttime desires.

This was a new sense of peace—one I hadn't felt since Dad took it away from me all those years ago.

By the time I was done, the record was covered in small notes. I couldn't wait to send it to Max. Hopefully, he would like it.

It was as close as I could get to spending time with him. He'd listened to these lyrics on repeat, and I hoped, had enjoyed them as much as I did.

I packed up the record, carefully wrapping it to make sure it wouldn't get damaged when I handed it over to Francine to deliver.

As it sat in the package, I knew I couldn't just send it and give nothing to the woman who had raised him for the last eleven years. Selena deserved something too.

But what?

I didn't know any more about her other than the fact that she liked to read. And even though I'd cemented into my memory the one day we'd had back in college, none of those things—the notepad she'd drawn on or the mint tea she'd nearly spilled on the table—would work in this situation.

What else did we have? We had the walk to my dorm. Her commenting on its cleanliness.

And her *sweater*. Disappeared into the depths after I'd kissed her.

I remembered her throwing it across the room. Back then, I'd been too focused on her to even care about where the sweater ended up, but I found it days later at the back of my closet when I was cleaning.

I never threw it away, mostly because seeing the thick, red fabric reminded me of the one woman who liked me when I was sober. As I slipped further and further into my drinking, the memory became one of the few good ones I had while not drinking. I *couldn't* throw it away. I felt the same way about that drawing she'd given me too. It was still tucked in my wallet after all these years.

But I was sure she'd drawn plenty of things for other people before. I doubted she even remembered it, just like I doubted that she remembered any details of that day in my dorm as much as I did. Hopefully, she would remember the sweater.

I found it after a few minutes of looking. I'd kept it in good shape over time, but I was more than happy to send it to its original owner. It was a fraction of what I wanted to do, but it was a start. It was something.

And I could only hope I'd be given more chances to do other things too.

Chapter Six

Selena

The next morning, I was getting ready when I heard the front door open. For a second, my heart stopped. What if it was Jax?

But then I heard Mom call to me. "Selena! I came to give you leftovers!"

I let out a sigh of relief and finished throwing my hair up in a bun.

"Hi, Mom," I said, giving her a hug and taking the Tupperware that was stacked in her arms. "You didn't have to come all the way over here. Don't you need to be at work?"

I heard a hiss and Meowcifer abandoned the couch to run to the back of the house.

"That cat is evil."

"She's sweet with Max and me."

"I'll believe it when I see it. But to answer your question, I can be a few minutes late for this client. He's very nice. I had far too many leftovers for just me."

"Thank you," I said, putting them in the fridge. That made the next few nights easier.

"Also, there was someone waiting for you outside. From Murray and Sons?"

I whirled around to look out the window. "Really?"

"Were you expecting something?"

"No, but I have an idea of what it could be."

"I spoke with the woman. She was gruff, but kind enough." She pointed to a box that had also been in her arms. "This is for you."

"Oh." It was a hefty package, much more than the letter he'd last sent.

"What's that?" Max asked as he walked downstairs.

"I'm not sure. I'll open it."

Please be something inconspicuous.

At first, all I saw was red fabric. I gently pulled it out, seeing a sweater that was a size smaller than I would usually order. I stared at it, wondering where I'd seen it before.

"Oh, it's so pretty!" Mom said. "It looks like the one you had in college."

My throat went dry.

No way. He had it? He *kept* it?

I had been sad when I realized I'd never see that sweater again. More than sad, because it had been so soft that I refused to take it off. But that was twelve years ago. How did he know to keep it?

With shaky hands, I picked up Tom's handwritten note.

I found your hoodie many years ago. It should be returned to its owner.

"There's more!" Max exclaimed, reaching into the box. He pulled out a record. "It's a Lila Wilde vinyl!"

Max didn't even have a record player, but he'd mentioned he wanted to collect her vinyl since they came with beautiful photos that he wanted to put on his walls.

"That was nice of him," I said. "I don't know how we'll play it, but—"

"Wait a second. It has notes on Post-its!" He squinted as he read them. "Mr. Tom listened to the album! And he wrote his thoughts."

"I should check if they're kid appropriate." I reached for it. All I saw were circled quotes and short notes in Tom's handwriting. I opened the vinyl, and when I did, a letter popped out.

Max scrambled to get it first. His eyes widened when he laid eyes on it.

For a horrifying second, I thought he'd found out the truth.

"It's to me!" Max exclaimed. "He said he wanted to let me know he really liked this album and that he wanted me to have the copy he listened to."

That was surprisingly sentimental.

"So, this man's name is Tom?" Mom asked, an eyebrow raised. I froze, knowing how this looked.

"It's not like that," I rushed to say.

"Men don't give gifts to women they're just friends with."

"That's a little old-fashioned," I said, but my heart rate was up. Getting back my hoodie and knowing that he'd listened to Lila Wilde for Max did unfair things to my brain. I'd always loved it when people *showed* their intentions with action. And he seemed to be doing just that.

Just like in one of my books.

No. Not going there. I didn't need to add fuel to the fire. My dreams were already wild.

"I give it a week," Mom said, winking.

I ignored the feeling of heat in my cheeks and pulled out my phone.

Selena: You kept my hoodie?

He answered immediately.

Tom: It wasn't mine to throw away.

I saw him type for a moment, stop, and then start again. No other answer came. I stared at the last text, biting my lip. What did he not send?

His letter from over a decade ago flashed in my mind. Maybe whatever was on his mind needed to stay there.

Yet, I couldn't help but think this was something that would happen in the pages of my favorite book.

Selena: Thank you. For both the hoodie and the record. Max loves it. Not many people would send something like that.

Tom: It's the least I could do.

I felt bold, so I sent something I usually wouldn't.

Selena: You were typing something earlier, but you never sent it. What were you going to say?

I saw the text bubble come up, disappear, and then come up again.

Selena: Just say whatever it is. No editing.

Tom: Okay.

Tom: I remember when I found it. I wanted to give it back to you, but I didn't know your last name so I couldn't ever find you. So whenever I was sober, I'd glance at it and think about how it could have been nice if we were something more.

Tom: Which is why it's still one of my biggest regrets that I don't remember the rest of it.

Holy *shit*. My face erupted into flame.

"Texting Tom?" Mom asked.

"No," I lied.

"As long as he's not as old as that man Luna is with, then I approve." Her smile fell from her face. "That reminds me. I had something else I wanted to talk to you about. You're making them a portrait? Really?" Her voice was flat, and it was far too close to how she spoke to Luna.

"Mom, please."

"Why would you entertain this?"

"It's a paying job, Mom. She's a client now. And besides, Luna is going to be in that relationship whether we support her or not."

"That doesn't mean we make it easy."

"She's not dumb. Eventually, if he truly isn't a good person, she'll see that."

"And what if they're married? What if they have a *child*? Could you imagine being tied to someone like Willie forever?"

I pressed my lips together, thinking of the version of Tom who had sent that scathing letter.

"Okay, then we can talk to her about being smart and safe."

"That's not enough."

"I need to get Max to school," I said, my hands playing nervously with my sleeves at Mom's disappointment. "We can talk about this later."

"You never want to finish conversations." She shook her head. "Fine. Get Max to school. But we *will* talk about this again."

I would do my best to make sure we didn't.

She walked out the door as I closed my eyes, feeling torn between stepping in to tell my sister she was possibly making a mistake and being able to pay my bills because she was overpaying me for this portrait.

When I got back from dropping off Max, Meowcifer was curled up on the red sweater on the table. I'd tried to train her not to get on countertops, but she never listened.

"What are you doing there?" I asked. "It probably doesn't even smell like me anymore anyway." I picked her up and gently put her on one of her beds.

She went back for the sweater.

"Huh. You must really like that. I guess I can't blame you. It *is* pretty soft."

Tom

"I'm not asking them that," I said into my phone. I was walking down the street on my way to the PATH office. "I'm just there to look at the system for the trucks."

"But you *have* to. If we can get them to cut us a little bit of slack, think of all the money we could make."

I rolled my eyes at the man on the other end of the line. I was very sure that Dale was still in contact with Dad and that he was relaying messages from him to me. They'd always been close ever since Dad bought out his company.

"No. They said we weren't cutting pay and we aren't."

"Todd would have done it."

"And *Todd* didn't get this deal in the first place," I hissed. "I'm sticking to what we agreed to. End of story."

There was something muttered into the line, something about me that I probably didn't need to hear.

I hung up, done with the conversation. This deal was going to change the trucking industry. PATH specialized in building self-driving technology that could be installed on nearly any car. And only a few months ago, Ruth had come up with a business plan that included the caveat that we couldn't lay off or dock the pay of our drivers. It was a small ask, and one that benefited many employees at our company. But people like Dale only cared about the money we could make.

And I vowed not to be one of them.

It should have been over. The technology was almost completed, and the business plan had been set in stone. Changing anything would result in more penalties and fines than it was worth.

But the idea of making money spoke loudly at Murray and Sons. I just didn't listen.

The new PATH office was a high-rise in downtown. It wasn't but a few blocks away from my own. Walking to and from had helped me keep my cool during the day.

Knox Price, the creator and CEO of PATH, had taken care to choose a building that not only blended into the skyline, but also had gardens lining the roads. It was well-designed—nice, but not overly fancy in the way Murray and Sons was.

Ruth was waiting in the lobby.

"Hey," she said, smiling. "Ready to see the product of all this hard work?"

"I am."

"Knox is waiting in the R&D department," she replied, leading me to the elevator. I wasn't sure what to expect, but seeing Knox inspecting a system of wires and screens seemed pretty on-brand.

"Everything good?" Ruth asked.

Knox didn't even look up. "Yep. Just fine-tuning things."

"That can wait. Tom's here."

He looked up instantly. "Oh, is it noon already? Good to see you, Tom."

"You as well."

"Let me show you the system. I think you'll like what we have."

I followed him deeper into the department and blinked when I saw a system of wires and pulleys suspended in the air.

"Obviously, it's not on the truck," Knox said. "But this is the mock-up."

"I didn't realize we were so close," I replied. "Is it functional?"

"More or less. We can have it tested as soon as next month."

"Great. I'm eager to get this on the trucks."

"We are too," Ruth said. "Having a win under your belt will look good against Dad."

"Good. We need everyone at Murray to see how good this could be."

"Is anyone giving you a hard time?" Ruth asked.

"No more than usual. They want me to screw you guys over."

"The contract is signed," Knox said.

"And I intend to comply fully. They just want more money."

"I hate business people sometimes," Ruth said. "Glad you're the CEO."

"Acting CEO."

"Dad isn't coming back."

I shrugged. My conversation with Dale had reminded me that Dad still had a lot of power in a lot of places. Our evidence was all in emails, but apparently, that hadn't been enough to remove him initially. He had said they were all jokes, and we were currently waiting on the women to testify in a court of law that they had been negatively affected by the harassment.

The court date was taking far too long, and I kept imagining all the ways he could somehow keep his slimy grip on Murray and Sons.

"Let me show you more about these," Knox said. "Any more talk about Todd Murray and I might go after him myself."

I forced myself to listen as Knox went into detail about the machines that were going to revolutionize the trucking world. He explained how they would work and how the drivers would interact with them on a daily basis.

The afternoon got away from us and the sun was sinking low in the sky by the time Ruth interrupted.

"We've been at this for far too long," she said. "Maybe we should all go home for the day."

"Already?" Knox said. "The day flew by."

"It's almost dinnertime and we deserve a break." It was the most un-Ruth-like sentence I'd ever heard.

But it was good. Both she and Knox did deserve to relax.

"I won't keep you," I said. "I should get back to the office anyway. It was great seeing you both."

The streets of Nashville were growing dark as I walked back. I had a laundry list of things I could do once I got to the office and I knew that staying at work late would keep me from drinking.

Yet, I still dreaded it.

Then I got a text.

Selena: I was not expecting that last text to be so nice. Thank you for that.

Tom: I'm glad. I was worried it was too much. I don't know what to say or what to do sometimes.

Selena: Join the club. Max wants to say thank you in person for the gift. Are you free for dinner?

Selena: Also, Martinez. My last name is Martinez.

Chapter Seven

Selena

"What did he say?" Max tried to look at my phone, but I moved it so he couldn't see.

"Hang on," I said. "He's typing."

Tom: Thank you for trusting me with your last name. And yes, I'm free. Where do you want to go?

"If he says yes, can we get Italian food?" Max asked. "What about that nice place near Centennial Park?"

"Um, I don't know if I'm in the mood for Italian." Or if I could afford it.

"Please? We haven't been there in forever!"

Another text came in.

Tom: I'll buy.

And that sealed the deal. The idea of something that wasn't fast food, or something I had to cook and then clean, made my mouth water. I wasn't turning him down.

"You got lucky. Tom offered to go wherever you wanted."

"Yes!"

It had been almost a year since I had the money to go anywhere fancier than a fast-food place. As we approached the restaurant, all I could think about was garlic bread. And pasta. And big portions that I would be able to have the next day for leftovers.

Tom was waiting by the entrance. He looked decadent in his perfect suit and tie. It fit so well, it had to be tailored.

And I was wearing leggings and a sweater.

"Hi," I said. "Sorry if we're underdressed."

"You two look great," he said. "I just look like this because I came straight from the office. Should we go in?"

Walking into such a fancy place made this feel different than it was. Jax had taken me to a restaurant this nice twice. Once with Max, the second without him. Things like this had always been reserved for special occasions only.

"Thank you," I said as we were seated. "You didn't have to offer this."

"It's no problem," Tom replied. "Look at Max. He's practically dancing in his seat."

Max was possibly the only one more excited than I was. He couldn't stay still.

"Still. This place is way more expensive than the last place we went."

He opened his mouth to say something, but shut it.

"What?" I asked.

"Never mind. It's...not a helpful thing to say."

"Say it. Don't hide it."

"Okay," he said. "I was going to say that this dinner, no matter what you get, is like pocket change to me."

"Ah, right. You're rich."

"But even if it wasn't, even if it were hundreds of thousands of dollars, I'd pay it. You two deserve whatever you want, no matter the cost."

My skin erupted in gooseflesh despite my sweater. How did he say things like that so easily?

It's like he's straight out of a romance novel, the romantic part of my brain said.

"I can tell I just said the wrong thing," Tom added at my silence. "I apologize."

"No, you didn't," I replied. "It was sweet. I'm just...out of it."

Trying not to see things the wrong way was cutting into what little I knew about social etiquette. *Great.*

"Good. If I ever do say something out of place, let me know."

I nodded then turned my attention to the menu. A steak caught my eye.

"So, Mr. Tom," Max said, glancing up at him, "you're really cool if we get what we want?"

"I am."

"And if Mom wants a delicious steak?"

My jaw dropped. "Max! Don't call me out like that."

"She loves steak, even though I think it tastes like salty shoes," Max said, and he folded his hands in front of him like he was making a business deal. "So, what do you say?"

"A steak is fine. She can have the whole menu if she wants."

I stared at him. My brain finally broke and all the delusional thoughts spilled over.

This could be my second-chance romance. He would be my knight in shining armor, the man who would whisk me away and make me fall in love with him.

"Can I interest you in our wine tonight?"

Our waitress pulled me out of my daydream. I came back to reality only to see the waitress offering a bottle to the two adults at the table.

Would he say yes? Would he cross one of the boundaries I gave him?

"No, thank you," he said immediately. "I'll just have water."

"Can I get an apple juice?" Max asked.

After writing down his order, the waitress looked at me, but my mind was too far gone to even begin to think of what I wanted.

"Mom likes Diet Coke," Max informed Tom.

"Then let's get that."

As the waitress walked away, I turned to Tom. "I was going to get water like you did."

"Is that what you wanted?"

"No." The word quickly slipped out of me.

"Okay then," he said. "Get what you *do* want." He gave me a nod and then turned to Max. "Did you like the vinyl I sent?"

"Liked it? I *loved* it. Oh! That reminds me." He stood and walked over to Tom and then did a dramatic bow. "Thank you, sir, for the kind gift. It was most appreciated."

"You're welcome," he said. Did his lips slightly turn upward? Or did I imagine that? "Though it really wasn't a problem."

"It meant a lot," Max replied as he returned to his seat. "I like to properly thank people."

"And I can say that I honestly enjoyed it. I'm glad you liked it too."

"See? This is why I like you. We get along, and you spoil Mom. That's boyfriend material right there."

Tom's eyebrows pinched together. "What?"

"Max," I began slowly. "What does that mean?"

"Nothing. I'm just pointing out a fact."

"Where did you get that idea?"

"I'm not dumb," he said. "I heard what abuela said. I can pick up on hints too."

Oh, God. I was *not* used to him paying attention to anything.

"He's just a friend."

Max's eyes darted between us, and it hit me that I'd sat next to Tom. I'd done it to monitor Max, but now I realized it looked entirely different from anyone else's perspective. I scooted my chair away, eyes level with my child.

We were interrupted when the waitress brought over the complimentary garlic bread. Whatever I was thinking flew out of my mind, and one look at Max told me he'd experienced the same thing.

"This is my favorite part!" Max said, eagerly grabbing a piece.

"The bread?" Tom asked.

"Yeah," Max replied. "Have you never had good garlic bread?"

"I don't usually focus on the taste of what I'm eating."

Max had stuffed an entire piece into his mouth, but paused at Tom's words. "That's so sad," he said, so full of emotion that I worried he might cry. Or maybe it was the bread in his mouth.

"It's not sad," Tom rushed to say. "I was usually listening to my parents or business partners. The taste was never that big of a deal."

"Now it is." Max set a piece of the loaf on Tom's plate. "Focus on it and taste it."

I was about to tell Max that it probably wasn't a good idea to make him try it if he didn't want to, but Tom instantly took the offered bread. Max leaned closer as he took a bite, almost as if he was waiting for a magic trick.

Tom ate it slowly. "Okay," he admitted. "That is really good."

"Right?" he said. "Mom has a way of finding the best places to eat. Oh, and she can cook too. But then we have to clean it up and that's just boring."

"That's part of the reason my dad told my mom to stop cooking. She kept disappearing to clean the kitchen. And the food she made wasn't classy enough."

"He told her to *stop* cooking?" I asked.

"Yes. She stopped a long time ago."

"Did she like it?"

"I think she did. She had a lot of family recipes that she had to get rid of."

"What?" I said incredulously. "She shouldn't have had to...where did he get the nerve?"

"Some men," Max said, sighing and shaking his head as if he possessed wisdom beyond his years.

"It's okay," Tom said. "I'm here with you guys where I know it's okay to enjoy my food."

"Yes," Max said. "Food is one of the best parts of life."

"I can agree. That bread already brought me some joy."

"If you want real joy," Max said, "get the chicken alfredo."

"Really? It's that good?"

"Amazing. I dream about it."

"Selena? Do you have any recommendations?"

I blinked, surprised to be included in their back and forth.

"The alfredo is great. I'm a fan of the steak, though. You can get the alfredo with it but...it's expensive."

He raised his eyebrows at me and I remembered his words.

"Sorry, I forgot nothing is too expensive for you."

"Mom, you should get it," Max urged, the biggest smile plastered on his face.

"Maybe I will."

"I'll get it too. And do my best to enjoy it."

"I can't wait," Max said.

Our waitress came over not too long after that to take our orders. I did as I said and got the expensive dish, and all I could think about was how excited I was to have exactly what I wanted.

Max and Tom talked in-depth about Lila Wilde while we waited for our food. Even I could admit, seeing someone connect with Max about something he loved was incredible. No one not related to him had ever made this much of an effort before.

He only stopped when our food arrived.

"You've gotta tell me what you think of the taste," Max said as he finished his first few bites.

"I love the garlic and spices. I like that it's mixed in well with the sauce."

Max beamed and asked more questions. I glanced around the dining room, relieved that he was having such a good time.

And that was when I saw my sister walking through the restaurant. She was in her best dress and her highest heels, hair curled to perfection. This was definitely a date outfit.

Her eyes ran across me and she stopped. She blinked and then did a double take.

And I knew I was *screwed*.

I stood. "Excuse me," I said, before I raced over to meet her.

"Selena?" she asked.

"What are you doing here?"

"I'm on a date with Willie. Who are you here with?" Her eyes went back to the table, to Tom. I held my breath when her eyes widened. "Is that...Tom Murray?"

"How do you know who he is?"

"Um, he was a legend at Vanderbilt when I went. He was the senior who every one of us freshman wanted to hook up with."

"Gross."

"What is he doing here with *you*? Are you on a date?"

"No!" I hissed. "We're...friends."

"Friends? You two? What would you have in common with a man like him?"

"What does that mean?"

"It means that he *knew* everyone. There wasn't a night that he was in his dorm. Unless he was with a girl or something. You've never been to a party in your life."

"That was over ten years ago, Luna."

"And? Some people don't change. Where did you meet him?"

I struggled to come up with an answer.

"Is everything okay?" a voice asked.

Tom.

"Oh, hi," Luna said. "Tom Murray. You look as good as ever."

I turned to watch him, wondering if he would do as most did. Whenever people saw me standing next to my sister, their eyes remained fixed on her, just like they should. She looked gorgeous and I was in an outfit one step above leisure wear.

But then his eyes turned to me. He repeated, "Is everything okay?"

I didn't know how to react. Why was he looking at me when someone far prettier was right there?

"Everything is okay," Luna said. "I was just shocked to see my big homebody of a sister out of the house."

"Oh. Well, Max wanted to come out."

"Oh, right. Max knows you too."

"He can meet my *friends*."

Luna's deadpan stare meant that she didn't believe me. My heart pounded. The restaurant felt too loud, and each noise hit my eardrums painfully.

"It was nice to meet you," Tom said, "but we're both starving so we better get back."

"Oh, okay, sure. Of course. I better get back to my boyfriend. He's in the fancy suit over there."

"Have a good night," Tom said, and his hand hovered over my back, as if to lead me to the table, but he abandoned the movement almost immediately.

What would it have felt like if he *had* touched me?

Even without the touch, just being seen with him was *so* going to get questioned tomorrow.

"Hi, Tia Luna!" Max yelled, waving at her. She gave him a quick wave back before returning to her own table. I closed my eyes as sounds pelted me.

"Mom?" Max's voice broke through my panic. "Are the paint levels low?"

"Very," I said.

"What does that mean?" Tom asked.

"It just means one of us is done with being in public," Max said. "Can we take this to go?"

"Of course," Tom said. "You guys go, and I'll finish up and pay."

I glanced over at him, wondering if his pursed lips meant he was mad that I was the reason we needed to leave early.

"Can't you come with us?" Max asked. "You can eat at our house."

"I don't know if your mom would be okay with that."

I glanced up. He'd been so kind, and I would hate to have to bail on him just because I got a little too anxious at dinner.

"Yeah, that's fine. As long as you don't mind coming to my neck of the woods."

"I'd love nothing more."

Tom

Selena lived in a small house on the south side of Nashville. I'd never been to the area, but it was cramped in the same way downtown was. Many houses had multiple cars on the street out front, and as I navigated around them, it reminded me of my drive to work.

Her Baja pulled into a gravel driveway and I followed suit. Max ran over to me the moment I put my truck in park.

"I can't wait to show you my room. Oh, and where I put my record!" He ran ahead and put a key into the lock, gesturing for me to follow.

Their home felt warm in a way all the places I'd ever lived hadn't. There was a small couch nestled in the living room with yellow walls that held dozens of pictures.

"So this is our house," Max announced.

"It's messy," Selena added, sounding as tired as she was when we left the restaurant. "Sorry."

She wasn't wrong, but I couldn't imagine it was easy to clean up after a kid when doing it all alone. It reminded me of my college roommate's side of the room, which had never bothered me.

Not everyone found cleaning relaxing like I did. And the only reason it was calming for me was because it was the only time when I could get my dad off my back.

I saw a black shadow slinking around the corner. Two green eyes blinked up at me.

"Is that a cat?" I asked.

"Oh yeah, that's Meowcifer."

"Be careful," Selena added. "She hates most people. That's how she got the name."

"Yeah, she attacked Mom's old boyfriend every day." A smile crossed Max's face. "It was awesome."

Meowcifer walked up to Max, tail in the air.

"Hi." Max leaned down to pet the cat. "She's so sweet when she likes you."

"How do I introduce myself?" I asked.

"You can put your hand out," Max said. "She might scratch it, though."

I leaned down and did as I was told. Meowcifer apprehensively walked over, watching me with narrow eyes.

"I'll get the first aid kit," Selena said, walking to the kitchen.

Maybe this had been a bad idea. But I at least wanted to try to connect with the cat Max obviously loved.

After sniffing, Meowcifer regarded me closely. I wondered how long I had before she attacked.

Instead, she rubbed her face against my hand.

"Whoa," Max said. "She likes you!"

"Really?"

"What?" Selena said. "She didn't attack him?"

"No, Mom. Look, Mr. Tom is petting her!"

I was. Her black fur was soft against my hand.

"That's...not possible. She hates everyone."

"Maybe he's special," Max said. "You're officially cool now, though. Meowcifer is picky."

"It's an honor."

Meowcifer moved from me and walked over to Selena. She meowed at her.

"I know, I know. It's your dinnertime. I can't believe you liked Tom, especially while hungry."

"Maybe it was the food smell on his hands," Max said. "Oh, Mr. Tom, can I show you my room now?"

"Of course."

"Just don't take too long," Selena said. "We still have to finish dinner."

"I won't," Max promised, and then gestured for me to follow him to his room.

The floor creaked under my steps, and I eyed the baby photos of Max on the wall. My heart lurched. I wished I had seen this. I wished I had been here. And the reminder of my own failure made emotion clog my throat. But I kept my composure as I followed Max to his room.

"So this is it," he said. "I have my bed and my desk, and then my Lila posters." He pointed to a very full wall where Lila Wilde was in different poses. "I put the record you gave me on my dresser. One day, I want a record player so I can listen along and reread everything you wrote."

I mentally filed that away for later. "I'm glad you like it."

"You really had a lot of thoughts for someone who doesn't like music."

"I don't have time for it," I said. "But I should. I forgot how nice it was to get lost in a melody."

"Right?" Max said, smiling. I could feel my own lips pulling back to return the gesture.

He told me more about himself, including his friends from school. He seemed so excited to have someone listen, and I hung on every word.

"I hate to break up the nice moment," a voice interjected. We both turned to see Selena leaning against the doorway. "But I think it's time to eat."

"Come on," I told him. "I still need to enjoy my food."

We went to the small dining room table. Selena had plated our food for us and set it out.

"This is nice. Thank you."

She blinked as if she had never been thanked before in her life. "N-no problem. I hate eating out of Styrofoam."

"The sound is the worst part," Max said, shuddering.

I'd eaten out of Styrofoam for most of my lunches. While I didn't hate it, I
also liked eating off of plates too.

"Do you have any homework tonight, Max?" Selena asked as we huddled
around the table.

He deflated. "Only in math. We're doing fractions again and Mrs. Mulligan
didn't explain any of it in a way I understand."

"Right. Well, we can try to find a YouTube video."

"I could help," I said. "Math was my best subject in school."

"Really?" Max asked, eyes bright.

"Yeah, I'll help you after dinner."

"Thank you," Selena said before taking another bite of food.

We all took our time enjoying our meals. I enjoyed every bite of the garlicky
deliciousness that was my alfredo.

After we were done, Selena took the plates into the kitchen before retiring to
the living room. Max brought his backpack downstairs.

As he talked about his homework, I realized that it all seemed far too complicated for a kid of his age to be learning. Luckily, I was still able to help, but it
took me a bit to figure out how to explain things in a way he understood.

Once I did, however, he caught on quickly.

"And I'm done!" he exclaimed. "Thank you. I feel like I finally understand
it. Now I just need you around all the time."

"You could always call me whenever you need help."

"Really? Are you sure?"

"Yeah, I don't mind. Call me any time."

"Thank you. I don't want to have to bother Mom with it anymore. She's
working really hard right now."

"Why is she working hard?"

He lowered his voice, glancing out to where Selena was sitting on the couch. "She tries not to tell me, but I know we're tight on money."

"Oh, I didn't know that."

"Yeah. She tries to hide it, but I see."

I slowly nodded, glancing at the back of her head.

"I should probably go relax for a bit before bed. Mind if I head to my room?"

"That's fine. I'll go talk to your mom." I stood and walked to where she was sitting. She was drawing on her tablet. Bright colors were everywhere as she filled in a portrait of a beautiful woman.

"You've only gotten better," I said softly.

She jumped and her hand moved to cover her art.

"I didn't mean to pry. I just saw it when I walked over."

"Do you need something? Did Max get his homework done?"

"Yes, he did. He said he wanted to go relax in his room."

"Oh, okay. He'll probably be going to bed soon then."

She glanced at the door and I knew she was ready for me to leave. I didn't want to overstay my welcome, but I did have one question. "Have you given any more thought to the child support offer?"

"Oh, um, yeah. I don't know if I'm going to go through with it."

"Why not?"

"I'm fine without it, and I mean, the at-home results aren't legally binding, so we'd have to go somewhere to get it done, and that means telling..." She hesitated. "I'm fine without it."

"I owe you for raising him alone."

"Don't worry about it. I promise, it's okay."

"I only want to help."

"Yeah, sure you want to help now, but maybe you won't always."

"The court would make me pay."

"Until you don't. A court order isn't a guarantee of anything. Especially when I can't afford a lawyer to fight it if you decide this isn't what you want again."

"But I'm not going to."

"I'm still working on believing that. Besides, I can't rely on someone else again. I need to be able to pay my bills alone."

"But—"

"Tom, I've spent far too long needing help. I want to pay my bills on my own, so the answer is no. My business is doing well. I have the card in case of emergencies. I'm *fine*."

I felt my jaw clench, but I knew better than to try and argue with someone who was telling me no. Images of Ruth screaming at me came to mind.

"Okay," I said, even though I hated it. "Then I'll head out."

She nodded. "Thanks for dinner. And coming over."

"No problem."

"And watch out for the stop sign at the bottom of the massive hill. It can be easy to miss."

"I'll be careful," I replied as I walked out the door.

I pulled out of the driveway, unable to calm the desire I had to do something for her—something more than a card she barely used.

I could never pay back the years I was gone, but I could do way more now.

As the night gave way to morning, I tossed and turned in bed, hoping for answers.

None came.

Chapter Eight

Selena

I knew I was screwed when Luna called out of nowhere. "Surprise," she said. "Mom is on the call too. This is an interrogation."

"No," I said. "No interrogation. I thought you two were fighting."

"We're not when we have something interesting going on!" Luna said. "Are you going to give us some answers willingly, or do we have to force the story out of you?"

"The story of what?"

"How you were on a *date* with one of the hottest men alive!"

"It was not a date."

Meowcifer jumped on my lap and I petted her nervously. I wondered if she could sense my stress.

"From what it sounds like," Mom said, "it was very much a date. And don't even try to divert us. This is about *you*."

I hated it when it was about me, when I was the center of attention. "There isn't anything to tell! I'm not dating him. I'm just..." Letting him see his son? *Nope.* Not an option. The moment they knew who Tom was, they would ban me from seeing him. They hated Max's father, even though they had no clue about his identity—and I didn't blame them.

I wanted to hate him too.

But I thought of the way he helped Max with his homework, and the way he'd come into my house with no air of judgment. Despite everything, I was starting to see him as someone I could like, and I didn't know how to stop it.

"She's thinking of him," Mom added.

"Guys, stop! It's nothing."

"If it's nothing, then can I date him?" Luna asked.

"No!" I snapped. "Y-you're seeing someone else anyway."

"I know. It was a test, one that gave us all the answers."

"Why do you sound so embarrassed?" Mom asked. "This is great! You're moving on from Jax."

"I'm...This is just private."

"We're your family!" Mom chided. "And we're happy for you. You deserve a great man who cares about you, and about Max. Unlike his *father*." She said the word like a curse. "You deserve a good man who treats you right."

"Oh, you know what? I think Max is calling. *Gottagobye!*" I hung up before they could say anything else.

For a moment, I listened to be sure Max wasn't actually calling me, then I picked my phone back up.

Hadley definitely needed to hear this.

After I caught her up, she laughed for so long I worried she was going to send herself into early labor.

"I'm so happy you find this so funny."

"Come on, they're pushing you to *date* him? It's hilarious!"

"I've made myself clear," I said. "They're going to kill me when they find out."

"You could just tell them."

"They'll tell Max at the drop of a hat."

"Maybe they won't."

"Remember the gender incident?" I asked.

"Oh, yeah," she mumbled. Hadley had wanted a gender-reveal party, so the results were handed off to me in order to plan it. Mom and Luna volunteered to help, but as soon as Luna learned Hadley was having a girl, she blabbed the secret by asking Hadley if she'd prefer a chocolate cake with pink sprinkles on the inside, or a vanilla one.

"They have no self-control," I said. "I'd prefer to keep telling them we're only friends rather than risk Max finding out and then Tom leaving. I've put Max through enough, especially when Jax was around."

"What happened with Jax wasn't—"

"I brought Jax into his life. I'm responsible for what he did."

"That's just not true."

"Even if it isn't, it doesn't change the fact that Jax hurt him. He's still strug-gling to go to school every day. Can you imagine what it would be like if he knew who Tom was and then Tom left?"

"I can. But doesn't Max like Tom? It's going to hurt either way."

I paused. She was right, as usual. "But at least it would be just *some guy* and not his *father*."

"What else does Tom need to prove?"

"Maybe that he can stay away from drinking and partying for a while? I don't know. I haven't talked to him about his life."

"It might be time to, then."

I blew out a breath. "You're right, but if I'm being honest...the people he knows and the possibility of what he might do in his free time is scary. I don't know if I *want* to know."

"Why wouldn't you?"

Because then I'll have to stop liking this side of him.

But that wasn't a good enough answer. It was the romantic in me that heard his words and twisted them into something more. And once I saw him with another woman, or worse, he left again, I'd be painfully reminded that this wasn't a romance novel and I'm not a heroine.

"I don't think I have a good reason," I replied. "I'll just have to ask."

Tom

Days passed.

Max, true to his word, either texted or called every now and again to ask for help. Some nights, we stayed up late in order to get his homework done. He always apologized, but I knew I wouldn't be sleeping anyway.

That, plus the PATH project, kept me busy.

Ruth and I had been diligently working on the road tests with the new trucks equipped with the self-driving technology. Our best drivers had tested them and a few bugs had been sent back to Knox.

It was common for Ruth to be around Murray and Sons these days. She was often either the messenger, or the executioner, if she ran into someone who wanted to screw over PATH.

It was good to see her in action, but our conversations had mostly been business. As much as I wanted to say I was fine with the superficial interactions, I wondered how she was doing.

After a long meeting, I was expecting her to head back to PATH and get out of the Murray building for a while. I often wished I could do the same.

But when I walked into my office, I saw her sitting at my desk.

"Wow," she said. "Finally in the CEO's chair. Never thought this would be happening."

"Shouldn't you be making your way back to PATH?"

"I've got all my work done. Besides, I have a gift for you."

Ruth stood and walked over to hand me a Ziploc bag.

"What's this?"

"Cookies. I made them."

"You?"

"Yes, me. Working for PATH has truly given me a good work-life balance."

"That's great."

"I sense a 'but' coming."

"How do you know that?"

"Your tone, mostly. Now, tell me what you're thinking." Her voice was firm. "Please," she added in a lighter manner.

"It's only that I thought you'd hate it considering what Dad said at that dinner."

"Oh, the 'women should be homemakers' thing? Who cares? He didn't even like it when Mom cooked anyway. You should try one. Knox says they're good."

My stomach rumbled as I grabbed a cookie from the bag. They were delectable. Soft and chocolatey. It was the closest thing to Mom's cooking I'd had in years. "This is incredible."

Her green eyes lit up. "Really? You like them?"

"Yes. You have a talent for this."

In another very un-Ruth-like move, she fist pumped. I blinked over at her.

"Don't give me that look. I'm too busy celebrating."

"Celebrating that I like the cookies?"

"Um, yes. I was worried you'd give me a critique on them like Barry did."

"No. I've recently learned to taste my food. I'm not going to complain."

"You're tasting your food now? Who taught you that?"

"Max."

"Did you ever find out if he is actually your son?"

"Selena shared the results with me, and yeah, he's mine."

"So you've met him, then?"

"Twice."

"Twice? It went well enough for a second time?"

"I'm getting to know him on a trial basis. He doesn't know who I am, though."

"Are you okay with that?"

"I am. For now, it's easier because his mom doesn't trust me. Plus, he doesn't hate me yet for not being there for his entire life. Once he does...then I don't know what's going to happen."

"Maybe he'll forgive you."

"Not for something this big. Could you imagine forgiving Dad for what he did to us?"

"Maybe, if Dad was at least trying to be better."

"Really?"

"Well, he'd have to be *really* trying. Besides, you haven't done half the things Dad did to us. Yes, you weren't there, and that was wrong. But you're trying to learn about Lila Wilde. And you're listening to him. You're not Dad."

"I was like him before."

"No, you weren't."

"Really? I wasn't? Ruth, I can barely talk to my own siblings. Everyone here is terrified of me. I had to be *told* to stop drinking."

"But you understood there was a problem that needed fixing. Dad knows that and has never attempted to change."

"The damage is done."

"We'll see about that," she said. "I don't think you're as bad as you say you are."

"I think I am exactly who I say I am."

"Then why even try with your son?"

"Because I'm selfish and want to see him."

"Okay, so if you're so selfish, then what do you want from him?"

"Nothing."

Ruth raised an eyebrow.

"All right, I get it," I huffed. "Maybe you're right."

"I'm right about a lot. You should ask Knox."

"I almost want to ask how the hell you ended up with him, but I know we don't have that kind of relationship."

"We could if you would just *ask*."

"I don't feel like I've earned the right to know."

"You don't have to *earn* anything. Siblings talk about their lives. So ask me."

"Fine." I sighed. I was excited to finally know more. "How did you and Knox end up together?"

"A friend of mine led me to the conclusion that I never hated *him*. I hated how Mom compared me to him all the time. Once I was over that then it was easy to fall in love."

"You have some good people surrounding you."

"I do. You should too. We've replaced the Monday night Murray dinners with a different kind of family time. It's with people we choose to be close to."

"That sounds very nice."

"You should join. You could bring your son."

"We might be getting ahead of ourselves."

"Then you could come by yourself. I know everyone would love to have you. I've been trying to get Barry to go for weeks, but he always says he's busy with his bar."

I could say the same thing. It would be easy to mention that I needed to run Murray and Sons. Maybe I could also add in something about investigating Dad to really seal the deal.

But the idea made a weight settle in my stomach. I couldn't bear it.

"I'll try to make it one of these days."

Ruth's face lit up. "Really?"

"Sure. Monday nights?"

"Yes! Maybe you can come next week."

"I'll do my best."

She fist pumped again.

"That is so odd to see."

"I fist pump now. Get over it."

I shook my head, trying to repress a smile. I couldn't believe how happy she seemed these days. It was a good look on her.

"I'd hug you," Ruth added, "but I'm pretty sure you'd spontaneously combust."

"I think you're right." I was pretty sure the last time we had all hugged was ten years ago, when a storm ripped through our neighborhood. That was also the night I realized I had to be the stoic one, never showing emotion.

"I need to go," she said. "I'll talk to you later?" Her voice was hopeful.

"Yes. We'll talk later."

I was only able to work for a few moments before there was another knock at my door. I told whoever it was to come in, and I saw my assistant, Asha, enter the room.

She didn't look great. Her eyes were red rimmed and her whole body seemed to shake.

"Um, s-sir," Asha started, wringing her hands. "My...wife is in the hospital. I asked one of the managers if I could go be with her, but they said I had to ask you since you're technically the boss of all of us."

All I could do was stare at her. Was this who I'd been as a person? Was I the kind of man that people feared *this* much? She shouldn't have to ask at all. An emergency was an emergency.

She took my silence the wrong way. "I-I don't have to, sir. I can just stay here."

"No," I said, putting my own self-hatred away so I could focus on what she needed. "Go."

Her eyes lifted to mine. "Really? Oh my God, thank you so much! I'll take my laptop so you don't experience any interruptions from me."

"No, leave your laptop here. You should fully be with your wife."

"But...it's during the day. Don't you need me to field all your calls and emails?"

"I'll just turn off the notifications. Don't worry about me. I'll manage."

"Are you sure?"

"Yes. Go."

She gave me a watery smile before darting out the door. After she was gone, I rubbed my eyes. My self-loathing returned and reached a new peak.

I needed to walk around the office and get some water. A distraction would be good.

As I arrived at the break room, I overheard Jason, a guy Dad hired, talking to someone else.

"I told Asha to go to Tom for final approval," he said, laughing. "There's no way she got the time off. She must have snuck out. He's going to fire her for that. Serves her right. Two women shouldn't be married anyway."

"Excuse me," I said coldly. Rage straightened my spine. "Are you talking about *my* assistant?"

Jason turned slowly. "T-Tom."

"That's Mr. Murray to you. You're the one that sent Asha to me?"

"I *am* the manager of the assistants."

"Since when is that a title?"

"Todd gave it to me last year."

Of course he did. "Interesting. So not only did you not do your job, but you sent her to me, expecting me to turn her down?"

"I-I mean, she doesn't *need* the time off."

"Yes, she does."

"Since when do we care about people like her?"

"I always have. I don't play games with the people I manage. Everyone here is equal and I don't appreciate having to step in for *your* employee where you failed. You're fired, Jason."

"For what?"

"I have a one-strike policy for assholes. And considering what I just heard? You just discriminated in the workplace, which is illegal. So get out."

"Y-you can't fire me."

"In case you haven't heard," I said, "*I* am your boss. And you've just given me all the justification I need. Do I need to drag you out myself?"

My muscles tightened, and I almost wanted to have to. It would feel good to kick him out onto the pavement.

But Jason paled and ran from the room. His friend opened his mouth, but no words came out. He followed closely behind Jason, looking like a child who'd just been caught with their hand in the cookie jar.

"Idiots," I muttered as I turned to the fridge.

That was where I found Francine leaning against the wall. "Wow. A one-strike policy, huh?"

"How long were you there?"

"The whole time. I go on lunch when they do. I like to keep track of all the shitty things they say."

"You have more?"

"I do."

"Send them to me. If my decision gets questioned, I'll have more evidence."

"Gladly. It's good to see someone standing up for those who aren't in the boy's club."

"I shouldn't have to. But I suppose this is the legacy my father left."

"There's one part of the legacy that isn't all too bad."

"Is it the free coffee?"

"No, idiot. It's you."

I blinked. "Was that a compliment?"

She shrugged. "I'm capable of them. I think I like you, Tom. I thought you were your dad's protégé, but you've proved me wrong."

"I just gave you the pay you deserved."

"And stuck up for Asha."

"That was the right thing to do."

"And yet that father of yours didn't do it. I bet you celebrated when he was marched out of those doors. I wish I knew who reported that bastard. It's the one mystery I haven't been able to solve."

"If anyone could figure it out, it's you."

"I have theories. It had to be someone close to him. The only problem is that no one here has the balls to go against him. Other than me, of course."

"You should look at his family, then," I said slowly. "One person in particular might have had a reason."

"Hang on a second," she said. *"You?"*

"I can't answer that," I said.

"I can't *believe*...I mean..." She cleared her throat as she tried to compose herself. "I oughta buy you a drink then."

"I don't drink alcohol. Not anymore."

"Doesn't have to be alcohol. I can offer you a nice water. Or a soda, if you're feeling fancy."

"I might take you up on that."

"Wow. I can't believe you had it in you."

"You cannot tell a soul," I said.

"Don't worry. I wouldn't dare betray the man who not only raised my salary and helped the best employee here but also had the balls to upstage Todd Murray. Your secret is *safe*."

She smiled and walked back to her office. I followed suit and heard whispers as I went.

"Jason is *fired*? That's the best news I've heard all week."

"Tom is just as ruthless as ever, but at least that guy deserved it."

"Maybe he's a little better than Todd was."

They weren't all compliments, but they were far better than what I was used to.

And it almost made me smile.

～☙

The urge to drink only showed its face at night, especially during the hours when everyone else was asleep. On good days or bad, I would crave the burn of alcohol once the sun set and I was at home for the evening. It wasn't even that late, but if I was already struggling, then it would only get worse.

Some nights, I would stay past business hours at work to avoid it. Others, I would spend the entire evening at the gym, trying to feel normal.

It felt so lonely, but so had most of my life. It seemed like the people around me could manage drinking in moderation.

I was simply not one of them.

Today had been a good day. There was no reason for me to be craving it so much. I'd gotten along with my coworkers, and even done something kind for someone who needed it.

So why was I still struggling?

I knew I couldn't sit with this for too long. I needed to get out of my bland and empty apartment and do something.

That was when my phone rang.

The moment I saw Selena's name on it, I answered.

"Hey!" Max's voice said. "So I have another question about math. We moved onto a completely different chapter and I couldn't understand a single thing my teacher said. Can you help me? Are you free?"

The need to drink lessened as I heard my son's voice. I'd been about to leave, ready to run off any of my problems.

Now I had something even better to do.

"Of course I'm free," I said.

"Thank God." Max sighed. "I didn't want to ask Mom again because she would feel so bad when she couldn't help me."

"I don't blame her. The stuff you're learning isn't easy."

"And she never liked math all that much anyway. Can we FaceTime? This is some intense stuff."

I turned on the lights and sat at my table. "Okay, show me."

It took over an hour for me to teach Max how to do his homework, but it was an hour that I was able to help someone that I cared about.

By the time we were done, it was late in the evening. "Okay," he said, "I think I get it all now, but my brain hurts. I need to sleep this off. Bye, Mr. Tom. Thank you again for helping!"

After he hung up, I couldn't stop the corners of my lips from dragging upward. My cheeks almost strained against smiling, but I couldn't help it. Max had completely changed my night.

And my life, if I was being honest with myself.

Chapter Nine

Selena

"Did your homework go okay last night?" I asked Max as we drove to school. "You crashed with my phone."

"Yeah, I got it done."

"How is it going? Did YouTube help?"

"I need Mrs. Mulligan to stop going so fast in class. Trying to figure out the homework broke my brain."

"I'm sure they have standards they have to meet."

He groaned. "Standards schmandards."

We'd figured out that Jax was in charge of cars on Wednesdays, which made us create a routine in order to avoid him. I pulled into the school and immediately darted to the passenger door to let Max out.

It had worked so far, and I hadn't had to talk to Jax since he said he was coming to the house. I didn't see him at that moment, but I was still locking all the doors and closing the windows. I felt paranoid yet justified.

"Really? You're avoiding me?" The voice made me jump. My eyes had lingered to make sure Max got into the building okay. Most students didn't enter through the secondary entrance, and it had been locked more than once.

"Jax?" I asked. "Aren't you on car duty?"

"I got out of it once I figured out you were hiding from me."

"I didn't want to be stopped all the time by you. I have things to do."

"What? Like draw your little pictures all day? That's not being busy, Sel."

The name grated on my ears.

"It's my job."

"Yeah, right. We both know that 'job' never paid your bills. I was nice enough to indulge it, but you'll never make it as an artist."

His words hurt. Back when I had a full-time job, I didn't know why I was struggling to go into work every day, why the lighting gave me headaches, or why I was so tired after simply sitting behind a counter all night.

"Admit it," he said. "You need me."

"I don't need you," I replied, but my voice was not firm. I wanted to make it on my own so badly, but sometimes, I wondered if it was possible.

Why couldn't I be like the badass women I read about in my novels? Why did *I* have to have help?

"I'm taking you and Max out tonight so you can remember what you're missing." The words pulled me out of my thoughts.

"Stay away from us. I told you, I'm done."

"You're never done with me, honey. I'm the best you ever had."

The best I ever had was Tom, but I'd never admit that.

Jax smiled, but his narrowed eyes felt threatening in a way I couldn't explain. He turned to walk inside, finally leaving me alone.

For now.

I didn't even know if he had come by the house the last time he did this. I didn't have the money for cameras and I didn't have the kind of friendship with my neighbors to ask. A part of me didn't think he would do it. Could the man I used to love really come to my house and violate my privacy?

But then I remembered the words he'd said to Max, and how he broke down the amazing boy I knew into an echo of himself.

He definitely could.

My head pounded as I thought of Jax showing up that night. I was going on night two of no sleep because of my increasingly illogical dreams and I could feel my body revolt as I put it through yet another round of stress.

I was hoping to con my overly anxious brain into letting me sleep tonight without the unhelpful dreams. Now that wasn't going to happen. I needed someone to be there just in case Jax made true to his promise to come over.

Someone to hold me accountable, someone who could stand up to him.

Hadley would be with Allen, so she was out.

But I couldn't tell Mom about this. Or Luna. All they would ask about was Tom.

I had no one in my circle who would be free on such short notice.

Well, *almost* no one.

Tom

"You should sign this for Asha." A card was thrown onto my desk. I slowly looked up at Francine who had come into my office unannounced.

"What's going on with Asha?"

"Her wife is still sick."

"She told me everything was fine."

"I think she's a little worried your kindness will run out."

"I see." I pressed a button on my desk phone, calling to connect with Asha.

"Hi, Mr. Murray," she said. "Do you need me to set up a meeting with someone?"

"I need you to come to my office." At Francine's raised eyebrow, I added, "Please."

Asha's workspace wasn't far from mine. Her job was mainly fielding calls, sorting my mail, and helping to organize my busy schedule. When Dad was here, she was a glorified errand runner.

I hid the card under my desk as she came in.

"Yes, sir?"

"I just wanted to let you know that I'm extending the senior manager employee sick policy to you."

"What policy is that?" she asked.

"The one that ensures you get paid if you need to take family leave."

"Oh, I have that, sir. But it only pays 60% and I can't—"

"I'm talking about a different policy—one for upper management. I'll extend it to you. This policy pays your full salary, Asha. If you need time off, you should take it."

Her jaw fell. "B-but I'm needed here."

"I'll have Julia at the front desk help."

"And I can too," Francine added. "Believe it or not, I don't mind working with this guy. If he can help you out, then I'll be sure to cover whatever Julia can't."

Asha looked between Francine and me. "Really? But I thought you hated him." Then her eyes shifted to me. "N-no offense."

"None taken."

"He's grown on me." Francine shrugged.

"I don't want you missing time with those who are important to you for this job. Nothing is worth that."

"Oh my God, thank you!" Tears spilled from her eyes. "I can't tell you how much this means to me. I'll finish up the day and put it in with HR—"

"I'll take care of that. Go."

She nodded, running out of my office.

Francine turned to me with a smile. "That was sweet."

I brought out the card and signed it. "She deserves it."

"She does. I'm glad you see it." Francine grabbed the card once I was done.

"Now I just need to get a few more people to donate to her meal train and then she'll be set for a week."

"What's a meal train?"

"It's a way to pay for the family's meals while someone is sick. I wanted to give her at least a week not to worry about cooking. We're three meals away."

"Where is it?"

"It's just online. Would you be willing to donate?"

"Yes, but I'm not stopping at a week. I was thinking a month."

Francine let out a laugh. "You weren't done. I told her to talk to you about it. I knew you'd help."

"I don't blame her for not believing you."

"That'll be the last time anyone thinks that. Now, if I'm helping you while Asha's gone, can I move my desk to one of these fancy-ass offices?"

I couldn't help but laugh at how much she sounded like Ruth.

"Sure. Take the office in the corner."

"With the view? You sure know how to spoil a woman."

"I try. Enjoy it."

She walked out of my office with a smile. A few minutes later, I noticed I was added on to the email chain that was wishing Asha and her wife well.

I spent the morning dividing up Asha's workload between Francine, Julia, and myself. No one knocked on my door until it was nearly lunch.

"Come in!" I called, and the last person I expected walked into my office. "Selena?"

"I sent her in!" Francine called from down the hall. "Julia was arguing with her again about being here. She kept saying you were too busy for her."

The shock wore off at Francine's words. "Thank you. Tell Julia I'm *never* too busy for Selena Martinez."

Francine smiled. "I'll make it clear."

Selena looked harried with her wide eyes and fast breathing. My heart stumbled in my chest as I watched her come into my office and shut my door.

"I need help."

"Name it."

"Are you free tonight? I need you to come to my house."

"For what? Is Max okay?"

"Max is fine. This is for me, mainly. I think my ex is stalking me. Or trying to stalk me."

My entire body tensed. "Excuse me?"

I'd never use this hard voice with her or Max. But I couldn't help that I didn't like what I heard.

Selena's eyes went wider at my tone. "It's not a huge deal. And maybe I'm being dramatic, but he said he was coming over to my house to *show* me I had made a mistake by leaving him, and it felt threatening. But if you're busy, I'll—"

I didn't miss a beat. "I'll be there."

"Oh," she said. "I feel like I should say thank you, but I also think you're mad."

"Not at you," I explained. "I just don't like the idea of anyone *showing* you anything without your consent. Is this the first time he's done this?"

"N-no," she said. "The night you met Max, he said he was coming over. I figured I could let Max meet you, and my ex wouldn't know where I was."

"He did it *then* too?"

"I don't know if he followed through. Whether or not he did, at least it pushed me to let Max meet you, which went well, so there was some good to it."

"We shouldn't be seeing any of this as good. He's pushing you in ways he shouldn't be."

"I know. And I don't know how to do confrontation. I keep telling him no, but then he blows past all of my words and...I don't know what to do. I just run."

She looked at her feet, as if there was something to be ashamed of.

"Selena, it's okay if you're not good at confrontation. You shouldn't have to be. A no is a no."

"He's always been like this. At first, I thought it was good that I was getting out of my shell, but then...he and Max started to not get along. I broke it off then. I'm sorry to ask. I feel like I should be able to handle all of this alone."

"Why?"

"Because *he* says I can't. He says I'll always need him. And if it's not him, then it's someone else." She let out an uneasy sigh. "I hate needing people. I hate inconveniencing them because I'm too weak to do it on my own."

"I don't think doing everything on your own is as fun as it sounds," I said slowly.

"But the *shame* is what's awful."

"Shame *he* put on you?"

"Maybe, but I always wanted to be independent. I had this idea of what my life would be like—a safe idea—and all of that blew up when I had Max. I'm not good at being an adult. I can't seem to raise Max the way he deserves *and* work forty hours a week. I don't know why."

"I'd rather you be a good mother than focus on work. Trust me, work isn't worth it. And neither was the business degree or the safe job."

"You remembered that?"

"I do, and I'm sure you would have done great in whatever you did. Just like you did with Max. You can't help that the world is expensive, or that it punishes women for just being women. My sister is an incredible person. Probably the smartest one I know. But she was held back by people who didn't think she could be incredible because of who she was." People like our own father. I blew out a long breath. "*You* are an incredible person too. I see your kindness and patience in Max, and to me, that's far more valuable than having money."

"T-thank you, but unfortunately, I can't give Max everything he needs without having a decent income. And my art barely pays enough. What I should have done when I kicked Jax out was get a real job. Not use my art as a career."

"But it *is* a career."

"One that doesn't pay very much. I can't exactly be a good mom if I can't keep a roof over our heads. But I *hated* working. I couldn't juggle both Max and that." She rubbed her forehead. "Everyone else seems like they can."

"It might *look* like they can, but those who try to do it all have something fall through the cracks. Just look at me."

"But I'm *so* broke."

"You're forgetting one thing. I'm here now. I can solve at least part of the problem. You've raised my *child*. I'm sure you could make it on your own, even if you worked a job you hated. But I couldn't bear seeing you *not* do your art, which you're amazing at, and then feel overwhelmed with trying to do it all when I'm *right* here. So if I can share anything with you so that you're happy, then name it."

Her eyes were wide but wet. I had no idea if my words had helped or hurt, but they were the truth, at least. "I-I think I want you to come over tonight."

"Is there anything else?"

"M-maybe I'll get better about accepting help. I don't know about child support but maybe...food. We'll start there."

"Okay," I said. "I would love to help you with those things."

"T-thank you," she eventually said. "For being here."

"I won't mess up my second chance."

She slowly nodded as she rubbed her temples. "Okay, now to deal with this headache."

"Have you eaten? Had water?"

"Yes and yes. I know what it's from. I haven't slept in two days."

"What? What's been going on to make you not sleep for that long?"

"Nothing. I just struggle with sleep. Sometimes worse than usual. I'll be fine."

"Go home and get some rest. What time does Max need to be picked up from school?"

"Three forty-five," she said. "I can catch a few hours and then get him."

"No need. I'll get him," I offered.

"A-are you sure? I'll need to add you to the list of who can pick him up."

"Are you okay with that?"

She bit her lip as she thought about it. "Yeah, I think so. I'll call on the way home."

"Okay, you rest and I'll take it from here."

She nodded, giving me a smile that stopped my world.

"Thank you," she said. "Again. You doing this helps so much."

I felt my own lips turn upward to mirror hers. "It's no problem, honestly."

"Wow." She sounded a little breathless. "Those have only gotten better with age."

"What has?"

"Your dimples."

My hand reached up to touch my cheek. I remembered my grandparents mentioning them when I was a kid, but I had forgotten I'd ever had them.

"And I made it awkward," she said, shaking her head. "Sorry. I'll head out. But *you*—you should keep smiling. The world needs more of that."

She bumped one of the chairs as she made her escape and then darted out the door. I could only stare at the area she'd left with a strange, warm feeling in my chest.

Chapter Ten

Selena

I should have been more concerned about Jax's possible appearance that night. But after calling the school and adding Tom to the approved pickup list, my thoughts were on one thing.

Tom's smile.

I'd seen it when we were in college and it had drawn me in then.

He hadn't smiled since seeing me again. He'd kind of half smiled when looking at Max, but nothing prepared me for the brightness of that full grin. And the dimples. *God*, the dimples.

I was in trouble.

I could see that grin every day and it still wouldn't be enough. And what was I supposed to do about that? I should hate him, but every moment was turning into a scene of a book that I wanted to be my life.

Especially after today.

My head pounded angrily, reminding me that I was in no place to figure out my feelings for Tom.

I needed a nap—that much was for sure. But how could I force my mind to shut up and let me sleep?

I lay down the moment I got home and hoped I could drift off. Meowcifer even cuddled up alongside me, which sometimes helped me sleep, but it didn't work now. I tried to walk off my energy, drink calming tea, and count sheep for hours.

No luck.

By three, I was annoyed and so was the cat. She'd started glaring at me every time I moved.

Just sleep, she seemed to be saying.

I could feel the exhaustion. No matter how many times I closed my eyes, drifting off evaded me.

I decided that maybe it was the clutter of my space that was making me unable to sleep. I went through some of the things on the floor and put them where they belonged. By the time I'd cleared out one corner, my exhaustion was back.

But my eyes caught on the box Tom had sent me; the sweater was still inside of it. Ever since I'd tossed it there, I'd find Meowcifer sleeping on it at least once a day. I wasn't even sure I could still fit into the sweater and considered donating it, but she seemed to love it, so I never moved it.

Maybe trying it on would have the same effect on me. It wasn't my most logical idea—that something my cat slept on would make *me* sleep—but I was desperate enough to try anything.

But as I pulled it on, I didn't notice the fit. I noticed how it smelled.

One sniff and I was back in that dorm with Tom on top of me. The sweatshirt smelled the same: earthy and woodsy, even now.

My heart skipped a beat. It was one of the best smells I'd ever breathed in, and now it did more than make me horny.

It made me feel safe.

I chewed on my lip as I walked to the bedroom. I'd always been sensitive to smells, and ones that I loved, I tended to be obsessed with. This was one of them.

I climbed into bed, pulling my soft blanket over me. If I nestled down, I could be enveloped in Tom's scent.

And I drifted off in minutes.

Tom

My truck rumbled into the parking lot of Max's middle school. People's heads turned, but I kept staring straight ahead, unwilling to make myself any more nervous by meeting any of the other parents' questioning gazes.

I saw Max loitering in front of the door and I got out of the truck to wave at him. For a second, his jaw dropped, then he ran over to me.

"Mr. Tom?" he yelled. "You're picking me up!"

"Hang on a second!" another voice boomed. A figure stepped in between Max and me. He was a shorter man who wore a green polo tucked into gym shorts. He had to be the gym teacher. Either that or Max's school had an extremely lax dress code. He eyed me up and down. "Now I can't let a student leave with a random stranger."

"Jax," Max moaned. "He's not a stranger. He's Mom's friend."

"You still have to have approval to leave with him."

"I do," I said. "Selena put me on the list this morning."

"Oh, she did, did she?" Jax scoffed. "Mrs. Rodney! I need you for a second!"

Another teacher walked over. "What, Mr. Carter?"

"Who is on Max Martinez's approval list for pickup?"

She checked her list. "Selena Martinez and...Tom Murray. She called and added him this morning."

"Yes!" Max said.

"Are you Mr. Murray?" she asked me.

I pulled out my ID. "I am. But you can call me Tom."

"Great! I've seen all I need to see. You can go, Max."

"Are we going home in that super cool truck?"

"We are," I replied. "Why don't you go check it out while I finish up here."

Max rushed off, not sparing the man next to me another glance.

Mrs. Rodney was already gone, helping another parent in line to pick up their child, by the time I turned.

"Who are you?" Jax asked.

"I believe you just heard my name," I said.

"The thing is, I know every one of Sel's *friends*. And you're not one of them."

"*Selena* and I met in college."

"I call bullshit, bud. Who are you and what do you want with *my* girl?"

"Your girl?" I asked, but then it dawned on me. "You're her ex, aren't you?"

"Ex is a temporary term. I've spent the last four years with her and I plan on getting her back."

"Funny. I haven't heard much about you. Other than the fact that you don't understand the word no."

"You know what's really funny? Why she would trust some *stranger* to pick up Max. She didn't let me meet him for a year."

"She probably had a good reason, considering Max didn't even like you."

"Max didn't like having a man in his life telling him what he needed to hear."

"Man in his life? You?"

"I was the only person who was like a father to him."

My fists clenched. "You were *not*," I said. "And you're definitely not now. From what I've heard, you did a bad job."

"Did I? I tried to warn him that his little obsession with the pop star was going to be weird. And that he needed to man up so girls would start paying attention to him. I said what no one else would."

"Because no one *should* say those things. He's a child."

"If Sel keeps babying him, then he'll turn out as one of those little f—"

"Don't you fucking finish that sentence." That was it. I'd reached my breaking point. Too many of Max's actions now made sense. How he seemed embarrassed about liking Lila Wilde, how he seemed genuinely excited when I didn't judge him for his interests.

I was looking at a lesser version of my own father. Jax could have put Max through what happened to me growing up and I wouldn't stand for that.

"You are going to leave Max and Selena *alone*. You are going to go back to your job as a mediocre gym teacher and never think of them again."

"And who are you to tell me what to do? You might look a little like the kid, but you're not his dad." He laughed, but then it died down as he looked at my features a little closer. "Wait, are you?"

"Huh. I'm surprised. You *do* have two brain cells to rub together."

"You're his dad? The rich guy who left?"

"The rich guy who came back and the one who will have you arrested if you don't leave Selena Martinez *alone*."

"Arrested for what?"

"Forcing your way into her life? Saying you're coming to her house after she says no? That's stalking."

"S-she's lying."

"No. I saw the fear on her face when she came to *me* for help. I know your type, Jax. And I will ruin you. You've already overstepped by making Selena upset, but now that I know you said those things about my *son*, I will gladly rip your life apart."

"So you just threaten people? Is that what you do?"

"That is *exactly* what I do to people who hurt the ones I love. So back off, *bud*. Before you mess with someone who can outsmart you in his sleep."

There was the look I was used to seeing: the pale cheeks, the wide eyes, the shaky lip. But this time, I didn't feel bad. I *hoped* he was scared.

"You're a monster," he said. "You're going to ruin Max."

"I might be a monster, but I am still *better than you*. So stay away. Because if you set foot on Selena's property, you will be in the back of a police car before you can blink."

A cold feeling of satisfaction slithered its way into my chest as I saw him scurry off. I took a deep breath, determined not to let Max see how angry I truly was. It took me a moment to get back to the truck. Max was watching me curiously.

"Is everything okay?"

"Everything is fine," I reassured. "Let's get you home."

"Okay. Where's Mom?"

"Getting some rest. She's had a long week."

Max gave me a small smile before his eyes roamed the cabin of the old truck. "This thing is pretty cool," he said.

"I got it when I was eighteen."

"Was it new then?"

I opened my mouth to ask him just how old he thought I was, but he gave me a wily grin.

"You're hilarious," I said. "No. It was already old when I got it."

He nodded, looking at the dash. "This looks so sleek. Why don't more people have older cars like this?"

"They're a lot of work, and they have no airbags."

"Oh, so if we get in a wreck then we probably die."

"P-probably." I barely managed to say it over the horror clutching at my chest. In the back of my mind, the offer from Knox to add safety equipment to the truck played back. At the time, I didn't want anyone else even touching this thing. However, now that I had my child sitting next to me, I was severely regretting not taking him up on it.

"Why did you get an older car?"

"I like working on them," I managed to say.

"Do you still like working on them?"

"Sometimes. It's been running smooth lately so I haven't needed to."

"Could you teach me?" he asked.

"Sure. Next oil change, I'll call you. But only if you want to."

"I...mean, it's a manly hobby."

"Max—"

"Did Jax tell you what he said?" he asked. "About me, I mean?"

"He told me a bit of it. But he's wrong."

"I mean, not really. Some of the kids *do* say I'm girly."

"Then they're wrong too. Fitting in at the cost of something you love is a one-way ticket to misery."

"So you don't think I'm weird for liking Lila Wilde so much?"

"No. I'm glad you have an interest that excites you."

"Thank you."

"You don't have to thank me for doing the bare minimum."

"Maybe to some it's the bare minimum, but it still means a lot. You really don't have to be so nice to me. I'm just the kid who's around. You're here for Mom."

"Not right now. I came to get *you* from school."

"I mean in general."

"No, I'm serious. You're a good kid. I like spending time with you."

"Really?"

"Yes. Really."

"I don't bother you when I call to ask math questions?"

"No, never."

"Or when I'm at dinner with you and Mom?"

"Not then, either."

"Wow, that's really cool." He smiled at me. "I didn't think I'd ever meet an adult like you."

I glanced over at him, returning his grin. "And I didn't think I'd meet a kid like you."

"So, about the truck...What if I really did want to work on it with you?"

"Then we would do it."

"Maybe we can work on Mom's car too. It makes some weird sounds."

"If she's okay with it, then we'll do that too."

"Yes! I'd love to help her out. I know she's stressed with how hard being an adult is."

"I feel the same way about helping her out."

"How late are you staying?"

"As long as I'm allowed to, why?"

"I know one thing that would help Mom."

"And what's that?"

"How do you feel about cleaning?"

Chapter Eleven

It was dark when I woke up. I could hear the sounds of an upbeat Lila Wilde song playing, which meant Tom got Max home in one piece.

I slowly sat up, rubbing the sleep from my eyes. I felt more like a human than I had in weeks. After giving myself a few minutes in the dark, I knew I needed to figure out what to cook for dinner; I was hoping we still had leftovers I could easily reheat for us.

And hope that Jax didn't show up.

When I opened the door, I expected Max to either be in his room or hanging out with Tom doing his homework. The last thing I expected to see was him mopping the floor.

"Max?" I asked.

"Mom!" he said. "We're cleaning."

"We?" I glanced in the living room where I saw Tom wiping off the dirty table. Meowcifer was next to him, looking up at him as if trying to use mind control to convince him to pet her. And like magic, I saw him rub her head the moment he was done with the task.

I couldn't look any longer. It was too cute.

I glanced over my living room. Gone were the piles of boxes I didn't know what to do with. Everything had been dusted and the house smelled…fresh.

"Oh my God," I said. "You both cleaned *everything*."

"Surprise!" Max said.

Tears welled up in my eyes. While Max didn't enjoy cleaning, he did enjoy helping, but I'd never sat him down and taught him how to do it right. I should have, considering I was the one who knew how to do it.

"I hope everything looks okay," Tom said. "I showed Max how to mop and—" He turned, freezing when he saw me, eyes going wide.

"What?" I asked. "Is there something on my face?"

"No, it's just…" He swallowed. "You're wearing the sweatshirt from college."

My face exploded in heat. I should have changed before coming out of my room.

"It still fits," I said, laughing awkwardly. "It, um, smelled nice."

It smelled like you, I almost said.

"It looks great."

"Aw," Max cooed. "This is too cute. But it also makes me want to barf."

I was grateful for Max's intrusion. I turned to him, ignoring the way my heart skipped a beat whenever I talked to Tom.

"Thank you for cleaning. Both of you. It looks so amazing."

"It was no problem," Tom said. "We needed something to do anyway."

"Did we have any…unexpected guests?" I asked.

"No. But we'll talk about that later."

"Have you seen Mr. Tom's cool truck?" Max asked. "I got to ride home in it today!"

"Only from a distance."

"He said he is going to show me how to work on it."

"You…want to work on cars?"

"They seem cool."

"Is this because of what Jax said to you?"

"No. I've worked through what Jax said. I want to learn because Mr. Tom likes it and I want to see if I like it."

"Oh," I said, blinking. "Okay, then you should give it a shot."

"I'll be sure he's safe," Tom said. "And you." He put down his rag and washed his hands before walking over to me.

"What do you mean?"

"I ordered a security system for your house. I'll have someone come install it. I don't trust him not to make an appearance."

"You ordered me one? But those things are—"

"No amount of money is too high for yours and Max's safety."

Heat rushed to my cheeks once again. If I didn't know any better, I would say he was *trying* to seduce me.

Let him! my romantic side screamed.

"Then thank you for that too," I managed to say. I didn't know what to do in the wake of all that he'd done for me since coming back into my life. He'd surpassed every expectation. I was supposed to still be angry, but I couldn't find it in me.

I could only hope he stayed. I could only hope that we were more important than his drinking and that he'd never be in the same place he was when he told me he needed to tend to his future.

"Whew." Max's voice pulled me out of my thoughts. "After all that cleaning, I'm super hungry and we don't have any leftovers. Can we order some food?"

I knew I should cook. After all, I had a clean kitchen to use. But I didn't have *anything*, and it was already late enough in the evening. The moment I thought about it, my exhaustion returned.

"How about pizza?" Tom offered.

"Yes! I love pizza."

"I don't know if what you get is considered pizza," I said.

"Come on. Pineapple on pizza is the best way to eat it!"

"I haven't tried it," Tom said. "I never would have thought to order that kind of pizza before."

"You should definitely try it," Max replied.

"You shouldn't," I added in.

"Please?" Max's face morphed and he looked eerily similar to a puppy begging for food.

Tom smiled back, showing off those dimples again. "I'll give it a shot."

"Does this face work on you? It never works on Mom."

"I'm just used to it," I replied. "Tom will get used to it too."

"I don't know," he said. "You look exactly like your mom when you do that. And I have a hard time resisting her."

I really needed Tom to stop being one of the most romantic people on the planet. I didn't think I would survive if he didn't.

"So cute," Max replied. "But still gross. Now I understand how Tess feels when his parents kiss."

Tom glanced over at me, his eyes wide for a second. Max had alluded to his best friend's *parents*.

And that was all too accurate.

"Let's order the pizza," I said, clapping my hands. "The sooner we do, the sooner we eat."

After it arrived, we all sat at the newly cleaned-off table. I silently marveled at how much better I felt when the area was organized.

"So, how did today go?" I asked Max.

"It went great. You should have seen Jax's face when Mr. Tom picked me up."

"Was he mad?"

"So mad. Then he ran off like a baby."

"Really?"

Tom's lips pursed. I blinked, trying to decipher if he was just tired or if he was trying to tell me something.

But if I stared for too long, Max would notice.

"Do you need help with your homework?"

"No, Mr. Tom helped me with it when we took a break. Everything else is easy."

Wow. He was really doing it all.

"Thank you," I said. "So much. I owe you one."

His eyes held mine. "It's the least I could do."

Technically, the least would be to stay away, but I couldn't say that in front of Max.

"Okay," Max said, pulling us out of our mini staring contest. "Pineapple on pizza time. You will officially be the coolest person ever if you like it." He handed Tom a slice.

"I'll do my best."

"But no lying! I want to know the truth."

"No lying. Promise."

"Swear on the pinky." Max held out his hand, pinky up.

"I solemnly swear on the pinky that I won't lie."

Max smiled, satisfied. "Good. Now you can try it."

Tom picked it up and took a bite. His eyebrows knitted, as if he was confused about it. "How does that work together?"

"You like it?"

"Kind of, yeah."

"You're not human," I said, but even I couldn't resist a smile at Max's excitement.

"It's sweet and savory. What's not to like?"

"Everything, actually," I retorted.

"He's just like me, that's all."

More than you know. The reminder made my heart skip a beat once more, and if this didn't stop, I might need to see a cardiologist.

But I doubted it would. If Tom continued down this path of being literally perfect, then I needed to figure out how to tell Max the truth, which was terrifying.

The idea bounced around in my head until we finished dinner. Max went up to his room, eager to have some alone time after cleaning and doing homework all night. Once he was gone, Tom started picking up.

"I need to tell you something," he said.

"About Max?" Was he ready to tell him? I didn't know if *I* was, but I knew it would need to be sooner than later.

"About Jax, really."

All thoughts of telling Max crumbled. "Jax? What happened with Jax?"

"He figured out who I was."

"What? How?"

"I made it easy for him. He stumbled onto it by accident, and then I confirmed."

"Did Max overhear it?"

"No, he was in the truck."

"Oh, God. Jax won't keep the secret. He'll tell Max the minute he can."

"We should get Max removed from his class, then."

"I-I tried before this school year started. They seemed reluctant unless there was hard evidence that Max was struggling."

"Isn't him forcing his way into your life enough?"

"In theory, yes. But it's a school requirement to take gym in his grade. They don't want him to fall behind."

"And Jax is the only option?"

"At that school? Yes. But we've gotten good at avoiding him otherwise."

"But he still finds a way. He jumped in the moment he saw Max walking toward me. This is something we need to face head-on."

"We?"

"He's my child too. And I know I haven't been here, but I still want a say when it comes to his safety."

"I agree I just...I don't know *how* to do this. I don't know how to stand my ground."

"Then let me do it. I am perfectly confident in being able to convince them to take him out of that class."

"Are you sure?"

"I am very sure."

"Okay, then. Do whatever you think will get him out of that class," I said. "Then we'll go from there."

"I'll swing by in the morning to talk to someone."

I watched as he took one more burden off my plate and I could picture a future where we worked as a team for Max, where I was no longer alone.

His phone rang and I saw him glance at the caller ID.

Asha, it read.

It was the reminder that I needed. Tom had a whole life, one that he didn't share with Max or me. He'd always been a playboy, never wanting to settle down.

"Hang on, Selena," he said. "Let me answer this."

I nodded as he walked outside as he hit accept.

"Hey," he began, his voice soft. "I'm glad I could help. I'd do it any—" The door shut.

I stared after him. How did I forget how he was in college? He had a reputation of being with a different woman every night. It should have been fine. He was single and we'd never once discussed the possibility of ever being more.

But it was a stark reminder that I still didn't know what he got up to when he wasn't here. I knew I wasn't owed that, but it felt like a fresh bruise had been poked. He was seemingly perfect around Max and me, but how did I know he wasn't still partying, breaking women's hearts, and involved in things I refused to expose Max to?

I'd never recovered from thinking Tom was my romance hero and then being sent that letter. That dreamer never truly went away, but I fought that side of me harder than ever before.

And this was why.

Dreams of romance were great until reality came crashing in.

Tom and I were co-parents. Those incredibly sweet things he said to me were things other women heard in different ways when he would take them home.

What a good co-parent would have done was tell him we needed to discuss our plan to tell Max. And I needed to. This was going to blow up in my face if I didn't.

But I didn't think I could even look at him. My hurt, caused once again by my own overactive imagination, made me want to run. Just like I always did.

I'd give myself twenty-four hours. When he came back in, I'd distract myself by opening some mail so I wouldn't have to look him in the eye, and then, by tomorrow, I'd know my place.

Tom

I walked back into Selena's house, still shaken by Asha's tearful thank you about my generosity. I didn't expect it to be acknowledged since I hadn't even told anyone other than Francine what my plan was. I felt closer to my team than I ever had before.

Selena was shuffling through mail when I entered the living room.

"You should head out," she said. "I'm sure you have other things you need to do."

It was a clear dismissal, and I knew not to overstay my welcome. "Let me just go say goodbye to Max."

I knocked on his door and waited for him to answer before I poked my head in. "I'm leaving for the night."

"Okay, thanks for hanging out. And for telling off Jax."

"I'm going to try and be sure he doesn't bother you anymore, okay?"

"That would be so cool," he said. "Thank you."

I gave him one last half smile before I shut the door. Helping both him and Selena had become one of the main things on my mind.

But I didn't know how.

As I walked back to the living room, she was frowning at a letter. On the top of the page, I saw a student loan servicer's name.

"Is everything okay?"

"Yep," she said, still not looking at me. "Everything is fine. Will you let me know how the school thing goes?"

"I will. See you later."

I turned to the door, finding Meowcifer gazing at me again. She'd followed me all night, though I wasn't sure why.

"I'll come back soon," I said to the cat. "It was nice hanging out with you."

When I reached to pet her, she leaned into the touch. I could feel Selena's eyes on me.

As I got into my truck, my mind replayed the expression she'd had when I saw her looking at the papers in her hand. It had to be a bill. Vanderbilt was an expensive school, and if she took out loans, they would be something she would be paying back for a long time.

Student loans could seem like a good deal, but their long repayment windows really hurt people over time.

And it was my fault she'd dropped out.

A plan half formed in my mind, one where I could help out Selena but still give her the independence she wanted.

It might blow up in my face, but I couldn't sit and do nothing.

"You're late," Francine said, following me to my office. "Have you ever been late?"

"Not really."

"Is everything okay with your son?" Francine asked. "Not that I'm supposed to know about that."

"You figured it out?"

"I read the clues, but I can pretend I don't know, if that makes you feel any better."

I felt the built-up tension in my shoulders, and for once, I wondered if talking about it *would* make me feel any better.

"It's fine that you know. And everything is mostly okay. But I had to stop at his school and remove him from a class with a teacher who was being inappropriate."

"Really? And how'd that go?"

"When they heard about how he was stalking Selena, they promised to investigate the situation and remove Max ASAP."

"Stalking? What kind of teacher is he?"

"Gym."

She made a face. "Gym teachers are either great at what they do and love kids, or get into that job because it's all they can do. There's no in-between."

"He is definitely the latter."

"Oh! Before you go into your office, I have to give you a warning."

"What kind of warning?"

"You have a surprise."

Frowning, I walked in, only to see a six count of donuts and a thank-you card on my desk. "What is this for?"

"Did you forget you paid off Asha's meal train and gave her full salary to go take care of her wife?"

"I didn't, but she called to say thank you last night. That's more than enough."

"You are so stubborn. You did a good thing. Now enjoy it. Or not. We didn't actually know if you liked donuts."

"I've never really had one."

"What? How could you not have—"

"My father only liked classy foods."

"Oh." She rolled her eyes. "Try one. They're from the best bakery in town."

I opened it up and picked a chocolate one. I offered the box to Francine. "You should have one too. Six is far too many for me."

"He even *shares*."

"Don't tell my siblings." I watched as she grabbed one. "Besides, I do need to ask something of you."

"Yes?"

"Do you know how I can pay off someone's debts anonymously?"

"I can find a way. Why?"

"Let's just say I may have found a way to help Selena with her bills without going through court for child support. She doesn't want that kind of help."

"And so your thought was to simply pay off her bills?"

"It's technically not child support."

She slowly nodded. "You're not the kind of man who half-asses anything."

"No," I replied. "I'm not."

"I like it. I'll help you find your woman's debts."

"Throw a couple of other people in there too. Maybe it's time I shared some of my wealth."

Chapter Twelve

Tom: Max is out of gym. He will retake it next year when they hire a new teacher.

The problem with remembering that your one-night stand was a very helpful guy was that it made it even harder to move past my developing crush when he, once again, saved me from something I apparently couldn't do on my own.

Needless to say, I wasn't feeling very good. Add that to me forgetting to make my student loan payment, and I was feeling like a useless adult.

"I don't think doing everything on your own is as fun as it sounds."

Tom's words played through my head. They helped, but the thought of him, of the things I didn't know about him, still hurt, and did nothing to help my mood.

Then Max came out of school looking sullen and my heart stopped.

"Is everything okay?" I asked. "Did they not take you out of Jax's class?"

"No, they did," he said. "It's an extra study period now. I tried to do my math homework and surprise, I don't understand it. Why does this always happen? I listen in class!"

"Oh, kiddo, I'm sorry."

"For once, I just want to understand it without it having to be explained to me a hundred times," he muttered.

"I'm sorry. Maybe we can move you out of honors math and into regular math."

He gave me a frown that shouted, *That was the worst thing you could have said.*

I looked back at the road, feeling entirely unhelpful.

"Can I borrow your phone?" he asked when we got home.

He usually borrowed it when he needed to relax by playing a game, but lately, he'd been doing more of it.

"Yeah, of course."

He disappeared into his room and I busied myself with the finishing touches of Luna's portrait.

It was not going well, which only made me feel worse. Luna looked great, but I still didn't understand how I could make Willie look like a silver fox unless I completely drew a different man.

Max came into the living room an hour later and flopped on the couch next to me.

"I'm hopeless," he said. "Take me out of honors math. I'm too stupid for it."

"Were you up there still trying to figure it out? I thought you were on the phone with a friend."

"I wasn't. I called Mr. Tom to see if he could explain it to me."

"You called Tom?" I asked. "Max, it's barely five. He had to be at work."

"He was, and he tried to explain it to me the best he could, but I still couldn't get it. I told him I was sorry for bugging him and that he should go back to work."

I was surprised he even answered. He was a CEO. He had to be incredibly busy.

"I'll try to help you."

"No, Mr. Tom is the *only* one who can explain it so I get it. But if he can't, then I don't even want to try to go back to YouTube videos. I'd rather be in a class where I don't feel like an idiot. I bet he's thinking about how dumb I am right now."

"We could try a tutor."

"Those are expensive," he muttered. "It's fine. Maybe math isn't for me."

I rubbed his back, wondering if pulling him was actually the right move. He wanted to succeed so bad and I wished I was in the position to help him.

"Why don't I make your favorite recipe for dinner," I said, "and then we'll go from there."

"I don't think anything will make me feel better."

"Can we try?"

He thought about it for a long time. "Fine."

I got up to start dinner. It had been a while since I last cooked, seeing as how Mom's leftovers kept us fed for a long time, and I missed it. Sure, my kitchen wouldn't be clean for a week after this, but if I could make something Max loved, then it was all worth it.

By six, I was putting the finishing touches on dinner when I heard a knock at the door. I rinsed off my hands and walked over.

When I opened the door, my jaw dropped.

"T-Tom?"

From his spot on the couch, Max finally looked up.

"Hey," he said, leaning against the doorframe. "Can I talk to Max for a minute?"

"Mr. Tom," Max said, rolling off the couch. "I'm so sorry that I called you today. I know you're busy but I was just so frustrated that I didn't get it."

"It's okay, Max." His voice was soft. "I wanted to say that I'm sorry I didn't have the time earlier to devote to your learning. Can we try again?"

"Tonight?"

"If you have the time."

Max looked at me, his eyes wide.

"Um, we should eat first," I said. "I cooked tonight."

"I can come back later," he replied, already taking a step back.

"Can he stay for dinner? Please? Mr. Tom hasn't had your cooking and it's *so* good."

I was supposed to give him distance. He had a whole life of his own.

But I couldn't say no to Max's hopeful face, *and* Tom had driven all the way over here.

"Sure," I said. "I made plenty, but only if Tom doesn't have any plans."

He shook his head. "My evenings are always free."

Always? What did he mean by that?

Tom Murray had a history of never having a free evening.

"It smells great."

"It's carne guisada," Max said. "Mom picked up the recipe from abuela but made it her own."

"This is one of my favorites for sure," I said. "But I make better waffles. Too bad it's not breakfast time."

"The secret is heavy cream," Max added.

"Don't give away all of my secrets!" I said, ruffling his hair.

"What? I trust him. He won't tell."

"I won't," he confirmed.

We sat at the table and it felt nice to serve my cooking again. Max, as usual, had his attention on Tom. "You've gotta tell me what you think," he said.

Tom took a bite, considering it.

There was a terrifying moment where I wondered if he would say he hated it. He did promise Max he would be truthful only the night before.

"It's delicious. Spicier than I'm used to."

"Let me get you some water," I offered. It was almost relieving to step into the kitchen. I felt like a schoolgirl inside, squealing because my crush liked my food.

It was embarrassing.

I took a shaky breath and sat back down, determined to be normal for this dinner. I needed to remember *reality*. Not my daydreams.

But I couldn't help replay what he had said earlier: he was free every night. I could have turned that over in my head for hours, but I was pulled out of my thoughts when Max said, "Don't you, Mom?"

"Don't I what?" I asked, forcing myself back into the present moment.

"Don't you think Lila Wilde and Blaze Matthews are secretly having problems?"

"Oh, yes. She hints at it in her music, but we'll never know for sure. I'm sure they'll stay together. I mean, they have been together for years."

"I just keep hoping," Max said, sighing. "She looks sad. I can't read many people, but I can read her."

"Maybe it's the fame," Tom replied. "I have a friend who is well-known, and he's never happy with cameras following him around."

"I couldn't imagine it," Max said.

A ghost of a smile crossed Tom's face.

"What?" I asked.

"My sister. She can imagine it. She's in a relationship with the friend of mine."

"Your sister is with someone famous?" Max asked, eyes wide.

"Yes," he replied. "They were seen together and immediately everyone knew he had feelings for her. It was written all over his face."

"What's her name?" I asked, eager to know more.

"Ruth. She's named after Ruth Bader Ginsberg."

"Ooh, I can't remember who that is," Max said.

"She was a judge on the US Supreme Court," I replied. "Very ahead of her time in a lot of ways."

"And Ruth is too. She probably got the best name out of all of us."

"Who were you named after?"

"A businessman of some kind. I don't even know who it was. It was all a part of my dad's hopes that we would work for him."

"Aw, come on, couldn't you be named after something cool? Like me? My name means 'greatest.'"

"That's an accurate name."

"And Mom's means 'the moon,' which is accurate, since she's up all night."

"I sleep *sometimes*," I said, rolling my eyes. "When you were a baby, you never slept either. So maybe I got it from you."

"Like the gray hairs."

"Tread carefully. I know your ticklish spots."

"Well!" Max said loudly, standing from his chair. "On that note, it's time to do some homework."

"You must hate being tickled if you're willing to do homework."

"I love homework, and despite what Mom says, I'm not ticklish."

I shook my head. "Okay, I'll let you believe that. Good luck on your homework tonight." I got up to clean some of the dishes I'd dirtied, but then I got distracted by an idea for the portrait.

What if I took inspiration from the beautiful man sitting in my dining room? He could look good with gray hair.

I went to the couch, finally feeling like I had a breakthrough with my work. I grabbed my tablet and got to drawing.

"Good job, Max," Tom said about an hour later from across the room. He had that soft voice again.

My heart squeezed and I kept my eyes firmly on my tablet. Did he have to be so sweet to Max? And to me? Some meanness would help me not equate him with a romance novel hero.

Max's homework went quickly after that. Once he understood the concept, he picked up the rest of it with ease. He seemed so happy to have someone who could help him.

"So, if you're free on weeknights, are you also free on the weekends?" Max asked.

"I can be, why?"

"My birthday is this weekend."

"It is?" Tom asked, glancing over at me.

I blinked and looked at the calendar on the wall. "Yep, he's right. It's his birthday."

"We usually have a party," Max said. "But I don't know if we are this year."

"We're having it. I'm making it work."

"Really?"

"Of course. And Tom can come, if he's free."

"Yes!" Max cheered. "You can meet my friends, and maybe this year I'll get a phone—"

"I think you're too young," I said.

"Aw, but Mom, all my friends have them."

And he was right. These days, kids had smart devices younger and younger. But despite all of that, I knew I couldn't afford the increase in my phone bill, and I was genuinely worried it was too soon.

"We'll see what happens," I said.

"But that's your way of saying no. I'm going to be twelve, Mom, that's practically an adult."

"It definitely is not."

"You could even put those safety settings on it. I just want to be able to call my friends."

"How about you give her some time to think about it?" Tom suggested, leaning forward. "It's a big decision. Cell phones are a lot of responsibility."

"Okay, but only if you promise to think about it."

"I promise," I said.

He nodded, appeased for the time being. "Thanks for coming over, Mr. Tom. I feel so much better."

"Don't want to drop down to normal math anymore?" I asked.

"No, I just said that in a moment of desperation," he replied. "As long as I have the best tutor in the world, I'm good."

"I wouldn't call myself the best," Tom added.

"You're definitely the best," Max said. "We should get you a trophy or some-thing."

I could see how the words affected him. His cheeks turned pink and he looked at Max in awe, like he was the stars themselves.

My phone rang and I saw it was one of Max's friends wanting to talk to him.

"Tess wants to chat," I said, handing him my phone. "But be done by nine. You need to go to bed."

"I will! Thanks again, Mr. Tom."

Max tightly hugged Tom, something that was so easy for him to do. I could see that Tom wasn't expecting it, judging by how his eyes widened and how he slowly put his arm around Max.

Unfazed by his own kindness, Max ran up to his room, only pausing to grab my phone. Tom stared off into space.

"Your first hug," I said. "I wish I'd taken a photo."

"I'm not sure that counts since he doesn't know the whole truth yet." Tom spared a glance up the stairs and then turned to me. "So, the phone thing."

"I know he probably should have one, but I can't exactly afford it."

"I'll buy it. I'll add him to my plan. And you, if you want."

"I can't—"

"I get that you don't want to depend on me, but the least I can do is make sure he can contact people. We don't have to tell him who bought it."

"But what if I need to change something on the plan and you're not avail-able?" Or *partying*, I wanted to say.

"You could add him to yours and set up autopay for it all on the card I gave you."

That was tempting.

I was close to saying yes, but a thought crossed my mind. "And what about when you have a night out? And then your kid texts you and you end up talking to him like you did to me in that letter?"

"A night out?"

"Your partying, Tom. I remember how you were. And I know that the drinking influenced what you said to me. Him having full, late-night access to you could lead to him seeing something he shouldn't."

"Oh," Tom said. "You don't know."

"Don't know what?"

"That I'm sober now. Permanently."

It felt like the floor fell out from underneath me. "You're *what*? For how long?"

"Six months now."

"But that was before you saw me again."

"Yes. I was asked to stop, so I did."

"By who?

"My brother and sister. They saw it had gotten out of hand. And they were right."

I thought I knew the kind of man Tom was. I thought I'd always known.

But apparently, I didn't know anything at all.

I nearly fell onto my own couch, trying to come to terms with the realization that he'd not touched alcohol in months. The one thing I was afraid of hadn't been in his life since before I reconnected with him.

"So this whole time you've never..."

"No. Never. And I hope I never do again. If I do, then you can block my number. You can even keep him from me, because I don't want to put him through that—*oof*!"

I pulled his massive body to me and hung on for dear life. "I'm so proud of you."

He went quiet, and in the back of my mind, I knew I was doing too much. We hadn't crossed this boundary, at least not since I'd seen him again, and yet I couldn't help but touch him now that I knew he was so far away from the one thing I feared most.

His arms slowly wrapped around me. "It's not that big of a deal," he said, but his voice sounded choked. "I should have done it a long time ago."

"No," I said, pulling away so I could look him in the eyes. "In college, you drank every night, and if you only stopped months ago, then it was an addiction. Stopping something like that is *hard*. You must have been irritable and tired and...I can't imagine. But you did it alone for *months*. That is an accomplishment."

He stared blankly at me. "How do you know so much about this?"

"My mom admitted my dad was a drunk once my sister started getting really into it. She lectured us on what it could do to people and it sounded scary. My dad never quit, and ultimately, it's why Luna and I have never had a relationship with him."

"And I carried on my dad's legacy of not having good relationships with kids. At least until I got my head out of my own ass about drinking."

"But you stopped drinking before I even asked you to. Don't make it any less than what it is. It's great."

He looked far from the composed man I knew.

"Are you okay?" I asked.

"S-sorry. It's just that...this is the first time I've ever heard someone say they're proud of me. And you said it *twice*."

"What?" I asked. "That's...you're a CEO."

"Acting."

"You're extremely smart."

"That's debatable."

"You have your shit together."

"Even more debatable."

"No, it's not. Who did this to you, Tom? Who made you so down on yourself that you can't see how successful you are?"

"It's really nothing."

"Tom, it's not nothing. I understand if you don't want to tell me, but you need to talk to someone you trust."

"I don't have anyone like that. You're probably the highest person on that list. I'd talk to Ruth but she...she was in the same boat I am. She and I were competitors for *everything* when we were growing up. My brother too. I'm sure that deep down, they both resent me in some way, and I don't blame them."

"Why would they resent you?"

"Because I did it all first. I was the favorite."

"And yet no one said they were proud of you?"

"What I did was never enough. They always wanted more from me."

"That's not how this works. You can't just keep pushing all the time. Why did they want you to be so perfect?"

"I don't know, but it was like that for all of us. Alcohol was the answer to making my anxieties disappear. Ruth had to toughen up to the point where she fought nearly everyone she came into contact with. And Barry will never want anything to do with us ever again. And I was the one who told them to be better. I enforced it, so I was the problem."

"Tom," I said, stepping close. "Your parents were the problem. Not you."

"But I took part in it. I didn't stand up for my siblings."

"And you can apologize for that, just like you did to me. And if I can forgive you, so can they."

"Selena, you don't have to pretend to forgive me. What I did was unforgivable."

"It was, but I'm gonna do it anyway."

"Why?"

I hadn't even really figured it out yet, but it all became clear as the words tumbled out of my mouth. "Because you're not the man who sent that letter to me. I don't see him when you're here. I see the man who *got down on his knees* to apologize. I see the man who was willing to send a credit card to a stranger to be sure he could help in some way. You've been patient and kind with Max, always stepping up every time he calls. You've been making good choices, Tom. And I see that."

He got that look on his face again, like a pitiful cat with a hurt paw. "I don't know what to say," he said quietly.

"Maybe you don't need words. How about another hug?"

He threw his arms around me again, pulling me to him like I was weightless. Normally, I wasn't a fan of this tight of a hug, but this one felt like a warm blanket being wrapped around me. My body fit into his like a key into a lock, as if we were made for each other.

"Thank you," he said. "I still don't feel like—"

"If you say you don't deserve it, I will sic Meowcifer on you."

It wasn't a very good threat. Meowcifer was laying belly-up on the couch, not having a care in the world.

"Okay, then. How about I am working on believing that I deserve that?"

"There you go," I said.

He let me go, but I almost didn't want to leave the embrace.

Don't make this weird, I told myself, and reluctantly pulled away.

"So, have you found any support groups for your new sobriety?"

"Support groups?"

"Yeah. People who are going through the same thing and may need to talk it out. A lot of people say it's crucial to staying in recovery."

"I hadn't looked into it, but I should. Just yesterday, it felt lonely."

"I'll send you some," I said. "Maybe it will help."

"Max helps too. I really enjoy helping him with math."

"Careful. You might be doing it until he graduates."

"I'd be happy to, but I wonder what he'll think of me once we tell him. *If* we tell him. I don't know how comfortable you are with the idea."

Two hours ago, I'd be nervous. But hearing about his efforts to be better lifted any worry I had.

"We should definitely tell him who you are. I've been meaning to bring it up with you anyway. How about the day after the birthday party? It's a few days out so we can prepare. We're going to have to go over *how* to tell him to minimize any…anger."

"Are you sure?"

"I'm very sure. The only reason I held off this long was because I was afraid of the drinking, but now I know it's not a problem."

"I should have told you sooner. I'm sorry, I…"

I held up my hand. "We're getting to know each other. It's fine to make a few mistakes along the way."

He took a long, slow breath. "I'm just now learning that. I agree, though, we should tell him this weekend. I'm just…nervous. Once he knows, I wonder if he'll hate me."

"We'll tell him the truth."

"All of it?"

"Yes. No more running." It seemed easier with him standing in front of me. "Besides, he knows what drinking is, and he's smarter than we give him credit for. If he knows everything, and we say it gently, then I think we can minimize the damage."

"He still might be angry."

The thought terrified me. "Yes, possibly. But we had his best interests in mind. We can tell him that, and we'll apologize. And I know from experience that you're great with apologies."

"The trick is to feel like an abhorrent person first."

"You're not an abhorrent person. You came over here to help Max."

"Maybe," he said. "I'm sorry. I'm just not used to kindness."

The thought broke my heart. "That changes now."

He nodded, taking in a nervous breath. "So, uh…do you need help cleaning up from dinner?"

"What?" I asked. "Oh, you don't need to worry about it. I made the mess. I just got an idea for a drawing—"

"Are you finished?"

"With drawing? Not yet, but I can pause on it."

"Don't. I'll clean up dinner."

"It's just a portrait."

"Your work is fantastic. Having you stop creating art in order to clean up dinner feels like a crime. Finish it, Selena. The world needs it."

Oh. My. GOD. The romantic in me screamed unintelligible noises.

All I could manage to say out loud was, "O-oh. Okay. Thank you. Are you sure?"

He gave me one of those smiles of his which made it all the better *and* the worse. His dimples were on full display and it did unfair things to my brain. "I can't be treated to a fantastic dinner and then have you do all the dishes. You cooked, I'll clean."

I could hear my heart pound and my tongue was too tied to say anything. All I could manage was an awkward chuckle while I gave him a nod.

What was happening to me? Sure, I was a romantic, but usually I could keep myself together long enough to have a conversation. I distracted myself by going back to my tablet and finishing Luna's portrait. I was *so* tempted to draw in Tom's dimples, but those were his and no one else's.

He had the story of a real hero. He'd been so hurt by his family, and yet he was saying things like *that* to me.

Inspired, I flipped to a new design and drew him instead of anything else. As I got the line art down, I didn't feel satiated. God, was he about to take over everything I drew?

"Night, Mom," Max said, pulling me out of my thoughts. "Oh, and Mr. Tom. I didn't know you would still be here."

"I'm happy to stay as long as your mom allows."

Forever then, my romantic brain murmured.

I shook off the unrealistic thought.

"Sleep well, kiddo," I said, giving him a kiss. "And be sure to brush your teeth.”

After he was gone, I turned to Tom.

“And that’s our night routine.”

“I should go and let you get some sleep.”

“I thought you were willing to stay as long as I allowed.”

“You have to rest, though. And I don’t know if you need me for that.”

That was not entirely true.

“I’ll be up for a while. I don’t sleep very well, remember?”

“Right,” he said. “Max did just make fun of you for that.”

“He’s not lying,” I replied, but then I remembered his whole life outside of this house. “But I bet *you* need sleep. You probably have to be at the office early in the morning.”

“I do need it, but I find myself in the same boat as you. I used to pass out because of drinking, but now I just...don’t. I might get a few hours here and there.”

“Oh, I’m sorry. It seems we’re two peas in a pod, then.”

“But I’m sure you enjoy your quiet time.”

“It gets boring after a while. But maybe it would be a little less boring if someone were here with me?” My heart wasn’t getting a break that night. It was already pounding as I waited for his answer.

“I do have some work I could do,” he said thoughtfully. “I have my laptop with me.”

“And I could read,” I replied. “I could even show you the Kindle you got for me.”

“I’d love that.”

We wound up on my worn couch, the old cushions seemingly pushing us toward each other. My thigh rested against his and our arms touched.

“So,” I said, but my voice came out a little too loud. “Um, this is it. I got a case for it too, because I broke my last one when Max was really little. But I love it. I have so many books on here thanks to that gift card.”

"What do you read?" he asked.

I paused, wondering if I should give the real answer. Reading romance was not embarrassing, not at all, but some people loved to twist it into being unintelligent or simple. Jax didn't read at all, but he viewed my hobby as he viewed Max's: frivolous, annoying, and a waste of time.

"I read romance," I said. "I like watching people fall in love."

"Romance?" Tom's eyebrows lifted. "I really don't ever have the time to read so excuse my ignorance. Is romance a popular thing to read about?"

"It's the biggest genre right now. A lot of them deal with hard issues, but they all have a happy ending. And in a world where everything sucks so much—" I shrugged. "—it's nice to know at least these will end well. And there's smut, which is always good."

"What's that?" he asked.

I shouldn't have brought it up. My cheeks grew warm. "Um, sex scenes. Between the characters."

"Really?"

"My favorites are when the women get doted on, which unfortunately, doesn't translate to real life."

His eyes met mine and he didn't answer for a long moment. I thought about that day in his dorm when he'd done exactly that. I wondered if he was still that way.

And if I didn't know any better, I'd say he was thinking of the same thing.

But that was unrealistic.

"So, that's what I like." I tapped my Kindle nervously. "But I'm sure you have work to get done."

"And you have a novel to read."

"Yep, so I'm just gonna..." I trailed off and dragged my eyes back to my Kindle.

I heard Tom pull out his laptop and begin typing. This was where I should have focused on the words and gotten lost in my book. But all I could think about was the way his eyes had nearly pierced me when I was talking about smut, of all things.

It had to be the tiredness. Maybe the unrealistic romantic in me was seeing everything in the wrong way. It didn't help that Tom's scent surrounded me and it was infinitely more powerful when it came from the source.

I felt safe and comfortable in a way that I usually only felt when I was reading. As we sat together, my nervousness was quickly being comforted by whatever magic his scent had over me.

My eyes closed a few times as I tried to focus on the words. I didn't have the energy to fight it and I even forgot where I was as I drifted off. I should have done this in my bed and not on Tom's shoulder, but I couldn't help it.

Whatever may come of this was a problem for in the morning.

Tom

Selena's head fell on my shoulder within an hour, and then I sat there, taking in her warmth rather than moving her away from me.

"I need to put you in your bed and leave," I said, even though she couldn't hear me. "If you were awake, you'd want me to leave."

She let out a breath of air and burrowed closer.

"I need to go." But I couldn't move. The only thing I could do was put away my laptop.

Meowcifer jumped into my lap, watching me with her bright eyes.

Stay, she seemed to urge.

"I can't," I replied.

In response, she promptly got comfortable. Everything about this begged me not to leave. This was the most relaxed I'd ever been, with the warmth from Meowcifer and Selena next to me.

"I should leave," I said one more time, but my head tilted back. "But I won't."

Meowcifer opened one eye. *Nice choice,* her gaze said. Then she closed them both and fell asleep.

I could hear Selena snore softly and it made my own eyes close. A drowsiness stronger than any alcohol washed over me.

And then it was the next day.

As the room turned golden in the morning light, I realized that I hadn't fallen asleep that easily...ever. Even when I was drunk.

We had only gotten closer throughout the night. I'd moved to where I was laying against the pillows by the arm of the couch. Selena's entire weight was on me and her head was tucked under my chin. Meowcifer was stretched out on the arm of the couch, as if guarding us.

Selena moved, lifting her head. Her warm eyes fluttered open, looking around with confusion.

Her cheeks flushed, but she didn't pull away.

"What happened?" she asked.

"We fell asleep," I replied.

"Both of us?"

"It seems so."

"I must have been exhausted. Sorry that I used you as a pillow."

"It's fine." It was more than fine. It was something I wanted to do again. I felt more rested than I had in years.

She moved, and her stomach brushed along a part of me that was much harder than usual. The friction made me close my eyes. It had been far too long since I had even *thought* about sex, but since I'd been hanging out with her, it was on my mind far more than it used to be.

After all, she was the only one I was completely sober with, and I remembered every detail.

"Oh," she said. "Sorry. I know it's a morning thing with guys. I'll get up."

The last thing my body wanted was for her to move, but I couldn't tell her that fast enough. She was gone in an instant.

"Want some tea?" she asked, running her hands through her hair. Her eyes glanced at my hardness and I threw a blanket over myself. I doubted she wanted anything to do with me after all these years, especially when she was reading books about people who were far better than I was.

"I usually go for coffee," I replied. When her nose scrunched, I remembered something. "But you don't like coffee. Or at least the smell of it."

"Your memory is both impressive and terrible," she remarked, smiling. "What else do you remember about that day?"

"Mint."

"Wow."

"Sober me doesn't forget much."

It was hard to forget it when the taste lingered on her lips as I kissed her. Everything about that day was hard to forget.

I could lose myself in every second of memory. I didn't, though, because Max walked into the living room.

"Mr. Tom? You're still here!" Max exclaimed. Then his eyes narrowed. "Does this mean...?"

"No," we both said at the same time.

"Dang it! I wanted to be able to tell abuela the good news."

"Not this time," Selena said. "And besides, as sad as it is, I'm sure Tom has to get to work."

"Unfortunately, she's right."

"Are you coming back tonight? We could hang out and maybe work on more homework."

The invitation hung in the air, and my eyes slid over to Selena, asking a silent question.

"Let's be sure Tom doesn't have plans," Selena said.

"Do you?" Max asked.

"I don't. I'd be happy to come over."

"Yes!" he said. "I can't wait. I like having you around, Mr. Tom."

"And I like being around," I replied, eyes still on Selena. I hoped she picked up on how much I meant those words, because she and Max meant everything. They would always be my priority.

Chapter Thirteen

"Oh, wow," Luna said as I gave her the print of her portrait. "You really nailed the silver fox."

I chuckled. "Yeah. I tried."

Fortunately, Luna hadn't caught *how* I'd nailed the silver fox. I'd managed to cover up a lot of Tom's features with Willie's, but if I looked hard enough, I could still see Tom's jawline.

And I'd love to say I'd only used inspiration from Tom on one of my pieces.

But I'd be lying. There was also a romance novel cover that I'd wound up using the drawing of Tom. I'd taken out his dimples, but the resemblance was uncanny.

And I like being around, he'd said earlier. A woman could easily pick up on the wrong signals when she was around a man saying things like that.

"Here is what I owe you," Luna said, shoving a wad of cash into my hand.

"How much is this?"

She waved her hand dismissively. "Don't worry about it. You did a great job."

"Thank you," I replied.

"But I require one more thing," she added.

"Do you want more prints of it?"

"Nope." She leaned forward. "I want to know what's going on with Tom Murray."

I should have seen this coming. "N-nothing."

"Yeah, right. You've let him meet Max. You get all red when you talk about him. When are you going to start dating?"

"We're not," I said. But was that true? If he wasn't drinking and was dedicated to being better, why *wouldn't* I?

"Come on, give me something."

I let out a long breath. "Fine. Here's something: I met him many years ago. We have a history."

"What? Why didn't you say anything?"

"Because it didn't end well, and I know that once you and Mom know, you're both going to hate him."

"What could he have done? It's not like he's Max's father or something."

"Right." I laughed nervously and my eyes hit the floor. I knew I was doing a poor job of covering it up. Would she notice my hesitancy? Would she call me out on it?

"Oh, come on," Luna groaned. "It seriously can't be worse than that, okay? Maybe give it a shot."

I was both relieved and annoyed at how my sister could be so surface level with me.

"We'll see."

"I can't exactly judge. Willie is like thirty years older than me."

"Right...How is that going?"

"He's busy with work, but when he's here, he's so *experienced*."

"I really hope you mean with your bills and stuff."

"I mean it *all*."

"That's...good? I guess?" I tried not to sound as grossed out as I felt.

"Thank you for this," she said, giving me a genuine smile. "I really love it."

"Of course." I said my goodbyes, knowing I needed to get home and go through my mail and catch up on bills. I drove home, mentally dividing up the cash I'd gotten between all the things that needed paying. After I pulled into the driveway, I checked the mailbox.

The first thing I saw was the result of the ancestry test I'd sent in. I pulled that aside and saved it for when Max was home. The next thing was a letter from my student loan servicer. I tore into that one first. I knew I'd missed a payment, so I was betting on this being a final notice before they trashed my already bad credit history.

I couldn't seem to get ahead on those things, and I was beginning to wonder if they would haunt me forever. With each minimum payment, my amount owed only went up.

But when I opened the letter, I didn't see a demand for money.

I saw a zero-dollar balance.

My loans were *paid off*. The letter was letting me know I was chosen as a recipient of a generous payoff that some billionaire had started.

Tears gathered in my eyes. There was no way I was this lucky. I logged into my account on my tablet and the balance showed zero there too.

For a long time, I sat in the pure relief I felt. It was gone. One huge bill that haunted me was wiped clean.

It was the best news I had gotten all week.

"Meowcifer," I called. "We can now afford the expensive cat food!"

She was stretched out on the table where the sweater used to be. She perked up for one second before laying her head back down.

Even if she wasn't excited, I sure was.

I continued to be in a good mood for hours, even as I went to pick up Max. I could splurge for his party this weekend. I could get a nicer cake and buy more decorations, because now my budget wasn't as tight as it used to be.

Pulling into the car rider's line, I thought that nothing could ruin my mood.

And that was when Jax knocked on my window.

Loudly.

My mood plummeted.

"What?" I said, rolling down the window.

"Did you really send your little baby daddy to get Max out of my class?"

My eyes shot to Max, and thankfully, he hadn't gotten close to the car yet.

"Shut up," I hissed.

"That man left you, and you're letting him walk into your life again?"

"You don't know the first thing about him."

"I know what he said to me, and he's not someone you should trust."

"I can trust whoever I want to. You're the one who threatened to show up at my house."

"That was the only way to get through to you."

"Mr. Carter!" a shrill voice snapped. Mrs. Rodney was storming over. "You are not supposed to be bothering this family."

Max was closely trailing behind her and Jax's eyes fell to him. "So you tattled on me?"

"That's it," Mrs. Rodney said. "You are out of line. This needs to be reported to Principal Smith."

"Come on!" he yelled, following Mrs. Rodney as she power walked to the office. "You can't—"

I stopped listening. "Did you tell on him?"

"Uh, yeah. He's not supposed to be bothering us. Besides, I have plans for tonight."

"Plans? Are you wanting to go to Tess's house?"

"No, but I need Mr. Tom to come over."

"Why?"

"Because this is an all-hands-on-deck matter."

Tom

"Our plans have changed," Max said the moment I walked in the door. "Mom, Mr. Tom, please sit."

I blinked. Selena looked just as baffled as I was.

We did as we were asked. Max took a deep breath. "I've been sitting on this information for too long."

"Information?" I asked. Meowcifer jumped on my lap, but not even her soft fur could calm my racing heart. What did Max know?

"Lila broke up with Blaze. She dropped a song about it today."

Relief hit me.

"Wait, what?" Selena said, leaning forward.

"Yes. I listened to it on Tess's phone at school. It's so...angry."

"Who's Tess?" I asked.

"Oh, my best friend. You'll meet him at the birthday party. He's a huge Lila fan too."

"Hang on," Selena interjected. "It was *angry*? I didn't think Lila did angry."

"I would argue that the anger is very subtle," I said. "At least in the softer albums it was."

"I'm not very good at subtle," Selena said.

"Here, let me play it for you."

I had just now gotten through about half of her discography, but even I knew this was nothing like she'd put out before. Selena's jaw dropped.

"She's *mad*," Selena said.

"I know! But she's also hinting that there may be someone else. I don't know."

I wondered if Barry would tell me if I asked, but I doubted it.

"So, like, is she happier now? What else happened? This *so* makes up for Jax being weird earlier."

"Hang on," I stopped him. "Jax was being weird earlier?"

"He tried to talk to Mom and I had to get another teacher to stop him."

My eyes slid over to Selena. "It wasn't a huge deal," she said meekly.

"Did it make you uncomfortable?"

"Well, yes, but—"

"Then it's a big deal to me."

"Don't worry, Mr. Tom," Max said, puffing out his chest. "I saved the day."

"Thank you again," Selena said, a fond smile on her face. "And don't look so worried. He's getting in trouble for it."

"And the school gave me a study period. I finished all of my homework. Except for math, of course."

It hadn't been easy getting the school to see that it was serious. It was only when I threatened to go to the police about Jax's behavior that they said they would investigate the allegations that he was harassing and stalking Selena, and pull Max from his class.

But I didn't want to tell Selena that. She had enough to worry about.

"Oh, one other thing," Selena said. "Your ancestry test came back."

"What?" Max's eyes grew large. "Really?"

"I'm pretty sure we also have it on an app somewhere," Selena said. "But the letter is more fun."

Max ripped into it. "Okay, so it says I'm almost half Mexican." He looked at Selena. "That's definitely from you, Mom. And the rest is...European? Mainly from Scotland."

Selena looked at me and I nodded inconspicuously.

"Must be from the other side," she said slowly.

"Interesting," he replied and then he glanced at me. "Oh well. Who wants to know more about a side that isn't even here?"

I watched Selena bite her lip.

"It's still interesting," I said.

"I like knowing more about Mom's side." He shrugged. "Thanks for getting it. Now I know a little more about myself."

"Um, no problem," she said, but her voice trembled.

"Can we go work on my homework now?" Max asked. "I want to get it done before I fully dive into that new Lila song."

"Of course," I said.

"I need to get some work done anyway," Selena said. "You two do what you need to do."

She retired to her room to work and possibly panic about that close call.

"Those were interesting results."

"It's cool to know a little about me," he said. "But I don't really care about the *other* side of the family."

"Why not?"

"That side's not here. It's cool to know that a little of me is from Scotland, but that's the end of it." He shrugged. "I try not to think about it too much." He would once he knew. We only had a few days until his party, and I was both anxious to get it over with and nervous about doing it at all. "Enough about that. What I really need to say is thank you for getting me out of gym. I didn't want to tell Mom, but he was the worst teacher."

"What do you mean?"

"He kept asking for information on Mom, and when I wouldn't answer, he would make me do extra laps."

"Are you *kidding*—" I nearly snapped. No, Max didn't need to see my anger. "That's not okay."

"No, but he would just say I was lying. When I finally told Mom what he was saying to me, he tried it then. Mom's smart, though, so she saw through it, but no one else does."

"What did he say to you?"

"He just kept saying that I was a burden on my mom."

"What?"

"My friends say that sometimes stepparents might feel that way, like they don't want to deal with the kid from another relationship, but I feel like that's not my fault."

"It definitely isn't."

"He just always hated me. I could feel it, even if I thought it was just me. I tried to ignore it, but eventually, he just started saying it. So I told Mom."

"And that was the right thing to do."

"But I feel like it made life harder for her. She works on her art a lot, but I know we're struggling for money. I feel bad for even wanting to have a birthday party."

I was glad I'd paid off her bills, because neither of them deserved to worry about any of this.

"Max, your mom isn't alone anymore. I will help her through everything, just like I will help you."

"Really?"

"Yes. Of course."

He smiled. "This is why I like you, Mr. Tom."

Chapter Fourteen

"Thanks for staying tonight," I said after Max had gone to bed. "I know Max appreciates it."

"It's no problem. It was much easier to help since I got a few hours of sleep."

"I can't believe people function like that all the time," I replied. "Thank you for...not making it weird."

"We both dozed off. What could be weird about that?"

"True. But it's rare for me to stay asleep." And even rarer for me not to have dreams. "I know you have to get back to your probably very nice apartment. I won't keep you all night this time. I just have one question before you go."

He blinked. "What is it?"

I inhaled nervously. My goal was to *not* make this as awkward as it felt. "What body wash do you use?"

Tom's eyebrows scrunched. "Why?"

"Uh," was my very eloquent response. "Science? I want to test something."

"What are you trying to test?"

My cheeks were on fire, but I couldn't lie to those intense eyes. "I like the way that it smells, and I'm hoping that it would help me sleep when you're not here."

"Interesting."

"And," I hurried to add, "Meowcifer loves it too. She always sleeps wherever you sit."

I pointed to the couch where she'd taken his spot.

"And you'll use it in place of yours?"

"Maybe, if it works."

"That's a shame, because I'm quite partial to how *you* smell."

The romantic in me cheered.

"We could swap."

"I prefer to smell it on you, though."

"Careful there," I said, chuckling awkwardly, "or I might think you want to sleep with me."

"I would happily do that."

It's happening! the romantic in me screamed.

But Tom blinked and took a step back at my silence.

"Just sleep, of course. I'd never ask you to do anything more."

"A-are you sure?"

"Yes. We don't have to do anything at all if you don't want to, either. I can just give you my body wash and leave."

"N-no. I like the suggestion. I'm just shocked you're even offering."

He gave me a smile, his dimples deepening. "Why would I have you settle for a body wash when I could just give you me?"

I could see why he'd had his pick of women in college. I thought that after everything, I would be immune to this charm.

I was not.

"I think I'd like that," I managed to say. "A lot."

Tom only went home to grab a change of clothes and the rest of what he would need to stay the night. While he was gone, I remained in the living room, staring at a wall as I tried to make sense of what had just happened.

By the time he returned, I'd made no progress.

After I got ready for bed, we both lay down on my full-sized bed.

There was no version of this where we wouldn't be touching for the whole night and I couldn't find it in me to complain.

I didn't do this. I wasn't a cuddler. Usually, I found it too overstimulating unless I was reading it in a book. But there was something about his subtle scent of moss and oak, something about the heat of his body in the cool air, and the feel of his hardness against my softness. Instead of being grating, it reminded me of the soft blankets I slept with every night.

This was the feeling I got when I was reading or drawing. This was comfortable and safe.

And it was because of him.

My usual comforts were a book or a blanket. Never a living, breathing man. Never someone who'd left me to raise a child on my own but came back even nicer than I remembered him.

The room was chilly and I wondered if I could get away with shifting closer to him. Meowcifer hopped up on the bed, which was rare for her. Usually, she slept in Max's room.

"So, is it working?" he asked.

It was easier to be bold in the dark. "I'm a little cold."

"Then come here."

He opened his arms. I wasted no time snuggling close with him. My head rested on his chest where I could hear his heart thump. His arm wrapped around my shoulders and I was enveloped in him.

I was out in minutes.

I woke up with the same desires from the previous night. Selena was pressed into me and my body wanted hers. But I remembered how she nearly jumped away the morning before, and I angled my hips away from her. She'd been understanding so far, but I didn't want to push my luck.

Her face was peaceful in a way I wasn't used to seeing in the daylight. She always looked like she was figuring something out, like everything around her was a little confusing. When she slept, however, she seemed truly at peace.

But the peace didn't last long. Meowcifer let out a loud meow at the door and Selena's eyes popped open.

"Cat food time," she said, yawning. "I can't believe it's morning. I think that's the first time I slept eight hours in years. My brain feels so rested."

"Mine too."

"Good. It would have been awkward for you to stay up all night while I probably snored like an old man."

I laughed. And then her cheeks turned red.

"I'll be back." She moved away, and I instantly missed her warmth.

When she didn't return, I decided to follow her out into the living room. It took me a few minutes before I was decent enough to get up. Selena was sitting on the couch with her tablet, focused on something.

"Is everything okay?"

"Yes, I just need to plan for Max's birthday party. This is the first year I can finally do something extra special for him."

"Why is that?"

"I have extra money from a few projects. Plus, my student loans got paid off by a generous donation."

"That's...great..." I said. So she knew about those. I wondered how she would feel when she found out about the other one.

"Yeah. Thank God. I really needed the breathing room. Now, I'll be able to ask for less from you. Hopefully, nothing after the phone."

"You don't have to not ask for things from me."

"I know, it's just..."

"Still feel like you should do it on your own?"

Her eyes shot back down to her tablet.

"I wanted my art to be able to do it," she explained. "Jax always said they were doodles, and I hoped I could prove that this was worth something."

"But it is," I said. "No matter how much money you make, your art *is* worth something. I knew that even twelve years ago."

"How do I know you're not just saying that to be nice?" she asked.

For a second, I wasn't sure what to say, but then I remembered what I had in my wallet. I slowly brought it out.

"You're not about to give me money, right?"

"No. But I want you to see this."

I pulled out the old piece of paper. It had yellowed over time, but I'd kept it in good condition. I unfolded it, seeing the work she'd done all those years ago in the coffee shop.

"No way," she said under her breath. She stood and looked at it closer. "You kept this?"

"I did. For a while, I forgot about it, but over the years, it was a great reminder of the woman who liked me for me."

"I couldn't have been the only one."

"You were the only one who got to see me sober and that's the real me."

"Even after all these years?"

"Yes."

"Why?"

"Because no one seemed to *like* me sober. Other than you. Plus, no one could hold a candle to you."

She blinked and bit her lip. "You either."

The words hit hard. I'd hoped that I didn't hurt her, and that her first time was as good for her as it was for me.

A moment passed between us—a delicate, hopeful moment.

"Um, anyway," she said, shaking her head. "I'm glad you kept it. And that you think my art is beautiful." She tucked her hair behind her ear and took a step back.

"It is. I'll tell you that any time."

I carefully folded up the drawing and put it back where it belonged, thinking over what had happened.

"But my art does pay for a lot. I get so down about it that I forget. I can pay for this party and I really want to."

"Of course. I'm glad it worked out."

I should have told her I was the one who paid off her student loans. I really should have.

But I didn't want to ruin what we had just had. It seemed so fragile—this unknown desire could be growing, and her knowing I'd paid for something might take a sledgehammer to it.

And besides, I could always tell her when she got her next zero-dollar bill.

Chapter Fifteen

Selena

"We're here to help clean!" Mom called as she opened the door.

There wasn't much to actually do. Tom often offered to do the dishes or tidy up for me if I cooked dinner, which lately, had been most nights. Ahead of the party, he'd done even more.

"Wait, what is this?" Luna asked, looking around. "It's spotless. Who are you and what have you done with my sister?"

"Tom cleaned it," I said, shaking off my emotions as I addressed my family.

"A man who cleans too?" Mom asked. "When is the wedding?"

"There is no wedding," I said. "He's been coming over to help Max with his homework. I cook him dinner and he cleans."

"Ooh, how domestic."

I turned back to the balloons I was filling up.

Max came downstairs. "This is the best birthday ever," he said to Mom. "Not only do I finally get the cake I've been wanting, but Mom and Mr. Tom are taking me out for waffles tomorrow."

Luna gave me a look, probably at the fact that Tom and I would be hanging out *again*.

But I shook my head. "I need to go outside and tie the balloons to the mailbox."

"We're coming with you," Mom said. "Especially since we have nothing else to do."

"Seriously," Luna said. "How did you get your boyfriend to clean?"

"He's my *friend*, and he offered."

"See, Luna?" Mom said. "Sometimes, age doesn't make a man more mature."

"We're not fighting today," I said, cutting them off. "It's Max's party."

"Oh, she's feeling direct today," Mom teased. "I can respect it. Is Tom at least going to be here?"

"Yep."

"Good! I finally get to meet him! How does my hair look?"

"Beautiful as always, Mom," Luna replied. "But I bet Tom only cares about Selena."

"Once again, we're just *friends*," I insisted. But even I knew friends didn't share a bed to get sleep. Well, maybe some did. But this wasn't *normal*. Was it?

But I pushed the thoughts out of my mind. The party was my focus, and then telling Max. Nothing more.

I could hear the rumble of Tom's truck in the driveway.

"He's here!" Max yelled, running out the door and down the front porch steps.

Tom climbed out, a box in his hand. I'd almost completely forgotten that we agreed to get him a phone in all the chaos of party planning. But my phone bill had already been switched to be paid by his card. There was now another bill I didn't have to worry about.

"Mr. Tom!" Max ran up to him and threw his arms around him. "You came!"

"Is that him?" a voice whispered.

I jumped and turned. Hadley was next to me. For a pregnant woman, she could still sneak up on people.

"Where did you come from?"

"My car. You were too busy gawking at that marvelous-looking man over there to notice. Those *dimples*." She fanned herself.

"He's...he's not that—" I couldn't lie to my best friend. "Okay, he's hot. But that's not what I need to be focusing on. We're telling Max the truth tomorrow."

"Really? He passed all your tests?" Hadley glanced over where Tom was listening to Max ramble on about his cake. "I can see why."

"He doesn't drink anymore," I said.

"Seriously?"

"He hasn't for six months. *And* he's looking to join a support group for it. He's turned out to be a really great guy."

"Then it's definitely time, considering how much Max seems to like him."

I looked over. One of Max's friends had arrived, and he was introducing Tom to him.

"We've got it down to the word on what we'll say," I replied, my chest tight at the sight. "I think it'll be hard to hear, but he'll understand once we explain."

"Good luck. And if you need me, Allen is on vacation for a while."

"Without you?"

"He said he wanted to go somewhere with his friends." She shrugged. "I was fine with it because it gave me some peace and quiet. I still have a few weeks before I'm due anyway."

I had never heard Hadley wanting or needing space away from Allen. This sudden change raised red flags. I opened my mouth to say something, but Max grabbed my attention as he ran up to me.

"Mom! Can I open Mr. Tom's present now?"

"It's the last one you open," I replied.

"I bet that means it's awesome," Max said. "Hi, Aunt Hadley. How are you feeling?"

"So good now that you ask," she said, smiling. "You're the sweetest kid ever.

You know that?"

"It's all a part of my plot. I want to hold the baby when they're here."

"You'll be welcome to." Hadley ruffled his hair. She then turned to Tom. "So you must be the famous Tom Murray. I'm Hadley."

His eyes moved from me to her. And just like with Luna, I wondered if they would stay. Both Hadley and Luna glowed. It was why my best friend had found someone quickly. I was waiting for whenever Tom would figure out who here had the main character energy that I didn't.

"Nice to meet you, Hadley." Tom's voice was level. His eyes moved right back to me.

My cheeks heated again.

"Oh my goodness," Mom's voice called. "Tom Murray! It's so nice to meet you."

Tom looked over to Mom. "Does she know...?"

I glanced over at Max, glad that another friend had arrived and distracted him.

"No, only Hadley does."

"I'm the special one," Hadley whispered.

"You are so handsome," Mom said as she walked over. "Selena is going to have to step up her game to match how amazing you look."

Ugh. Here we go.

"I like it when she's comfortable," he said. "She looks beautiful no matter what she wears."

Hadley elbowed me, eyebrows raised. I pushed her away.

"That is so sweet," Mom said. "I'm Carmen."

"Tom," he said, shaking her hand. "But...you already knew that."

His face fell, and I wondered if he was playing that social mistake over in his mind just like I would.

Mom plowed on. "Oh, you have an awkward streak just like she does. It's a perfect match."

Hadley raised her eyebrows even higher and I rolled my eyes.

This was going to be a long party.

Tom

"And this is Tess," Max said, gesturing to the last friend he'd had over. "He's my best friend. I've even been over to his house."

Tess was a kid with thick glasses and a Lila Wilde shirt. Max had introduced me to his other friends, too many to remember, but I knew this was the friend he was closest to.

"Nice to meet you," I said, giving him a small smile.

Inwardly, I was struggling. My mind was stuck on what I would be telling Max at breakfast the very next day. I'd been thinking about it nonstop for the last few days. I'd gone over everything, how to word it, how to react to his anger, and how to move forward from there.

It wasn't going to be easy.

I could see that Selena was affected by the stress too. She was running around, looking more and more agitated as time went on. I was reminded of that day in the restaurant when we'd run into Luna.

I decided to step in to help when I saw her glaring at the cake.

"Hey," I said, putting my hand on her back. "Is everything okay?"

Just like last time, she seemed to relax when I touched her.

"This is...a lot," she said. "And with tomorrow..."

"I know," I replied. "I feel it too. You could step away and—"

"It's time for photos!" Carmen called from the living room, cutting me off. "Max, get over here!"

"We do this every year," Selena explained. "I don't want to miss this. It's a photo in front of our door to see how much Max has grown. One day, we'll put them all together in a time-lapse."

Carmen was positioning Max in the middle of the doorframe. They took photos while I watched on the sideline, wishing we'd had a tradition like this growing up. I'd have loved to see our growth in pictures like this. Instead, all I had were haunting memories.

"Okay, now you and Tom get one," Carmen said motioning to me and her.

"That's not necessary," Selena said.

"I want it for the future! It's our first time meeting him. We should remember this."

"Yes!" Max echoed.

"I don't think Tom even likes photos," Selena argued.

"With a face like that?"

Selena narrowed her eyes.

"I'll do it," I said. "But only if you want to."

She turned to me, eyes wide. "Are you sure?"

"It's just a photo." I shrugged. "And I want to remember this too."

She slowly nodded and we situated ourselves in front of the door with a respectable distance between us.

"Get closer," Carmen called. "Act like you like each other."

"Mom," Selena hissed.

I moved slightly closer to her, and I could feel her sweater against my arm. "How's this?"

"Put an arm around her!"

"Is that okay?" I asked her.

Her cheeks were red.

"It's fine," she said as she leaned into me. I wondered if we could have had this for years if not for my own stupidity. Drinking seemed so useless now that my body touched hers.

"Yes!" Carmen said. "Young love at its finest."

As soon as the photo was taken, Selena stepped away. "She always says the most embarrassing things," she muttered.

My body was still buzzing from having her close to me. Selena went back in the house and I turned to Carmen.

"Can I get a copy of that?"

"Of course," she said. "It was one of her best. You bring out the good side of her."

I doubted that, but I didn't mind pretending that I did—even if it was only for one more day.

"All right, time for cake!" Selena called from inside the house. I could barely hear her through the storm door.

The kids all ran inside and I followed along. I saw Selena's friend, Hadley, slowly walking up the stairs.

"Here, let me help you with that," I said.

"Oh, such a gentleman." Hadley accepted my hand. "I tell you, pregnancy starts taking a toll nine months in."

"I can imagine," I said. I wondered how Selena had handled it.

"Selena was a trooper," Hadley added, as if reading my mind. "She was determined to pretend that nothing bothered her, but we all knew it was hard."

"I wish I could have seen it."

"Me too. I have a feeling you'd have seen right through it. Just like you do now."

"I just want to be there for her."

"And you're doing a pretty good job of it." She winked and walked inside.

Did her friend like me? I expected her to hate me.

We all gathered around Max in the living room and sang happy birthday. He basked in the attention and blew out his candles with a giant smile on his face.

After cake, Selena let him open up gifts. Most of them were Lila Wilde related, but I could tell his eyes kept falling on my present.

Finally, he got to it, and he nearly jumped to grab it. "It's heavy," he said.

I saw Selena take a breath before telling him to open it. The minute he did, everyone in the room gasped.

"Is this...a phone?" he yelled. "Like a real cell phone?"

"It is," I said. "Happy birthday, Max."

Luna and Carmen were staring at me with wide eyes. I didn't do well with the attention. Maybe I should have given this to him later.

"It's an iPhone!" one of Max's friends said.

"And now you can have my present," Selena said. I frowned over at her as she grabbed something out from under the table. It had been hidden by the tablecloth.

"A Lila Wilde phone case!"

"If you're going to have a phone that nice, it needs protection."

"Thank you! Thank you!" Max said, giving us both hugs. He ran back to his friends, eager to show off his new device.

"Did you put parental controls on that thing?" Selena asked.

"I did when I opened it. I'll send you the invite so you can see what he does."

She nodded. "It feels like he's too young for this."

I could see why Selena said that gift was last, because the party was consumed by it. The kids were crowding around Max, showing him how to use his new device.

"Apparently not," I said, gesturing to the group around him.

"What a gift," Carmen said when Max was fully entertained by his friends.

"Seriously," Luna added. "I'm surprised Selena even agreed to it."

"He needs a phone," Selena said. "And Tom offered."

"What do you do for work, Tom?" Carmen asked.

"He's the CEO of Murray and Sons," Luna said. When Carmen and Selena turned to her with matching raised eyebrows, she added, "It's on Google."

"I'm only acting as the CEO."

"Oh, that's just semantics."

"I suppose that's true."

Luna smiled, but I barely noticed. Selena was looking at her feet, body hunched like that day in the restaurant when she'd needed to go home.

"Are you okay?"

"Yeah." But she didn't meet my eyes. "It's just a little loud."

"Then let's step away for a bit," I said. "Excuse me," I said to Luna and Carmen as I led Selena to her room.

"That's better," she said, sitting on the bed. I watched her carefully as she looked up at me.

"Is there anything else you need?"

I watched as she played with her hands. "Probably not. I think my thoughts just took a downhill turn out there."

"What happened?"

"Sometimes, when I get overwhelmed, I latch onto the wrong thing. It's nothing."

"It isn't nothing to me. Tell me."

"Hadley and Luna...They're interesting, aren't they?"

"I suppose so. They care about you."

"You know, one day, you're going to realize that they're more interesting than I am."

"Excuse me?"

"It's fine when you do. I know that I'm not on their level."

"On their level?"

"It's dumb."

"Nothing you can say will be dumb. Tell me."

"I read a lot of books," she explained. "And all of them have a main character. She's always beautiful and perfect. And I don't see that in myself. But I see it in them. They're these amazing, outgoing personalities, and I'm just...in the background—like a side character. And I keep waiting for you to notice that people like Luna and Hadley are so much better than I am."

Selena looked at her hands again, sighing as she shook her head.

"But I only see you."

"What?"

"To me, *you're* the most beautiful woman in the room. You have the best sense of humor and a kindness that I admire. I understand you might not see yourself as the main character of your own story, but there is a part of me that hopes you're a main character in mine."

Selena blinked, her jaw falling open. "M-me?"

"Yes, you." I gave her a warm smile. "It couldn't be anyone else."

Her eyes were wide. "But I don't dress up."

"You don't have to."

"I just read and draw all day."

"You're doing what you love. I love the focus you have when you're doing those things. It's one of the things that drew me to you in the coffee shop."

"I don't...I don't know what to say."

"You don't have to say anything. I don't say what I do expecting a reaction. I just want you to know exactly how I feel."

She nodded, eyes meeting mine. I was lost in her gaze, analyzing every single detail of her: the curve of her cheeks, her upturned nose, her endless eyes. She was getting closer, leaning into me. And I couldn't help but do the same. What would her lips feel like against mine? Would she even let it happen?

But then the door opened.

"We have a situation," Hadley said, out of breath.

"What is it?"

"Jax is here."

Chapter Sixteen

Selena

Jax had a bottle in his hand and was pounding on the screen door. Every movement looked like it was going to knock him over.

"Why is he here?" Max asked, eyes wide as he witnessed what a shitty man my ex was.

"I don't know. I'll get him to leave." I made my way to the door, Tom hot on my heels. The moment Jax saw me, he wasted no time.

"Of course you invite Mr. Perfect and not me!" His voice rattled around in my ears. In the background, I heard Meowcifer hiss. She must have come out of hiding to do it.

"You need to leave," Tom said, his voice hard. The tone sent a shiver down my spine, and it wasn't even directed at me.

"Why? I deserve to be here. I wasted years of my life on that kid."

"Wasted?" Tom said, his jaw clenched.

"And it's that attitude that made me dump you," I said. "You're ruining his party."

"Ruining his party? You ruined my *life*."

"How did I ruin your life?"

"You got me fired. I have to live in a shitty apartment because you kicked me out of the house. And worst of all, you canceled my Netflix subscription. How *could* you?"

I blinked. The worst of everything was the *Netflix* subscription?

"Get your own Netflix," Tom snapped. "And get lost before I call the police."

"You," Jax said, pointing. He swayed on his feet. "You are the *worst*. You took her from me."

"I didn't have to do anything. You did this to yourself."

"Oh, that's real rich. You're not better than me."

"You need to get the hell out of here!" Mom snapped. "You're not ruining Max's birthday by—"

"Ruining it? I haven't even gotten started." His eyes slid to me. "I could topple this party with one sentence."

"Don't," I hissed quietly. I hoped, foolishly, that there was some sense of kindness in him.

Jax looked at Max, who shrunk away. "Haven't you figured it out yet, smarty-pants? Tom is your dad. The same man who left you."

Max's jaw dropped. I could feel a hush fall over the house before Tom dragged Jax out and slammed the door behind him.

"What—M-mom?" Max's voice cracked. "Is that true?"

I opened my mouth to answer, but no words came out. Everyone's eyes were on me, expecting an answer.

"That's why he looks so much like you!" one of his friends said.

Max looked back at me and my heart broke as I saw the betrayal spreading across his face. His brows were low, making him look so much older than he was.

He took off for his room and his friends all followed. I reached out, but I had more problems than just my child.

"Tom is Max's *father*?" Mom asked. "The one who never stepped in? *That* bastard?"

"And you trust him now?" Luna snapped too. The betrayal on Max's face leaked onto theirs.

My heart pounded. My breaths came out fast. Why couldn't I do anything? Why couldn't I *move*?

"Oh, *shit*!" Hadley called. "I think my water just broke."

Tom

The moment I called the police, Jax took off sprinting like the coward he was. My only other option was to beat the shit out of him like I wanted to, but I knew I couldn't make this any worse by losing my cool when things were already bad.

While Jax disappeared around the corner, the door burst open. Hadley was being supported by Carmen and Luna. She was moaning loudly, clutching her stomach.

"I need you guys to take me home," she said. "We wanted a home birth, and Allen isn't here to come get me."

"Okay, sweetie," Carmen said. "We'll get you there."

Luna glanced up and saw me. Her smile from earlier was gone and she glared at me as she helped Hadley make her way to her car.

"You drive, Luna," Hadley said. "I'll sit in the back. Carmen might want to bring her own car."

I wanted to help, but I had a feeling if I stepped any closer, Selena's family would kill me.

"I can get myself in," Hadley added.

When Carmen and Luna were in their own cars, Hadley looked at me from the back seat and gave me an exaggerated wink.

Was she...faking labor?

The car pulled away, and as it did, the police arrived. I told them how Jax had been threatening Selena and how he'd shown up drunk to a kid's birthday party. They said there wasn't much they could do since he was gone, but that Selena could put a restraining order in place if he showed up again. They left soon after, and my mind was filled with all the things I needed to get done.

I was glad that I'd gotten a security system installed. At least we'd have evidence.

Walking inside, I wondered how to broach the topic with Selena, but those plans disappeared the moment I saw her.

She had sunk to the floor. Tears streamed down her cheeks as she stared blankly at the linoleum. I usually didn't know how to handle emotions like this from someone I felt so much for, but refused to let her suffer without stepping in.

"Hey," I said, sitting beside her.

"I've messed up so bad," she cried. "I should have told him sooner. I should have stopped Jax, or *God*, helped Hadley to her car. I just froze!"

I didn't know what to say. It felt like that night when Ruth was in my apartment all over again.

But I refused to leave her like this.

Just say something.

"In a way, I did too," I said softly.

"I should have just told him the truth from day one. Why did I lie?"

"We didn't lie. It was just withholding the whole truth."

"I'm not sure that's any better. I should have just told him."

"Because you thought you were protecting him. You didn't trust me, and it was fair not to."

"But now look at what happened! You stayed and he found out from *Jax*, of all people."

"I know. We owe him an apology. And an explanation."

"I failed him, which I promised never to do."

"Maybe we both should have made different decisions, but we didn't know what would happen. We didn't know what we do now. All we can do is be there for him and try to put this back together. You're not going to do this alone. When we have the chance to, we'll tell him everything and ask for his forgiveness."

Another sob escaped her and I put a hand on her back. I watched to make sure she wasn't going to jerk away, and when she didn't, I applied more pressure.

"I'm sorry I was here crying and not helping Hadley," she said. "I need to check on her."

"I don't know that you need to. When we were out there, she winked at me, and then told your mom and Luna to take her home."

"Why would she go home?"

"She said she wanted a home birth."

"No, she doesn't. She—*oh*. She's faking it."

"It would make sense. She got your mom and Luna to go with her."

"So I could have space. God, she's the best. She doesn't freeze when things get hard."

"You were overwhelmed. It's okay."

"Nothing feels okay," she said. "It feels like the apocalypse. Everyone hates me."

"I don't," I said.

"You should. I kept you from telling Max."

"You did, but it was easier talking to him without him knowing what I'd done. Maybe that makes me a coward, but at least I had a little bit of time before he knew it all."

"You're in good company, then. I think I'm a coward too. And I don't know how to stop."

"My sister once told me change starts with one choice. We could make one now."

"Okay," she said. "I think...I just need a second."

"Take all the time you need."

"Can I...hug you?" Her voice was small.

My throat grew dry. Of all the people in the world, why did she want *me*? I was responsible for all of this because of my actions all those years ago.

But I slowly opened my arms and she leaned into me. Her head rested on my chest and I wrapped myself around her, as if I could somehow protect her from the fallout of our own mistakes.

"I'm here." I hoped the words were comforting. "You're not alone."

She tightened her grip. I sat there, holding her, content to be here as long as she needed me.

Eventually, when her tears had stopped, she pulled away. "Thank you." Her eyes then trailed down my shirt. "Oh my God. Your shirt is stained. I'm so—"

"I don't care about a stupid shirt more than I care about you."

"But you're always so put together."

"I'd gladly let you stain every single thing of mine if it means I get to be here for you."

And there it was. The upturn of her lips that made my heart skip a beat.

"We need to talk to Max," I said. "Probably without his friends here."

She took a stuttering breath. "We do."

We walked to Max's room and she knocked on the door.

"Go away!" Max called.

I could see how the words affected her. She looked near tears again, but I grabbed her hand and nodded. She gave me a sideways glance, lips forming a watery smile.

After another deep breath, she spoke again. "Max, we need to talk. Please open the door."

I heard him groan and then the door opened. He was angrier than I'd ever seen him, and all his friends were staring at us with wide eyes.

Selena's grip on my hand tightened.

The attention. She didn't like the attention.

It was time for me to step in.

"I believe it's time for all of you to go home," I said. "We need to talk to Max."

"So, you're kicking my friends out? I can't even talk to them about this?"

"Of course you can," I said. "You have a phone now. After we talk, you can call all of them to process. I encourage it, actually."

Max glared, but I held firm. His eyes traveled over my face, no doubt seeing the similarities there.

"My mom is already on her way," Tess said. "What's Max's number?"

They all got their phones ready and I recited the number to them.

It took a while for their parents to pick them up, and Max stayed on the couch, huddled with his friends like we were the enemy.

I hated seeing it, but I had to push on.

"Are you hungry? It's been a while since we had cake."

"I'm fine." His stomach growled. "Okay, maybe I'm not. But you're not going to charm me with food."

"I'm not trying to. I just need to take care of you too."

"Because you're my dad."

"Yeah. Because I'm your dad. And I want the best for you."

He looked down, jaw still ticked. He took a moment, then said, "I want pizza. With pineapple. Please."

Chapter Seventeen

Selena

I couldn't stop staring at Max's glare. He'd never been like this, even when Jax had lived with us. He was a gentle kid, not an angry one.

Until now.

"When were you going to tell me?" Max asked after he had eaten two pieces of pizza. "Or were you gonna hide it from me forever?"

"Tomorrow," I said. "We were telling you tomorrow."

"Why tomorrow? Why not the moment I met him?"

"Because your mom didn't know she could trust me yet," Tom replied.

"Why couldn't she trust you? You were like...super nice. *Too* nice, almost."

I chewed on my lip. I wanted to run and hide, but I couldn't—not after already doing it for so long. "When I first met Tom, he was...different. Nice, but he did some things that weren't great, including turning me away when I told him I was pregnant with you."

"I didn't just turn your mom away. I told her to never contact me again."

Max's eyes shot to Tom. "Why would you do that?"

"I don't know," he said. "I wish I did, but I only have a guess."

"How could you not know?" he snapped. "You did it, right?"

"I did, but I…I don't remember a lot of my life. Back then, I was drinking, just like Jax was today, but it was every night. And when you do it as much as I did, you can have memory problems."

"I was worried he'd drink one night and hurt you like he did me," I said.

"What did he say?"

I pulled out my phone.

"I have a picture of it saved." I scrolled for a moment, going back years. Back then, I'd snapped the picture with shaky hands to remind myself never to trust a man like him again. Now, it felt like it was from another life.

When I read it out loud, I could feel Tom's eyes on me.

"Goddamn it," he muttered when he heard it.

"You said that to my mom?" Max asked. "That's…that's horrible."

"It is."

"How could you?"

"Max," I started, "it was twelve years ago. He's not that person anymore. He doesn't drink and he's trying to be better."

"Why are you defending him?"

"She doesn't have to." Tom said it matter-of-factly. "No one should defend me. I was an idiot. I don't have an excuse. I've apologized to your mother so many times. But I know that one day, she's going to see sense and hate me again."

"Stop it," I said, turning to him. "I'm not going to see sense, because I don't need to. Tom, you're not going anywhere. As long as you're not drinking and you're trying, then we're good. You got Max's tablet, his phone, defended him from Jax, and got him out of gym."

For a moment, no one spoke. Tom looked at me as if he'd forgotten all the good things he'd done.

But then Max broke the silence. "Do you know how embarrassing it is to hear it from *Jax* in front of everyone?"

"It must have been mortifying," I said. "I'm sorry."

"How did he even know? Other than the fact that we look alike."

I looked over at Tom. "He figured it out when I was going off on him that day outside your school. He didn't like that I put him in his place after what he said about you."

"So he *did* say something to you. You looked so mad."

"Yes, I was. I didn't like what I'd heard he was doing. And I definitely didn't like what he said about you."

"You *have* to feel that way," he said. "You're my dad. Wait, how do we even know for sure?"

"I mean, *I* know for sure," I said. "He was the only person who it could be. And we did a DNA test a while ago."

"When? We just did the ancestry one."

"I also did a paternity one."

"Really? That was a cover-up too?"

"Yes," I said. "I'm sorry." I'd already said it once, yet it didn't feel like enough.

"Are there any more lies you want to tell me about? Is my name even Max?"

"Of course it is. There is nothing else."

Max looked down at his half-eaten pizza. Meowcifer jumped up, sniffing his plate before going to sit in Tom's lap. "I can't believe she likes you," he muttered.

"I don't understand it either."

"I'm going to my room. I don't think I can talk anymore tonight."

I hated that he needed space from us, but I knew better than to keep him somewhere that he didn't want to be.

"Okay," I managed. "Let us know if you need anything."

He sullenly walked away.

I watched him go, tears gathering in my eyes.

"I think we did the best we could," Tom said. "Especially considering how he found out. He just needs time."

"Yeah," I said, wiping away a stray tear. "You're right."

"Thank you for what you said, about not getting rid of me."

"I meant it."

"I don't know if I deserve it."

"That's my choice to make, and I stand by my words. You're not that man anymore. You made one choice to be better, and then you kept making more choices." I stared into his emerald eyes, noticing as they grew wet. "Come here," I said. "I think it's your turn for a hug."

Closing my arms around him, I realized just how comfortable this was. I could stay next to him forever, just like this. Beneath us, Meowcifer purred.

"Do you...want to stay the night?" I asked. "We could present a united front with Max tomorrow."

And I'm starting to think my life is better when you're here.

The thought wasn't as terrifying as it should be. But it was true. I slept. I drew more. I felt more alive.

This version of him was exactly what I needed.

"Of course I'll stay," he said. "Besides, we need sleep. We've all had a long day."

Tom

"Maybe we're not going to get sleep tonight." Selena's voice sounded withdrawn.

"It was a bad day," I replied. "I'm not surprised."

"My mind keeps going back to what happened," she said. "I can't escape it."

"We've done all we can."

"Does thinking that help?"

"Nope."

She propped herself on her elbows.

"Then what does?"

"I don't know. Usually this would be when I would drink. Maybe work on the truck if something needed fixing. Or work out."

"Gross. Mostly to the working out part."

"It calms me down."

"Does anything else calm you down?"

"Music used to." *You do, now,* I wanted to say.

"That's a good one."

"I don't know if any of it is going to help at the moment. What calms you down?"

"Drawing and reading, but I'm too tired for it. Maybe we should try some music."

"I...I don't know if I can." The idea made my entire body tense. I felt on edge in a way I hadn't in a long time—just like the moments before the storm that tore through my neighborhood when I was a kid.

"Why not?"

"My love for music was killed by my father and now it's only barely been brought back by Max. I don't think it would help me at all since it has so much negative history tied to it."

"Wait, what happened with your dad?"

"I got a B on a test once and he berated me for being distracted with 'silly sounds' for hours."

"What?"

"You don't have to be offended on my account. Everything is just a fact of my life. I try not to dwell on it too much."

"But doesn't it hurt?"

"I learned a long time ago that I don't have time to feel hurt. Things happen and I move on."

"You didn't do that with Max."

"I did, in a way. Compartmentalizing it was the only way I could look you in the eyes."

"But you can't do that forever. You have to feel things eventually."

"I'm fine."

"I don't think you are," she said. "And that's okay. Neither am I." She reached out, placing her hand on my arm. It was a warm reminder, like a lighthouse in a storm. "Do you want to talk about it?"

"I don't want to make this about me."

"You're not. I'm asking."

"Then, this isn't something you need to hear after a day like today."

"Maybe not, but I don't think running from things has done me much good either, has it?" She let out a long breath. "We'll have to figure out what to say to Max tomorrow. But for now, we can make sure that we're okay."

"I *am* okay."

"I think we've already established that you're not. What happened, Tom?"

"I've lived a privileged life. Sure, my dad was terrible, but I was always taken care of."

"Having money doesn't erase emotional damage. It's like you think you have to keep everything, including yourself, together. Did your dad teach you that?"

"No. It was a lesson I learned myself."

"When?"

I closed my eyes, and I was back at home, so many years before, after the tornado had ripped past our house. Ruth was sobbing as she watched the neighbor search for her husband. Barry was shaking, gripping her hand like it was a lifeline.

"Did you ever hear about the tornado in Franklin? About twenty years ago?"

"I think so. Why?"

"That tornado hit my neighborhood. We were in it."

"What? Were you okay?"

"We didn't get hurt. Ruth, Barry, and I all were huddled in the closet. I covered them, hoping I could do something. But the damage was done. Maybe not to the house, but to us. My siblings were terrified. I was too, but I couldn't let them see that. I couldn't let them see anything. Even years later."

"Tom, you would have only been twelve. Where were your parents?"

"I'm not sure, but when they reappeared, they wanted us to be past it. I quickly learned that I was the only one who gave a damn about how my siblings felt. My dad was an angry man, and my mom spent all her energy keeping him together. Someone had to do that for Ruth and Barry. I kept my composure, hid my own fears to protect them. But it only wound up pushing them away."

She scoffed. "I'm sorry, but that wasn't your job. Your parents didn't help their kids emotionally *ever*?"

"No. They expected us all to toughen up and deal with it. We were as good as what he produced, and a good production worker doesn't stop to be afraid of anything."

"That's *horrible*."

"It's just how it was. Ruth was terrified of storms after, and they would get on her for it. Even if I didn't understand *why* she was scared of them back then, I knew she needed at least some form of protection. If I did what my parents wanted, it took a little bit of the pressure off of them. Especially with my dad. When he was focused on me, he wasn't on them. I couldn't offer much, but I could offer that. But it was never enough. *I* was never enough."

"You didn't have to be," she hissed, sitting up. I followed suit, wondering how I'd managed to upset her. "Tom, that was your *parents'* job. Their kids were in a tornado and they didn't fucking comfort them? They told them to toughen up? What kind of parenting is that?"

"It's what they did."

"And *why* are you blaming yourself when your parents failed you?"

"Because I was *there*. I should have done more, said more—"

"Tom, of course you were there. You were a victim just like your siblings were."

"Victim is a strong word."

"It's not. You were hurt because of them. That's why you drank so much, wasn't it? You found one thing that helped and *had* to have it just to deal with all of this."

"Yes, but if I were stronger—"

"There is no being stronger. Everyone has a breaking point."

"But my breaking point hurt you."

"I forgave you for that."

"You shouldn't have."

"Well, too bad. That's my choice too, and I've not regretted it *once*. And maybe some of this responsibility, for you, for your siblings, should be on your *parents*. Not you."

"It was only on us when we were problems."

"You guys were never not their *problem*. You were their *kids*."

She was right. I knew she was. But if I let go of all the blame, if I truly *felt* everything I'd bottled up, I didn't know if I would ever stop.

The emotions clogged my throat. Walls I'd spent years building around me were at risk of fracturing after I was shown the slightest hint of compassion. Was this all it took to break me down?

Or was it *her*?

I couldn't let this happen. I wasn't important here. She was. Max was. I was an afterthought.

"Tom, don't. I know you're about to make this about me or Max. You always do, but you don't have to this time. You can feel whatever you need to. You're safe here. You're safe with me."

"I'm not going to burden you with my feelings."

"It's not a burden when I *want* to know them. You are important to me. Your feelings especially. *Please*. Feel them."

Her words ripped through the brick and cement that protected me, leaving only me and the torrential downpour of my emotions I'd hidden for so long.

Decades-long anger and pain were like thunder. I was angry. I was scared.

But most of all, I was hurt.

Hurt by Dad's expectations, by his refusal to see Ruth for what she was, and his disdain for Barry's existence. I was hurt by being close to him, listening to him tear apart my siblings for being human. I was hurt by him whenever he'd turn all of that onto *me*.

He'd once told me I was the only kid who'd met his expectations.

And it *didn't matter*.

None of it did. Because at the end of the day, he was a terrible man, a terrible *father*, and we would never be good enough for him. I didn't get any passes for doing what he asked. I only got asked for more.

Get your brother and sister in line. Do this project. Go yell at this employee for m e.

There was always more needed of me.

Arms wrapped around me. "It's okay, Tom. Let it all out."

The words felt like a different kind of protection. Instead of cold, empty walls, this was a warm blanket on a cold night. It didn't protect me from the storm inside of me, but it made it easier to bear.

I held fast to her warmth as the storm roared. And then, just like that night, it faded.

My chest ached and I was more exhausted than I'd ever been.

I realized I had been crying into Selena's neck. I hadn't cried since before the storm when I locked those emotions away for good.

"I'm proud of you."

A chuckle escaped me. "You keep saying what I wish my dad would say to me. And each time, I was doing the exact thing I wasn't supposed to."

"And what is that? Being a human?"

I slowly nodded. "Yes."

"How could it be a bad thing? Humans can grow and change. Just like you did."

Maybe I had. Maybe Ruth had been right. All those small choices had added up.

"I don't want Max to ever feel like this. I will *never* make him wonder if I care."

"And that's why I forgave you," she said.

A feeling I didn't know possible wormed its way into the chasm that was my heart. It was warm and shaped like her.

It felt a little like...*love*.

"Come on," she said, gently pulling me back to lie on the bed. "I think you need some sleep."

I need you, I thought. And maybe, for once, I had exactly what I wanted.

Chapter Eighteen

Selena

When Max got up, he immediately looked out the front windows. "He's still here?"

Max didn't use a name, but I knew exactly who he was talking about.

"Yes," I replied, locking my tablet. "Tom stayed the night."

"Why?"

"Because he wanted to."

"I mean, why would you let him? Especially after what he said to you."

I slowly inhaled. After last night, I felt like I truly understood Tom. And I needed Max to know how much he'd changed. "Do you want to see what he said to me after he saw you?"

"I doubt it's going to change anything," he muttered. "But fine."

I still had the letter in my mess of a purse. I plucked it out and handed it to him.

Max read over the words. "This...this sounds like him. The him I know. That other letter doesn't."

"I know. Because it was a different version of him." I knelt to look at Max. "I wouldn't let him be this involved in your life if I didn't trust him. And I do."

"But he hurt you."

"Yes. And I moved past it. The more important thing is that he didn't hurt *you*."

"No! You're important too, Mom."

I closed my eyes, torn between feeling pride at Max's defensiveness over me and sad that Tom's past made Max so angry. "I am important. After I got this letter, I went to see him. This snobby lady at the front desk tried to turn me away, but the minute he saw me, he said I was important to him, and that he was always available for us. And he has been."

"Because he feels bad."

"He could have bought us an 'I'm sorry' card if he *only* felt bad. But coming over here to help you in person when you were struggling with your homework? Taking us out to dinner when you asked? That was him wanting to spend time with you."

Max looked at his feet and then at me. "Has he ever been like Jax was to you?"

"No. Never."

"That's good," he said, biting his lip. "I'm still mad, but I trust you. Sometimes, you're smart."

"Smart? I just made the biggest mistake by not telling you sooner."

"That's why I said *sometimes*."

"Fair enough. But I promise you'll know the truth from now on. Both Tom and I agreed on it."

"Okay." His eyes went to the kitchen. "Are you making breakfast?"

"I was about to," I said. "Waffles, for you."

"What's that smell?"

"Coffee, for Tom."

"But I thought you hated coffee."

"I do, but he likes it and I wanted to do something nice for him." And he would need it after the night he'd had.

Max nodded. "Can I flip the waffles when they're ready?"

"Of course. It's all yours."

For a while, we lost ourselves in making the batter and cooking the waffles. Eventually, Tom came into the living room. Meowcifer followed him.

For a man who had lost it only eight hours ago, he looked far more put together than I would have. He was in a shirt he'd brought from home and jeans that looked nicer than anything I owned. But when I looked into his eyes, I saw the exhaustion.

He had to be feeling terrible. I was no stranger to the emotional hangover.

"Coffee?" I offered.

"But you don't like coffee."

"It's fine," I said. "I had a French press deep in my cabinets anyway. Have some. We're making waffles."

He slowly walked into the kitchen, eyes falling on Max, who wouldn't meet his gaze. I opened my mouth to say something, *anything* to help them through this transition.

Nothing came to mind.

I busied myself by making Tom a plate. He took it with a tight smile and folded himself into the chair farthest away from us, as if he didn't want to bother Max with his mere presence.

Max watched it all. "Is he…mad at me for being mad?"

"No, it's not you."

"Then what happened?"

"His parents happened," I whispered. "They were not good people."

"What did they do?"

"Let's just say they were worse than Jax. Far worse. And he lived with them his whole life."

"Oh. So…should I forgive him?"

"Someone having a hard time doesn't excuse what they've done. It's just a reason. You can forgive him if you feel like you're ready."

"When did you forgive him?"

"When I knew he'd worked on changing himself," I replied. "He doesn't ever want to hurt you. What happened yesterday was not how we planned it to go."

"How were you going to tell me?"

"We planned to take you to breakfast and gently explain it. I wanted to tell you how unsure I was at first, but exactly why I trusted him."

"That sounds way better. I hate Jax."

"Me too," I replied. "Hopefully, we never have to deal with him again."

He nodded as he flipped the last waffle. Then he made himself a plate and sat across from Tom. I followed to make sure everything went well.

"I'm still mad at both of you," he said. "But eating a waffle in my room is a bad idea."

"I understand," Tom said. "Take as much time as you need."

"How was the food?" Max asked.

"Amazing as always," Tom replied.

Max looked down at his plate and all conversation died off.

Tom eventually stood, most of his food gone. "Let me put this away and start a load of dishes. I'll have to head out after. I have some paperwork I need to get done for tomorrow."

I followed him to the kitchen. "Are you okay?"

For a moment, I thought he would lie and say yes. But then he shook his head. "Not in the slightest."

"Me either."

Tom

"I'll be honest," Knox said, eying my truck with interest. "I'm surprised you're letting us do this."

"I have a vested interest in the safety of my occupants," I said. And doing something for the safety of Max, who could be riding in the truck at any time, was the only way I could force myself to come into work. I felt heavier, like I was buckling under the weight of everything that had happened Saturday. I'd slept as well as I always did when Selena was around that night, but staying in my own place last night had left me exhausted.

But I had work to do, especially when it came to making my truck safer for Max.

Months ago, before I knew about him, Knox had offered to install a new safety system for older cars. I'd turned him down, unwilling to let someone else work on something I cared about so much.

But after having Max in it, that had changed.

I didn't think Knox would even be present for this, but I should have known he had a hand in almost everything that PATH did. He was the head inventor, after all.

"So," Knox began, "how are things?"

"Fine," was the automatic answer.

"Cool. That's great. How is Max?" The name was like a punch to the gut. I could feel my teeth clench as I fought to keep it together in front of him. He, of course, caught on. "Not great, huh?"

"He just found out he's my son in a less-than-ideal way and he's not happy."

"I can tell it's taking a toll on you."

I could feel the pull of my emotions again. But I'd be damned if I was going to melt down in the PATH office.

"Can we talk about the truck?"

"Right," Knox said. "The truck. Let's go to the garage so you can meet the guy I have working on this."

I nodded, grateful that he didn't push.

An older man in an oil-stained flannel and jeans was waiting on us. He smiled when we walked in. "This must be Tom Murray."

I almost winced at my own last name. "Yes. It's nice to meet you."

"I'm Ronald."

I had to resist the urge to say my own name back, just like I'd done at Max's party. Maybe I shouldn't have left my apartment at all. I was obviously not in the right headspace.

"He's a little nervous about having his truck worked on," Knox added.

I was nervous about a lot of things, and the truck was definitely on that list.

"I can see why. She's a beauty." He held out his hand and gave a firm handshake. "It's a 1976 Chevy C10, right?"

"Yes, it is."

"Did all the work yourself?"

"How did you know?"

"You're worried, like anyone is when they're letting someone else work on their pride and joy. And Knox told me a little about it."

"Sorry," Knox said. "I wanted to be sure Ronald knew how much this means to you."

"It's fine," I replied. "Installing a safety system is a little out of my wheelhouse."

"We take videos of all the work we do, especially on these older ones. Let me show you exactly what I'll be doing."

He led me to the truck, showing where he'd be putting each accessory. None of it was invasive, and seeing the plan made me feel a little less anxious.

"I appreciate your thoroughness," I said. "I trust that you'll do a good job."

Ronald smiled. "Good! You're much easier than some of the other customers we've had. Knox, you had me worried for nothing."

"What?" Knox had been looking at his phone. "Oh, you're done explaining."

Ronald's eyebrows furrowed, as if Knox usually didn't get so lost in his device.

"I can let you get to work, Ronald," I said. "I'm sure you're both busy."

"No, not at all." Knox's voice was almost rushed. "You should stay and chill for a bit." He glanced at the door. "For at least two minutes."

"Why for two minutes?" I asked suspiciously.

"Just for funsies?"

"I think I'm good," I said. "Can you call me when it's done?"

"I will," Ronald said, and I turned to leave. As I walked down the hallway, I thought over my interaction and hoped I didn't give away just how terrible I was feeling.

That was when I heard heels clicking.

"Don't you fucking dare!" Ruth called, and I knew she was yelling at me. "You can't come to this office so upset that *Knox* notices and then try to leave!"

I didn't turn to her, content to look at one of the office doors. "Knox told you."

"Yes, he did. And we're going to talk about it this time. No more hiding."

I didn't know why she cared so much. I'd never been the brother she deserved.

But as that thought crossed my mind, I could hear Selena's words in the back of my mind.

"You were a victim too."

Is that why Ruth tried so hard? Had she already figured it out?

I was terrified of turning to her—terrified of letting anyone see me like this.

But it only took one choice to change. So I turned around.

The minute Ruth saw me, her eyes widened.

"Can we...go to your office?" I almost hated her shocked stare, but the silence was even worse.

"Yes," she said immediately. "Follow me."

Her office was, unsurprisingly, next to Knox's. When she walked through the hallway, everyone smiled at her, and then me. I tried to smile back; I really did. But nothing seemed to make my lips move upward.

She walked into her office and shut the door. "Is it Dad?" she asked. "Did he do something?"

"Nothing recently. I'm just coming to terms with...all the decades of the emotional abuse."

"Oh, this is one of *those* days."

"You talk like you've felt this way before."

"Because I have. My best friend at my old job finally got it out of me why I harbored such hatred for Knox—because of how they measured my success up against his—plus everything else they're responsible for. She let me know just how fucked up it all was. What we went through is not how functional, supportive families work. And the next few days after she told me that were...hard."

"When does it get better?" I asked, almost desperately. "I can't feel like this forever. I'm struggling not to drink and I need to be there for—" At the thought of Max, I closed my eyes, pain hitting me in waves.

"Do you want a hopeful answer or the truth?"

"The truth." Though I knew it wasn't good news.

"Okay. Then for me," she began, "I'm always a little sad about it. I moved on, surrounded myself with better people, and it helps. I feel like a human again, but I also carry around the scars. I'm still scared of storms. Sometimes, I get so angry with Knox when he figures something out before me. I try to be better, and each day I *get* a little better, but it's hard."

"I don't know how to stay sober then," I said. "I don't know if I can."

"What's helped you so far?"

"Max. Selena. But Max is angry with me right now, and I can see that me being around is making it worse."

"Why is he angry?"

"He knows who I am. And knows about the original letter I sent."

She sucked in a breath. "The really bad one?"

"Yeah. I don't expect him to want me around for a while."

"So, you're alone and feeling everything bad right now. Yeah, I can see why you'd be struggling."

"What do I *do*?" I asked.

"You find your support system," she said. "It can't just be Selena and Max.

Has there been anyone else that you've enjoyed being around?"

"Francine is sometimes pretty nice to be around. And I've been meaning to join a support group for drinking. Selena brought it up before all this happened."

"That's a great idea. Let's find you one now."

She gestured for me to sit and she turned her computer screen around so I could see. She searched through the myriad of options, looking at reviews for each one.

"What about that one?" I asked, pointing to the result in the middle of screen. She opened the website and we both read about their program. They also offered therapy for those who needed it.

"They have so many great reviews," Ruth said. "This might be the one."

"Sign me up," I replied. She didn't waste any time. In minutes, I was scheduled for one of their sessions in the next week. "Thank you."

"This is a good step." She smiled. "I'm even in a type of therapy for my fear of storms."

"Really?"

She nodded. "The noise-canceling headphones help, but I want to get past that too. It's been tough, but it's work that we all need to do. Support, from people we care about, goes so much further than punishment."

"I'm figuring that out."

"And speaking of support, you always have Knox and me. Plus his family, if you ever need more."

"I highly doubt they'd ever want to meet me."

"No, they've asked about you a lot. Lynn and Benji are amazing people. They're my family now too."

I could tell by the smile on her face that she must have really liked them. I wondered if they were the ones who had brought out this softer side of her.

Maybe that was what I needed too.

"I already said I'll try to come. Now I definitely will. You're right. Being alone isn't for me."

"That's the right spirit."

"I just can't promise I'll be fun. I feel so overwhelmed with everything. I can barely work, even."

"You're overwhelmed?" she asked. "I might be able to help with that."

She went to her desk and pulled out a set of headphones. "Knox gave me the final prototype of these, but the original ones are still working."

"What are they?" I asked.

"The noise-canceling headphones I mentioned. Well, kind of. They have the capability of blocking out certain sounds, but they can also block out everything. Maybe try listening to music and using this."

"I think I will. Thank you, Ruth. You're a far better sister than I deserve."

"Hey, don't say that. You deserve a lot."

"I keep getting told that."

"Maybe one day you'll believe it, then."

Chapter Nineteen

Selena

At three, I was getting ready to pick up Max after school when I got a call I wasn't prepared for.

"So," Hadley said, "I think I'm really in labor now."

"What?" I asked. "Really?"

"Yes. I should have told Allen to stay. This…" She paused for a moment. "This sucks."

"It's not fun," I said.

"Can you come over? I know you have to pick up Max but—"

"I'll ask Tom to do it. It's fine."

"Doesn't he work?"

"Um, yes, but—"

"I might have a few hours. The contractions are still five minutes apart."

"Five minutes?" I asked. "You need to go to the hospital when they're that close."

"Do I? I can wait."

"I'm calling Tom. You call and tell Allen."

I hung up before she could convince me out of it. I immediately called Tom.

"Hey," I said. "So Hadley is in labor. For real this time. And her husband is out of town. I need to go be with her. Can you get Max from school?"

"That's...Shit, I have a meeting at four thirty."

"Oh, okay. I'll call my mom then. She might ream me about the party but—"

"I'll bring Max to work."

"Um, can you do that?"

"I'm the CEO. They can't tell me no."

"Are you sure?"

"Yes. He can come here and stay in my office. No one will bother him."

"Okay. Thank you."

I hung up and got in my car, trying not to think of all the ways Max would hate this. I felt bad for sending Tom when things were still so rocky between them, but I refused to let my best friend go through labor alone.

"What do you mean you have a party tonight?" Hadley yelled into the phone when I walked in. "I'm in labor! I don't care if it takes days for me to have the baby—you have to be there!"

"I'm here," I said.

"Fuck you, Allen," she said as she hung up. She then clutched her stomach. "He's saying first-time moms take way too long in labor and that he wants to wrap up his trip first."

"*What?*"

"I can't...I don't even want to deal with this right now. Will Max be okay?"

"Tom has it covered. Let's just get you to the hospital."

"I'm going to kill him," she muttered as I helped her to the car. "I am going to ream his ass if this baby comes and he's not here."

"I will too," I said as we started on our way to the hospital.

I watched Max's shoulders sag when he saw I was the one picking him up.

"Sorry," I said as he climbed in. "You're stuck with me today."

"Where's Mom?"

"Hadley is in labor. She went to be with her."

"I thought she was in labor a few days ago."

"She faked it to give us time to talk," I replied. "But now we think it's real."

"Okay," he said, looking down at the dash. "Did you do something to the truck?"

"I got a safety system installed. I don't want anything to happen to you if we ever do get into a crash, so...I had someone work on it."

"That's really nice." He said it quietly, as if it almost pained him. My heart sank and I focused on the road.

"Not to add on to your bad mood, but I'm not done with work for the day, so we have to go back to my office too. But I only have one meeting. We'll leave as soon as I'm done."

"Fine," he said, looking out the window. I didn't know how I was supposed to focus on work with my angry son taking up all of my mind, but I had to.

We drove through the houses and into downtown. As the buildings grew denser, he turned to me. "Where do you work again?"

"Murray and Sons."

"Like the big trucks I see around? Wait, *Murray* like your last name?"

"Yes. It's my family's company."

"Is it fancy?"

"Unfortunately."

"B-but I'm not dressed to go to a fancy office."

"You're a kid. You don't have to be."

"But like...important people will be there."

"It's going to be okay. If any of them say anything about you, let me know."

It didn't seem to help, and Max chewed on his lip up until we pulled into the parking lot under the building.

"This is nice."

"Don't worry about it. It's all just for show."

"Still," he said as we walked toward the elevator. I pressed the button for the top floor, noticing how Max couldn't seem to sit still.

"It's going to be fine," I said, putting a hand on his shoulder. We walked past Julia, who did a double take. As we walked in, more people turned. I ground my teeth together, annoyed at the attention. I could feel Max's shoulder tense as we walked toward my office.

"Well, who is this little cutie?" Francine asked in a soft voice.

Max glanced up at me.

"This is Max. Max, this is Francine. She's one of my best employees."

"Um, how about *friend*?" Francine said. "I swear, he thinks everyone hates him. It's so nice to meet you, Max."

"You too," Max said. He wasn't as pressed to my side.

"You're in luck. Usually, Francine is mean to everyone."

"Oh, you little—" She rolled her eyes. "I'll get you back for that."

"I'm just kidding. Francine does a lot around here, and she's been helping while my assistant is out caring for her wife."

"I'm a permanent edition to this floor, though," Francine added. "So, anytime you come visit, you can hang out with me. Especially while your dad is in all those boring meetings."

"You know he's my dad?"

"I know everything, kid."

"She does," I added. "Let's get you settled. You can play a game if you want."

"I should do my homework."

"You're in a new place. I'd imagine it would be hard to focus."

"I have a deck of cards in my desk," Francine offered. "I can teach you poker."

"Why do you have a deck of cards in your desk?"

"You never know what can happen, Tom," she said. "Or when you'll need something to do. I'm just happy I'm not playing solitaire for once."

"Do you want to go hang out with Francine?" I asked.

"Yeah, I think so."

"I'll leave my door open until my meeting. Come in if you need me."

It was hard to leave him, even though I trusted Francine with anything. I kept an ear on things, just to make sure they were getting along, but all I heard were laughs.

Just like I had assumed, focusing on work was difficult, but I managed it. By the time the meeting started, I knew that Francine and Max shouldn't have any more problems.

I hopped on the call and the grim face of my lawyer appeared.

This would not be good news.

"I'm not going to waste your time, Tom." His voice was tight. "One of the witnesses no longer wants to testify."

"Why?"

"No idea. Todd was forbidden from interfering, but the woman in question is now ignoring our calls. I have my suspicions, but no proof."

"Son of a bitch," I muttered. "What about the other victim?"

"She is still willing to testify, as far as I know. But if the same thing happens to her, then we don't have a case."

"Can you warn her that the other dropped out? Maybe let her know about the suspicions?"

"I can let her know the other witness dropped out. That is the best I can do."

"Then do it."

"Todd is a very intimidating man," the lawyer said. "He can scare almost anyone."

"Not me."

"It's too bad you aren't the one with the case, then."

"Other than being a terrible father, I'm afraid he didn't do anything illegal."

"Then let's hope this last victim has the same drive as you."

I rubbed my eyes once I was off the call. If Dad somehow managed to win this, I would either be fired or would never know peace again. I almost preferred the first option. If I were fired, then maybe I could start over somewhere that wasn't tainted with my family name. But I wanted at least one thing with the Murray name on it to mean something *good*.

"How'd the meeting go?" a voice asked.

"Francine?" I asked, looking up. "Where's Max?"

"He's currently chowing down on some of the snacks I keep in my office. He's fine. But judging by the look on your face, you're not."

"No. One of the women dropped out."

"Why? They had a good case."

"My guess? She was either paid off or intimidated out of it."

"Maybe both," she said with a shrug. "So there's only one?"

"For now."

"There has to be a shitload of illegal stuff that man did. He didn't know how to keep his nose clean."

"Maybe, but I don't have anything else."

"Let me do some digging. Maybe I can find something."

"Digging into what?"

"Financials, mostly. If we find something there, then he could be removed."

I pressed my lips together. "He kept it all printed out in his office. It's under lock and key."

"Yeah, I know. Locks can be picked if someone wants it bad enough."

"If you help me with this, and we lose, he will fire you when he gets back."

She shrugged. "If I go down fighting on your side, then I'll have no regrets. Let's do it."

"Okay then. Get into that cabinet."

"I'll do it tomorrow. You're done for the day, right? I assume you want to spend the evening with your kid?"

"I do."

"He's a good one."

"That all goes to Selena."

"Yeah, maybe. But I see some of you in him."

I wanted it to be true more than anything.

Max was quiet after I retrieved him from Francine's office. He'd been snacking just as she said, but it was unusual for him not to be talking my ear off.

Until he found out who I was, at least.

"Are you okay?" I asked.

"It's been a long day," he muttered. "Can we go home now?"

"Of course."

Traffic made the drive longer, and I caught Max glaring at every loud car that drove past us. I wondered if my truck was making things worse too.

He went right to his room when we got to Selena's.

But her house wasn't quiet either. One of the neighbors had a lot of people over. Who had a party on a Monday night?

I was decent at ignoring loud sounds. I had to be in order to do my homework while Barry and Ruth were fighting. It seemed to have worn on Max, though. I sat on the couch, thinking over every interaction I had with him. Had I caused this somehow? What could I do for him to make it better?

Eventually, I went to check on him. I couldn't sit by and do nothing any longer.

"Max?" I said, voice raised so he could hear me through the door. "Are you okay?"

"Yes," he replied, but the response was tight in a way I hadn't heard before. "I'm fine."

"Are you sure?"

"Yes, Mr. Tom! I just want to be alone. Everything is so *loud*!"

I blinked at his tone. A part of me felt the need to bark back, but I knew that wouldn't help.

He'd said things were loud, and he wasn't wrong. Was he bothered by the noise? That was when the idea hit me.

I walked out to my truck, grabbing the headphones. When I walked upstairs, I followed Knox's directions and then knocked on Max's door.

"Mr. Tom, *please*—"

"I have something that might help."

There was silence, minus the booming music, then his door opened. He winced at the bright lights and I noticed the ones in his room were off. I fumbled for the nearby switch with my free hand, and when the hallway went dark, the door opened fully.

"What?" Max asked softly.

I put the headphones on him without another word. For a second, his face scrunched up, but then his eyes went wide.

"I can't hear anything," he said loudly.

I opened my mouth to speak, but then realized it would be futile. I gave him a thumbs-up, which he returned.

Max retreated into his room, and once I was alone, I felt unease settle in my chest. Was this normal? Did some kids react to noise and light like that?

I needed to bring it up with Selena once she was home, if she was even in the mood to talk after Hadley going into labor.

But for now, I couldn't walk away from his door. Not if something was wrong. So instead, I sat on the ground, listening in for any sign that he needed me.

Hours later, Max emerged from his room. I'd still been sitting in front of his door, turning over every interaction in my mind, trying to see if I'd somehow done something wrong. Meowcifer sat with me, and giving her attention kept me from being completely swallowed by my thoughts.

Max didn't expect to see me, judging by the way he jumped when his eyes met mine. The headphones were still on his head, but his hair was mussed, as if he had slept.

Slowly, he slid them off. "Mr. Tom?"

"Are you okay?" I asked in a quiet voice.

"Yes. These really helped. Thank you." He handed them back to me, but his eyes never once reached mine.

"What happened?"

"Nothing that is that big of a deal," he said. "It was just a long day."

"Did I do something? Other than…you know, having you come to the office. And…everything else."

He shook his head.

"But if I did, you could tell me."

"It was just too loud. Everything was."

"Okay."

"I know it's weird. Most kids my age don't have meltdowns like toddlers when things are loud."

"Max, it's fine."

"Is it? Right now, you're being nice because you know I'm upset, but people don't *get* people like me. Eventually, they'll all end up like Jax, who hated me every time I got like this."

"Jax was an asshole, last I checked."

"I don't think you're supposed to say that word in front of me."

"Sorry, it's just how I feel. Max, it's okay."

"I don't want to be a problem," he said, and he went to turn away.

"Max," I called, but he was already back in his room. I sighed and then pulled out my phone.

Tom: I won't bother you if you're upset. Let me know if you need food or anything.

Max: Okay.

He didn't text for the rest of the night. I ordered pizza, texting him once last time that he could get some if he wanted. He emerged thirty minutes later to grab a plate and two slices and went right back to his room.

I lay awake on the couch, trying to figure out what to do, but I came up with nothing.

Chapter Twenty

Selena

Ariana Anderson was born at midnight, only seven hours after Hadley called her husband.

Allen hadn't shown.

I'd experienced birth before, and while I may have forgotten some of the details, I remembered how empty it felt to be doing it without Tom.

And I felt it again as I watched Hadley go through the same thing.

This wasn't supposed to be how her life went. She was supposed to have her happy ending. Allen had even mentioned it in his vows.

But apparently, that had changed.

Hadley had alternated between looking at her daughter in awe and sobbing.

"How could he not be here? He knew I was in labor and yet still chose to be with his friends."

"I'm sorry, Hadley."

"God, and the nurses keep giving me *looks*. I'm mortified."

"If anything, it's on him and not you."

It didn't make her feel better. After hour three, she took off her wedding ring.

By hour four, her mother, Ada, finally arrived in the city. She'd been on a trip with Hadley's dad halfway across the country, but she'd dropped everything to get to the hospital as soon as possible.

And Allen still hadn't shown.

"He's not here?" Ada asked. "I thought he'd—"

I shook my head and she instantly went to Hadley's side.

"You should go and check on Max," Hadley said.

"No, I can't leave."

"You can. You helped me give birth, and I can't thank you enough, but I can't watch you run yourself into the ground for me. Get some sleep. Be sure Max is okay."

"And I'm here," Ada added. "We'll all get through this together."

It took more convincing, but eventually, my own tiredness won out. We'd taken my car here, and I was grateful to get home in it.

The engine sputtered to life and I knew it probably needed something on it fixed, but that was an issue for another day.

I got home at four in the morning. Tom was at the table, laptop in front of him.

"I'm back."

"How's Hadley?" he asked.

"She's...sad. Her husband didn't show up for the birth."

"Why wouldn't he? It's his child."

"He said that labor usually takes too long and he didn't want to miss out on his time with his friends."

"That is the worst excuse I've ever heard."

"I agree, and so does she. There was a new life brought into this world and it just felt *sad*." I sighed. "I've already been through a birth like that. I never wanted it for her."

"With Max?" he asked.

The air felt cold. I turned to him. "Yes, but you were a different person. I didn't say that to make you feel—God, I'm sorry."

"I'm the one who's sorry. I should have been there. I would have *loved* to have been there."

And I didn't doubt it. I only wished his father hadn't squashed this version out of him all those years ago.

"He was a cute baby. Sensitive, but cute. He still is, in some ways."

"Did it wind up having to do anything with sound?"

"Yes, why do you ask?"

Tom closed his laptop, rubbing his eyes. "After I got done with work and brought him home, he was quiet. I thought it was because of me, but then the neighbors were having a party and he was...not himself."

I sucked in a breath. It had been a long time since Max had gotten overwhelmed like that. I almost had myself fooled into thinking it could never happen again. "Did he say anything to you?"

"He said I didn't do anything wrong, but I feel like I did. Maybe I shouldn't have taken him into the office, or—"

"Tom, you didn't do anything wrong." I sat at the table across from him. "Max has always had issues with sounds, but it got better over the years. It was way worse when he was a toddler. He started talking late. He wouldn't eat anything other than mac and cheese. Eventually, his pediatrician noticed it and sent me to get him evaluated for autism."

His brows knitted. "Autism?"

"It's a developmental disability. But even that doesn't feel like the right word for it. He just works a little differently than others. When he gets incredibly overwhelmed and tries to push past it, he gets angry. It hasn't happened in years because we did a lot of therapies and I'm careful about getting him home if he shows signs of being overwhelmed, but if someone was having a *party*..."

"Then he truly couldn't relax," Tom finished.

"Exactly," I said. "I sometimes hate this neighborhood. The people are nice and it's somewhat safe but it can be loud. I used to cover Max's ears with a blanket when they would do that. I'll talk to him when he wakes up. I'm sure he's still in a bad mood."

"So, if I were able to make it quiet, it would have helped?"

"Yes, but my neighbors do not stop a party for anything."

"I don't mean it in that way. My sister gave me something when I saw her earlier today. They're headphones that block everything out."

"I've heard of those. They're just expensive."

"These are a prototype that her boyfriend is working on. They're really meant to block out only certain sounds, but it has a function to block out everything. It seemed to help."

"Now, that is new. Wait, this is the sister with the famous boyfriend?"

"It is. I don't know if you've heard of Knox Price. He owns PATH."

"PATH...you mean the self-driving technology PATH?"

"That's the one."

That was a *big* name. I knew he had to have powerful connections, but not that powerful. "Um well, thank you. She just gave them to you?"

"She thought it might help, and it did."

"That was exactly what he needed. You handled it perfectly."

He nodded, but his eyes didn't meet mine. "I still wonder if maybe I've done something wrong before now. Something that I don't know about."

"No, you didn't. I would have told you if you did."

"I know, I just...hate the way he's looking at me. Like I could hurt him with one word."

"We all can, but we do our best. You can't agonize over everything. You'll exhaust yourself."

"I want to be a good dad. And after everything I've seen, I don't know if I know how."

I put my hand on his shoulder. "Be yourself. It's worked out so far."

"That's the problem. Being myself hasn't exactly worked out for me."

"I think it will with us."

He nodded, eyes on the floor. "It's late."

"Technically early, but we'll call it both."

"We should sleep."

The words hung heavy in the air with the silent question that followed.

"You're always welcome here," I offered.

"I just don't know if Max will want to see me. But I need sleep. I have a busy day."

"Then stay. We'll deal with the morning when it comes."

Tom

Max hadn't come out of his room by the time I was awake again. I had to leave for an early meeting, but Selena promised me she would talk to him about the day before.

I'd felt distracted all day. Even in my meeting, I constantly zoned out of the conversation.

It didn't help that it was all the same things I'd heard in dozens of other meetings.

"Tom, what do you think?"

I looked up. Dale was talking about revenue again, as if our announcement about the PATH partnership hadn't raised enough.

Despite some of the truckers being worried about their job security, the only thing that soothed their ruffled feathers was our promise not to dock their pay. If we hadn't kept that detail, I wondered if we would have had a mass exodus of our employees.

But Dale didn't see it that way.

"I think we need to put our focus onto the PATH partnership," I said, bringing my focus back to work. "We don't need to worry about any more revenue building until this is done."

"That isn't how this company works."

"It is now. We didn't even need to have this meeting. It's eight a.m., guys. Next time, set up one for later and spend the morning with your families." I stood, walking out of the meeting room without another word. I heard Dale's footsteps behind me.

"You need to be more business focused."

"I am business focused, but I'm only working on one thing at a time."

"And thinking about that boy you brought in?"

I stopped, turning to him with a hard glare on my face. "I'm not talking about this with you."

"It just feels like your focus isn't here where it should be. Todd wouldn't make that mistake."

I was well aware of that fact. "Todd isn't your boss right now. I am, and I firmly request that you get out of my business and focus on your job."

"Does Todd know that he's a grandfather?"

"Do you know how to listen?"

"It's a shame to see the family business not be so family oriented anymore. Your father made you and you threw him away like he was nothing. I hope the same doesn't happen to you someday."

I stared at him. There had to be a reason he was saying this now.

And it was possibly because of the victim who had withdrawn her case.

"Dale, don't you have something better to do than to make enemies with the CEO?" Francine's voice was hard as she approached us.

"Acting CEO," he corrected.

"Bold move. When he's the actual CEO, you might regret saying that. Now buzz off. I need to talk to the boss."

I glared at him as he walked away. Once he was gone, I took a deep breath to steady and calm myself. Then I turned my attention to Francine. "Was that an excuse to get Dale to leave or do you really need to talk to me?"

"Let's go to your office. This needs to stay private."

We walked together, but my heart raced. Had she found anything to keep Dad out of power?

"Don't get excited," she said as soon as the door was shut. "I've been through five years and haven't found anything too suspicious. Nothing illegal anyway. Some transfers have me raising my eyebrows, but he has notes that *say* it's legal. But I did find a laptop." She pulled it out. It was an older model and I'd seen it before.

"At least we know he complied with the order to leave it here," I said. "Though it was supposed to be left with security."

"What are the chances he has something on here?"

"High."

"Think you can crack the password?"

"I can try." I gestured for her to hand me the laptop and I opened it.

"A lot of people use their kid's birthdays as passwords."

"Not him."

"What about his wife?"

"Doubtful." I closed my eyes, trying to remember any hint of what it could be. I'd seen him log into this laptop many times when he wanted to talk business during the family dinners. It was a short password, only eight characters.

Francine could be right that it was a birthday. *His* birthday.

I typed it in. It unlocked instantly. I shouldn't have been surprised. After all, he was the only person who was perfect in his own eyes.

I handed it back to Francine. "Let me know if you find anything."

"Oh, I'll find something. I have a good feeling about this."

She walked out of the office and I focused on work. It was near five when I got a text from Selena.

Selena: Sooooo, you can't come over tonight.

Selena: I mean, you can. But my mom and Luna are here. And I can tell this is an ambush.

Tom: Are you okay?

Selena: I can handle it. I think. I'll let you know when they leave.

Damn. My support group wasn't until tomorrow, leaving me with no plans, and the last thing I wanted to do was go home.

But maybe I could make something happen.

Tom: Ruth, are you busy tonight?

Ruth: Family dinner was moved to tonight, so yes. But you're invited, as always, if you want to come hang out with me.

Tom: I think I'll take you up on that.

Chapter Twenty-One

Selena

As Mom and Luna glared at me from the couch, I also texted Max.

Selena: You're lucky you asked to hang out with Tess. Your abuela and tia are here to talk about Tom.

Max: Yikes. Good luck?

"You can't stay on your phone forever," Mom said. "You have to face this eventually."

"Maybe if I had a warning, I would be a little more ready to talk."

"No warnings," Luna cut in. "You're the queen of avoiding things you don't want to talk about."

They weren't wrong about that, but after seeing how my choice affected Max, I didn't know if I wanted to avoid anything anymore.

I took a deep breath before saying anything else. "Okay, what do you want to know?"

"Have you lost your mind?" Mom began.

Instantly, I felt like a little kid again. Mom came on *hard* whenever she didn't agree with one of our choices. "Wha—how is that your first question?"

"It's a valid one."

"Actually, it's not a valid one. If you want answers, then you need to ask real questions. I understand you're mad, but if this isn't going to be a productive conversation, then you can leave and we can deal with it later."

My pulse pounded in my ears as I said the words, but I wasn't going to be reamed in my own home. Sticking up for myself was hard, but I managed to stand my ground.

I may not have been looking Mom in the *eye*, but her eyebrows were easy enough to look at.

"So," I said, shifting uncomfortably at the attention, "what's the real first question?"

"Did you always know?" Luna asked.

"Yes."

"Then why didn't you tell us when you first got pregnant?"

"Because Tom's family is powerful. Mom, you were on a warpath. We couldn't afford the lawyer bills if we did fight it."

"And you were okay with just letting him leave?"

"I had to be. He sent me enough money to pay off the medical bills and put the down payment on this house."

"He sent you money?" Mom asked. "I always wondered where that came from. You said the state paid for it."

"Well, there *is* a program for that."

"So you lied rather than ask me to calm down?"

"When has anyone asking you to calm down worked?"

"She has a point," Luna added. At Mom's withering stare, she shrugged.

"I don't understand why you would let him back into your life after this." Mom directed her attention at me again.

My instinct was to lie, but I pushed past it. "Because he genuinely sounded like he was sorry."

"He *better* be sorry."

"He also sent a letter saying what he'd done was inexcusable, and he, um...sent me his credit card."

"What?" Luna asked. "A credit card? What's the limit?"

"Don't take his guilt money," Mom hissed.

"I went to his office to give it back."

"Why would you do that?" Luna moaned.

"It's what she should have done," Mom said.

I squeezed my eyes shut, overwhelmed by their differing opinions and priorities.

"Don't worry, Luna. He didn't let me give it back. Instead, he..." My face heated when I thought about it. "He got down on his knees and apologized to me."

For once, they didn't have anything to say.

But eventually, Luna caught up. "Was it hot, at least?"

"Luna Maria!" Mom hissed.

"It's a valid question."

"We're not like..." I trailed off, thinking of this morning. "It wasn't like *that*."

"That kind of explains the restaurant," Luna said. "It doesn't explain how he looks at you."

"Like he's full of guilt?" Mom added.

"Like she's the only woman in the world. Mom, I know you saw it too at Max's birthday party."

"Maybe I did, but I'm not happy about it."

"Guys, that's not how he looks at me."

Luna gave me a flat look. "Then you're blind."

"It's not! We're co-parents. And maybe I draw him a lot and *maybe* we sometimes sleep in the same bed, but it's as co-parents."

"Oh, no. You're infatuated." Mom shook her head. "If you get pregnant again..."

"It's not like that!"

"If it were anyone else," Luna started, "I'd say bang it out, but you already did that and had Max."

"I am well aware of that, thank you, Luna. You know what question you should be asking? How does he treat *Max*? Not me, him."

"I mean, we all saw how he acted at the party. He cares about him."

"At least there's that," Mom muttered. "But it was foolish of you to even let him in. And it's foolish of you to continue!"

"Okay," I said.

"Okay?" Mom pressed.

"I hear you. I know what you think, but...I'm going to do it anyway."

Luna's jaw dropped. Mom narrowed her eyes.

It was terrifying standing up for myself. Of course I was worried I was making a mistake. I always was. But in the thick of that worry, I had hurt Max. And I refused to do that anymore.

"Fine," Mom said. "But I don't want to hear about it when he breaks your heart."

She turned and walked away, a tactic she usually used on Luna to try and get her to change her mind.

I didn't fall for it, no matter how much I wanted to. Luna gave me one more glance before she followed Mom. I stood in the living room, heart racing for a good ten minutes.

But I was pulled out of it by a knock on the front door.

I opened it, seeing someone from the post office waiting for me. He shoved a piece of paper in my hands to sign before driving off, muttering something about how he was running behind for the day.

All I was left with was a massive packet from my mortgage company marked urgent. I tore into it immediately. That should have been the usual monthly payment, unless they were transferring my mortgage *again*, in which case, it was going to be a nightmare to figure out how to make a new online account to make payments.

But what I saw was nothing like that.

It was the deed to my house, along with the notification that my mortgage was gone.

Paid off.

Balance zero.

I dropped the deed. I had to be dreaming. There was no way I wasn't. There was no way this was *real*.

With shaky hands, I picked it back up. It was, in fact, real.

I ran to my tablet and logged into my account. The balance was zero. There was no note, no reason—it was gone.

A call to the mortgage loan servicer was only slightly more helpful. I'd been the recipient of a donation, one that paid off multiple people's homes. I was lucky. That was all there was to it.

But how did I get lucky *twice*? What person could have paid off both my mortgage *and* my student loans?

And that was when it hit me. I knew *one* person who could easily do it, and he'd been offering help from day one.

Tom

When I parked my truck, I had to take a moment to breathe through my nerves before I walked into the house. My radio, which was usually off, played a soft tune that gave me just enough to focus on to help calm me down.

When I looked up, Ruth was waiting for me on the porch. "Have things gotten better?" she asked as I climbed out of the truck.

"Kind of. Max had a bad night, maybe because of me."

"I doubt it was you," she said. "Was anything else going on?"

"He got overwhelmed. I asked Selena about it and she told me he has autism."

She raised her eyebrows. "Oh. That is one subject I don't know anything about."

"Neither do I."

"I know someone who might. And she and her husband just pulled into the driveway."

I turned and saw a modest, older Toyota. A woman who was the spitting image of Knox got out of the car.

"Hello!" she called, looking as if she was on top of the world. "You got Tom to come!"

"I did!" Ruth walked over to the woman.

And then she hugged her.

I'd hardly ever seen my sister touch anyone, but the way she embraced the other woman was familiar, as if they'd known each other all their lives.

She seemed so happy these days. I wanted to feel what she did.

Then the woman pulled me into a tight hug in the same way she had Ruth. For a second, I didn't know what to do, but I let go of my fear and hugged her back.

"Sorry," she said, pulling away. "I'm Lynn. I just have heard so much about you that I feel like I know you."

"You know about me and you still hugged me?"

"Oh, I've heard nothing that was that bad," she said. "Wow, you look so much like your sister. Your family's genes must run strong."

"With the exception of our younger brother," I said.

"We'll have to get him here next so I can see for myself," Lynn replied.

"Is it my turn to introduce myself?" a male voice asked. He was Lynn's age and wore a cable-knit sweater.

"Of course," Lynn said.

"I'm Benji, Knox's dad."

"Nice to meet you, sir." I held out my hand, desperately hoping I wouldn't offend him tonight. I had never been good with fathers.

"Sir?" he asked. "While I'm honored by your respectfulness, I must say I'm *sir*-prised you didn't just call me Benji."

I opened my mouth to apologize, but then the joke registered.

Behind me, Ruth snickered. "Was that in your pun book?"

Benji shook his head. "Made that one up on my own."

"There is a joke *like* that in his pun book," Lynn said.

"What does a knight do when he's done fighting?" Benji asked me.

"I'm not sure."

"He *sir*-renders."

Ruth cackled and I couldn't help the smile that graced my face. I could see Max loving these kinds of jokes.

"Benji is amazing," Ruth said. "Nothing like Dad." The last part was said under her breath, but it helped to hear.

Ruth led us inside the house where I saw plants everywhere. Knox was setting a farmhouse table, smiling warmly when he saw his family.

"Hey, guys," he said. "And Tom, glad you could make it. How's the truck running?"

"Everything is fine."

"Good, I—"

"No more work talk," Ruth scolded. "If you've got questions on how it works, ask him tomorrow."

"Fine," Knox said, sighing, but he looked the furthest thing from exasperated. Lynn took Ruth into the kitchen and I listened as Benji and Knox talked about life.

For a moment, I felt out of place and wanted what usually helped me when I felt this way. I could probably think of something to say with the buzz of alcohol in my system.

"What are you doing over there?" Benji asked. "Come and hang out!"

I blinked, unsure if he was talking to me.

"You can join us," Knox said. "I was only telling him about my plants."

"I don't want to intrude."

"We invited you. You're not intruding."

"You can help me keep count of how many he got this week," Benji added.

"There were only four," Knox said before he turned to me. "I like taking care of them."

"We all have our things. I like puns. You like plants. Ruth likes smashing heads and cooking."

"That she does," I said.

"What about you?" Benji asked.

"I like cars and...when I was younger I liked music. And I think I also like cats."

"Cats?" Knox said. "Do you have one? Or five?"

"No, but Selena and Max have one. A black cat named Meowcifer."

There was silence.

Then Benji cackled. "Lynn! You've got to hear this cat's name. It's the greatest thing I've heard all day."

I let out an uneasy breath.

"You okay?" Knox asked.

"Yeah, sometimes I just wonder if I've somehow said something wrong."

"You did good," he said, clapping my shoulder. "They like you." Knox offered me a seat at the table, which I took. "So, don't tell Ruth, but I found something at the store." Knox's voice was low.

"What?" Benji leaned in.

He pulled out a box.

"It's called Uno Show 'Em No Mercy."

On the box, there were various cards, all aimed at making UNO even more ruthless than usual.

"Do you *want* her to kill us both?" I asked him suspiciously.

"I love seeing Ruth mad," Knox said. "Especially when it's just for fun like this is."

"Okay, then she'll kill *me*."

"You could just watch."

I considered it, but I knew I wouldn't be okay with missing out. "But that's no fun."

"Lynn and I will be sure no one gets too mad," Benji said, sitting alongside us. "Don't worry. We've played Monopoly, which is known to ruin relationships just as much as UNO."

"How did it go?" I asked.

"Lynn beat us all. She must have been reading up on strategy. Knox and Ruth landed on Boardwalk and it bankrupted them."

"It was pretty epic," Knox added.

"Then let's do it."

Ruth came out from the kitchen to say dinner was done. After we all served our food, Knox showed her the new game we were going to play.

"Oh, yes," she said, laughing. "I'm going to kick your ass."

"Or maybe I will," Lynn said. "That's now an option."

"Tom, are you playing?" Ruth asked.

"I was thinking about it, but if it's too competitive then..."

"No," she said. "I want you to join. It'll be fun to just play a game together. It's not like we're competing to see who gets the highest grades in math which will win our parents' approval."

"Yeah, that's true."

"As the adult-iest adults here," Benji said, "we approve of you *all*."

Ruth smiled over at Benji. "Thank you."

Her eyes slid to me, as if checking to see if I was okay. Benji's kind words would have taken me out emotionally if Selena hadn't gotten to it first.

At the thought of her, I found myself wishing she and Max were here.

After we finished dinner, Knox shuffled the cards and dealt us our hands. I started out with so many action cards, I wasn't sure how I was going to be able to play nice for a bit.

But then Lynn hit me with a draw four.

So I passed it on to Ruth, who gave it to Knox.

"Damn it," he said, drawing a pile of cards.

"I don't know how any of us are going to win," Benji said, hitting Lynn with a draw ten card, which she passed on to me.

"Did you even shuffle this right?" Ruth said moments later as she was drawing to get cards to use. "All I have are green!"

"Maybe you just have bad luck," Knox teased.

I laughed when she glared at him.

We went around the table repeatedly, always hitting each other with something, but never truly getting mad about it. It became fun after I realized there were no stakes.

After Lynn won the first game, I found myself finally able to relax. Then when she won two more games, I could barely remember I even had a problem at all.

I found myself not even playing to win, but just to have fun.

By the time the games were over, I'd laughed at Ruth's incredulous expression when she continually lost to Lynn, and Knox's feigned annoyance when Ruth kept making him draw cards.

"Who did you say could maybe help me with Max?" I asked Ruth after everyone at the table had dispersed.

"Oh. It was Lynn. She works with a lot of people in her job. Come on." She stood and gestured for me to follow her into the kitchen.

Lynn was washing dishes when we walked in.

"Can we ask you something?" Ruth said.

"Of course," she said, putting down the dishes and giving us her full attention. "What's going on?"

Ruth looked to me and I took in an unsteady breath. "Do you know anything about autism?"

"I do," she said. "A few of my clients or their kids have it. Why do you ask?"

"Max has it."

"Your son, right?" At my nod, she continued. "Well, it depends on how his manifests."

"Yesterday, he was really affected by sounds. He snapped at me, actually."

"What did you do?"

"Ruth gave me a pair of Knox's noise-canceling headphones," I said. "I guess they can also block out all sounds. I gave them to Max."

"That was *exactly* what you should have done," Lynn said. "You didn't snap back and you found the root cause and solved it."

"Is there anything else I should know? Anything I should avoid?"

"It all depends on him. As long as you continue to treat it as you just did, you're going to do a fine job. People with autism are human. We don't have to walk on eggshells or treat them any differently as long as we listen and not make light of it when they see something differently."

"That makes sense. I'm just terrified I'm going to screw this up. It's not like Ruth or I had a good example of parenting growing up."

"That's such a shame. You and Ruth are very good people."

She was so effortlessly kind even though she barely knew me.

"T-thank you," I said, clearing my throat.

"How about this? I can give you mine and Benji's number and if you ever have parenting questions, you can ask us."

"I—that would be great."

As she wrote down her number, I saw Ruth give me a thumbs-up from across the room.

I could see why she liked this family so much. My phone dinged as I got in the truck.

I had one ominous text.

Selena: Come over. Now.

I rushed to her house, mind awash with all the things that could have happened that day. Had her mom and sister upset her? Was she okay? Was Max okay? Had Jax come back?

What I didn't expect was to see her sitting on the couch with two letters in front of her. A quick glance showed me the name of the loan servicers Francine had helped me find.

My mind calmed. This, I could deal with—her or Max being hurt, I couldn't.

"Did you do this?" she asked, slowly looking up at me. "Are you why my house and student loans are paid off?"

There was no point in lying. "Yes."

She nodded, lips pursing as she accepted the information. "Why?"

"Because it's what you deserve."

"What I deserve? Or was it pity?"

"Why would I pity you?"

"Because I'm broke and live in this tiny house? Because I'm not like you?"

"That wasn't it."

"Then tell me why."

"You said you didn't want to depend on me and that you wanted to live off your art. That's fair, so I found a way that didn't involve you depending on me. And then I helped other people because I'm sure they deserve it too."

She blinked. "You just wiped away people's debts just because you could?"

"Yes."

"Why?"

"Most of my wealth comes from my family taking advantage of others. I didn't want that to continue with me."

Her lips pressed together. "Wow."

"Are you angry?"

"I'm not angry. I just...I don't know *what* to feel. These were my debts. *I* should have paid them off. But I could never seem to get ahead on them and it made me take a gig that caused problems with my family. Now, I can just take jobs that really inspire me. I know I should thank you, but this all seems too good to be true. Are you going to hold this over my head? Or ask me for anything in return?"

"Of course not. This is a gift because I wanted you to be free of something that burdened you. I would never ask you to repay that."

She let out a disbelieving laugh. "That's *exactly* what a hero would say in a romance book."

"I'm no one's hero."

"I'm starting to think you might be mine." The words lingered in the space between us and my heart raced at the implication. "You came into my life and did all of this for me, and I haven't done anything to deserve it."

"You spent the last decade raising our child on your own. That is more than enough."

She blinked and then shook her head. "You can't be real."

"I don't think I know what that means."

She stood, walking over to where I was. "I dreamed about you, you know. Before you came back."

"You did?"

Her eyes were wet. "Most days, it was me dealing with my anger. Maybe I'd be able to yell at you or something. But other times, they were me imagining that you came back to me. And then you did."

"I hope I'm at least half the man I was in those dreams."

"You, the real you, is better than I could have ever dreamed up."

"I...I don't—"

Whatever stuttered thanks I could manage was swallowed when she hugged me. I blinked, trying to accept that I wasn't a disappointment this time.

I'd gotten something *right*.

"Thank you," she said, her words muffled into my shirt. "Thank you for all of this."

"I'd do it any time."

I tightened my arms around her, additional words failing me.

"Remember how you said I was your main character?" she asked as she pulled away.

"Yes."

"I think you're mine too." Her hand drifted to my hair. "If you're okay with that."

"I am more than okay with that."

Selena's eyes moved to my lips. "Are you also okay with picking up where we left off? Before Hadley told us Jax was here?"

"When we were...?"

She nodded, a small, almost nervous movement.

"Yes," I breathed out. "I'd love to finish what we started."

Her hand tugged my face down, pressing my lips to hers. I thought I was dreaming the moment we touched, but I was never creative enough to imagine how perfect it would actually feel.

That day in my dorm was burned into my memory. But as I felt her lips against mine again, I knew this would linger for far longer. I didn't have just one day with her worming her way into my heart. I had months of her kindness, her beauty, and her forgiveness.

I brought her impossibly closer, snaking my hand around her waist to press her body into mine. Her tongue swiped across my lower lip and I opened myself to her. The kiss turned frenzied after that, and I felt her pulling me toward her bedroom.

How far was she wanting us to go? I'd happily lose myself in her, but something about this, especially considering what she'd just found out, felt wrong.

"Wait," I said. My body didn't want to stop. It was humming with electricity, begging me not to hold off any longer.

"What? Did I do something wrong?"

"No, it was...it was great. But I can't sleep with you right now."

"Why not?" Her lips turned downward.

"I want to, more than anything, but I'm worried that you feel like you have to because I paid off your debts."

"No, I've wanted this for weeks. I really like you."

"But why now?"

"Max isn't home and you just did something so kind for me..." She trailed off. "Okay, I see what you're saying now. But what you did will always be there. I'm grateful, of course, but I also want you."

"I want you, more than anything. But only for the right reasons."

"Then what do we do?"

"Give it a week," I said. "Let's give you time to accept what I've done, and if you still want this, then I'd be more than happy to pick up where we left off."

"A week. Like a week where I don't see you?"

"No, a week to think about sex. If you need space, I'll give it to you but—"

"I need sleep, and I only seem to do that when you're around."

I looked into her eyes, knowing I couldn't stay away either.

"Then I'll be here, just like always. But for sex, I want to wait."

"Okay," she said, slowly stepping away from me. "I'd be happy to wait, because I know my mind won't change."

I nodded, internally battling with the desire to throw away everything I'd just committed to—something I knew she'd be okay with if I had.

Selena's eyes left me and she checked her watch. "It's getting late anyway, and if we're waiting, then someone needs to go get Max. He's at Tess's house. And dinner needs to be made."

"I'll get Max if you cook dinner."

"I think I'll take you up on that," she said.

Max came out of his friend's house shortly after I'd pulled into the driveway. I attempted to make some small talk with Tess's mother, but it seemed she was a little wary of the man who'd come back into Max's life.

And I didn't blame her.

Max didn't even look at me. He silently put his backpack in the truck and climbed in. I gave Tess's mom an awkward goodbye and got in too.

I spoke first, desperate to fill the emptiness.

"Is math going okay?"

"Tess helped me with it."

"Oh, okay. That's good." I tried to keep the disappointment out of my voice, but I failed.

Max glanced over at me for only a second. Then he turned to me, sighing. "He tried to, at least. But he kind of just repeated what Mrs. Mulligan said."

"Do you need help?"

"Yeah, probably. If you're okay with that."

"Of course I'm okay with that."

Max turned his attention back to the view out the windshield. I focused on driving and the quiet radio in the background. I knew I needed to be patient and give him time, but I miss how we used to be—before he knew about my screwups.

But I knew this was going to happen, and I was the one who'd turned Selena away. I deserved this.

"So..." Max said, his eyes still looking ahead. "Can I ask you something?"

"Yes."

"And I want a real answer."

"Okay."

"When we first met, you were *so* nice to me. Was that because you had to be because I was your son?"

"What do you mean by that?"

"I mean, you kind of have to like me, sort of like Mom does. And I guess that's fine, but I thought you liked me for *me*. Not because you had to."

"Max, of course I like you."

"But you *can't* hate me or anything."

"I can't?"

"Yeah. I'm related to you, so you *had* to deal with the Lila stuff. You wanted me to like you so you probably pretended I wasn't a total loser with it."

"I didn't pretend."

"You had to. I'm your son."

"Max, I *do* like music. Listening to that Lila Wilde album made it where I could use the radio in the truck again. I wanted to connect with you by taking interest in what you liked."

"But you had to. If I was some random kid, if you were dating Mom or something, then you wouldn't have."

I stared at the road, going over his words. I could see it all from my perspective, where I'd met him after so long and wanted to connect. But what if it had been different? What if I had been there for Selena and not him?

"I would have," I started. "I would have liked you either way."

"Are you lying?"

"No," I said. "I'm not. I think you're underestimating how amazing you really are. Let's say I was just around for your mom, do you think I wouldn't notice just how much you do for her? You're selfless in a way that I've never seen from someone of your age. When you found out, you were mad on your *mom's* behalf. You get that from her, and I'd admire it whether I was related to you or not."

"R-really?"

"Yes. And you're funny and so smart in school. A blind man could see it."

I glanced over and he was looking at his hands. "Thank you for saying all of that, but...do you really like what I like? Or do you just *have* to?"

"I do like Lila Wilde and I do enjoy the food you've had me try. I've never lied about any of that. It's not a requirement for me to like what you like just because I'm your dad."

"It kind of is, though."

"No, it's not."

"How do you know?"

"Because my dad doesn't," I admitted. "He doesn't like anything about me. It's why I didn't listen to music, or really taste anything I ate. He wanted me to be a certain way."

"Why?"

"I don't know. Me and my siblings were just something for him to use. Anything we loved was a waste of time. And I never want that for you. I love you for *you*, Max. Even if you weren't my son. You're a great kid, and I'm lucky to even be around you."

The cab was silent other than the rumbling of the old engine.

Did I take it too far? Did I upset him?

Finally, Max spoke. "Y-you said love."

"I did," I said. "And I do. I'm lucky to be able to know you."

"I think...I think I'm tired of being mad," he said. "But I don't want to be lied to again."

"Never."

"Okay," he said. "Now, can we please change this radio station? What is this—emo country music?"

Chapter Twenty-Two

"Good morning," Tom's voice said from behind me.

I'd been slowly waking up from my dreamless sleep. My small bedroom had become idyllic in the last six days, and I'd slept well each night.

"Mm, morning," I muttered. He was holding me against his hard body.

There was no semblance of space between us. My legs were plastered against his, my back meeting his warm chest. I was surrounded by his calming scent.

I felt at home.

I'd never thought home could be a person. It seemed impossible when people either loved those around me or left when I became boring to them. I knew without a shadow of a doubt that it would break me if Tom ever left, and that was a terrifying attachment to have.

"One more day," I said. I'd taken to counting down the days until his embargo on sex was lifted.

"One more day," he agreed, his lips ghosting on my cheek. I leaned into it and his mouth moved down to my neck. My eyes fluttered closed, thighs clenching around nothing.

"You're killing me."

I felt him smile against my skin. "Do you want me to stop?"

"No," I said. "But I can't take this waiting. Six days I've woken up with you so close to me. I want more."

"One more night," he whispered. "Just to be sure."

"Can't we just say fuck the rule? I've processed you paying off my bills. It was great. Now can we—"

"One." A kiss on my cheek. "More." My jaw. "Day." He finally landed behind my earlobe, his voice barely above a whisper. My skin erupted in goosebumps.

"Tom," I groaned. "You're torturing me."

"Maybe I'm torturing us both. Do you know how hard it is to wake up next to a woman like you and not have my hands all over her?"

"Your hands are on me right now."

"Not where I want them." His words were spoken into my neck, his breath ghosting over the sensitive skin. His hips rolled forward, his hardness pushing against me.

God, I wanted that.

"Can't you break your rule just a little? Please?"

"You are a bad influence."

"I just...you were so good that day in the dorm. The best I've ever had."

"Really?"

"Y-yes. I know I wasn't for you, but you were for me."

He gently rolled me over, his eyes dark. "Selena, let's get one thing straight. Of all the women I spent nights with, you were the *only* one I was with as *me*. And I never forgot a second of it."

"You didn't?"

"No. You weren't just the best I ever had. You were *everything*. Which is why I want this to be for the right reasons."

"Tom," I started. "I don't want you because you paid off my debts. I want you because you're *kind* and patient and so many other things I can't name. You were amazing back then, too, especially in bed." I could feel my cheeks heat as I said it. "But now that I know you, I know I want more."

"Are you sure?"

"I'm so sure," I whispered.

"Then I'll break the rules a *little*, just for you."

Anticipation curled up my spine.

"What kind of rule breaking?"

"One where I make you feel as perfect as you deserve. Maybe this time with my fingers. And other times, with different parts of me."

My already warm body grew hotter. "Please. I'd love that."

The smell of him made all of it more intense. I wanted him to fill every part of me. Tom's hand trailed down, tracing at my sides and my hips, until it found my thighs. Each touch left sparks in its wake. They fizzled across my skin, making me want more of him.

I silently prayed that this wouldn't be like the other times—where I'd come but feel disappointed afterward. I'd never seemed to reach the peak that I had all of those years ago, and I didn't know why.

But then a hand drifted underneath my layers and all thoughts vanished. I was wet for him already, and one single brush of his fingertips on my center had me moaning.

"Still as sensitive as ever," he said, his mouth on the shell of my ear.

He knew me, even after all this time. His touches against my clit were gentle and never made me jerk away. I was gasping with each caress of his hand against me.

This felt exactly like that day in the dorm. Tom's careful movements were exactly what I needed and my body responded to him in ways it hadn't with any other man.

His mouth slotted over mine. I kissed him hungrily, desperate to hold on, like he was a dream that could float away at any moment.

This didn't feel like it was about him. There was no rush to the finish line, no impatient groans when my orgasm wouldn't happen fast enough. There was no pressure, only sensation.

This is impossible, I thought. *It's not supposed to feel this good.*

His tongue invaded my mouth as his fingers still made delicate yet earth-shattering movements. I jerked my hips into his touch, feeling my body tighten in anticipation of a breathtaking release.

"T-Tom, I'm gonna—" I could barely get the words out. "Don't stop."

He didn't. Instead of changing it up like most men I'd been with, he continued with the same movements, giving me the perfect stimulation until I fell over the peak of the mountain I'd climbed.

His mouth closed over mine again and my moans were swallowed into his kiss.

As the pleasure faded, he pulled back to look at me. I blinked out of the haze I'd been in, and my first thought was that maybe this had all been a dream and I was overdue to wake up.

But I wasn't sleeping. Real life had somehow become better than a dream.

"You have to be one of the most gorgeous women I've ever seen," he said, his eyes tracing my face.

I blinked. That was not what I expected him to say. "I—what?" was the useless response I came up with.

"You're beautiful all the time," he said. "From your brown eyes to your shy smiles. But that was more beautiful than anything I'd ever seen."

"Thank you," I said, the words hitting me harder than I expected.

"Sorry if that was too forward, I—"

"Mom!"

We jerked away from each other at Max's voice.

"What?" I said, suddenly standing.

"Meowcifer is begging for food again and the bin is empty!"

"I've got it," I called, and then I turned to Tom. "S-sorry, but I should—"

"Go," he said. "I'll be out in a few."

I darted from the room.

"Please tell me you have more cat food," Max began. "I think she might eat us if you don't." And true to his word, Meowcifer was staring him down.

"It's in my car," I replied. "I'll be right back."

By the time I'd gotten cat food in the bowl, Max had gone back upstairs. I only had a second to catch my breath before Tom came out of my bedroom.

"So," Tom said, causing me to jump and turn. "Breakfast?"

My mind went to all the things we had yet to do, and I was tempted to drag him back into the bedroom.

But he'd asked for one more day, and we had plans anyway.

"Of course," I replied. "I'll make waffles again."

"She's so tiny," Max said, leaning over to gaze at Ariana.

Hadley had reached out and asked if we wanted to visit. I'd been calling most days to see if she needed help, but she always insisted that she was fine. Her mom wasn't around when we'd arrived, and surprisingly, neither was Allen.

I knew better than to ask.

"You started out this small," I said.

"Can I hold her?"

I looked over to Hadley, who nodded.

Max gently took the baby and I coached him on how to hold her.

"This is so cool."

Hadley smiled, but it didn't reach her eyes. She had been struggling with what to do about Allen in addition to adjusting to life with a newborn. He'd been showering her with gifts ever since he missed Ariana's birth, but the smoke screen had cleared, and I didn't know if my best friend would ever trust him again.

Besides, he wasn't even at the house.

"Mr. Tom," Max said. "Look at this."

"You're doing great," Tom encouraged.

"You can hold her too," Hadley offered.

"Oh, I couldn't—"

"You're welcome to. I trust you."

Max looked up at Tom, and I could read the question from my spot on the couch.

I should have prepared myself for seeing Tom with a newborn. He cradled Ariana like she was the most precious thing in the world. He was massive compared to the tiny bundle in his arms, but he hunched around her, like he needed to protect her from the world.

I was torn between an immense sadness at what he missed and a desire to make a second baby with him just so I could see this more often.

The second one was a pipe dream. A very tempting one, though.

"Don't drool too much," Hadley said to me under her breath.

"I'm not."

She laughed, a welcome sound in the midst of all the drama she'd been going through.

"It's good to hear you laugh," I said. "I've missed it."

Her smiled faded and I hated myself for even bringing it up.

"Selena, I...I have something to tell you."

"What's wrong?"

"Nothing is wrong. Other than my marriage. I'm leaving Allen."

"Really?"

"Yes. I can't move past what he did."

"I think it's a good idea."

"You do? I thought you'd be sad."

"I am, but for you. Not him. You need to do what you need to do. I've always wanted you happy, even if he didn't like...never mind." I shook my head, not wanting to make this about me.

"No, what? Did you not like him?"

"Don't worry about it."

"I will. Was there something you noticed before this?"

"Well, yes. He didn't like me very much."

She blinked, as if considering it. "I thought that he just wanted my attention when he was around, but now that you say it...I can see it."

"I'd never tell you to leave someone you love because they didn't like me, but I did start avoiding coming over when he was here, or even reaching out when he was home. I didn't ask for help because I didn't want you two to fight about it. I would have dealt with it, though, if he'd been right for you, but after he wasn't there for Ariana's birth..."

"It wasn't right," Hadley said. "He's always been a little bit of a jerk, but it just took until now for me to see it. I'm sorry he made you feel like you couldn't ask for help, and that I didn't notice."

"It's okay. I once thought all of that was normal, but then—" My gaze slid over to Tom, who was watching us with sad eyes. "—then I saw that maybe a partner *should* get along with your friends. And now I know better."

My words didn't help. Tears escaped her eyes.

"This just makes it so much harder."

"Makes what harder? Leaving him?"

"No. Leaving *Nashville*. I'm moving back in with my mom. In Atlanta."

I blinked. "Oh."

"I'm sorry," she blubbered. "I just don't have money to stay here by myself. I haven't had a job in years, and I'm worried he'd come looking for me once I'm gone. Otherwise, I'd have asked to stay with you."

I reached over and grabbed her hand. "It's okay. You have to do what's right. Atlanta isn't that far away. I can visit."

Before my support system had grown, I would have been beside myself at my best friend moving away. There was a time when Hadley was the only one who knew everything about me, but now that Tom was here, and everyone knew who he was, things felt easier.

And I'd never ask her to stay for my sake.

"You're not mad?"

"No. I'm happy you're doing what's best for you."

She wiped at a tear. "I am too. My mom is willing to help with Ariana, and I need that right now. I'm struggling to stay afloat."

"When do you go?"

"I was thinking tonight. He's working late."

"He's already back at work? I thought he got a few weeks off."

"I told him to go. He complained about Ariana's crying and that was when I knew."

My heart dropped, but I knew I couldn't delay her. This was what was best.

"I'll help," Tom said. "Packing goes faster with extra hands."

"Thank you," she said. "That means a lot."

I nodded, watching as Tom handed Ariana back to Hadley. He asked where the boxes were and took Max upstairs to help get the rest of her clothes. I watched my friend who I knew deserved the world. I'd always thought she had gotten her happy ending a long time ago when she'd met Allen, but maybe things weren't so cut-and-dried.

Maybe she had more of a story to live, and maybe I wasn't the side character like I always thought.

"We'll talk on the phone, right?" Hadley asked. "Every night? And I can come visit for the holidays?"

"Of course," I said. "And we'll come stay too."

"I love you," she said. "Thank you for not being mad."

"I only want you happy," I said, thinking of Tom's words to me. "So go find your happiness."

"So, Auntie Hadley is leaving, huh?" Max let out a long breath. "That sucks."

"She'll still visit," I replied.

Max helped grab stuff from the closet while I built boxes. Hadley had told us she only wanted enough to live for a few weeks, but she wasn't in the physical condition to do it.

"But not every day. She sounded sad, though. So this is for the best. It just feels like I'm losing an aunt."

"We'll make an effort to visit her. Besides, you have another aunt."

"On your side? Oh, you told me her name once." He thought for a moment. "Ruth!"

"That's right. There's Ruth, and I have a brother too."

His eyes grew wide. "What's his name? What are they both like?"

"My brother's name is Barry," I said. "Ruth is...well, it's hard to describe her, really. She's smart, and sometimes scary looking, but she's secretly really nice."

"And my Uncle Barry?"

"He is a bit of a loner. He figured out what our parents were doing way faster than Ruth and I did. He works downtown."

"Will I ever get to meet him?"

"I hope so," I replied. "You'll get to meet Ruth, that's for sure."

"When? How soon?"

He was bouncing off his feet, and after that day at Knox's house, I felt comfortable letting it happen.

"They do a weekly dinner at Ruth's boyfriend's house. How about then?"

"Yes. Now, for the most important question." He put his hands in front of him and leaned close. "How much can I talk about Lila Wilde?"

"As much as you want," I said. "They won't judge."

"So, they're like you. I'm excited to meet them."

"They'll be excited to meet you too. But for now, let's get Hadley's stuff packed."

"Okay," he said, resuming his work. "But if she lives in Atlanta, how will we get there? I don't think Mom's car can make that trip. And I think I'll shut down mentally if I make that drive in your truck. No offense, it's just so loud."

"We'll figure it out," I replied. "We can always rent a car."

"But that's for rich people." His eyes went to me. "Oh yeah, I forgot. I have a rich dad now. Do you have a vacation house? I hear rich people have vacation houses."

"I haven't taken a vacation in years, so no. My dad does, though."

Max's nose scrunched. "I don't want to go on vacation with him."

"Trust me, neither do I."

We finished packing Hadley's things, just enough to get her by. Her mom came over in a truck to help pick it all up. Hadley loaded Ariana into her car seat, not once looking back at the house.

She did, however, look back at Selena.

"I'll visit. I promise."

"And we can come visit you," she offered.

"At least you're not alone this time," Hadley said, eyes moving over to me.

"Don't worry about me," Selena said. "You guys drive safe."

She gave her friend one last hug and then Hadley and her mom drove off.

"Are you okay?" I asked.

"I'm as good as I can be," she said softly. "Ready to go home, for sure."

"I'll go home with you. I have my first peer support group tonight, but I can cancel if—"

"No, go. If it helps you, then definitely go."

"I'll come over after."

She gave me a smile. "Works for me."

The place Ruth found was nice. When I'd asked to only start with group sessions, they didn't push me for anything else. If this went well, I'd probably look into their other services.

There were colorful walls and comfortable chairs. The group I was in was smaller, with only five adults in it, including me. I was told this was a group for people who wanted to completely cut alcohol from their lives. Some only wanted to lower their intake, but I knew that wasn't the path for me.

I watched as my peers filtered in. One was a young woman with blonde hair tied into a braid. Another was an older man with bags under his eyes. He was thin and frail looking. Another woman in her mid-forties with long box braids walked in and sat at the front of the room. And lastly, a young man who was maybe ten years younger than me took a seat. He looked so young. I wondered how he'd found himself here.

"Welcome," the older woman said, standing from her chair. "I'll be your guide this evening. Now, we have two new people with us tonight, so I want us to introduce ourselves to get to know each other. We usually start with our names and why we wanted to quit drinking. I'm Shannon. I started my journey over fifteen years ago when my husband and I got divorced as a result of my dependence on alcohol. I've spent a long time struggling with my part in the end of our marriage, and I've channeled my energy into helping others."

A few of the participants smiled in her direction, like they were old friends who'd heard this many times over.

"Albert, would you like to go next?" Shannon turned to the frail-looking man next to her.

"Yes." He slowly stood, wincing as he did so. "I stopped drinking two years ago when I was diagnosed with liver disease. I've struggled with it because I was raised in a family that loves to drink for fun, but my health is the most important thing right now."

"And you're doing great," Shannon said, smiling. "Stacey?"

The young woman with a braid stood. "Hi, I'm Stacey. I used to drink a lot in college. I don't really have some of the same things going on as you guys do, but I wanted to stop to feel like I had more energy. And I needed some help from others in order to do that."

"She's always willing to lend an ear," Shannon added. "We love having her. Now, for our newest guests. Sunny, would you like to go?"

I was relieved that I didn't have to go first. Even though all of these people had their legitimate reasons for being here, I wondered if they would judge me for mine.

"Hi," Sunny said sullenly. "Um, I'm here because my friends said it would help. My dad, uh, only really talked to me when he was drinking. So I would drink to get his attention. But lately, I've been getting so drunk I black out, and one of my friends said I was *so* mean during it." He sunk into his chair. "I've got to stop. Whether my dad likes it or not."

I blinked, seeing myself in the young man. Maybe, in another life, I could have gotten help at his age.

"It's good that you're stopping now," I said, unable to refrain.

"Thanks," Sunny said. "What about you?"

My nerves had me shaking. "I'm Tom. I drank so I wouldn't feel any emotions about what was happening in my life, and I did it so much that I don't remember my college years. I pushed away a woman who was pregnant with my child, and because of that, I missed eleven years of his life."

I expected for someone to curse under their breath or to look at me with narrowed eyes.

Instead, Shannon sighed. "I'm sorry to hear that. I hope we can help you learn better ways of dealing with emotions other than using alcohol."

"I want to be better. For them."

"We all have someone," Albert said. "I want to live to see my grandkids be born."

"I want to be able to have a healthy relationship," Shannon said.

"And I want to finish college," Sunny added.

"Let's write down those reasons somewhere that we can keep them. Albert, Stacey, and I have already done that."

She handed Sunny and me a piece of paper and we wrote down what we said. I put it in my wallet, tucked right next to the picture Selena had drawn of me. It felt right having it there, like the reminder I'd been craving.

"Now, let's talk about our weeks," Shannon said. "We can say anything we're going through with no judgment."

I listened to all of their stories, amazed that I wasn't alone in the struggle. Many of them had issues with the cravings or social pressure to cave in and have a drink. Hearing it all made me feel like I was a little less alone.

And that staying sober could be possible with help.

Chapter Twenty-Three

Selena

The next morning, I woke to the feeling of the bed dipping and Tom pulling me to his body.

"Sorry," he said lowly. "I went ahead and fed Meowcifer so she wouldn't wake you or Max up."

"S'fine," I muttered, still half asleep. "Thank you."

Tom's lips pressed to my shoulder, and as much as I wanted to sink back into sleep, I knew he was far too distracting for that.

"It's been a week," I said. "We made it the one more day."

"You just woke up and that's the first thing you thought of?"

"Yes. It's hard not to when I'm waking up next to you."

I could feel his hand, which was resting on my hip, tighten at my words.

"Before we even consider this," he began, "I need to ask this one more time. Do you feel in any way that you *have* to do this because of what I've done?"

"No." It was one of the easiest answers of my life.

He nodded and there was a moment of silence as he regarded me.

And then he rolled me over and kissed me.

His lips slotted on mine and it felt like coming home. Like a cup of hot chocolate on a cold day or reading a book after a tough week. A part of me assumed I'd never be able to kiss someone and it would feel like this.

Tom hovered over me and my nipples hardened to tight peaks. My body knew he was going to make me feel good and I was ready to finally return the favor.

I ran my fingers through his hair, keeping my mouth on his. I couldn't help but moan as his hand drifted to cup my breast and his tongue darted out against mine.

I had plans for him. I would make him feel just as good as he had me. This morning would be about him because he deserved to feel as good as I did.

But as most of my plans did, they fell apart when Tom slid his hand under my shirt, gently rolling my nipple between two of his fingers.

His mouth left mine. I had a second to catch my breath and try to remember exactly what I wanted to do to him. But his hand moved from my breast and trailed down my sides.

"T-Tom," I said. "It's your turn to feel good."

"And what makes you think I don't feel good when I see you come apart?" His mouth found the most sensitive part of my neck as his fingers slid over the front of my shorts. "The sounds of you when you come is all I want to hear right now."

This was it. This was how I died. And he had only barely touched me.

"I want..." I gasped when he ran his finger along my pussy through the soft cotton. "I want to feel you. All of you."

"We'll get there," he said, pausing only to kiss where my neck met my shoulder. "But I'm a fan of making you come multiple times before I do. How about a three-to-one rule?"

"Three?"

"Or four. I'm flexible."

"Two. I need you, Tom. I need you in me."

"Fine. Two. And then we'll aim for you coming on my cock. That'll make three."

"Yes," I said, both to his proposition and the way he finally touched my clit through my shorts. His fingers slowly moved the material aside.

Tom's mouth made its way back to mine while his fingers slowly traced my core. Despite how tight he had me pressed into the bed, his hands were as gentle as ever, never once overwhelming me.

My tongue met his again. I closed my eyes, lost in the torrent of sensation. He'd figured out the perfect way to move, the perfect tempo, to unravel me in mere minutes.

I let out a moan as I began to dissolve. My body fluttered. My eyes closed. All I knew was the sensation pulsing through me.

Tom's hand slowed and I started to jerk away from his movements. I felt my brain start to come back online, and somehow, my body was ready for more.

"Are you sure you don't want to fuck me now?"

"I will when I'm good and ready," he said. "But now I think we need less layers on."

Tom gave me just enough room to pull off my tee. He planted his mouth on the exposed skin.

"If I have less layers, then you should too."

"Fair enough." His shirt came off and I was blessed with the sight of his toned chest once more. I ran my hands along his skin, noticing how his jaw ticked at the sensation.

My shorts were the next to go, and as he slowly dragged them down my legs, I could feel his touch leaving a trail on my skin. I needed more of him. My hand reached for the elastic band of his pajama pants and I silently begged him not to stop me.

When they were off, I couldn't resist feeling his hard cock through his boxers. It had been twelve years since I last held it. That was far too long. I ran my hand up it while my core clenched in anticipation.

"I need you," I said. "I need this." I tightened my grip.

He groaned at the feeling and his hands moved to take the boxers off.

We paused only to get a condom, and after it was on, I lay next to him, bringing his mouth to mine. I was aligned with him and I could feel his cock at my clit. I couldn't help myself. I rocked forward and the delicious friction made me see stars. His hand came to rest on my hip, and for a second, I wondered if it was his way of stopping me.

I stilled, but then he pulled me the slightest bit toward him, giving me more of that perfect pressure. My moan was muffled by our kiss, but I got the message, and I resumed my movements.

Every now and again, the tip of him would catch on my entrance, and after the fourth time of the tiny preview of him being inside of me, I was propelled to the edge of another intense orgasm. I moved faster, almost desperately, as I tumbled over the peak.

I paused with his cock right at my entrance as I came again. My body jerked and my vision went dark, wholly lost to the sensation.

"Fuck," I said. "That was..." I didn't have adequate words.

"Beautiful," he answered for me. "It was beautiful."

"I only want more," I said as I remembered where he was situated. Tom was barely in me and my body was begging for an encore. I shifted forward, pushing him in further.

"We need a better angle," he said, rolling me onto my back. For a second, he slipped out of me, and I felt achingly empty without him.

Tom didn't waste any time after we reoriented. He pressed into me again, but this time he was able to slide in farther. My hands moved to the back of his neck and tightened as he slowly pushed inside.

Nothing I'd ever experienced before was like this. No one could ever come close to make me feel as complete as I did when Tom Murray was fully inside of me.

I could feel my walls tighten around him, as if they were near yet another release, one like no other.

"Move," I pleaded. "Please. I need you to move."

He was slow at first. He had a languid pace as he pulled all the way out of me and then pushed back in. My legs crossed behind him, keeping him near me as he moved. He picked up speed, his thrusts becoming more and more powerful, as he continued to wreck me from inside out.

My eyes fluttered closed as my body gripped him like a vise. This was unreal, better than anything I'd ever had before.

"Oh, God," I moaned. "I'm so close."

"Come for me, Selena. I want to feel it."

That did it. Those words made me topple over the edge.

My core tightened and heat erupted from my body. All of me twitched as it came apart for a third time. I fluttered around his hardness and he moaned, his thrusts becoming more erratic as he came too. His forehead met mine and his cock pulsed inside of me.

I almost wished that I could have felt it with nothing on.

But that was a dangerous thought.

"You're incredible," he said, and I dimly realized this was the first time I'd ever heard him be out of breath.

"No, you are," I said in response. "That was the best sex I've ever had."

"It was for me too. It's never felt like that except for that day in my dorm."

My heart squeezed. I always thought I'd made up the chemistry we'd had on that day.

But now I was questioning that.

"You felt it too?"

"I always did. I looked for you in the coffee shop after that. I regretted letting you go, which is why what I sent after doesn't make..." His brow furrowed.

"Let's not ruin a good morning by thinking about the past."

I gave him a smile before we both got up. I thought I was safe from the questions Tom had posed, but then I couldn't help but think about what he said as I made breakfast.

If he'd wanted me even then, why did he turn me away? Why did he send that letter?

The answer was the drinking. It had to be.

Otherwise, none of it made sense.

The night of Tom's family dinner, we drove my car since it had a back seat. I silently begged for it not to make the odd sound it had been when I turned it on. But, as always, my car didn't cooperate.

"That sounds like the alternator," Tom said.

"You know what it is?"

"I do, and it's an easy fix. I can do it for you."

"Can I help?" Max asked from the back seat.

"Sure," Tom said. "I owe you a lesson anyway."

"How long will it take? I'd hate to not have a car for a few days."

"Not long, but if it does take longer, you could drive my truck."

"Really? You'd trust me with the truck?"

"Of course. I'd trust you with anything."

My stomach flipped as he gave me an easygoing smile, acting as if it wasn't a monumental thing that he trusted me with his most prized possession. "Okay, thank you."

By the time we pulled in, he'd ordered the part for my car.

His sister lived in a beautiful two-story home, and I instantly felt underdressed. Nerves hit me. Would I fuck this up somehow? What if they hated Max and me?

"It's okay," Tom said as we climbed out of the car. "We can leave if they say anything out of line. But I don't foresee that happening."

The words helped more than they should have. "What are the chances they do that?"

"Low. These people are some of the nicest I've met. I wouldn't take you two anywhere else."

I took in a breath and nodded. I was terrified to meet these people, but Max didn't seem to share the same sentiment.

It didn't help that the day had been rough from the moment I got up. Luna had called, complaining about how Willie wouldn't propose, and then afterward, I'd tried to work, only to be distracted by a loud fight my neighbors were having.

The day seemed cursed and I desperately hoped it wouldn't carry over.

A young woman with flowing dark hair and Tom's green eyes met us at the door. She had a sharp nose and jawline, but smiled when she saw us. "You came!" she said to Tom.

"Hey, Ruth," he replied, giving her a hug. She turned to us with a smile.

"Welcome," she said. "I'm Ruth."

"Nice to meet you," I said, putting on my usual smile whenever I met some-one new. "I'm Selena and this is Max."

Ruth's eyes slid over to Max and I could see her smile widen. "Wow, you look so much like your mom."

I blinked. No one ever pointed that out.

"Really? I hear that I look like my dad."

"In some ways, but not in all of them. You have your mom's skin tone and face shape."

"Thank you for noticing," I said. "Most people don't catch that."

"I try to be observant. Why don't you all come in? Barry should be here soon."

"Barry's coming?" Tom asked.

"I finally wore him down. And I said you were bringing Max."

"Great," he said, but I could see his jaw tick.

"I'll keep you two from fighting," Ruth said. "But I think you'll do great."

I put my hand on Tom's arm and he took a breath, seemingly calming down.

"You have such a pretty house," I said. "So many houseplants."

"Thanks, but it's not mine. It's Knox's."

I'd known that. Tom had told me and I'd completely forgotten. I cursed my brain. Why couldn't it work in social situations? I wanted to impress these people, not make silly mistakes.

"But you live here now, right?" Tom asked.

"Mainly. My apartment is too boring to go back to. Would it have killed our parents to teach us some decoration?"

"Probably," Tom said lowly.

An older couple sat in the living room. "Hey!" the man called. "The guests of honor are here!"

Guests of honor? I glanced at the door, expecting to see someone else behind us.

"It's so nice to meet you. I'm Lynn. I'm..." She trailed off, looking around. "Where is Knox?"

"He better not have snuck into his office," Ruth said. "I will drag him out—"

"I didn't sneak away to work," a male voice announced. "I forgot to water one of my plants."

"This obsession with plants is getting out of hand," Benji muttered, yet he smiled.

"Hi, Tom. This must be Selena and Max." Knox smiled at us. "Welcome. Can I get you anything?"

My mind unhelpfully reminded me that he was technically famous. And I didn't know half of what was going on here socially.

"N-no," I managed to stutter out. "I'm good."

"How many plants to you have?" Max asked.

"I lost count."

"It sort of makes me feel like I'm in a jungle, but with less bugs. I love it."

Knox looked at Benji. "He sees my vision."

"Okay, he sees your vision, but does he like puns?" Benji slowly turned to Max. "What do you call an illegally parked frog?"

Max took the question very seriously. "Hang on. Don't tell me. I know this one." He scratched his head. "Oh! *Toad.* You call it toad because it sounds like towed."

"I'm impressed."

"I had this sub once who made puns the whole class, and I had to ask him what each meant. That one was my favorite."

"You know what? I think you're my favorite kid."

"Hey!" Knox interjected. "Wasn't that me?"

"You're not a kid anymore. You're my favorite adult. Behind Ruth."

Out of the corner of my eye, I saw her stick her tongue out at him.

"Ruth and Knox used to hate each other," Tom explained. "Then they somehow fell in love."

I watched as Knox didn't seem to get mad at her teasing at all. Instead, he pulled her close and gave her a kiss on the forehead.

All of these people had a dynamic that I didn't know how to break into. They were all so comfortable with each other, and I felt like I belonged in the background.

Like a side character.

And that was fine. At least it was something I was good at.

I stayed quiet and observed everyone until Barry walked in.

He was the only Murray sibling who didn't have green eyes and dark hair. He was relaxed in a way I'd never seen Tom. Especially now. My shoulder brushed Tom's and I could feel his tenseness.

"Barry!" Ruth said, a smile on her face. "Welcome."

"This is a nice place," he replied. "I see why you never leave."

Barry's eyes slid to Tom and then to Max.

"Hi," Max said, giving a small wave.

"So, this is the fellow Lila Wilde fan I've heard so much about?" Barry asked.

And that did it. Any shyness disappeared from Max. "Fellow fan? You like her too?"

"She's my favorite singer."

I glanced over at Tom, who was looking at Barry like this was his first time seeing the man in front of him.

"What?" Ruth asked. "I had you pegged an alt-rock kind of guy."

"Alt-rock has its place, but I'm a big fan of her softer stuff."

"Yes. All her softer stuff screams unhappiness. Not that I want her unhappy, but I like the depth of it."

Barry raised an eyebrow. "That's a very smart way to say it."

"I get it from my mom."

"Oh." Barry chuckled. "Not your dad?" Then his eyes widened. "Wait, did I just—"

"He knows," Tom said. "Don't worry."

"My friends kept telling me I looked like him," Max added. "I would have figured it out eventually."

Barry nodded, and he looked up, eyes catching on me. "You must be Selena. It's nice to meet you." He held out his hand, and I remembered the few things Tom had told me about him. His smile was more real, yet it held the same sadness I'd seen in Tom's.

"You too, and I'm sorry."

"About what?"

"About the people who raised you. They sound like they weren't the best."

"He told you?"

"After a while."

"Then he trusts you. Good."

Lynn and Benji introduced themselves to Barry, and I took a moment to analyze what I said. Had I overstepped?

"Don't worry about it," Tom said. "Things have always been tense between the three of us."

"Was I that easy to read?"

"I do the same thing all the time. It never helps."

Max was enamored with Barry and spent time asking him all about Lila. I thought he was going to talk poor Barry's ear off.

Half an hour later, dinner was ready.

Ruth was an excellent cook and the conversation was lively. Between Max and Barry talking, Benji cracking jokes, and Knox subtly annoying Ruth, I knew everyone was having a great time.

And I was the only one overwhelmed.

After dinner, I had to step away into the cold night air. I leaned on my car, begging my brain to function normally. I liked these people, but I couldn't think of a damn thing to say. I always did this whenever I'd had a bad day and I didn't know how to fix it.

Eventually, the door opened and Tom emerged. I looked at my feet, trying to think of a way to explain my random exhaustion. Jax used to say I was just too used to being home and I needed to get out more.

"Sorry," I said.

"The paint is low," he replied.

I stared at him blankly. "What?"

"It means you're socially tired, right? Max said it some time ago."

"Yes, he did. And you're right." I sighed. "But Max is having fun. And I am too, but it's so loud. I wasn't very good at starting a conversation anyway. I felt like I was doing better melting into the background."

"You're never just in the background. Not to me."

"I can be. Seriously, it's fine. Your family is here."

"Let me rephrase, then. I *can't* ever see you in the background. You're always on my mind, even for the last twelve years. I meant what I said. You're never a background character to me. You're everything."

I wasn't able to look at him, but the heat in my cheeks warmed me even in the cold air. He stepped close and I found myself leaning on him. One of his hands ran through my hair and I could feel a little of my exhaustion lift.

I'd fallen back into old habits on instinct. Somehow, his words had pulled me out of it.

"Thank you," I said, stepping away. "I needed that."

"I also thought you might need these." He held out headphones.

"Aren't these for Max?"

"He seems to be doing okay. I think you need them."

"I don't. I'm a grown adult, and I don't even have autism. Save them for him."

"I'm sure Ruth has more if he does need them. Besides, I hear autism is genetic."

"How did you hear that?"

"Lynn. She works in a salon and learned about it from her clients with special needs."

"I don't—I mean if it is hereditary, then it didn't come from me. I made it through school just fine. I didn't have meltdowns about noise, even when Luna was driving me up the wall. I just went to my room."

Despite my words, something uncomfortable churned in my gut. I may not have had meltdowns, but I wanted to. I just didn't *let* myself have them. Mom was as patient as she could be, but I knew from a very young age that I didn't want attention, so I kept everything to myself.

I'd always thought I was so much like Max. It was as if we were the only ones who could understand each other.

And now I was seeing why.

"Selena?" Tom asked. "Are you okay?"

"Oh no. I see what you're saying now." I pressed my palm to my forehead. "I was just so focused on Max being okay that I never thought about what it meant that I was so similar to him. Tom, what do I even *do*?"

"I'm still learning about it myself, but Lynn seems to know a lot."

"Maybe I should talk to her."

"She's smart. I see where Knox gets it from. I'm sure she'd be willing to hear whatever questions you might have. Want me to get her?"

I nodded, relieved that he was willing to go inside when I couldn't. Moments later, Lynn came out.

"Hi," her voice was soft. "Tom mentioned you wanted to see me?"

"Um, yes." A car drove by, breaking my focus. "But now I don't even know how to word what I wanted to say."

"Put these on," she said, handing me the headphones Tom had already offered. "They might help."

It didn't feel like anything would help, but I tried it anyway. The world went silent when I slipped them on. Things became clearer and I could finally think.

"Now, I don't know how these fancy things work, but you *should* be able to hear me."

"I can," I said. Another car drove by, but I didn't hear it. "This is *amazing*."

"These are going to help so many people," she said. "Do they make things better for you?"

"Yes, they do. I can think. And now I remember what I wanted to ask you. You work with kids with autism, right?"

"I do. And adults."

"I know how it works. I've worked so hard to help Max succeed in school, but what would happen if it were missed in someone? Especially an adult?"

"I had a client who had the same thing happen. She had a child, and the child got diagnosed early. Over time, and with the help of friends, she started to see that she had some signs of it too, but they were different. She'd spent her life learning to hide and mask it. She was always seen as introverted and quiet. She would push past her shyness and try to be social, and it worked, but it was tiring."

My heart pounded. It was like she was describing me.

"What did she do?"

"She started treating herself like she did her child. She did research and found that autism in adult women manifests differently than it can in others. Eventually, she got diagnosed by a professional. And it's all helped."

Flashes of my childhood played in my mind. I was told I was the normal one in comparison to Luna. I wanted to be good in school and at home since Mom was so busy with her. So, I learned how to pretend to be normal, how to mask what I truly felt.

I blew out a long breath. "Maybe I need to do the same thing. God, how did I not see it?"

"You were busy making your son's life better. And he's amazing, Selena. So bright and happy. Maybe it's time to give yourself some attention too."

"I think you're right. Thank you." I glanced at the door, wondering if the headphones could help me there too. "I want to go inside, but I don't think I can take these off and do it."

"Then keep them on. None of us are going to judge you." Her eyes were steady on mine, making me doubt that she was lying.

"Okay," I said. "Let's go back inside."

The get-together was going as if I never left. Instead of being overwhelmed by the amount of conversation, I only heard whoever I was facing.

"How are they working?" Knox asked when he saw me. "This is the first calibration of this kind and I want them to be perfect."

He turned sharply to his right and I realized Ruth had said something to him, but I didn't hear it.

"It's just a few questions. I'm being social, I promise." He turned back to me. "Sorry, she wants to make sure I don't work myself to death."

"That's sweet. I could maybe come by your office with some notes."

"Please."

"These are life-changing. I haven't felt this relaxed around this many people since before Max was born."

"I'll send you a few extra," Knox said. "That way you, Max, and Tom will have a pair each."

Ruth walked up, asking about what I did for fun. It was far easier to think of something to say when I only had to focus on one person. Instead of staying in the background, I was able to step forward and socialize.

Maybe I'd been overwhelmed all this time.

It helped that Ruth was interesting to talk to. We discussed romance books since she was intrigued by them. After, Benji and Lynn told us stories of when Knox and Ruth were rivals, and later, I was able to ask Knox what plants I had the least likelihood of killing.

Max was the star of the show, blending in with the family as if he had always been a part of it. He kept Barry's attention for most of the night.

Somewhere along the line, I realized I felt almost like I was at home.

Tom

"Careful," Barry said as he finally approached me for the first time. "I hear people can tell when you stare."

"I wasn't staring," I said, but I knew the truth. After Selena finally came in from outside, I was making sure she didn't need me.

So far, she seemed more like herself than ever.

"Sure you're not."

This would be where I would snap back and a fight would ensue. From across the room, I could see Ruth eying us warily.

But I chose not to take that path.

"I'm just worried about her. She got overwhelmed and I don't want her pushing herself for my sake. I think we all know that forcing anything doesn't exactly work."

"That was a very eloquent and caring answer. I almost don't recognize you."

"I'm still me. I'm just trying to be a better version of that."

"Still sober?"

"Yes. And I've been going to group sessions too. It helps knowing it's not just me. Eventually I'll add in therapies too."

"All of this has been good for you," Barry said. "I can see that."

"It's been easier than I thought. I think our parents missed out on the biggest motivator of all."

"What's that?"

"Love and support. It does wonders."

"I don't think they're capable of love," he said, shaking his head. "And besides, being alone works too."

"Does it?" I asked. "Has it motivated you?"

"My life is fine. I've got it all under control."

I doubted it, but I knew better than to push. "Okay. But if it's ever not, just know I'm always there."

"I have a feeling you don't want to know about anything happening in my bar."

"Drinking might not be good for me, but family is. At least the parts of it we choose to keep."

Barry looked at his glass of water, his lips pursing. "I'll keep it in mind. Thanks."

He walked away, moving over to talk to Max. While I was happy to let him connect with his nephew, I also wondered if he did have something going on, something he wasn't ready to share.

The day the first PATH-assisted truck rolled out of the warehouse was a day for celebration. After months of testing, the truck was set to make a long-haul trip and one of our veteran drivers had stepped up to lead it.

All of the employees involved with the project gathered at the warehouse to witness its launch. Ruth and Knox had joined, excited to see their biggest copiloted project move forward.

"You had a good idea, Ruth," I said once the truck had disappeared down the road.

"I have those every once in a while. Did you see the news is here?"

"I did. The press from this has completely changed the game for us. Many forward-thinking companies want to work with us to move freight."

"Sometimes, good things do come to those who do good things. How's revenue?"

"Up. Just as everyone wanted."

"I bet Dad is *so* mad. Has he tried to come back by the office?"

"Nope. I was sure he would once this got closer to being done."

"Maybe it's for the best," Knox interjected. "The less you guys see him, the better."

"Yeah, you're right." Ruth's eyes drifted to someone behind me. "Oh, shit. The news is coming."

"And that's my sign to head out," Knox said.

"Is he not a fan of the reporters?"

"Public speaking. And news people are close to it. I'll handle this. You're welcome to join me in bragging, if you feel up to it."

I never did much with the media, but then again, we'd never done something so noteworthy where I had to.

Maybe it was time for me to show off what we'd done here.

"Sure, I'll do it."

Ruth gave me a bright smile and together we faced the camera.

As I talked to the news anchor about the project, I realized that, for once, things at work felt stable and secure. My home life was the same way. It was like I was on top of the world.

But later that day, my lawyer walked into my office, face grim.

My heart sunk. "Don't say it."

"I have to," he said, sighing. "The last witness dropped out of the case. There are no charges of harassment against your father remaining."

"Shit," I said. "So he's going to return?"

"His lawyer is already working on it. You will be asked to step back into your old position and allow him to return."

"That's not going to last long. He's going to fire me once he's back."

"I'm sure a man of your talent will be able to find employment again."

I knew he was right, but I couldn't help but feel that, for a moment, Murray and Sons was something more than just the family business. People were taken care of, employees were happy, and I'd been the one to do that.

But it seemed it was only temporary.

Chapter Twenty-Four

Selena

I was pretty sure Tom worked on cars when he was stressed. He had come home from work, part in hand, and gotten under my Subaru with only one muttered hello and a call for Max to join him.

I'd stayed inside to feed Meowcifer and draw another cover I was working on, but I was worried about him. Eventually, I gave up on my task and went to watch him and Max work.

He was answering questions that Max posed with his usual patience, but his tone was tight. If it was enough for me to notice, then he was probably going through something serious.

"How is everything going?" I asked.

"They gave me the wrong part," he said, sighing. "I'll have to take it back in."

"It's late," I told him. "Maybe you two need a break to eat."

"The parts store is going to close soon, and you need a car."

"You said I could borrow your truck."

He looked at his truck, as if calculating something in his head. "Yes. You should keep it here. I shouldn't drive it to work anyway."

"Why not?" I asked.

"Don't worry about it," he said. "Max, can you help me clean up?"

"Yes!" Max said, jumping up from his place on the driveway. After everything was put away, Tom handed me the keys to the truck. I watched as Max ran inside to call and tell Tess about his adventures in car repair, and then I turned to Tom.

"What's going on?"

"My dad is returning to Murray and Sons."

My throat tightened. "What? I thought he'd harassed people."

"He managed to get the victims to drop the case. He's turning it into a smear campaign, saying that I did it to steal the family company from him."

"Have you talked to him? Did he tell you this?"

He opened his phone and showed me a statement from Todd Murray.

> *I have been the victim of an attack planned by my own family. My son, once my pride and joy, made up fictitious lies about me to take over the family company so he could institute his controversial and dangerous ideals and ruin what I've built. I am happy to say I am returning to my rightful place as CEO tomorrow and ensuring this will never happen again.*

A shiver ran through me. That post sounded eerily familiar in a way I couldn't explain.

"Wait, that last line, is he hinting he's going to fire you?"

"Probably."

"Are you going to be okay?"

"Yes. I have stocks in the company and in other places, and I highly doubt he will buy me out of them, so I'll remain a shareholder. Plus, I have other companies interested in having me work for them."

I nodded. I couldn't imagine what he must have been feeling. Being faced with his father again, after all that man had done, couldn't have been easy.

And yet he'd *still* been patient with Max while he asked questions.

"Well, whatever happens, wherever you wind up working, you'll do great."

"Thank you," he said. "I just wanted this one to mean something more than just being the family business."

"I'm sorry." I reached out to rub his back. "Is there anything you can do?"

"I have Francine looking into him, but once he's back, he'll fire her too."

"The woman who delivered the letters?"

"Yes. She's my right-hand woman at work. She hates my father as much as I do, but she hasn't found anything yet. And maybe she won't. He could have covered his tracks so well no one could find what he did. Maybe he outsmarted me."

"All he wins from this is a company. And you have so much more than that."

He blinked, as if this was the first time he'd thought of it that way. "I think you're right."

"This time I know I am. You may have been raised to be a trophy, but you aren't like that anymore. Even if the worst happens, you have us."

"I'll make sure of it," he said, turning those green irises on me.

"Let's go get cleaned up. We can have dinner and let tomorrow be tomorrow."

"I think I can work with that," he replied.

I kissed his cheek. "I just need to check the mail. I've been better about checking it since *someone* paid everything off."

His lips turned upward. "Glad to help."

When I opened my mailbox, I found a book waiting for me.

One of the authors I worked with had sent me an advanced copy of their novel. I smiled when I saw it. Seeing my work take shape was rewarding in a way I couldn't place.

My eyes drifted over the cover and they stopped on the drawing of the man.

I knew I'd taken inspiration from Tom, but I didn't realize how much. It was *exactly* him. Anyone who saw him would know.

My face flamed and I instinctively covered the image. God, this was embarrassing. I'd drawn that *so* long ago. Before I'd even known he'd stopped drinking.

"Selena!" Tom called, poking his head through the door. "Are you coming?"

"Y-yeah," I said. "Just got a fun package."

"What is it?" he asked as we walked inside and he went to the sink to wash his hands.

"It's a copy of a book I did the cover for. The author sent me one."

"Can I see?"

My cheeks heated. "Um...sure."

I turned it to him, biting my lip. Maybe he would give it a once-over, like most people did when they saw my drawings.

But I should have known better. His eyes traced over every line I'd drawn. He looked at it like it was a masterpiece in a museum. I could see the moment he recognized his own face mirrored on the cover.

"This looks like..."

"You? Um, yeah. I was just inspired by..." I trailed off, gesturing to his face.

He was quiet and I dragged my eyes up to look at him.

His cheeks grew pink and I blinked in surprise. Had I finally embarrassed him? He then took out his phone.

"What are you doing?"

"Ordering a copy for myself. I want to add it to my collection."

"Your collection of me being weird and drawing you?"

"It's not weird. I love to see the version of me through your eyes. Your art is incredible. I love it."

I love you, I wanted to say, but tamped it down.

Was it too soon? I had no idea, but I was already feeling embarrassed that I'd liked him for this long. The last thing I needed to do was be turned down right after.

"This made my day so much better," he said, holding up the book.

I stood on my tiptoes to press my lips into his. I could have stayed there forever, up until I heard Max say, "Guys, I'm begging you. This PDA has got to stop. I'm staging an intervention."

Tom

The next day, I dreaded going to work, but I couldn't put it off any longer. It was close to nine, and I knew Dad was waiting on me so he could fire me publicly. I'd tried to put on a brave face, but I was terrified of seeing him again.

"After this, you're done," Selena said, adjusting my tie in the living room. "No more of him."

"I know," I said. "I just need to make it through this first."

She stood on her tiptoes and kissed me gently just like she had the night before.

"You've got this. Meowcifer thinks so too."

I looked down, and as usual, the cat was staring at me. "I think she just wants me to pet her," I said, reaching down to rub her head.

"You can't tell me she doesn't help."

"She does," I replied.

I went to the front door, only to find someone waiting when I opened it.

Francine had bags under her eyes and didn't look like she'd slept at all. Her hand was raised as if she was going to knock at any moment.

"Oh, good. You're here. Both of you."

"Is everything all right?" I asked.

Her lips pressed into a thin line. "No. No, it's not."

"Is it my father?"

She slowly nodded. "Can I come in?"

"Of course," Selena said. "We have some extra coffee if you want some."

"That would be great." Francine gave her a small smile. She sat on the couch, and moments later, Selena brought over a mug.

"Do you need me to step out of the room?" Selena asked. "If this is about work, I can make myself scarce."

"No," Francine said. "You should hear this too."

I glanced over at Selena, who looked as confused as I felt.

"Oh, okay." She sat across from Francine. "Then what's going on?"

Francine reached for her bag and pulled out Dad's laptop.

"Why do you still have that?" I asked. "He's back at the office today and is going to be looking for it."

"He's not at the office. I've forwarded what I found to the lawyers already."

"You found something?"

"Yes. Money stuff, but that's not why I'm here."

"It's not?" I asked.

"Tom, you should sit. You're not going to like this news."

I already didn't like it. Anything that had Francine like this couldn't have been good.

"Okay," I said, sitting next to Selena. "What did you find?"

"Todd made a lot of risky financial decisions with company money. Those transfers I found were to himself, but he labeled them as business expenses."

"That doesn't sound right," Selena said.

"Most of it benefited him. I found transfers lining up with when he purchased a new car or when he was buying another vacation home."

"Is that why he always wanted more revenue?"

"Yes, and those transfers weren't recorded as profits, which will open up a large investigation into him by the IRS."

"That's good, right?" Selena asked. "I mean, it's not *good*, but it keeps him out of the company."

"Yes, you're right. But there is one other thing he labeled as a business expense." Francine's eyes turned to me. "That was *you*, Tom."

"Me?"

"There were very old transfers that aligned to when you were in college. He was paying your tuition with company funds, possibly because he saw *you* as an investment. But there was one that didn't align with the others. One that was...to you, Selena."

"To me? I've never talked to Todd Murray in my life."

"I'm not saying you did, or that you *knew* you did." She turned to me. "Did you know your father had access to your college email?"

"What?"

"Google saves passwords for ages, and he never cleared them out. He had your login saved and all of your emails were in his work inbox. He was BCC'd on all of them. Including the ones Selena sent. Did you ever share your password with him?"

"He...gave me one to use. He said he didn't want me to get hacked while in school and I stupidly trusted him."

"So he logged in using that."

"So he knew about Max? Then why would he never say anything? Why would I have even told Selena to stay silent then?"

"Because you didn't," Selena said, but her voice was soft. "You didn't tell me anything. It was all Todd."

Francine nodded. "That's my guess too. He was decent at covering some of his tracks. He could have deleted them from the inbox so Tom would never see them."

"So, the check I got was from the company too?"

"Yes. I found the documentation of the transfer."

My world tilted under the weight of this news. This whole time I thought I'd been the one to turn her away, but it was my own father. He looked at me for twelve years, knowing I had a son, and *never* mentioned it to me.

"I'm so sorry," Francine said. "But this makes sense. You're a lot of things, Tom, but you were never the kind of man who would abandon his own child. You were cranky and rude, but never cruel. Todd, however, is."

"Tom showed me what he said on social media last night," Selena said. "It sounded familiar. This must be why."

I thought I knew rage, but never had I felt it course through my body like fire. My jaw clenched, my muscles tightened.

How *could* he?

"That *fucking* bastard."

Selena's hand landed on my shoulder. "Tom, I know this is—"

"He hid Max and you from me. He paid you off as *me*, so you would never come looking."

"I know but—"

"I need to go." I stood and turned to Francine. "You said he isn't at the office?"

"Right. They didn't allow him back in the building this morning. They told him they found new evidence."

"I bet he's at the house then. I'm going to see him."

"What?" Selena asked. "Why?"

"Because I need him to look me in the eye and tell me what he's done."

"I'm coming with you."

"No," I said firmly. "I don't want you anywhere near him. This is my fight. Besides, you'll need to pick up Max from school."

"But my car..."

"You can use my truck. I can take a cab over there. Unless Francine wants to drop me off."

"Since I have his laptop, I don't want to be anywhere near him right now. And my inbox is already flooded with questions from the lawyers. I should probably answer those."

"Someone should be there for you," Selena said. "That's why I want to go."

"He's a monster, Selena. The worst person I know. And if I can keep you from him, I will do that. I can't let him anywhere near you. Please stay here."

Her lips pressed together. "Fine. But you still shouldn't be alone. Can we call

Ruth?"

Chapter Twenty-Five

Selena

Ruth answered on the third ring.

"Hello? If this is another scam call, I swear—"

"It's Selena," I said. "Not a scam call."

"Oh, hi," she said, her voice infinitely kinder. "What's up?"

"Um, do you know how your dad is a jerk and ruined all your lives?"

"How could I forget? Wait, is this about that stupid social media post, because I will get Tom a job at PATH here if—"

It was time to rip this off like a Band-Aid. "Your dad is the one who turned me away and sent me money all those years ago. Not Tom. We just found out this morning."

"He *what?*" Ruth's voice rose.

"Tom's going to confront him, and I don't know how fast you and Knox could get to wherever your parents live, but I think you need to be sure he doesn't kill his father."

"*Fucker.* I can be there in about thirty minutes. Don't worry, I'll make sure our lovely father is the only one doing illegal shit. Thanks for letting me know."

"Wait! Where is your dad's house? I need to know in case..." I struggled to come up with a reason.

"In case it takes a while?" she guessed. "I'll tell you. Don't worry about it."

I scrambled to get a pen to write it down. Once I had it, she hung up to go deal with her father.

My body was buzzing with anxiety. I tried to be patient and kill time, but I couldn't sit still, and I kept wondering what was happening at his parents' house. I stared at the address, asking myself why I didn't just follow them to make sure everything was okay—to make sure *Tom* was okay.

An hour later, my phone rang, and I jumped to answer it.

But it wasn't who I was expecting. "Selena," Mom began, "Luna has finally found some sense and is leaving that old man. Can you believe it?"

I'd completely forgotten about Luna and Willie's relationship. "Mom, I can't—"

"I was thinking we should have a girl's day. Maybe go do our hair, get our nails done."

"Mom," I snapped. "Today is not the day."

"What's going on?" she asked. "Is it Tom?"

"I'll kill him!" Luna yelled in the background. "I'm already in a mood."

"N-no, it's not Tom." I took a breath. "It's his father. He's the one who sent the money and turned me and Max away. Tom never knew."

"What?" Mom asked. "What do you mean?"

I told her everything, about all the evidence, about all the ways I'd doubted it was him. When I finally caught her up, she was cursing in Spanish, sounding as mad as the day I'd told her Tom hadn't answered my emails.

"So, where is Tom now?" Luna asked over the sound of Mom's rage-filled words.

"At Tom's dad's house. He's confronting him."

"Is that a good idea?"

"No, but I sent his sister to help."

"His sister who also has been hurt?" Luna asked. "Maybe you should go."

"I can't. I need to get Max from school."

"We'll get him," Luna said. "You're obviously mad but keeping calm right now. That's probably what he needs."

In the background, Mom was threatening Todd Murray with castration.

"Staying levelheaded is not a skill all of us have, obviously," Luna said.

"M-maybe you're right."

"Go help him. We'll keep Max happy for the time being."

"Okay," I said. "I'm going to go. Thank you, guys."

"Let me know where I can find him!" Mom broke in. "I'll end his days!"

"We need to focus on Max," Luna said, taking the words out of my mouth. "You've got this, Selena."

I hung up, heart racing. Meowcifer made a noise by the door.

"I'm going to find him," I told her. "And I'll bring him back." I gave her a few pats on the head before I grabbed the keys to Tom's truck. The old truck roared to life and rumbled in my ears, but I didn't give myself any time to overthink me driving his antique.

Pulling out of the driveway, I headed right for where all the action was.

I was so out of it, I almost missed the cursed stop sign at the bottom of the hill. Luckily, I was able to stop in time.

But I wasn't watching out for anyone else but me.

Behind me, someone obviously wasn't paying attention. I only had a second to catch the fact that they were *not* slowing down.

Then they hit the back of the truck. I heard metal on metal, a sickening crunch, and my head was thrown toward the steering wheel.

The moment the cab dropped me off, I was storming in. I hadn't been here since the fateful night Ruth had snapped on everyone and walked out for good, and being back should have filled me with dread, but I was too angry to feel anything else.

"This is insanity!" Dad was yelling. I heard something slam. "I am tired of weathering these baseless lies about me!"

I rounded the corner. Mom was tucked in the corner, attempting to look small. Dad was next to the dining room table, his briefcase and its contents strewn on the floor around him.

"You," he said when he saw me, "you have a lot of nerve coming here!"

My fists instantly clenched when he addressed me.

"Selena Martinez."

Dad's anger melted off his face. "So you *do* know that name."

"Do you admit it?"

Before he could answer, the front door opened. "Tom!" Ruth called and she ran into the room. "Don't do anything rash, at least not without me."

"So you invited her too?"

"Ruth?" Mom asked. "You're here?"

"Not for any good reason," she said. "Oh, by the way, meet my boyfriend, Knox." She looked at Dad. "Watch what you say."

Mom made a choked sound as Knox came into the room. If it were under any other circumstances, I'd have cared more. Mom always loved Knox, possibly more so than Ruth.

"He doesn't scare me," Dad said.

"Really?" Knox asked, his voice harder than I'd ever heard it. "I hear my lawyer is giving you a run for your money."

"What is going on?" Mom asked. "Why are you both here?"

"I'm here for moral support," Ruth said, and she turned to me. "Has he admitted it yet?"

"He was about to."

"I suppose you know then," Dad said. "About her *claims*."

"Claims of what?" Mom asked, looking between us desperately.

"They weren't *claims*. Selena Martinez was pregnant with my child."

Mom sucked in a breath. "What?"

"And Dad posed as me and paid her off. Using company money."

"Really?" Knox said. "That is *very* frowned upon."

"She was supposed to get rid of it," Dad replied. "I'm guessing she didn't."

"Do not refer to my son as *it*," I snapped. My voice rattled against the walls. I took one step closer. "And of course she didn't."

"She took the money. And I guess she didn't heed my warning."

"Oh, that you would take it back if she ever spoke to me? She thought *I* said that. Do you know how much I apologized for words I didn't fucking say?"

"Todd," Mom said. "Is it true? Does Tom have a son?"

"Unfortunately," Dad said in a measured tone.

"And you kept him from all of us?"

"You don't understand. None of you do. I had *three* kids. Three! And only one was worth a damn."

"Hey," Ruth snapped. "I did what you asked. You wrote me off for being a girl."

"And I stand by it! I stand by *all* of my decisions because I wanted *success*. You'll get pregnant by Knox and never want to work again." He turned to me. "And *then* I saw the same softness in you. You would quit everything for that child. And I refused to let you throw away all that I've built for you."

"Max is my future," I said slowly. "He always was."

"Let me guess, you coddle him. You treat him with all the smiles and happiness you wish you had. Let me be the first to tell you, he will be a *failure*. Just like you."

Ruth spoke first. "You son of a—"

I held up my hand, eyes still on Dad. "Raising my son with love and affection will be the greatest failure I ever experience."

Dad blinked and then scoffed. "I refuse to believe that you would be okay with failing after all I did for you."

"You're not better than us, considering you *failed* at making me like you."

Ruth snickered, which only seemed to make Dad angrier.

"And what? You'll ruin my company too?"

"I'll make Murray and Sons better than you could ever imagine it to be. I've already started to. You've seen what the PATH project did for revenue."

"Yeah," Ruth added. "Everyone is talking about what Tom and I did. Revenue is up. You had no part in that."

"Exactly. Me and your *daughter*, who you wrote off from the beginning, did what you couldn't."

He turned red in the face. "You're wrong. You're wrong about all of it."

I knew he would deny it, but as the weight of everything he'd done hit me, I realized this man was not my father. He was only a man who'd ruined my life.

"Let me make something clear, *Todd*. I don't care what you think. You'll never be able to convince me that what you've done was right. I will raise my son with kindness and patience. I will run Murray and Sons the same way. And I will do it all *despite* everything you taught me. You were never my strength. You were a weakness. You always have been."

He breathed heavily; his mouth opened, but no words came out. He was finally out of things to say.

"I couldn't have said it better myself," Ruth added. "Well, I have one other thing to say. Fuck you, Dad. Mom, grow a pair and finally leave him."

That got his attention. "She will never leave me. I have her domesticated, something you never learned."

"You're wrong." Mom's voice shook. "These last few months have been the worst of my life, you know that? You're a terrible husband, a terrible father, and I regret ever marrying you."

He raised his hand.

"Don't you dare," I said. "Or you'll be adding domestic assault to your list of problems."

"I'm leaving," Mom said. She ran past him, standing between Ruth and me.

"You'll have nothing." The words were hissed. They were the last ones of a man losing everything.

"I'll have myself," she said. "And I'll be free of you. That's enough."

"Fine then. Take everything away because I dared to push you all to be better. I should have never cared."

"You didn't care either way," I said. "You're just losing your trophies."

We all turned, walking out the door despite the words he yelled at our backs. "You won't get away with this! I will be back at Murray and Sons. I will beat this ridiculous case you have and I'll—"

The door shut.

And we left Todd Murray behind.

Knox let out a long breath. "Do you know how hard it was for me not to hit him?"

"Join the club," I said dryly.

"We got him to admit it," Ruth said. "And I recorded it, like I always do when I confront assholes, so you'll be able to use this if he still tries to get Murray and Sons back. I'll send it to you."

"Thank you," I said. "We should get out of here before he comes outside."

"Ruth," Mom said, as we walked down the porch steps. "Does your offer still stand?"

"Yes," she said.

"Then I'll take you up on it. Please."

"What offer?" I asked.

"To pay for the lawyer in case Mom did leave," Ruth said. "A lot of women get stuck in marriages and they can't afford a way out. I didn't want that to stop her."

"It's more than I deserve," she said. "Thank you. You kids are far more giving than Todd or I ever taught you to be."

Ruth and I exchanged glances, unsure of what to say.

She was still our mother, but she'd let us stay with Todd for far too long. She followed in his ways and pit Ruth against all of us.

"Where will you go?" Ruth asked.

"My parents' place, out in the country. I'd been thinking about leaving him for a while, but I never had the courage. They said I could live with them. It's rough life but it's home."

"Knox and I can give you a ride," Ruth said. "Do you want to go too, Tom?"

I wasn't sure, but before I could answer, my phone chirped. It was a different noise that I'd never heard before.

"What is that?" I muttered.

"That's a PATH notification," Knox said. "For the airbags."

"Airbags? But Selena has the truck."

I pulled out my phone, seeing the notification that my vehicle had been in a crash bad enough to deploy the airbags. The system had automatically called 911 when the occupant didn't seem conscious.

And the only occupant had to be the one woman I couldn't lose.

"I let her borrow my truck," I said, heart kicking into high gear. "I need to get where she is."

"Take my car," Knox said. "I'll order another to pick us up. We can walk down to the nearby gas station so we're away from Todd."

"Okay. How fast can it go?"

"Normally, I wouldn't be able to answer that question. But there's an emergency mode. I'll activate it." He threw the keys at me and I took off.

I needed to get there. I needed to know Selena was okay.

Because if she wasn't, and she was hurt while I was with *Todd,* of all people, I may never be able to forgive myself.

Chapter Twenty-Six

My forehead rested on something softer than the metal that was the steering wheel. I slowly pulled away from it, ears ringing. I heard a loud dinging noise, yet it sounded like it was so far away. Blinking, I tried to get my brain to function, but everything felt off. I pulled back from the material and saw the PATH logo.

I pushed it away, trying to make sense of what had just happened. I was on my way to be there for Tom. I had stopped at the cursed stop sign, but someone else had missed it and slammed into me.

I opened the door and stumbled out of the car.

"Whoa there," a female voice said. I blearily noticed that ambulance lights were flashing. They hurt my already pounding head. "Let's get you checked for a concussion."

"I'm fine. I think."

"Did you hit your head at all?"

"It hit the steering wheel." As I said it, I realized it wasn't true. "No, it hit the airbags."

"I don't think cars that old have airbags."

"But it did. It had the PATH logo on them."

"Can someone go check and see if that's true?" she called out. Another man jogged over. She shined a light into my eyes, which made me push away.

"Your eyes are normal at least."

"She's right! Truck had airbags."

Wait a minute.

Had?

"How bad is the damage?" I asked.

"That doesn't matter. What matters is you."

"No, it definitely matters. That's not my truck, it's my..." I wanted to say *boyfriend's*, but I wondered if that word would even apply anymore after he saw this. "It's special to someone. He's going to kill me if it's damaged."

"We need to worry about you," she insisted.

"I'm fine."

"Let's get you to the ambulance to double-check."

I gnawed on my lip as I was guided over. I tried to turn and look at the damage, but it wasn't visible from my angle.

Minutes later, and after a battery of tests, she finally gave me some good news. "Somehow you don't have a concussion. And you're not injured. I've seen many accidents in older vehicles where that is not the case."

"It's got some system in it," the other guy said as he walked back over. "PATH or something?"

"The owner of the truck knows someone at PATH," I said.

"Then you owe them one. I think whatever it is just saved your life."

I stood, walking over to survey the damage. The car that had rear-ended me was totaled. Bent metal was all that was left of the front and the other person involved was being cut out of the car.

Then I finally saw the truck. The bed was bent inward, the old metal giving way to the collision.

My knees buckled.

The paramedics ran over to me, but I didn't know how to tell them that this wasn't a physical injury. It was all emotional.

I was pretty sure Tom was going to dump me over this. I'd come to help on the worst day of his life, but somehow I'd managed to ruin one of the first things he ever cared about.

I sat in silence and let them help me back to the ambulance.

Tom

I'd never seen so many police cars and ambulances in this part of the neighborhood. People were on their porches, jaws agape, as they witnessed the aftermath of a serious accident.

My heart was in my throat as I pulled up to it. My eyes were on the ambulances and everything stopped when I saw Selena.

I couldn't see if she was all right, but she was at least on her feet. Someone was helping her walk over to the emergency vehicle. I threw the car in park and ran to her.

"Selena!"

She jumped and turned, her brown eyes that I had dreams about wide as they saw me. "T-Tom." Her voice was soft and wavering.

"Are you okay?" I asked.

"Do you know her?"

"Know her? She's the woman I plan to spend the rest of my life with, so I would say so."

Selena let out a sob. "Not after this."

The EMT looked concerned. "I thought you were all right."

"I am. This is all emotional. Physically, I'm fine."

I turned to her, inspecting every inch of her face. I didn't see a scratch on her.

"I've got her," I said. "I'll call if she needs anything."

Selena leaned into me, as if hiding from the noise and chaos. I took her weight gratefully, leading her to the back of the ambulance. Apparently, the other driver wasn't as lucky as Selena had been and was receiving medical care. My eyes slid over the truck and I eyed the tough metal of the steering wheel, covered by the airbags that had saved her.

She'd been rear-ended at the bottom of the hill. That could have killed her.

"I'm sorry," she blubbered, face landing on my shirt. "I'm so sorry."

"What are you sorry for?"

"I wrecked something you love."

The words did not compute. "What?"

"I wrecked your truck!" she exclaimed. "The one thing you love! And on the worst day of your life! I'm an idiot. I should have stayed home and never come after you."

"You came after me?"

"I didn't want you to be alone," she said. "I don't care how evil your father is. You shouldn't have had to face him without me. I wanted to be there for you."

It hit me then. She'd left the house to be *with me*. She cared enough to face a man who'd hurt her when she normally hid away from conflict.

"Selena," I said, moving her to where I was facing her. "You didn't wreck what I love."

"But the truck—"

I put a hand on her mouth, gently quieting her. "You didn't wreck what I love," I repeated slowly. "Because I love *you*. You will always mean more to me than the truck."

"M-me?" she asked.

"Yes. You."

She let out a breath, eyes wide as she took in my words. "God, I just had the most romantic moment of my life and I'm crying through it?" She wiped at her face.

"It's okay. And this isn't going to be the most romantic moment of your life.

I'll make sure of that."

She slowly nodded. "Thank you. I was *so* scared you would—"

"You're everything to me. You and Max."

"Damn, where do I find a man like you?" the EMT asked. "This is like one of those romance novels or something."

"Yeah," Selena said, a smile finally crossing her face. "I'm lucky to have him."

"You're lucky in a lot of ways." The EMT pointed to the truck.

"Did the airbags work?" I asked.

"Yes. We owe Knox one," Selena added.

"I owe him a lot of things. Putting those in was the greatest thing I ever did." I wanted to say more, but a cop came over and told her he needed a statement.

"They missed that stop sign while I was at it," Selena said. "So they hit me going full speed."

My grip on her tightened. "That sign needs to be a traffic light."

"You're not the first person to tell us that. I've been getting the runaround from the traffic safety department for years."

"Give me their number. I'll handle it."

"More power to you," the cop said, writing down the number. His eyes moved to Selena. "Glad you're okay. This was a nasty one."

"Me too."

"Are you the owner of the truck?" he asked me.

"I am."

"Can you give me the info of that safety package you got? I have a classic car at home and after seeing this, I think I'll look into it."

I happily did. And once all the statements were given, and the other driver was on their way to the hospital, we arranged for my truck to be towed. I kept Selena in my arms, grateful that I hadn't lost her in the mess of this.

As long as I had her, everything else was going to be okay.

Chapter Twenty-Seven

Selena

"I may not have a concussion, but I definitely have a headache from all the crying I just did."

"Lie down and rest," Tom instructed me. "I'll get you some water."

I followed his orders and pulled out my Kindle. When he brought me the glass of water, I gulped it down. He sat with me while I recovered, only taking his attention off me for a few moments to answer emails on his phone from his employees asking what was going on.

"I bet they're happy you're staying their boss," I said.

"I think they might be. All I know is that I'm making changes. Big ones."

"How did it go with your dad?"

"He isn't my dad," Tom said. "Not anymore."

"I'm sorry," I replied, putting my hand on his shoulder.

"He never really was anyway. He was only the man who kept wanting me to be like him."

"I'm glad you're not."

"I am too," he said, giving me a small smile. I lay against his shoulder, where I dozed on and off until Mom, Luna, and Max walked through the door.

"Are you sure you don't know whose fancy car that is?" Max asked as he walked in.

"No clue. I don't even know if your mom is home yet."

"I am," I said from the couch. "And I actually don't know whose car that is."

"It's a friend's," Tom said.

"You're both here?" Max asked. "But where's the truck?"

I looked at Tom, biting my lip.

"Probably at an auto shop by now," he answered.

"Auto shop? Don't tell me it broke down."

"No, your mom got hit in it."

"What?" Luna asked.

"Are you okay?" Mom added.

"I'm fine. No concussion."

"But what about the truck?" Max asked.

"Max," Tom started, "your mom is far more important than the truck is. Even if it were totaled, I'd rather she be okay."

Luna turned to Mom, eyebrows raised.

"I-I'm sure you want her to pay for the costs, right?" Mom asked. "It must have been a nice truck."

"No, I don't care about that. Like I said, all that matters is that everyone is okay."

"There is one other thing," I added. "Max, we need to tell you something."

"Please don't tell me that DNA test was fake and I'm not really Mr. Tom's kid." The words blew out of him, and Tom and I looked over at each other, confused.

"No," I said. "That's not going to happen."

"It's been a bit of a whirlwind these past few weeks," Max replied. "Anything can happen."

"That's true. But don't worry. We know for sure you're Tom's son."

"Anyone can see it," Luna added. "Except us, apparently."

"Do you remember that letter I read you," I said to Max, "that Tom sent me all those years ago?"

"Um, yeah. But I thought we all agreed that he wasn't that person anymore."

"Well, he wasn't that person then, either. Someone else sent that letter."

"What?"

"My father did," Tom added. "Though, I won't be calling him that anymore. He never earned the title."

"Oh," Max said. "That's really sad."

"It's okay," he replied. "I'm just grateful that you guys gave me a second chance when you thought I had sent it."

"So, then no one has any reason to be mad then, right?" Max asked. "We can all maybe get along?" He turned to Mom with a hopeful, wide-eyed expression.

"Maybe Max has a point," she said. "Maybe we should move on. Especially since you made sure my daughter was okay."

"Technically, Knox Price invented the system," he replied.

"You still had the idea."

"And Tom stepped in the moment he found out about Max," Luna added. "You can't forget about that."

"Are you on his side now?" Mom planted balled-up fists on her hips.

"What? I want my older sister to get her happy ending. At least I can see one after dating an old fart for far too long."

Mom rolled her eyes but then looked over at Tom again. "I'm sorry your family did that to you. You're on the road to being a good father yourself and I don't want to stand in the way of that." She held out a hand. "Truce?"

"I would love that," he replied, shaking her hand.

"Welcome to the family," she said. "Now, if I ever see Todd Murray, you will have to keep me from going to jail."

"I'll do my best. But you'll have to get in line."

"Behind you?"

"Behind my sister Ruth and my brother Barry."

"Oh, Max has even more family. I'd love to meet them one day."

"I think you can. You know, they do these lovely dinners on Monday nights. Maybe we should go."

"I might take you up on that."

Tom

When Max asked me to help with his homework in his room, I had a distinct feeling that it was not all about his school assignments. Usually, we'd be at the dining room table if we were working on his homework.

"So," Max said, nervously playing with his sleeves. "You really were a decent guy this whole time. I should have known when the cat liked you."

"I still don't get why she does."

"They have a sixth sense. She knew. And I wish I did too. That was the one thing I didn't get," he said. "You didn't sound like you in that letter."

"And I didn't even know who I was," I said. "I'm sorry for all the confusion."

"It's not your fault. Apparently, it's your dad's. Is he why you look sad sometimes?" He wasn't supposed to see that I was sad at all. He was the reason I smiled, even. "I'm not blind. Mom used to look the same way, until you came around."

I let out a long breath. "Yeah, it's one of the many reasons I look sad sometimes. But he can't hurt me anymore."

"I'm sorry. I guess some people don't care about their kids. Not like you do."

"It's an honor to care about you, Max."

"Y-you know, I can't exactly call you Mr. Tom anymore. Putting 'mister' in front of your name feels weird."

"Then what do you want to call me?"

"What you are. My dad."

My heart stuttered in my chest. "Are you sure?"

"Yeah. Because you're definitely my dad, and the best one I could ask for."

Emotion clogged my throat. I hadn't even let myself think of being called "Dad" by Max. I thought I'd lost that luxury when I hadn't been around. But now that it was an option, I knew I couldn't turn it down. "Thank you, Max. I would love nothing more."

Max jumped forward and wrapped his arms around me. His grip was tight, as if he was afraid I would leave at any moment.

But I never would, not if I could help it.

"Thank you for giving me a chance to be your dad."

"Thank *you* for being the best dad ever."

The hug lasted for minutes, but it felt like seconds. Max pulled away, asking if we could listen to music together until it was time for dinner.

We ordered in because I knew Selena didn't feel up for cooking, and we ate at the table. Carmen and Luna joined, making it livelier than all the dinners I'd been to with Mom and Todd. I could see a future where it was even bigger, where we would have Ruth and her found family over too—and the thought made me so grateful that I had started with one choice all those months ago. I only needed one to change everything.

After dinner was over, Carmen and Luna left, saying they needed to get the rest of Luna's stuff from her now ex-boyfriend. They hugged us both, and Carmen's grin in my direction reminded me of the first time I met her, when she didn't know about my past.

"That was fun," Max said once the door shut. "But I need some alone time before heading to bed."

"Don't stay up too late," Selena called.

"I won't. I'm too tired to. Night, Mom." He gave her a hug and then turned to me. "Night, Dad."

The term warmed my heart in a way I didn't think possible. "Good night," I said, feeling my face break out into one of the largest smiles I'd ever had.

When Max went back to his room, Selena turned to me, eyebrows raised. "Since when is he calling you Dad?"

"Since earlier, when I went to his room. He asked if he could."

"I knew you were in a good mood," she replied. "And I'm happy to see these." Selena reached a hand up to trace a dimple.

I brought her closer and pressed my lips to hers.

"Before we get too carried away," she said, pulling back, "I need to put dinner up." She turned to go to the kitchen, but I saw her wince and rub her neck. "I must be sore from the wreck."

"Go lie down," I replied. "I'll put the food away."

"I'm not even going to fight it. God, I need a neck rub."

"I'll do that too," I offered. "Just give me a few minutes."

Her cheeks turned pink as she blushed and went to the bedroom. I made quick work of the chore before joining her.

Selena was sitting up reading a book, still grimacing as she rubbed her neck.

"Turn around," I said. "I'll take care of you."

My hands touched her shoulders and I carefully rubbed her neck and back.

"Mm, harder," she said.

With my hands on her, my brain took the words the wrong way and blood rushed to my cock.

No, I reminded myself. *She's in pain and that's not the solution.*

I continued my movements, tracing the plane of her back with my hands, listening to her deep breathing as I worked to loosen her muscles.

"You're incredible at this," she said, her voice breathy. "Maybe you were a masseuse in another life."

"You'd be my only patient." I couldn't stop myself from leaning down to kiss her shoulder. She scooted back to lean into me and her ass came to rest against my growing erection. "Sorry." I resisted the urge to let my hips jerk forward. "I know you're not feeling—"

"After that back rub," she said, looking over her shoulder at me, "I'm feeling up for anything."

"Are you sure?"

"Yes," she said, and she rotated her body to where she was facing me. She was pressed against my hardness, which strained against my dress pants. She rolled over. The moment she was on her back, she kissed me.

God, she was perfect. I may not know how I managed to land the woman of my dreams, but I would do my best to make sure I treated her like the perfection she was.

My hands ran down her sides, desperate to feel more of her. My body wanted every inch of her. My head spun with ideas of ways I could have her moaning, which had quickly become my favorite sound.

"Let me take care of you."

She didn't argue, her eyes staring up at me. I hovered over her, kissing her mouth, her jawline, and then the spot on her neck that always made her let out a breathy noise that was indented in my mind.

"P-please," she said. "Touch me more."

"I'm getting there," I said, moving down her chest. Her loose V-neck sweater gave me perfect access to her beautiful breasts, which I kissed the moment I saw them. My mouth covered her nipple and she arched her back into the sensation.

"Oh, fuck," she whispered. Her hands moved to keep me there and I nipped at them until she was gasping for breath.

But then it was time for me to make my way down lower. My mouth kissed her rib cage, the area just above her belly button, and then her hip.

When I finally hooked my hands around the waistband of her leggings, she pulled them off before I could.

"Impatient?" I asked her, but I loved this needy side of her.

"I need you."

"Then you have me." I couldn't deny her any longer. It had been too long since I'd tasted her, and the musky sweet flavor was so satisfying. I could stay here forever, worshipping her pussy with my tongue. But she was already worked up by my mouth in other places. Her legs tightened around my head and she rode herself over the mountain of a body-shaking orgasm.

Selena was beautiful every moment of the day, but this was something different. There weren't words for how she looked when her body was convulsing from pure pleasure, but it was burned into my eyelids and I had dreams about it.

She was gasping as she came down from her high. "You better be about to fuck me," she said.

I moved one of my fingers to her entrance. "Like this?"

"You know that's not what I meant."

"I do." I pressed one inside. She gasped and I could feel her tighten around me. "But I have a feeling you wouldn't complain about this either."

Selena didn't answer. She was lost in the feeling again. I pumped my fingers inside of her, hooking them upward to hit her G-spot. She was writhing, hands gripping her sheets. Her white knuckles told me she was once again close.

I brought my mouth down to her clit, circling my tongue over the swollen bud. She made a broken sound and I could feel her pussy clench, liquid rushing from her as she orgasmed again.

I kept moving until she yanked away from my movements, her body sensitive after two orgasms.

"Did you get some inspiration from one of my romance novels?" she asked as she caught her breath.

I looked up at her. "I don't need a book to tell me how to make you feel good. Not when you make sounds like you do."

"Okay, maybe I *did* enjoy that," she said as she calmed down. "But I'm ready for you to fuck me this time."

"Are you—"

She rolled us over, displaying strength I hadn't seen. She took off my pants with one fluid movement and then sat on my lap.

"Is that a good enough answer for you?"

"Message received," I said. "Do you want to get a condom?"

"I'm on birth control," she said. "And I got tested after breaking up with Jax."

"I did too, after I got sober," I replied.

"Then screw the condom." She leaned forward to kiss me and I pressed my cock against her soaked entrance. Her hips moved down as she slowly accepted every inch of me.

Her eyes met mine as I was fully inside of her. They were darker than I'd ever seen them. "This is what I wanted," she said.

My head was spinning from her tightness. I needed to move, to fill her up with nothing in between us. I thrusted my hips upward and her eyes rolled back as she got more of what she wanted. I pumped in and out of her and she bounced as a result of my movements.

This was where I needed to be, buried inside of her and watching as she felt all of me. She was like a vise, gripping my cock, which sent me tumbling toward release. Her hips moved in time with me and her pussy fluttered around me as she built to another orgasm. I bit my tongue to hold out for her. I wanted to feel her come before I got my own release.

"T-Tom," she said, driving her hips into mine. "I'm gonna—"

"Do it," I said. "Come on me, Selena."

Her mouth dropped open and her core clenched tighter around me. I could feel every pulse of her orgasm, and it sent me into mine. I filled her with my own seed, holding her down so she took every last drop.

Selena slumped against me, nearly gasping for breath. "That was...I don't have words."

"You don't have to," I said, bringing her in for a kiss. She pressed her lips harder into me and I felt my spent cock jump in anticipation. "We're doing that again in the morning."

"Please," she said. "But I think I need sleep first."

"Good thing I'm here, then."

"Good thing you're *always* here."

When I walked into work the next day, the last thing I was expecting to see was my office decorated in balloons and a massive banner that said "Congratulations!"

"What the—"

"Hi," a female voice greeted. I turned to see Asha. "I did this last night. Do you like it?"

"Y-you're back? How is your wife?"

"Much better," she said. "My first day back was yesterday, and we were all worried that Todd was going to show up."

"He isn't."

"We know. This is just a little something for you to say we're happy you're our boss permanently."

"Thank you," I said, touched.

"Is he here?" I heard Francine's voice call from the hallway. "I want to get these in his office before..." She walked in, a large box in hand, groaning when she saw me. "Damn it. There goes the surprise."

"I am still very much surprised," I said.

"But nothing would have beat you seeing this on your desk." She opened the box.

I saw my face made out of icing on cupcakes. Underneath it said, "You're now CEO! You're stuck with us for life." A laugh escaped me. "You had time to make these."

"Walmart sure did. I took yesterday off so I could sleep. I figured you had it in the bag."

"I think I did," I said. "Speaking of which, I have a surprise for you."

"Oh?"

"Another promotion, to senior manager. I trust you with a lot and your title should show that."

Francine's jaw dropped. "Seriously? Are you sure?"

"I'm sure. You had a part in saving this company, so you deserve the title with it."

"I'm truly honored." She set down the box. "Fuck this thing. I'm giving you a hug."

I only had a second before she was wrapping her arms around me.

"Oh, I want to join too!" Asha exclaimed.

"All right, all right. Thank you both," I said.

"Thank *you*," Asha began. "Murray and Sons is a better company with you at the head of it."

"Murray and Sons isn't too accurate of a name anymore. Maybe it's time for a rebrand."

"Going bold on your first official day," Francine said. "I like it. What do you want to rebrand to?"

"Just Murray, I think."

"Yes," Asha said. "It feels more modern."

"We also need to do something about all the guys here loyal to Todd," Francine added.

"I'm sure a few of them already turned in their notices," I replied. "But I'll let you monitor some of the external emails. Especially if they send them to Todd. If you see anything, let me know and I'll take care of it."

"Sounds perfect."

"Speaking of good change," I added, "how about we see if we can electrify all our trucks?"

"You're gonna keep us busy," Francine said, but she was smiling. "I'm ready, though."

"Me too," I replied. "Call a meeting. Let's make these changes immediately."

Epilogue

Selena

Two Months Later

"Keep your eyes covered," Tom said. "I'm just getting the door."

"What surprise could you possibly have for me this time?" I asked. "You've already taken me out to some of the nicest restaurants in Nashville. Plus, the ones in Atlanta whenever we visit Hadley, not to mention the springtime walk in the cherry blossoms. What else could you do? And at home, no less?"

"You'll see." He brought me inside and positioned me somewhere in the living room. I heard him try to move Meowcifer as he walked in, only for her to circle his legs. "Just give me one second and I'll pick you up," he told the cat. "Okay Selena, open your eyes."

The first thing I saw was bookshelves. At least five of them. I blinked, thinking I was somehow teleported to a bookstore. I looked closer.

"Are these...romance books?"

"All the ones on your Kindle, yes," Tom said as he made true to his promise to pick up Meowcifer.

My jaw dropped. He wasn't lying. Every single romance novel I'd read was on the shelf, plus some I hadn't.

"Tom, this is hundreds of books."

"I told you that the day of the wreck wouldn't be the most romantic moment of your life. And it's a late Christmas present."

"You bought me a new car for Christmas. *And* fixed the old one up for Max to have when he's old enough."

"*Second* Christmas present. Or maybe it doesn't have to be a holiday present at all. I just like to spoil you year-round."

My eyes watered as I looked at all of them. I'd always wanted to be surrounded by books and art, and now my home felt like a little library.

"This is amazing," I said, bringing him in for a long kiss. "Thank you. I don't even think I could fit any more into this living room."

"There are ways."

"Like what?"

"Getting a bigger living room."

I stared blankly. "In a different house?"

"Yes. If that's what you wanted."

I thought about it. While I'd liked this house for when I was younger, Max and I were quickly running out of space—even more so now that Tom basically lived with us.

"Where would we live?"

"What if we moved into a house closer to Ruth and Knox? It's such a perfect neighborhood. And it's near where my mom's trying to move to."

"That's exactly where I was thinking."

I bit my lip. I'd been dreaming of that neighborhood ever since we started regularly visiting it. We spent a lot of time in that area now that Mom got along with Tom and joined in on the now-massive family dinners. Mom had taken to teaching Lynn, who couldn't seem to cook anything edible, how to be at least a little better in the kitchen. The two women got along great, especially since Lynn had started cutting Mom's hair.

I loved being near Lynn. She'd helped me find a place to get on a waiting list to get tested for autism—something I'd been nervous about.

"We could even have a little guesthouse for your mom and Luna to stay in if they wanted to," Tom added.

"Maybe we'll do that after we're married."

"I could go for that any day now too."

My heart pounded. Sometimes, I felt like we were moving too fast and yet not fast enough at all. I wanted forever with him, and I'd known it for months now.

"I love you." Even though they were words I said every day, I meant them. "I can't wait to marry you one day."

"That day might be coming sooner than you think. Now that we have house plans, I'm tempted to accelerate other things."

"I would be okay with that."

He kissed me, his lips slotting over mine like they were coming home. I melted into him, feeling for once, like I had gotten the happy ending I never thought possible.

Tom

Mom was living in western Tennessee. I hadn't ever made the drive out here, but I was glad to do it with Ruth. It was the truck's inaugural drive after getting fixed and I was happy to have it back.

Heading out to the country in it with Ruth was more relaxing than I'd ever imagined. She played Lila Wilde and sang to every lyric. Apparently, our grandparents still owned a decent plot of land and did local farming. Both Ruth and I had thought they had given up farming after Mom insisted they move on to more profitable endeavors. Instead, they had moved to a new place and told no one.

Both Ruth and I kept loose contact with her after the divorce. Barry had yet to do the same thing, but I couldn't blame him. Sometimes, I felt so angry for how she'd treated him and Ruth. Sometimes, I hated how she was Todd's enforcer. All those years had done damage and it was easier to rely on people like Lynn and Carmen, who'd never hurt me in those ways.

Maybe one day I'd be closer with her, but for now, distance was best.

When she'd called and invited us, neither Ruth nor I were very excited about coming out. We didn't know what she had planned, but she said she desperately needed to talk to us, so we made the journey.

Mom was waiting for us outside, but our grandparents ran out to give us hugs.

"You've all grown so much!" Grandma said. "Ruth, you're so beautiful."

"And Tom!" Grandpa said. "You're a foot taller than me!"

"It's great to see you guys," Ruth said, smiling. "How have you been?"

"Good, good. Come on in for lunch. We made bologna sandwiches."

It had been a long time since I'd had one, but it felt familiar in a nice way. I'd missed this kind of life, and I knew Ruth did too.

Grandma and Grandpa caught us up on everything that was happening in their tiny little town. I didn't know most of the people they told us about, but it was interesting to hear anyway.

Mom was quiet while we were there and I kept wondering just what she was thinking. Did she regret coming back? Did she wish she was still with Todd?

"Can I speak to you both outside?" Mom asked after we'd finished lunch. Ruth and I looked at each other, frowning in concern. We walked outside into the warm spring air. Mom wrung her hands.

"What's going on?" Ruth asked. "Is everything okay with the divorce?"

"As good as it can be. He was done with me after I walked out, but that's not why I asked you to come out here. I was hoping Barry would be here for this."

"Barry isn't much for family stuff," I replied. "He has his own life."

"Much like his father."

I frowned. Was that an insult? I knew Barry wouldn't take any comparison to Todd lightly.

"Do you see that house over there?" she asked, pointing to the neighbor's place.

"Who lives there?"

"A man by the name of Wilfred Simmons. He's a very good friend of Mom and Dad's, but before their friendship came to be, he was a classmate of mine. He was always the popular boy when I was in high school. He could have had every girl he could dream of. But he only wanted one."

I looked at Ruth, raising an eyebrow. Did she bring us out here to tell us about her high school life?

"He sounds nice, Mom," Ruth said.

"He was. He was my best friend, but I...I left when I thought I could have a better life. With Todd, I mean."

"Are you saying you're still in love with him?" I hedged.

"I don't know. I haven't talked to him since coming back. I'm terrified to tell him about...well, what I'm about to tell you two. You kids need to know first."

"Need to know what?" Ruth asked, her voice laced with a desperate edge.

"There was one time when I thought about leaving your father. You kids were very little. I came here and ran into Wilfred. He lived in that house alone and said he was waiting for me. We had one night, but I...I thought it didn't leave a mark. Then I turned up pregnant."

"What are you saying?" I said lowly, but I was starting to put the pieces together.

"I'm saying that Wilfred and I have a baby. And that baby is Barry. He's not Todd's."

Ruth sucked in a breath of air. "What? Barry is...oh, that explains his looks."

"He looks just like Wilfred. The blond hair, the eyes." She looked at her feet. "I didn't tell anyone because I thought having a stable life with Todd would be safer. And when Todd started questioning it, I fell in line to prevent him from looking into it further. It was all wrong, I know that now, but I can't go on without someone knowing. Barry deserves to know, but he doesn't want to talk to me, which is exactly what I deserve."

Ruth paced the front porch we were standing on, running her fingers through her hair. "He's going to be so mad. We have to tell him."

"I don't know if he'll talk to you."

"He will if we call a sibling meeting," I said. "And go to his bar."

"Please," Mom said. "Tell him. I would go, but I don't think he wants to see me. Nor will he ever, once he finds out."

"We'll...we'll talk to him," Ruth promised. "Do you have any more secrets, Mom? Anything else that could change our lives?"

"No. This is the only one."

"Well, I guess this is our rodeo now." She turned to me. "Ready to go ruin Barry's day?"

"No." I looked over at Mom who was still near tears. "But he needs to know."

"This better be good," Barry said when we knocked on the door.

I never thought I would set foot in another bar. Thankfully it was closed, but seeing all the liquor bottles made me uncomfortable. The people in my support group would have told me not to go, but this was a bit of an emergency; this was family business.

Barry looked like he'd just woken up. His long, blond hair was messed up on one side and I was pretty sure he had a hickey on his neck.

"Sorry to interrupt your night of fun," I said.

"Night of fun?"

I gestured to his neck. He rolled his eyes and tugged his T-shirt up higher.

"It's fine," Ruth said. "We have bigger problems than a hickey."

"Bigger problems? Is this about Mom leaving Dad?"

"It's about Mom, yes," Ruth said slowly. "But not about Dad. Well, kind of a dad."

"You're confusing me."

"Just give us a second," I said. "We're still dealing with the shock of it too."

"Shock? Why are you shocked?" His eyebrows lowered and his expression turned dark. "And why did you come here today of all days? Do you guys know?"

"Know what?" Ruth said. "No, it's not—we're here to talk. About you and someone else. Something big."

"How did you find out?" he ground out.

"Mom told us!" Ruth snapped. "Stop being all weird and listen for a second."

"No. This is bigger than just us. If people know, then she's going to be mad, and if she's mad, then she's gone."

"She?" I asked.

"Wait," Ruth said, brows knitted, "Are you seeing someone?"

Barry's eyes narrowed. "Don't you already know?"

"I know about something *Mom* told us about Dad. Not anything about anyone else."

"Oh," Barry said, and he let out a breath of relief. "Good."

"Good?" Ruth said. "You haven't even heard it yet. Barry, this is life-altering news. We wouldn't be here for something small."

"Whatever it is can wait until later, okay? I have something that I need to get back to."

"Barry," I said.

"No. I'm not having you guys ruin it by bringing more family drama for her to see."

"It's okay," a different, softer voice said. "Whatever it is sounds important."

"Shit," Barry muttered under his breath. He turned to the stairs where I could see someone hanging out. "Go back to bed. It's nothing."

"It's obviously not nothing," the woman said. "And they know someone is here."

"Wait," Ruth said. "I know that voice."

I thought about it. Whoever it was had a melodic voice that even *I'd* heard before.

"You might as well come on out," Barry said, his tone flat. "Ruth is going to figure it out any second now."

Ruth's eyes widened. "Wait. Barry, are you sleeping with—"

"Lila Wilde?" the voice said, and she fully came into view. My jaw dropped as I saw her dark hair come into view. "Yes. Yes, he is. And now that you two have seen me, you're about to have to sign the most extensive NDA you've ever seen. Sorry about that."

Bonus Epilogue

Character art for Max!

Max

"Do you have any chips?" Tess asked. He played with a Rubik's Cube on my bed while I finished up his part of our group project.

"Yeah, I think so, but you can go look."

"I don't know if I can. Your dad is the only one who's here."

"And?" I asked.

"And he's kind of...scary."

It wasn't the first time I'd heard that. Even the day of the birthday party, when I'd been angrier than I had been in a long time, most of my friends didn't dare speak directly to Dad because of how he looked. I seemed to be the only one who knew the man underneath it.

"My dad isn't mean or anything," I said.

"I know. And I know you forgave him and all, so he has to be kind of nice, but he's quiet. *Too* quiet."

"Come on." I grabbed the Rubik's Cube, and by extension, Tess's hand. "Let's go ask him together."

We walked downstairs where Dad was working on something on his laptop. With his thick eyebrows and perpetual near-glare, I could see why Tess was scared.

"Can Tess have some chips?" I asked. Dad looked up slowly, eyes catching on where I still kind of held Tess's hand. I dropped it like it was on fire, but I wasn't sure why.

"Sure," Dad said. "I think your mom got a few different kinds."

"What's your favorite?" I asked, even though I knew.

"Barbecue," Tess replied, his voice quiet.

"She got those. Help yourself."

Tess went to the pantry meekly, which was unlike him. I looked over at Dad.

"Can you crack a joke or something to make him feel better?" I whispered.

"Why? Is he not feeling well?" he asked.

"He's nervous because you're scary."

"I'm scary?"

"Not to me! Just to everyone who doesn't know your great sense of humor."

"My sense of humor is mostly me laughing at your jokes."

"Can you make that Toe-ny Stark pun I told you?"

"With what context? Stealing your friend's toes?"

I groaned as Tess came back into the room.

"Thank you," he said, and then turned to me. "And thank you too. For trying to get your dad to make a joke."

"You heard that?"

"Yeah," Tess replied, and then faced Dad. "Toe-ny Stark?"

"When I first met Max, he asked me if I would sell my toe for a million dollars."

Tess's eyes lit up. "That's *my* joke! I put it in there!"

"Oh, so you stole it," Dad said to me. "Maybe it's Tess's jokes I've been laughing at this whole time."

"I come up with some on my own!" I insisted. "Sometimes."

Dad laughed, and so did Tess. "It's okay," Tess said. "You can steal my jokes. Sometimes."

"Can we get a number of how many is too many?" I asked, rubbing the back of my head. "Because I've stolen a lot."

"You can steal some from Benji," Dad reminded. "He's an endless supply."

At the mention of the pun-filled guy, I turned to Tess with wide eyes. "You should definitely meet Benji. He's so cool! We know him through my aunt."

Tess had heard me talk about all of these people before, but he always seemed shy around my new family, especially after the party.

But he smiled. "Okay. I'll meet them sometime."

"You're always welcome," Dad said with a smile. "I'd never keep Max from his friends."

"And hopefully you don't have feet as gross as Jax's," Tess said.

"They're not," I reassured him.

"I don't know how I feel about this conversation." Dad looked slightly grossed out.

I stuck out my tongue. "You don't know how awful it was to live with unwashed feet."

"Are you sure you're still hungry?" Dad asked Tess. "I wouldn't be."

"I'm always hungry," Tess said.

"If that's the case, then I'll order some pizza for us."

"Please no pineapple," Tess begged, shaking his head. "It's gross."

"Worse than Jax's feet?" I asked.

"Yes."

"Hey!" I protested. "Don't knock my pizza!"

Tess shook his head as he started to go back upstairs, complaining once more about the flavor of pineapple on pizza. I went to follow him, but not before giving Dad a thumbs-up. I could tell he'd just charmed my closest friend.

Want more?

Get access to a bonus epilogue from Selena's point of view here!

What's Next?

Pre-order Barry's book here, coming in late 2024!

Looking for another read?

Check out these other books by Elle!

Forces of Nature
Ruth Murray thought she had seen the last of Knox Price when she walked away from him at their high school graduation.

After always coming in second place, she was ready to be done with their rivalry and make something of herself.

But then he went on to create PATH, a company that retrofitted cars to self-drive, cutting automobile accidents in half. His name was in everyone's mouths, especially her parents, who still compare her to him even ten years later. His success is a sore reminder of her own stagnant career.

When he mysteriously steps down as CEO of his company, she hopes this will be the reason he finally disappears from everyone's minds.

Until she walks into work and sees Knox is the newest executive of her company and, technically, her boss. All she can hope is that he doesn't remember their little rivalry, because he now has the power to make her life a living hell.

Knox Price should be on top of the world.

He's created an invention that saves lives, made his parents proud, shares his company with his best friend, and has more money than he knows what to do with.

And yet, he feels nothing.

He's a robot, pretending to be human but never actually feeling a thing. It's taken over his life, so much so, that his best friend suggests for him to step down and find passion in helping a different business build something great. When he returns to his hometown, he's content to spend extra time with his parents and work on a new app for a company he doesn't own.

That's when he sees the woman he could never forget.

Ruth Murray is as feisty and hardheaded as ever, and instead of feeling the emptiness he's grown used to, his heart starts beating again from the very moment he sees her.

The only problem? She hates him and he doesn't know why.

With the media clawing to get more information about him, and a ruthless boss out to fire Ruth for any reason, he should stay away from her. But the longer he's around her, the more he realizes he can't keep his distance.

Forces of Nature is a dual-POV, standalone book that will be part of an interconnected three-book series. It features the rivals to lovers, forced proximity, and only one bed trope. Spice and a HEA for the two leads is guaranteed!

CONTRACTUAL OBLIGATIONS

When Lily is offered a ticket out of the career and life she hates, she takes it. Even if it means signing a contract to marry the attractive but aloof Sebastian Miller for five years.

Her job is simple: play the happy house wife in person and on social media and she will get awarded a million dollars of her inheritance. That money is more than enough for her to start a life on her own and away from her controlling parents. It should be easy.

But four years in, she's more than ready to be done with this marriage. She's pretty sure her husband hates her, and she longs for the freedom the end of their contract will bring—a freedom that is threatened when she's called to meet Sebastian's father, the orchestrator of this whole sham. She worries he will try to extend their contractual marriage.

What he does is worse.

Forced to move across the country due to a promotion for Sebastian is her worst nightmare, but her only choice is to pretend to be fine.

She prepares for the last year of their marriage to be more cold indifference, but being stuck in a new city shows a sweeter side of Sebastian that Lily never thought possible. Gone is the indifferent man she knows and in his place is the kind and patient man of her dreams.

But their clock is ticking—only one year of their marriage remains. Will they find love or will contractual obligations get in the way?

FAILURE TO THRIVE

Riley Emerson is probably the last person anyone would expect to be a nanny. For starters, her life has fallen apart. Her boyfriend just cheated on her. She lives with her mom, and she might have a drinking problem.

But Oliver Brian is desperate. His daughter, Zoe, has refused to go to sleep for anyone else in four years and with his career Oliver can't always be there for her. Riley is only supposed to watch Zoe for one night, but somehow she gets Zoe to bed on her own. He's so shocked that he offers her a job on the spot.

Riley needs the money, and Oliver needs the time for himself. It's a match made in Heaven... until feelings get involved.

UNDER ANY CONDITIONS

What happens after the happily ever after?

Riley and Oliver are finally together. Things should be perfect, but Riley struggles with the ghosts of her past while Oliver finds himself trapped in a workplace legal battle, which puts him face-to-face with someone he'd rather forget.

While Riley wonders if she isn't good enough, Oliver knows she's the one for him, but they have a lot of work to do if they want to figure out how to merge their very different lives into one. Does love persevere under any conditions? Or will it crumble under the weight of someone's past?

TO MAKE MATTERS WORSE

Violet Moore is not having a good week.

It starts with a fight between her and Charlie Davis—the usual bane of her existence—and ends with a drink thrown on her. Then, she somehow agrees to be *fake friends* with the same man to ensure her best friend's wedding goes off without a hitch. And last but certainly not least, her apartment collapses, and the only person with an open room is Charlie himself.

Violet isn't sure what's going to be worse: the wedding or her living situation.

There are few people that are more confusing than Violet Moore.

Charlie has never understood her, but the quick-witted, five-foot-three school-teacher has a huge grudge against him. Why? He has no clue. He's not proud of his immature spats with his former college friend turned enemy, but he can never seem to stop himself—not when it's her he's fighting with. He's content to get this wedding and their fake friendship over with so they can go back to their normal fighting lifestyle.

Then he finds her crying and needing a place to stay, and it changes all of his plans. Feelings he had long since buried rush to the surface, and he finds himself unable to stop thinking about the beautiful, but confusing, Violet Moore.

They haven't agreed on anything in six years, but can one wedding, a

ruined apartment, and being stuck in one house somehow bring them together?

Thank You

Every time I write one of these, I am overwhelmed with gratitude for the incredible people in my life who have made this possible.

To Kasey, who always tells me what I need to hear in these edits. My works have come so far with your help.

To Allie, thank you for making my vision come to life. I still remember that day in Starbucks when our first cover finally came together, and it's a moment I am excited to have again!

To Josh, none of this would be possible if you hadn't swept me off my feet when I was nineteen. Your dedication to me and desire to grow together have been the backbone of every novel I write. You were the first romance hero I dreamed of.

To Lizzie, thank you for helping this novel come together. I loved sending you screenshots of lines so we could scream together. Your input while writing has helped me develop this into what it is.

I have so many other friends who have helped me with this as well. Morgan, Jewels, Cass—I love you all. Thank you for being here for me.

And last but certainly not least, thank you to my readers. I can never understate just how much you guys have changed my life. It is my greatest honor to write these novels for you. Thank you thank you THANK YOU!